Of Blondes, Betting, Booze and Bolshevism

Charles Marks

Clink
Street

London | New York

Charles Dickens' "It was the best of times, it was the worst of times" is a wonderful opening line to a great novel.

Implied in Dickens' statement is the duality of life being simultaneously good and bad: a dialectical truth.

Witness then the contradictions in the life of the present novel's central character Charlie Gaily.

The middle class upbringing of an only child is seen to leave our hero totally unprepared for the travails of later life. However, at the same time one sees how those early years pave the way for what is to follow. Leading a coddled existence at home, at school and in his early working life made Gaily vulnerable to what in the vernacular would be termed "good ideas at the time". Loneliness and isolation made Gaily seek out excitement in a lifestyle fraught with danger.

The social conditioning of the individual leads to major decisions in life the repercussions of which will reverberate for many years. Such decisions affect not only the person concerned but those around them.

The role of the individual in society is seen to be at once as part of the social whole but at the same time as a single unit in what can be an extremely hostile environment.

When the whole of society seemingly conspires against one man the odds may seem overwhelmingly against him. How he adapts to the situation will determine how well or even if he survives. Many objective situations in life are so stacked against the individual he simply cannot win no matter how valiant his efforts, how strong his mettle. One school of thought emanating from America has it that the individual is capable of achieving anything to which he puts his mind. Such is simply not the case. A product of a hostile environment can be destroyed by the very environment which created both the individual and his objective situation or circumstances.

In Charlie Gaily's case he was placed in an invidious position for twenty years of his life after a series of disastrous decisions combined with circumstances over which he had no control. His ability to survive and eventually prosper was not just testament to strong character and will but predicated the need to develop these qualities or perish.

Such are the fortunes of war. When an individual soldier or indeed an entire army lack basic fighting qualities they have to develop these qualities not obtained from their training on the battlefield itself while continuing to survive: not an easy task when all seems hopelessly lost.

Gaily was not born great. Gaily attained greatness as a result of having greatness forced upon him.

This story belongs to Charlie Gaily: a likeable left-wing larrikin with a love of racing, beautiful blondes and Resch's beer.

Charlie Gaily's first memories are portrayed in sepia photographs of him as a toddler.

An only child, he spent a large proportion of the glorious summer months in a backyard wading pool in suburban Sydney - always under the watchful eye of one or both of his parents. Sydney was his city of birth and would be his place of residence for the first thirty-four years of his life. The wading pool and the adjoining Hills hoist (outside clothesline) were symbols of suburban life in Australia in the sixties as was the Victa lawnmower which its manufacturer claimed "turns grass into lawn".

Gaily's parents had only come down from "the bush" a few years prior. The big city was daunting with its size and unfriendliness: both of which would only increase with the passing of time. His mother would cry herself to sleep in the couple's little flat in the suburb of Kensington when first they ventured outside the country towns in which they had been born.

Some solace was to be obtained from moving out of their little rented flat in "Kenso" and renting a brick veneer house in the outer suburb of Baulkham Hills although eventual home ownership was high on their list of priorities.

Gaily's father was severely traumatised through having served in the Royal Air Force during World War II. Australia having no air force of its own during the second war Australians were deployed to England in support of the war effort. Working as a wireless operator on Lancaster bombers flying over Germany Mr Gaily served with distinction receiving the Distinguished Flying Cross for his efforts. His act of bravery in saving a comrade's life while under enemy fire earned him a military decoration second only to the Victoria Cross in prestige. However, the traumas of war service did irreparable damage to someone really still only a boy when the war ended. These days the term "Post Traumatic Stress Syndrome" would be used and professional counselling offered. In 1945 service personnel were expected to come home and simply get on with their lives. Ted Gaily was no exception.

A sensitive, quiet man Charlie Gaily's father instilled in his son all the classic attributes of introversion.

Mrs Gaily was therefore the dominant force in the Gaily household. Like most women of her time she was serious and hard-working with little time for humour or fun.

"Life is a serious business, Charles", Mrs Gaily would say when her son acted like a child rather than an adult.

Despite this Mr and Mrs Gaily were "good parents": a fact of which the young Charlie was reminded not a few times.

"She's a good woman Charles", Mr Gaily was fond of telling his son.

Frugality was the cornerstone of the Gaily family's existence.

The benefits of frugality were repeated ad nauseam in almost litany-like fashion.

Although staunch Labor (sic) Party supporters the Gailys were obsessed with home ownership. The post-war economic boom allowed the majority of Australian families to own their own house: unthinkable for previous generations. Great political mileage was gained by arch-Conservative Prime Minister Bob Menzies. Menzies created "the great Australian dream" as being the ownership of "a house on a quarter acre block with a white picket fence". Despite their general loathing of political conservatism Mr and Mrs Gaily were at one with Menzies on this particular question.

A series of pithy little sayings quantified the Gaily financial world view.

"A penny saved is a penny earned Charles", Charlie Gaily's mother would tell him.

Despite being keen racing followers Gaily's mother would never bet, his father rarely so and then no more than a tenner.

"Only the bookmakers win Charles", his mother would say: this despite his parents having known very successful professional punters.

A degree of snobbery was involved with Gaily's mother in particular regularly sneering at the lives of others.

"We always eat well, Charles", Mrs Gaily would say. Red salmon was popular in the Gaily household, pink salmon being for poor people.

The hypocrisy of wowserism was never more evident than with regard to the subject of drinking.

"Some people spend all their money on drink", was another of Mrs Gaily's favourite sayings.

What was not juxtaposed was the smoking of forty cigarettes per day by Mrs Gaily and a lesser number by her husband when he was not smoking a pipe.

Another contradiction involved Mrs Gaily's differentiating between "house clothes" and clothes worn outside the house: a good example of what Shakespeare termed "the outward show". Similarly, Mrs Gaily went through a phase of rolling her own cigarettes while reserving her favourite Rothmans for public occasions.

Ted Gaily suffered his wife's views largely in silence - choosing the path of least resistance. He was old enough to be able to remember the hardships and deprivation of the Great Depression: an experience which led him to occupy the left of the political spectrum. He remembered the unemployed men carrying their swags from rural property to rural property in the bush during the thirties and the introduction of a subsistence dole ("susso" as it was called). Never again did he want to see a repetition of those events.

Ted Gaily's war service reinforced his political views. Capitalism's solution to economic depression was to send the finest of its youth into a military conflagration six years in duration.

Mr Gaily never discussed the war except to occasionally opine, "There were atrocities on both sides".

What the young Ted Gaily had witnessed one can only imagine. However, his equating of Allied methods with those of the Axis powers contradicts the history of World War II written by the victors.

With the cessation of war Ted Gaily was able to complete his articles and become a solicitor. In the 1940s it was possible to obtain the equivalent of a law degree without attending university.

Mr Gaily's experiences as an articled clerk were to embitter him towards drinking as his employer Tim Boys was an inveterate drunk.

Just back from war Ted Gaily was often left to effectively run the office while the boss went to the Post Office Hotel for a drink.

Tim Boys was a brilliant man but went on long binges confirming Ted Gaily's opinion of him as an alcoholic. When sober Boys would commence his day reading law journals before breakfast. When on a bender he would skip early morning reading and breakfast in favour of the Post Office's beer. Like a lot of heavy drinkers Boys did not like to mix eating with his drinking. Two or three days would pass without solid food followed by a big feed of fish and chips to soak up the grog.

In this environment Ted Gaily had his introduction to the civilian workforce. As soon as his articles were completed he scarpered.

The only positive occurrence during this phase of Ted Gaily's life was his meeting the woman who would become his wife.

Having moved from the country town of Quirindi for work Ted Gaily spotted an attractive young brunette walking her fox terrier in the streets of Tamworth, Tamworth being a larger town more conducive to office work than its smaller neighbours.

The young woman was a secretary with the local council. After a short courtship they married and moved down to Sydney. Their marriage was to last fifty-five years.

Although initially requiring some adjustment the couple were able to obtain jobs with ease in post-war Sydney. Ted Gaily become a solicitor employed by a local council and subsequently the railways. His wife obtained secretarial work with a multinational corporation.

Eventually the newlyweds were able to chuck in their jobs thus allowing Ted Gaily to establish his own legal practice with his wife as his secretary.

From the rented house in Baulkham Hills the Gailys were soon able to purchase a house in the adjoining suburb of Castle Hill. The middle of the twentieth century saw Castle Hill as still being semi-rural – located on what was then the fringe of the Sydney metropolitan area. The couple were therefore able to purchase a large house built on five acres of land – some compensation for their having reluctantly moved to the "big smoke".

In this idyllic setting Charlie Gaily was to spend most of his school age years.

His father was able to establish a magnificent garden while his mother kept house. The war having taken its toll at an early age Ted Gaily's career ambitions were limited to maintaining his small legal practice specialising in wills and conveyancing. The office was open from the dot of nine in the morning until the dot of five in the afternoon. Mrs Gaily was able to pare back her hours and eventually learnt to drive a car in order to pick up her son from school. The Gailys therefore were able to structure their lives around the needs of home and family: no mean feat at the best of times.

Leaving his father to tend the garden and his mother to keep house Charlie Gaily developed a love of reading which was to stay with him for life. At first his parents would read to him, the degree of difficulty increasing as the months progressed.

From nursery rhymes to the wonderful Australian children's stories of the day Charlie Gaily quickly developed a love not only of reading but of the English language. The children's stories featured the adventures of archetypal Australian characters with a strong emphasis on the Australian bush with its unique flora and fauna. They nurtured both a love of nature and a sense of identity with one's country sadly lacking in contemporary Australia.

By the time he reached school age Charlie Gaily was a proficient reader in his own right with a literacy level to rival most adults. The seral progression of the education he had received in the home ensured by age five he was already appreciative of classical literature. The solid grounding provided by his parents complemented the further knowledge which would be imparted by schoolteachers in the years ahead.

School was a hoot

Charlie adopted a carefree attitude to his formal learning in order to minimise stress. He required not his father's war service to not push himself too hard in any area of life. This lack of drive seemed like a good idea at the time but would tell against him in later life. Were there a short cut available Charlie would find it. Many years later a supervisor referred to a still young Charlie Gaily as having "cunning beyond his years". Yet this energy would have been better spent in performing a task to the best of his ability.

Kindergarten was largely devoted to play, eating and

naps. However, the arrival of infant school signalled the beginning of the serious formal learning process. It was here Charlie's solid grounding at home would hold him in good stead.

School also meant organised sport and daily contact with other children. Both held their challenges.

Charlie's parents were extremely supportive of his sporting ventures. Swimming and tennis lessons paved the way for later competition in those sports.

Soccer was the chosen winter sport for the majority of boys with a strong junior competition in the area. However, Mrs Gaily would not have a bar of it. Yet again her snobbishness came to the fore.

"They only play soccer because it's free", she informed her son.

Soccer was the sporting equivalent of pink salmon so the money continued to flow for tennis and swimming lessons and tins of red "Sockeye" salmon.

For all his efforts Charlie Gaily was never going to excel in the sporting arena. What small achievements came his way were as a result of training which only served to allow him to partially catch up to the naturally gifted athlete. His swimming would stand him in good stead in terms of maintaining a high standard of aerobic fitness throughout his adult life. A season of football (Rugby League) would eradicate from his system the desire to play that particular sport despite a lifelong devotion to the St George District Rugby League Football Club which began at age nine.

As for tennis playing that game developed a lifelong devotion to admiring good sorts in short dresses and miniskirts.

Speaking of girls school provided Charlie with his first significant contact with people outside his family circle.

The classic introvert would never be completely comfortable in the company of others. Despite being imbued with good social skills from the earliest stage of his life Charlie Gaily would never overcome the isolated existence of an only child growing up in the solitude of the five acre suburban block. Sport and political activity would assist to draw him out as the years went on. The socially acceptable medium of booze would also play its part in lubricating his gregarious instincts. However, Gaily would always struggle to mix with people regardless of how much his peers liked and respected him.

This latter struggle is a major problem in the development of the individual's personality. On the one hand the developing individual wishes to assert their individuality as a unique entity; on the other hand the individual seeks to be accepted by peers, family and society in general. The breakdown of society is occurring as a result of individuals placing their personal interests as individuals above those of society.

Charlie Gaily was to become an introverted left-wing intellectual. The problem here is of the individual placing the needs of society so far above his own as to be as unbalanced as the selfish introvert.

In the post-war Australia into which Gaily was born suffering should have been eliminated: consigned to the dustbin of history. Instead of a better society coming into being on the strength of the post-war economic boom the hedonistic mob have allowed the multinationals to quarry Australia while the extroverts partied in apolitical bliss. Ironically their unwitting allies have been holier than thou lefties who viewed a decent standard of living as being too bourgeois to accept. Not for them good clothes and pleasant homes. In the late twentieth century so-called "grunge" would become fashionable as relatively wealthy people voluntarily accepted a lower standard of living and quality of life. The gains made by generations of battlers were eschewed by this fake left who equated poverty with principles.

Charlie Gaily would never be a trendy leftie. He would eventually adopt the politics of the Old Left. Having been brought up to appreciate the finer things of life the allure of socialism would always be to raise people up - not drag them down to a Lowest Common Denominator.

This would be a few years down the track. The immediate priority was school.

After kindergarten came twelve years of actual school. The first six years consisted of infant and primary school, the second six high or secondary school.

The first six years were designed to impart basic literacy and numeracy skills. High or secondary school allowed the student to concentrate on mathematics and science or the humanities (English, history, etc.).

Charlie Gaily's parents had provided him with a head start in his education. However, the vast majority of his peers came from similarly stable, supportive families so standards at the Castle Hill schools were commensurately high. Exceptions only serve to prove rules and a stable domestic environment is a huge advantage in promoting academic achievement.

There were two exceptions to the rule at "Casto". One was the wards of the state who lived at what was termed Govo' House. The other was the Aboriginal kids who resided in the nearby Aboriginal mission.

Both groups stood out like a dog's ears at schools with a preponderance of Anglo students from economically privileged backgrounds.

The Govo' House boys (there were no girls) were tough whitefella kids who had come up the hard way. Some of them made a good fist of their schooling – driven as they were to escape their pasts. Their lunches consisted of Govo' slabs: sandwiches which bounced if accidentally dropped on the ground.

The Aboriginal kids were a sad lot reflective of the treatment of the Aboriginal people since the English colonisation of Australia. Most of them were male, none of them any great stakes in the classroom. The one thing they were generally good at was sport. Even here they encountered difficulties as good coaches cost money. Transportation around a vast area such as the Hills District can also be difficult without parents who are willing and able to drive a car.

The end result for the Aboriginal boys was that they had to make do with the resources provided at school.

Play in infant and primary school largely consisted in games which could be organised by a teacher with no specific training in this area. In high school sessions were dedicated to sport and Physical Education. The P.E. teacher possessed training specific to physical fitness and had a good general knowledge of a range of sports. However, general sports supervision often fell to a teacher who with the best will in the world had no formal training.

The Aboriginal boys displayed great ability in running and swimming short sprint distances but lacked the endurance which only consistent training will bring. In all the twelve years Charlie Gaily attended school in Castle Hill not one Aboriginal made it through to the end of their final year. One poor devil got burnt to death whilst at home on holidays.

Charlie's parents did what they could to assist the situation during their son's high school years by occasionally driving a couple of the Aboriginal boys to swimming carnivals. A tea (as the evening meal was still termed in

Australia) of a steak dinner and dessert was provided prior to the carnivals. In their patronising middle class way the Gailys were seen to do what they could for the disadvantaged youth, Ted Gaily having to be careful not to express deep-seated prejudices which were a legacy of his country origins.

The six years of infant and primary school went quickly for Charlie Gaily. Having already learnt the alphabet together with basic literacy and numeracy he was just able to coast his way through. In this environment Gaily excelled. There was no pressure and he could become confident- if not a little cocky- at his own ability. In years to come he would "choke" under pressure but for the time being he was safe.

It was during these formative years Gaily had daily contact with people his own age for the first time. He would always be awkward and shy with new acquaintances. Later life would provide the facade of confidence afforded by the successful gambler's swagger. Drinking would provide Dutch courage.

His mother was not normally a sociable woman but an offshoot of her son's starting school had been the creation of a social outlet for her too. One of the other mothers had attended school in Tamworth so auld acquaintance had been able to be renewed. As a successful businesswoman in partnership with her husband she also carried a degree of cachet in what was a small tightly knit community. Her son's starting school was good for Mrs Gaily at both a business and a personal level as socialising was a very rare occurrence for the Gaily family.

Despite having started school life was still a fairly lonely affair for Charlie Gaily. His parents would drive him to school in the morning and his mother picked him up in the afternoon. There was little in the way of organised activities after school apart from swimming lessons. Homework was never too arduous with television and books the main diversions. Fairy-tales had already given way to the likes of Dickens and the great Australian children's writers such as May Gibbs and Norman Lindsay. Walt Disney and Hanna-Barbera cartoons were favourites as far as television went. A lot of the American-made cartoons such as The Flintstones were very clever and Mr Gaily and his son would often watch them together after Mr Gaily's arrival home from work. A shared sense of humour would create a bond between father and son.

Still Charlie saw little of his schoolmates outside of school hours and this would set the pattern for his life as a loner. Occasionally the son of his mother's schoolmate would come over on a Sunday night and the two boys would watch Disneyland together. On these occasions tea was allowed to be eaten away from the dining table: a major concession to informality.

Eating away from home rarely occurred. Other people were considered "dirty" and restaurants had yet to gain the popularity they hold today. Takeaway food from the cake shop or fish shop adjoining Mr Gaily's office was a treat reserved for school holidays.

"We prefer our own food, Charles" was another of Mrs Gaily's favourite statements.

Eating at home reflected the Gailys' obsessions with the need to be both thrifty and clean.

Charlie never accepted the thrifty part but made up for it with his obsession for cleanliness. Personal hygiene was to become a central part of his neurotic personality. It would affect every facet of his life in the development of his overall personality. His mother's obsession with cleanliness would modify his behaviour to such an extent he would avoid eating with his hands and eschew unheated food prepared by hand. His mother would actually frown upon rigorous exercise because it involved breathing through the mouth as well as the nose.

However, as will later be seen the most telling aspect of this behavioural modification would be in Charlie's choice of woman. His mother unwittingly drove him into the arms of courtesans.

Suffice to say when explaining the difference between the singular and plural "tart" is sour but "tarts" are sweet.

By the commencement of high school the hormones were beginning to be secreted in record amounts. Castle Hill High was no exception to any other community of young people thrown together by the hand of fate.

The seventies was a wonderful time to be young. Unfettered by the prudishness of liberal "political correctness" the youth of the day were - unbeknownst to them - living through the highpoint of human existence. The post-war economic boom was to reach its crescendo with its concomitant full employment, the Vietnam War was to attain a successful conclusion with the liberation of Saigon and the radicalisation of Western society as a result of the various new social movements which the anti-war movement had inspired would have ramifications for years to come.

In the midst of all this Charlie Gaily commenced his high school years surrounded by brilliant, inspiring teachers and dishy schoolgirls who had obvious difficulty squeezing into their uniforms. Not for the last time in his life Charlie had struck the double.

High school in the seventies was therefore very different from high school today.

The teachers were articulate, literate, numerate, motivated. They commanded respect without having to resort to force. The exceptions were sadistic throwbacks to a Dickensian past whose impotence led them to seek solace in inflicting pain on defenceless children during what were thankfully the final days of corporal punishment.

The teachers did actually teach. They were not mere facilitators of a dialogue of the deaf between an illiterate teacher and an illiterate class such as occurs today. They were gifted people who viewed their work as a profession rather than merely being a job.

The main impediment to the boys' ability to learn was the presence of girls. Given his sheltered existence thus far Charlie Gaily had never seen anything like it in his short existence. His sexual being had begun to evolve.

Life had become a giant peep-show. Sitting behind his favourite girlies on a daily basis for six years would make Gaily a voyeur for life. One a blonde, the other a brunette, he was able to watch their bodies mature through puberty until attaining early womanhood. Mrs Gaily never needed to worry about starching her son's pyjama fronts as they were stiff with the ejaculate of wet dreams every morning.

The most peculiar thing about the situation was that Gaily never masturbated during his school days hence the profusion of wet dreams. As masturbation was a taboo subject both at home and school it never occurred to him to stimulate himself by hand. It would take the experienced hand of a prostitute years later to achieve manual orgasm.

Despite extreme ignorance the teenagers' sexualities developed free of inhibition. This ignorance was actually of assistance in drawing out the instinctive and primal urges which motivate human behaviour.

Gaily felt no guilt in ogling the pretty girls who sat in front of him in class just as the exhibitionistic minxes felt no shame in flaunting their new-found sexual powers. The girls' summer uniform in particular barely covered their knicker-clad bottoms- making every day a lingerie exhibition which would stay in Gaily's memory for the rest of his life.

This experience cemented in Gaily's mind the role of the short dress or miniskirt as his major sexual stimulus for arousal.

For the rest of his life the question would arise in his mind whenever he saw a good sort in a mini or short dress, "What colour are they?"

The girls did nothing to discourage him. One was an English girl with a peaches and cream complexion, an hourglass figure and naturally platinum blonde hair which cascaded over her shoulders and back. The other was a petite Aussie brunette who wore the shortest uniforms in the entire form.

Never a word was said as the game continued day after day, month after month, for six deliriously erotic years. It was as if no one ever noticed what occurred in the corners of the classrooms inhabited by three of the brightest students to grace the halls of Castle Hill High. No acknowledgement was ever made by either the girls or Gaily as to what occurred. In years to come Gaily would pay big money for titillation of a far inferior quality.

What with the girls in front of him constantly dropping pens or rulers on the floor, putting their hands up to answer questions or resting their heads on their desks Gaily's ability to concentrate was severely tested.

His happy-go-lucky attitude would stay with him all his life but this would have two negative results. Firstly, he was destined to be an underachiever until forced by circumstances to realise his full potential. Secondly, he would become what psychiatrists would once have termed a smiling depressive as a result of his constant underachieving. The happy-go-lucky attitude was thus a facade masking deep-seated inner conflict which would not be resolved until well into middle age.

Throughout high school Gaily's fortes were modern history and English. His speaking and writing skills put him at the top of his form year after year. His grasp and interpretation of history were in line with his development as a left-wing intellectual. In his final year he was voted by his peers as the student in their year most likely to become Prime Minister.

His sporting achievements were on a lesser scale but still read well. His prowess on the tennis court and the football field as well as in the swimming pool gave the impression of a well-rounded scholar. Again though underachievement was seen to effect.

Early in his teens Gaily developed what today would be termed an eating disorder. His weight dropped several stone and did not normalise until leaving school. A sensitive child, he had been severely hurt by taunts over his allegedly being overweight.

The problem was compounded by the death of his swimming coach when Gaily was aged fourteen. The coach had been a steadying father-like figure to him – a real man's man compared with his own father who despite being a decent fellow was a bit of a milksop in his son's eyes.

The swimming coach had been larger than life having served in the Spanish Civil War, played football for South Sydney and been a professional boxer. He had witnessed the strained relations between Gaily and his mother and once expressed it in terms of the boy having to carry the weight of the two people through the water. By her own admission Mrs Gaily did not like children and had only borne a child in order to have an heir to the family estate.

Mrs Gaily's personality was depressing and repellent. Her attitude towards her son's weight loss was to threaten to have him force-fed. People like this drain one of the joy of life. It was to his credit Charlie Gaily turned out as well as he did.

The loss of the swimming coach also meant the breaking up of the squad at the local swimming pool. The coach's reputation had meant that at its peak two hundred young people would train for up to two hours per morning swimming twenty-five to a lane. With his excellent social skills the coach had been able to bring people together and create bonds amongst individuals. Having trained an Olympic gold medallist he was able to dine out on his reputation for the rest of his short life. Unfortunately he dined a little too well and not wisely to the fatal detriment of his liver. His legacy lived on as a result of the benefits he had brought to the local swimming club and its individual members.

Apart from developing his swimming skills Charlie Gaily derived two additional benefits from having participated in squad. Firstly, there was his introduction to the joys of Resch's beer. Secondly, there had been a reinforcement of his penchant for blondes.

One of the enduring memories of the coach's reign at Baulkham Hills was the regular delivery of his Resch's Dinner Ale. As the coach lived on and rarely left the pool premises the local off-licence would deliver two cases of D.A. stubbies (half bottles) to the pool each week.

Gaily had admired the coach to such an extent that if Resch's D.A. was the coach's beer of choice then it would also be Charles Gaily's. Unfortunately Resch's D.A. was an acquired taste for the more mature male palate. It was a bitter real ale. However, with much perseverance Gaily developed a taste for D.A. that would last until the beer's untimely deletion.

The belle of the swimming squad was a beautiful champion breast-stroker with the requisite long blonde hair and hourglass figure. A year older than Gaily she was as big a tease as Gaily's classmates.

For two lots of Christmas school holidays they had worked together on the pool reception and assisting in the kiosk. When business was quiet the girl's favourite method of gaining Gaily's attention was to lean across the reception counter allowing her little dresses and minis to ride up her beautiful round firm knicker-clad buttocks. If her aim was to gain Gaily's attention it was a ploy with a one hundred per cent success rate. Again he was allowed to look and not touch: a recurring theme in the evolution of his sexuality. The girl always wore frilly red or black knickers and would provoke Gaily by bringing her buttocks tantalisingly close to his face. The poor fellow did not know how to respond so just admired in silence without attempting to touch. A misplaced word or hand may have spoilt the magic of the moment.

A German woman whose daughters also swam at the pool was also employed on reception. When she would catch the girl flashing her knickers she would put the girl over her knee and spank the offending backside. There was obvious mutual consent between the giver and the recipient of the spanking. Gaily would watch these actions in silent awe with the memories etched indelibly in his mind.

The pool had certainly provided its share of kinky eroticism.

Tennis was another sport which provided ample opportunities for seeing ample opportunities. All that bending over and stretching out made mixed doubles Gaily's favourite form of the game. It was as much a spectator sport for him when he played as when he watched from the sidelines. Television and newspapers also provided far more risqué coverage of the ladies' lack of coverage than is the case today.

Sport was therefore a big part of Gaily's school years with the girls involved a major attraction.

Despite their inadequacies his parents did their best to support their son's sporting endeavours by driving him to a swimming pool or a tennis court most every day.

One season of football (Rugby League) was enough to get the desire to play out of Gaily's system and the all-male environment lacked the appeal of swimming and tennis.

From an early age Gaily identified strongly with the stereotype of the Australian male: a beer-drinking man's man. This romanticised image played a major role in his being attracted to football as a spectator if not as a player.

At the age of nine his parents took him for the first time to see his beloved St George play at the Sydney Cricket Ground. In years to come they would traipse all around the Sydney metropolitan area to see Saints play home and away and at the Cricket Ground. The club had enjoyed their greatest successes only a few years prior to the Gailys starting to follow them so some famous names were reaching the conclusions of illustrious careers.

His parents tried to involve themselves in their son's interests although he could never have spoken openly to them about the main attractions of swimming and tennis. They could never discuss openly anything of a sexual nature and never displayed any signs of affection towards each other in their son's presence. Sexual repression was big in the Gaily household.

Gaily's father chose to follow the local club Parramatta on purely parochial grounds. His mother gave a hint of her sexual repression choosing to follow the Manly club based on the good looks of their star player.

Footie fans provide a good example of how people live

their lives in a vicarious fashion. Someone who may never have pulled on a boot can experience all the highs and lows of their heroes, be shocked or titillated by gossip, yell advice to players and officials from the safety of the side-line and do it all again the following week until the end of the season. They can support their club financially by taking out memberships and buying merchandise. These days they can also bet with their hearts not their head by gambling on the multiplicity of betting options available.

Not only did Charlie Gaily begin to live his life through his football club but sexually too he had drifted into a pattern of behaviour which provided gratification without active participation.

The line between fantasy and reality was already becoming quite blurred. In later life it would become further blurred by the introduction of prostitutes into his life. Then the line between client and friend would be so blurred life would become filled with fantasy so detached from reality as to be potentially fatal in terms of its physical and financial impacts.

For the time being Gaily could dream about football and girls without any significant consequences. However, adult life would throw up challenges for which he was totally unprepared.

After twelve years attending school in the one suburb one would hope to forge bonds of friendship which would last a lifetime. Despite being generally popular with his fellow students he was not to remain in regular contact with any of his old schoolmates come the parting of the ways.

By the senior forms of Years 11 and 12 Gaily's sights were set firmly on his future: in particular his political future. This was already bringing a new circle of people into his life in the form of fellow political activists: his "comrades".

Ted Gaily had repeatedly promised to bring his son home a copy of the Communist Party of Australia's newspaper Tribune. In the seventies the paper was still freely available alongside the mainstream dailies in the Sydney Central Business District and from individual sellers on the C.B.D.'s busiest streets. Mr Gaily had already introduced his son to Marxism at the age of fourteen by presenting him with a copy of the Communist Manifesto. The budding intellectual fell in love with the ideas presented by Marx and Engels in their famous thesis.

Living in an outer suburb one would have had to either have a postal subscription or travel some miles to obtain a copy of "Trib" as it was affectionately known. Ted Gaily's failure to procure the goods resulted in an interesting quirk of fate.

Although not unsympathetic to Marxism Mr Gaily was a left liberal. He had in fact written letters to the Sydney Morning Herald in opposition to Australia's participation in the Vietnam War. The gist of these articles had later been plagiarised he was to claim when the Herald's editorial policy shifted in line with a shift in public opinion.

As a passive man whose own life had been dramatically altered as a result of the Depression and subsequent war service he was a staunch supporter of the A.L.P. Although not as politicised his wife supported her husband in all things.

As liberals they had allowed their son to develop his own views while providing a guiding hand. They had gone so far as to provide him with beer on a daily basis despite themselves being teetotallers.

In 1975 the dismissal of the Labor Federal Government by the Queen's representative the Governor-General had caused a huge stir amongst the Australian people. The withdrawal of Australian troops from Vietnam had just been announced after ten years of anti-war demonstrations. A shift to the left of the political spectrum was taking place in Australian society. The trade union movement was strong and militant.

In this context a series of pro-A.L.P. rallies were organised throughout Australia. Rallies in Sydney were held in Hyde Park and on the steps of the Sydney Opera House. Amongst the tens of thousands of people attending were Charlie Gaily and his mother.

The rallies were addressed by A.L.P. and trade union leaders. Some of the unionists were Communist Party members or sympathisers (so-called "fellow-travellers").

Also attending the rallies were members of the various fringe dwellers of the left: the avowed followers of Leon Trotsky.

The "Trots" are small in number but big on rhetoric. What they lack in numbers they attempt to make up for by physically driving their members into the ground and financially bleeding them white. Historically undercover intelligence agents direct budding left-wing activists into one or other Trot sect in the knowledge they will be burnt out and lost to the movement forever. In the apparent absence of a Trib seller it was the newspaper of one of these dubious organisations Mrs Gaily purchased for her son.

First impressions count. On the train going home Charlie Gaily pored over his first copy of the Indirect Inaction newspaper of the Trotskyite Workers' Party. The paper provided simple solutions to complex questions. It was written in a style designed to appeal to young minds. The language was bold and optimistic. It portrayed the

T.W.P. and their co-thinkers overseas as leading the working class towards the promised land of socialism. Photographs showed T.W.P. members out and about building the revolution by selling newspapers and handing out leaflets. Revolution was just around the corner. Any minute now a gigantic Trotskyite broom would sweep away the old forms of government and replace them with Trot parties in every corner of the globe. It was breathtaking stuff. Join now and help lead the revolution or miss the bus: all this from a tiny sect with less than a hundred members throughout Australia.

However, to the impressionable young mind it sounded perfectly plausible. It captured the imagination with its romantic simplicity.

It certainly managed to capture Charlie Gaily's imagination. With no other point of reference the Trot newspaper seemed to bring to life the inspiring words he had read in the Communist Manifesto. Here was a practical application of the words of Marx and Engels applied to today's conditions. Marx had written "...philosophers have only interpreted the world,...the point, however, is to change it". The T.W.P. was that force for change: no doubt about it. They were the vanguard of the vanguard. If the poor benighted working class would only stop listening to the sell-outs in the A.L.P. and the Stalinists in the unions Australia would go socialist tomorrow. It was just a matter of selling more papers and recruiting more members because not many people had actually heard of the T.W.P. otherwise they would already have joined. We are correct and everyone else is wrong so our victory is inevitable because all history is on our side.

"It all sounds too good to be true", Charlie told his mother.

"If something seems too good to be true it probably is,"

replied the wise Mrs Gaily.

However, as Trotsky's erstwhile comrade Vladimir Lenin opined, "The workers learn from their own experience".

Charlie Gaily's experiences with the T.W.P. were to provide a very harsh lesson indeed.

The Christmas school holidays had just commenced. The swimming coach had died two years prior, the squad had been cast to the four winds and the beautiful girl in the miniskirt had left Gaily's life forever along with the allure of spending one's holidays working at the pool. Politics was about to shove swimming aside on the centre stage of Charlie Gaily's theatre of life.

Over tea with his parents the night of the rally Gaily could speak of nothing else but the myriad pearls of wisdom contained in the pages of Indirect Inaction.

"Christ I wish I'd bought him that copy of Trib", thought his father, too timid and polite to express himself out loud.

Gaily could not wait to visit the offices of the T.W.P. to meet his new comrades. As was inevitably the case his parents acquiesced to his demands. His mother agreed to accompany her son to the T.W.P. head office the following day. Charlie drained his glass of Resch's Dinner Ale with alacrity and shortly after bid his parents good night. His dreams that night were a heady mix of blondes and Bolshevism.

The next morning Mrs Gaily rose early in order to prepare breakfast and traipse back into town with her son.

Mrs Gaily had never seen her son so excited: not even when St George had almost won the premiership a few years prior. He exuded the brash confidence of youth without the worldly experience to back it up. Mrs Gaily hoped her son would not be disappointed.

Travelling into the city by public transport involved both a bus and a train trip. It was a long, arduous journey. Charlie Gaily amused himself by rereading Indirect Inaction; his mother read the Women's Weekly.

The T.W.P.'s tiny office was located in a fire-trap in Sydney's Haymarket. Mrs Gaily had always referred to this end of the town as "the dirty end of town". The T.W.P. office merely confirmed her opinion. The entire building should have been condemned years prior. Most of the neighbouring offices were vacant and the building possessed an eerie silence.

One first had to ascertain how to gain access to the building. As the custodians of humanity's future the T.W.P. were obsessed with security. This was because in their own deluded imaginations they posed such a threat to the ruling class as to warrant constant surveillance. Successive governments of the day would have liked nothing better than to breach their own laws pertaining to civil liberties in order to quash this imminent threat to bourgeois democracy. (In reality the occasional Australian Security Intelligence Organisation agent deployed to infiltrate the T.W.P.'s ranks found them a scruffy mob of dole bludgers and ratbag students.)

Access to the building could only be obtained by first making contact with the relevant office via intercom. Having identified herself to the anonymous T.W.P. voice Mrs Gaily and her son ascended the rickety timber stairs to the T.W.P. office. Here the owner of the anonymous voice cast a suspicious eye over mother and son through the ironically named spy hole.

"Petty bourgeois" he thought to himself before opening

the office door to the well-dressed mother and son.

The Gailys had never witnessed such squalor. Amidst the gloom one could barely discern the tall, gaunt man in his thirties dressed in an old perspiration-stained business shirt and tatty jeans. The musty, foetid room had never seen direct sunlight – nor had the T.W.P. functionary by the look of his pasty skin. A single light bulb revealed books and newspapers strewn over a table which looked in far more imminent likelihood of collapse at the hands of the T.W.P. than was Australian capitalism. A few yellowing posters clung for dear life to the walls recalling rallies and marches from the T.W.P.'s glorious past. The walls had not seen a coat of paint for years, one's shoes stuck to the filthy carpet and the ceiling looked an even money chance of caving in prior to the demise of the table. A few nondescript pieces of broken furniture completed the picture, every object in the room being coated in a thick layer of dust. This was the headquarters of the Australian revolution's government-in-waiting.

Mrs Gaily almost fainted at the sight and smell of the place. After recovering her composure she explained how her son had obtained a copy of Indirect Inaction and was keen to obtain more information about the T.W.P.

The functionary launched into a set spiel as to how the T.W.P. represented the historical continuation of the Russian Revolution, how the crisis of leadership had been brought about by the Stalinists and reformists, how T.W.P. membership was growing by the minute and how they would soon be the mass party of the working class because capitalism was "ripe for revolution if not a little rotten". He then sold the Gailys a copy of History of the Russian Revolution by Trotsky, loaded Charlie up with back copies of Indirect Inaction, invited him to a meeting of the Trotskyite Youth Alliance on Saturday and ushered mother and son out the door.

Once outside Mrs Gaily broke one of her own rules of etiquette and smoked a cigarette in the street. While his mother dragged on a Rothman's her son flicked through the books and newspapers.

"If I wanted to be a Communist I would join the Communist Party, Charles", Mrs Gaily opined.

"They are Stalinists, Mum", Charlie replied, picking up on the T.W.P. line.

"Very well, have it your own way," said his mother as they walked back to the railway station.

Saturday again rolled around and for the first time in his life Gaily was allowed to travel into town by himself.

After much fussing his parents saw him off at the bus stop.

"Be careful, son" said his mother, brushing away tears.

His father shook his "little man's" hand and wished him "all the best".

After two hours' travelling Gaily arrived back at the Haymarket. The same rigmarole ensued as occurred when in the company of his mother but eventually he was allowed in and traversed the rickety stairs which were to become all too familiar over the ensuing four years.

When Gaily entered the room the three young men and three young women who had been sitting on broken chairs drinking beer all got up to warmly shake his hand. Most had only been members for a few months at most so they still possessed the ardour of the new recruit. The exception was one of the girls who introduced herself as being the full-time organiser. She offered him a stubby of beer which he gratefully accepted. To drink under age was to challenge the hegemony of bourgeois morality.

The beer was also Resch's and the room was stiflingly hot and humid.

One of the young blokes gave an educational talk on the history of the Russian Revolution. The organiser gave a glowing report about their growing membership and escalating sales of their newspaper Young Trot. A general business item discussed good places to sell the paper during the following week.

After the meeting Gaily was offered another beer and asked if he wanted to join. Seeing signs of indecision the organiser urged him to join the struggle straight away as the revolution was due any tick of the clock and he would be negligent in his duties if he failed to join at next week's meeting. One of the girls was a pretty blonde in a miniskirt. He said "yes".

The next Saturday saw Gaily nominated and elected unopposed as a T.Y.A. member. For the next four years his Saturday afternoons would belong to the T.Y.A.

A typical Saturday would involve being picked up from a railway station by one of his comrades in an old bomb car, being driven to a suburban shopping centre, selling copies of Young Trot for two hours then going into town for the branch meeting.

Leaflets would be distributed publicising meetings on what the T.Y.A. saw as the main issues of the day. Petitions were used as a means of accumulating mailing lists. If a person agreed to be put on a "contact list" T.Y.A. members would visit them during the week to try to talk them into joining. Failing this they could be sold a newspaper subscription. Older people would be referred to the T.W.P., where a similar system was in train.

It was a lot of work for a very meagre return. No wonder membership turnover was so high. Gaily saw the faces come and go. The new recruits would initially come in full of enthusiasm, gradually become disenchanted, become less and less active then finally disappear altogether.

When Gaily questioned the high turnover of members he was told in no uncertain terms that most people did not have the mettle to be revolutionaries and that the demands on members sorted the wheat from the chaff, culling the dilettantes from those who would go on to lead the revolution.

Despite growing disillusionment himself Gaily stood solid. After about a year he was approached about joining the T.W.P. This was seen as an indication of a T.Y.A. member having served their apprenticeship well. Gaily was by then well-read in the theory of Trotskyism as enunciated by the T.W.P. and articulated by their co-thinkers in the United States. Gaily agreed to join the senior organisation.

Another reason for Gaily's standing within the sect was the freedom he had shown with his parents' money. The T.W.P./T.Y.A. had a pledge system in place whereby members were expected to part with as much of their income as they could possibly afford for the good of the cause. The amount of a member's weekly pledge was portrayed as a yardstick of their seriousness – a measure of their commitment. In Gaily's case it had merely been a measure of his ability to cadge off his parents. It would be a different story upon his venturing into the workplace.

Gaily was on the verge of completing his secondary school education. His parents urged him not to waste his talents: to go to university – or at the very least teachers' college. The Trots also wanted him on campus.

However, this was one of the rare occasions in Gaily's life where he asserted himself. Charlie Gaily did not fancy the stress of further formal studies. Despite matriculating to all universities Gaily just wanted to get a job, join a union, make a wage and have a few beers: so he did.

Gaily's first job was as a public service clerk. It was an easy little job in town which enabled him to proudly carry his first trade union ticket and have a beer in the pub after work and on weekends.

Gaily quickly got to know the office's union delegate. He was a boozy, worldly, likeable fellow to whom Gaily took an immediate liking. His name was Mark McMartin.

McMartin was everything the bookish Trots were not but would have liked to have been. Despite his starched white collar he was of the working class. He had attended the school of hard knocks. He had been through university but as he liked to tell people he had "been pushing a wheelbarrow at the time". McMartin could see that Gaily was not as fanatical as some of the madder Trots he had known in his time and invited Gaily to attend union meetings with him. Gaily jumped at the opportunity.

The meetings were long, boring affairs as befitted a public service clerks' union. The one bright spot was "tea money": an allowance paid to reward members for attending meetings. However, tea was hardly the drink of choice. After meetings the tea money was converted into beer.

Most of Gaily's nights were now spent at meetings and ended with the ritual beer drinking until the pubs closed at ten o'clock. Gaily would often fall asleep on the train going home and sometimes miss his station.

Gaily's parents had moved house so their son would be in close proximity to a railway station upon his entering the workforce – or as they had hoped commencing university. Whilst still living at home Gaily tried to curtail his drinking but did not try too hard.

On one occasion Gaily fell asleep and missed the last train back to his local station. His father was none too pleased at being rung after midnight but felt obliged to pick the boy up and drive him to ensure his son got to work on time the next day.

The cream puff bureaucrats of the T.W.P. had noticed Gaily's increasing drinking with alarm. Gaily had proven even more generous with his own money than with that of his parents. A large slice of his income went towards the upkeep of the sect's officials – whose only other source of income was social services. With his high workload and financial generosity milch cows like Gaily did not walk in the T.W.P. door every day.

One of the amateur psychoanalysts suggested to Gaily his excessive drinking might be due to his overbearing parents. The solution would be to move into a "party household" – in other words a flat or house shared with other T.W.P. or T.Y.A. members.

Gaily agreed to the suggestion. It proved an absolute disaster. Within a month the fellow with whom he was sharing a flat moved out. His mother purchased the flat from the T.W.P. owner and thus became her son's landlady.

Another suggestion was to attend A.A. meetings. Gaily attended a couple to placate the bureaucrats, chug-a-lugging Resch's tinnies on the way. However, one had to be ready to take decisive action of this nature. Down the track he would cut back but for the time being he enjoyed his drinking too much.

The T.W.P. leadership comprised half a dozen ego-driven no-hopers with delusions of grandeur and aspirations to power.

Just as Gaily had started to make inroads as an activist in the public service union the T.W.P. directed their cadre into what they termed "basic industry". Suddenly people of middle class background with no experience of manual labour were being told to resign from the jobs they held at the time and go into some of the dirtiest, most dangerous jobs in the blue-collar sector including the steel industry, car manufacturing and rail sectors.

The Trots had and have no idea as to the need for laborious, long-term work in a given area of work in order to achieve political goals. They flit from flavour of the month to flavour of the month. They concentrate on a campaign for a short while, sell a few papers, recruit a few members and move on in a never-ending slash and burn exercise.

The plan was to colonise key sectors of industry, gain positions within the relevant unions and obtain significant leverage within and ultimately leadership of the unions despite a lack of numbers. It was a complete disaster.

Immediately all the openly homosexual members recruited during an upturn in the gay rights movement resigned. They simply did not want to get their hands dirty.

A handful of others did as they were told and were promptly sacked for being politically outspoken while still in the probationary period of their employment.

Gaily could see what was coming. A group of people with no intention of heeding their own directives was telling their rank-and-file they had to cease their present employment and go into dirty, dangerous, poorly paid and insecure jobs for the expediting of the revolution.

Gaily had always held the long term approach to his union work. One had to spend years to build one's power base. A compromise was put to him to obtain a job in the postal industry. This would enable Gaily to remain in full-time permanent government employment and obtain continuity for the purpose of long service leave. Another T.W.P. member was already working in the area and he would be working in a large, strongly unionised workplace. It was actually not a bad proposition so on this occasion Gaily accepted what was being put to him.

It would also provide a breathing space. The T.W.P. bureaucrats were continuing to hound him about his drinking so by being seen to be going along with their ideas he had hoped they might leave him alone for a while. One of Gaily's weaknesses was excessive loyalty to those who did not deserve it.

Gaily continued to attend T.W.P. and T.Y.A. meetings and sell their papers. Although sufficiently disillusioned to resign his memberships he did not know where to turn. As someone who believed fervently in the need for a Marxist party he sought a star to guide him. If that star was not to be the T.W.P. then another star had to be found.

As Gaily commenced work with Australia Post an alternative star beckoned. Shining ever more brilliant the red star of the Communist Party of Australia heralded a new dawn in the political life of Charlie Gaily.

After years of having it drummed into him that the C.P.A. was "Stalinist" Gaily had difficulty equating the T.W.P. line with his own experience. The C.P.A. members he encountered were all decent people – more in keeping with his own view of the world than the lumpen Trots.

Gaily's new place of employment was the Sydney Mail Exchange. Once through the mailsorting training school he would encounter one of the greatest assortment of lefties under one roof on the planet.

However, the Inland training school was hard going. Prospective mailsorters had to learn the names and locations of more than two thousand suburbs and towns throughout the state of New South Wales. To facilitate the learning process the school provided printed notes in the form of stories which incorporated the names of towns in a particular area.

One of the training school supervisors could see Gaily was struggling so sat down next to him and gave him a hand. Mailsorter training involved placing cards with place names on them into the relevant pigeonholes in a sorting frame. The supervisor suggested Gaily put the cards for each region in front of him in the order in which they appeared in the stories. This simple memory technique etched the names of the towns in the trainee's mind and helped link town names with regions. The technique worked and Gaily passed the final training school examination with flying colours.

The six weeks of training did not pass completely without mishap. Training school hours were divided into morning and afternoon shifts in order to mimic the hours trainees could expect to work once on the floor. One afternoon after a morning shift Gaily went to one of his favourite haunts – the Great Southern - and consumed an excellent sufficiency of Resch's in a short space of time. Upon boarding his homeward-bound train he promptly fell asleep and went on a long journey through the suburbs of Sydney before awaking at the railway station whence he had boarded the train several hours prior. Looking up at the station's clock tower he saw it was after six o'clock and not realising it was night and not morning ran back to the Mail Exchange and into the training school.

"Sorry, I'm late", he gasped to the afternoon shift supervisor.

Realising immediately what had occurred the supervisor merely smiled and advised Gaily to go home. Never another word was spoken on the matter but occasional knowing looks would be exchanged between Gaily and the supervisor in the years to come.

On another occasion Gaily and some of the other

trainees went to a club after work. With the pubs closing at ten one had to go to a club in order to have a drink after this time.

After another excellent sufficiency of Resch's Gaily fell asleep at the table. One of his workmates attempted to arouse him from his slumbers by slapping him on the face.

Thinking to put him in a cab he sought Gaily's suburb of residence from him.

"Where do you live?" the workmate repeatedly asked.

"Seven West," replied Gaily – giving the name of one of the rural postal regions.

This farce continued until Gaily was at least capable of staggering into the night for parts unknown. The training school was obviously playing on his subconscious mind.

Such were the joys of postal training school for trainee Mail Officer Charlie Gaily.

At his medical the examining doctor – of Chinese origin – could smell quite clearly the beer on Gaily's breath.

"Have you been drinking?" asked the doctor.

"No," came the reply, Gaily having just chug-a-lugged three bottles of Resch's Pilsener.

"Are you sure?" asked the doctor.

"Maybe one or two last night," replied Gaily.

"You have a most euphoric personality," quipped the doctor.

Thus was the post office's most recent recruit passed fit to start.

Gaily's leaving the public service had been tinged with sadness. At this stage of his life Gaily saw a decency about humanity which he appreciated and sought to nurture. With a worsening of the objective situation Gaily knew that basic human decency could either be transformed into political radicalism or swept away to be replaced by a dog eat dog individualism. Gaily was still optimistic the former would prevail.

The people with whom he had worked at the little public service office were just that: decent human beings. The supervisors would rather have had a feed than a fight – turning a blind eye to the fact Gaily processed fewer forms than other clerks. The union delegate was a good bloke but not a radical. Still many a beery tear was shed at his farewell party at the Occidental Hotel.

There were bigger fish though to fry. The Trots were right about one thing: with the left short on numbers it was necessary to spread oneself thin.

The left was never going to make any advances with people bludging on the welfare state while mouthing a lot of platitudinous rhetoric. The main vehicles for social change were the trade unions and it was incumbent upon anyone of Gaily's age who considered themselves a Marxist to get a job, join a union and seek to organise the troops for the clashes ahead.

The Mail Exchange was a bastion of trade union militancy. So powerful had it become the Federal Government of the day sought to close it in order to break the backbone of the postalworkers' union. Gaily's father referred to the Soviet Union as "like one big Mail Exchange" (when it was almost too late Gaily would realise what a wag his father had been).

Into this seething cauldron strode Mail Officer Charlie Gaily.

If Gaily had wanted action he got it straight off the bat. For fourteen years the Mail Exchange workers had been able to control the postal industry in New South Wales due to the centralised nature of the postal network. The vast majority of articles posted within Australia's largest state had to pass through the exchange in order to be processed.

In an attempt to break the union's power the Federal Government ordered Australia Post to redirect a large volume of articles to outlying centres for processing. In the event of this ploy succeeding the flow of mail within New South Wales could not be halted simply by the exchange workers going on strike or imposing bans: the union would require a more co-ordinated state-wide approach. The government knew co-ordination of the entire state would be difficult to effect given the relative conservatism of postalworkers outside Sydney. By seeking to undermine the exchange's industrial clout it pre-empted a move to close the exchange altogether and create a fully decentralised postal system.

Two new pigeonholes had been created on the sorting frames into which letters were sorted. These were labelled with the names of the two centres on the New South Wales south coast to which articles were to be redirected for processing. Similar modifications occurred on racks used for larger articles.

An overseer was required to ask each sorter under his/her charge whether or not they were prepared to redirect the post to the south coast centres. An answer in the negative resulted in the worker having their pay suspended for not following their employer's directive: No Work As Directed No Pay (N.W.A.D.N.P.).

Every single mail sorter at the exchange refused to redirect articles. The fight was on.

Mass meetings were convened by the union. Over three thousand were employed at the exchange and other members of the union were involved in acts of solidarity.

At the first meeting convened the union president told

his members "If yous lose this yous'll be nothin' better than process workers".

The dispute lasted for six weeks. Although not on strike it was six weeks devoid of wages. Large sums of money were borrowed in order to survive.

At the end of the six weeks the workers were demoralised and vanquished. The bypass had been effected in their absence due to the union's inability to co-ordinate state-wide action on an ongoing basis.

The exchange workers returned to their normal rostered duties "nothin' better than process workers".

This had been Charlie Gaily's first taste of industrial action. This and similar defeats in other industries set the trend for the future. The gains made by the Australian trade union movement on the back of the post-war economic boom were to be gradually eroded.

When Gaily entered the workforce the percentage of workers in trade unions was over fifty per cent. This figure has gradually dwindled to be around twenty per cent today.

There is a direct correlation between the degree of unionisation and the quality of life and standard of living enjoyed by a nation's people.

The Mail Exchange boasted virtually one hundred per cent of union members amongst its ranks. The couple of dissidents were labelled "scabs". No one would talk to or work with them. Legally it was impossible to enforce a closed shop. However, when every single workmate sends you to Coventry you soon get the message.

Working conditions at the Mail Exchange were second to none. In the public service Gaily had worked a thirty-five hour week. In the post office it was a thirty-six and three-quarter hour week. At the Mail Exchange though there were five (in reality ten) minute breaks to wash one's hands prior to meal breaks and knocking off, five minutes grace to bundy on (ten on the early morning shift) and two ten (in reality fifteen) minute tea breaks per shift.

These and other conditions of employment were not written into the industrial award so could be annulled at any time. They were based on "gentlemen's agreements" – which presuppose one to be dealing with gentlemen.

The wages on the other hand were surprisingly low despite the postalworkers' pay rates being tied to those of the metalworkers – the metalworkers' union being the most powerful union at the time.

The base rate had been allowed to fall behind as a result of an acceptance of overtime as being a condition of employment. Once the bypass came into being overtime was significantly reduced thus reducing the amount of take-home pay upon which people had come to rely.

Shift loadings of fifteen per cent applied to most shifts with night shift being an entity unto itself and carrying a thirty per cent loading.

Gaily had always believed conditions to be more important than pay but this was easier for him to say than most as at a pinch he would always have his parents upon whom to rely.

The atmosphere of the place was pretty relaxed with a blind eye turned to a lot of things. This included "mailies" going to the pub during working hours.

Two pubs were almost equidistant from the Mail Exchange: the Surry Club and the Woolpack. To go to one or other when one was meant to be working was termed to make a "run". It involved leaving the building via a fire escape and down through loading docks onto street level. There were blokes at the Mail Exchange who had made more runs than Don Bradman.

Gaily refrained from making runs as he found he could consume an excellent sufficiency of Resch's without putting his job at risk – there being a six month probationary period for new employees.

Drinking was a huge part of the culture of the workplace. Australians used to identify much more strongly with their pub of choice than is the case since the advent of poker machines and the push towards a younger crowd at the expense of older drinkers.

Gaily became an adherent of the Surry push as opposed to those who frequented the Woolpack. The "wallopers" (overseers) and management types were discreet enough to drink at the Norfolk.

The drink of choice was Resch's. It was still "the beer we drink round here". When sunbaking on the Mail Exchange roof Gaily could look out over the Resch's Waverley Brewery. The standing joke amongst the mailies was "we call it Wreckers because it wrecks you". Despite about a third of the workforce being female it was a very blokie culture which prevailed.

This is not to say the women themselves were blokie: far from it. There were a few obviously lesbian women but their attitude was that their sexuality was a private matter even if one could guess without being told. (Now Gaily was mixing in broader circles he would discover a lot of lesbians and male homosexuals thought the camp element which pervades the Sydney Gay Mardi Gras and overseas equivalents did more harm than good.)

Amongst the straight women there were some real stunners: some who modelled on the side, some who could have so done. How they had found their way to the Mail Exchange was hard to imagine but the exchange brought together a diverse assortment of people who did not quite fit into mainstream stereotypes. It was an "inclusive" workplace prior to that term becoming popular.

A lot of the attractive younger women worked in the

coding section. This involved processing small letters by entering keystrokes pertaining to a letter's postcode on a keyboard.

Those not in coding worked in manual sections- which included the loading of trucks on the docks. Watching one of his new workmates bending over to lift a bag presented a very interesting spectacle due to the brevity of her mini-skirt.

The older ladies did not know where to look: some others did not share their problem.

The one woman Gaily could not abide at the Mail Exchange was his fellow T.W.P. member Lyn Bogan.

Bogan was a proper pain in the neck (or another part of the anatomy Gaily was too polite to mention). She was always snooping around to see what he was up to and would reprimand him loudly in front of other people. Regular reports were made by her to the T.W.P. executive about his drinking and general behaviour.

The larrikin is a likeable character whose existence has been threatened by Americanisation and social conservatism under the guise of liberalism.

The old barmaid at the Surry would often sing "Charlie Is My Darling" in his honour upon seeing Gaily enter the pub. Bogan looked forward to hearing dirges sung in his memory.

Gaily had continued to remain an active member of the T.W.P., selling papers and attending meetings. His weekly pledge was only matched by the sole doctor the T.W.P. had as a member. The doctor's income was at least twenty times that of Gaily.

There was no doubting his commitment. Being popular with his workmates Gaily would sell copies of Indirect Inaction to people who vehemently disagreed with its political line. These included the Mail Exchange's resident Communist.

However, something had to give. One night he was called to appear before the T.W.P. executive. The so-called executive was in fact several scruffy individuals with clothes by St Vincent de Paul. None of them had ever had a job outside the T.W.P. They obtained their incomes from social services topped up by mugs like Gaily.

In four years of membership Gaily had barely got to know their surnames due to the Trots' obsession with security and the pretence of their having to adopt an underground form of organisation in the event of their being suppressed by the state for their subversive activities. They really kidded themselves.

It was a put-up job. Gaily was deemed to not be the type of person the T.W.P. wanted representing them in the post office.

"They only have two members in the whole place", Gaily thought to himself. (There was no point in saying anything aloud as the decision had already been made.)

Gaily listened inattentively to a litany of allegations – waiting for the whole dreary affair to reach its predetermined conclusion.

All the allegations centred around his drinking.

"These clowns have nothing better to do than sneak around pubs checking up on me", he thought.

He looked with contempt at these would-be leaders of men in their dirty, unironed, ill-fitting clothes. Earlier in the evening he had parted with several hundred dollars he was said to have owed.

Gaily mused as to the real reason for their decision. He did not have to look far. They felt threatened by someone better dressed, better spoken and actively engaged in political work which they could only discuss at a pseudo-intellectual level.

Finally the clique advised him his membership had been lapsed. Gaily showed no emotion despite having devoted thousands of hours and thousands of dollars to the sect over four years. He had no intention of wasting his time in appealing against the decision. This would only result in formal expulsion. He had seen it all before where an individual who did not quite fit the mould was isolated and demoralised until they either resigned or were shown the door. It was small circle politics and was the main reason the Trots would never amount to anything.

Gaily reluctantly shook each of his erstwhile comrades' hands and wished them a good night before descending the rickety stairs for the last time.

As he entered George Street he felt a huge weight lift from his shoulders. It was a beautiful summer's night in the best city in the world. Gaily went to the Great Southern for a schooner of Resch's to celebrate his newly found freedom.

Life without being in a political organisation would be strange and new. It would leave a huge void in Charlie Gaily's life as Gaily believed fervently in the need for a Marxist party suited to Australian conditions. Unfortunately his first attempt at locating such an animal had proven a disaster. Having had his fingers badly burnt he would tread warily on the second attempt.

Thankfully history abhors vacuums. Gaily was already in contact with the post office's grand old man of the C.P.A. Brian Timothy.

As a Senior Mail Officer Timothy had his own desk adjoining a rack of airmail bags on the third floor of the

Mail Exchange. His job involved writing out consignment notes for inclusion in each bag as it was tied off by the mail officers sorting articles into the bags.

As the holder of various unpaid positions with the union he was often off the job attending to union business. As long as the management were made aware of intended absences they had no problem with what was an established work practice. Timothy was highly respected by union and employer alike.

Gaily and Timothy were already on good terms and often had tea-breaks together. Each week they would exchange newspapers: an Indirect Inaction for a Trib.

Timothy had known Gaily's break with the T.W.P. was just a matter of time. He had witnessed the younger man becoming increasingly demoralised.

He also had to put up with Lyn Bogan's carping backstabbing of her supposed comrade. On these occasions Timothy would bite his tongue but he knew from years of experience how badly the Trots treated their own.

Gaily asked Timothy about joining the C.P.A. Being a much larger organisation than the T.W.P. the C.P.A. had a Postal and Telecommunications branch. Timothy said he would discuss the matter with the branch secretary.

The following week Timothy invited Gaily to a branch meeting. It was held at the Party headquarters in Dixon Street.

The P and T branch consisted of three postal clerks and Brian Timothy. It was one of thirty branches within the Sydney District. Of these thirty fourteen were industrial branches. As late as the early eighties the Party could still boast five hundred members in Sydney and two thousand throughout Australia.

The branch secretary was a small, nuggety man who walked with the aid of a stick. He was an official with the postal clerks' union which at the time was still separate from the main postalworkers' union the A.P.T.U. His name was Dennis Jack. Timothy had told Gaily Jack had had polio.

Timothy had also told Jack Gaily had been chucked out of the T.W.P. for excessive drinking.

"Bloody wowsers," Jack laughed. "We would give him a Stakhanovite medal." (This was an award for services to socialism in the Soviet Union.)

Jack's favourite call to arms was that the role of the Communist was "to apply the tactics of Che Guevara in the workplace".

This was hardly the politics of reformism.

Nearing the end of the meeting a General Business item accepted Charlie Gaily as a member of the Communist Party of Australia subject to District Committee ratification. Gaily considered it a wonderful if slightly belated twenty-first birthday present.

After the meeting the five branch members went to the Party pub the Criterion until closing. The Resch's had never tasted better.

The C.P.A. was much more of a mainstream party than the little Trot sect. The Party had influence far beyond what its numbers would suggest. Its members included many people famous for their contribution to Australian society. The Party had a rich history dating back to 1920. It was acknowledged by left-wing A.L.P. Members of Parliament as a decisive ginger group. It was part of what was still termed the international Communist movement.

One of the first internal gatherings Gaily attended was a Sydney District Conference. Delegates from all branches met over two days for discussion and the election of a new District Committee.

The theme of the conference was "Build the Party". There was no hint of the liquidationism which would eleven years later result in the Party's dissolution.

Gaily had been delegated by his branch in order to give him experience of the Party's workings. Articulate, cultured people spoke with passion about issues pertaining to the unions, locality work, the peace and women's movements and other international issues. Gaily was able to provide his branch with a very positive report.

One of Gaily's duties as a delegate was to vote for the incoming District Committee. As a new member he was not familiar with all candidates so another delegate gave him a hand.

Mitch Rodney was to become a lifelong friend. After the final conference session they went for a schooner of Resch's.

Rodney and Gaily were part of a peer group of twelve to fifteen C.P.A. members which stayed solid for the eleven years of Gaily's membership. They also remained in contact after the Party's dissolution.

When the Party revived its youth wing this group formed the nucleus of what was called the Young Communist Movement.

The Y.C.M. produced its own magazine Groundswell. Members were encouraged to write, type and assist in the actual production of the magazine. It was a joyous time in Gaily's life.

The C.P.A. had severed formal ties with the so-called socialist countries years prior but the tenuous links which still remained provided the opportunity for travel to overseas conferences.

Gaily turned up opportunities for travel to these conferences in deference to more experienced and better credentialled comrades. However, he was at least prompted to obtain a passport for future reference.

Timothy had warned Gaily that he would encounter a lot of older people in the Party. There was in fact a good spread of ages with a leaning to the very old and the very young as a result of the Cold War.

Those that were of his parents' generation included former officials of the Builders Labourers' Federation. They were legends of the labour movement.

Gaily sought out their company at the pubs where they drank: the Coronation as well as the Criterion. One of them sagely advised him to concentrate on one area of activity rather than spread himself too thin.

Despite this advice Gaily threw himself into both his trade union activity and a new area of activity for him: the peace movement.

The peace movement had come into being as a result of the Ban The Bomb movement in the fifties. The world had been shocked by America's unnecessary bombing of Hiroshima and Nagasaki in 1945. The war was as good as over, the Nazis had been defeated and the Japanese were ready to surrender. Ban The Bomb centred around a mass petition campaign spearheaded by the Communists to ensure that never again would nuclear weapons be used.

As had occurred in World War I America had come in half way through proceedings after having sold arms to both sides. Their bombing of civilian populations at the end of World War II was the opening gambit of the Cold War. It was the most thinly veiled of threats to the Soviet Union.

At the beginning of the eighties there were two influential peace organisations in Sydney. One was the Association for International Co-operation and Disarmament.

The other was the Australian Peace Committee.

Within the C.P.A. the preferred option was A.I.C.D. as the A.P.C. was deemed pro-Soviet. Some of the older comrades in particular retained strong sympathies for the Soviet Union and therefore supported the A.P.C. Gaily joined both but this proved at times to be something of a juggling act.

Peace activists in the C.P.A. organised their activities via the Peace Collective. The collective often split along A.I.C.D.-A.P.C. lines. It was in fact impossible to make co-ordinated interventions in campaigns as Communists due to fundamental political differences.

Central to the problem was one's attitude to the role of the Soviet Union. Did it represent a counter- hegemonic force to United States imperialism or not?

From one's answer to this question flowed one's attitude to a range of other problems which had their origins in the Party's splits in the sixties and seventies.

Old wounds had never healed and those people who had left to form their own separate Communist organisations had never been fully forgiven by the most trenchant supporters of the C.P.A. leadership.

Particular vehemence was reserved for the Socialist Party of Australia - which had been formed as a result of differences towards the Soviet military intervention in Czechoslovakia in 1968.

Peace Collective discussions often became bogged down but because it was a collective and not a committee decisions were not always made by a formal vote. The collective was a useful forum for discussions but individual members sometimes carried their differences into public forums. This could result in Communists speaking and voting against each other.

Gaily thought this a deplorable situation in what was ostensibly a Marxist party operating along democratic centralist lines. Under the circumstances all one could do was one's best.

Gaily did just that – helping to organise all the big marches and rallies held in Sydney throughout the eighties.

A regular feature of this activity was pasting up posters. With a paintbrush in one hand, a bucket of wallpaper paste in the other and a swag of posters over his shoulder Gaily was a one man paste-up team. If anyone wanted to keep him company so much the better.

The three big days of the year for which marches were scheduled were Palm Sunday, May Day and Hiroshima Day.

Gaily sat on the respective organising committees for all three events and often took leave from work to perform clerical work. When not representing the Party he would be delegated by his union's rank-and-file group or the newly formed Western Suburbs Peace Group.

The peace group had been formed by local A.L.P. members but had lapsed into inactivity. Gaily obtained mailing lists from the peace movement and posted out invitations to a meeting to people in the area. He remained secretary for nine years during which time the group became an integral part of the community.

The peace group also offered an opportunity to become closer to his parents. The group's coffers were swelled by regular donations of pot plants from Gaily's father. The plants were sold at the group's monthly stalls and Mr Gaily requested no reimbursement.

It gave Ted Gaily great pleasure to help green the gardens of the western suburbs and at the same time assist his son in one of his more worthwhile endeavours. His wife would type the group's newsletter so the group assisted in bringing the family closer.

All this activity did not go unnoticed by the young women in the Party. With his long blonde hair, blue eyes and fair skin there were worse catches to be had.

Linda Burnley was a new member of the Postal branch. With her very long blonde hair, blue eyes, hourglass figure and peaches and cream complexion she was the epitome of the English rose. Memories of school days flooded back at the sight of Linda. Were Gaily to finally lose his virginity let it be to someone like this – and a Communist from northern England to boot.

Linda was slightly older and more sexually experienced. One weekend she arranged for the two of them to spend a weekend together at the Carrington Hotel in Katoomba in the Blue Mountains – a very picturesque area just outside Sydney. With its open log fires and rural atmosphere the Carrington was the perfect venue for seduction.

In the afternoon the couple were able to walk hand in hand through nearby bushland.

At night they were able to laugh at the memory of an old wharfie who opposed the use of night shifts with the words, "The nights are for love"…And so it proved to be…

In the hotel room the English girl struggled to remove her tight jeans and white t-shirt. Her large firm breasts and buttocks strained against the garments as though willing her to remain clothed. Gaily had implored her to wear a miniskirt but Linda paid lip service to her feminist convictions by denying the request.

Breasts, buttocks and erect penis all stood in unison pointing towards an imaginary heaven. The girl threw herself on the bed, removed her brief white cotton knickers and parted her legs. As she did so she led Gaily by his penis- guiding him to the Promised Land.

Two minutes later the act had been consummated in a somewhat clinical manner. The offending virginity was lost and gone forever.

Linda made it quite clear that favours such as the one just bestowed were just that and not to be expected on a regular basis. They would sleep together on several more occasions but it would never be quite the same.

When Linda turned up at the Surry one night one of the other drinkers was a Trot but thankfully not of the T.W.P. persuasion.

"You Stalinists get all the best sorts," he joked, using a most non-Trot turn of phrase.

There was a certain cachet in being seen in public with a beautiful woman. However, beautiful women can get sick of hanging around pubs.

On Gaily's twenty-second birthday a mob of C.P.A. members including Linda joined him at the Criterion for drinks. Linda looked decidedly bored.

One of the comrades was an older man of mixed Aboriginal and Indian heritage. He had been with the B.L.F. in their glory days but now made a living as a professional Aboriginal.

He sauntered up to Linda and asked, "Like a curry?"

The two of them took French leave and that was the end of Gaily's fling with Linda.

Ironically the next year Linda moved permanently to India to be a part of their women's movement amidst the poverty of Bihar. In the meantime she entertained the men of the C.P.A. – much to the chagrin of one or two wives.

Gaily and Linda stayed in contact for many years but eventually the tyranny of distance became too much. Gaily could only imagine from the letters he received what Bihar must have been like. He preferred to leave it to the realm of imagination. Living in the western suburbs was bad enough.

Linda had given Gaily a taste of the pleasures of the flesh. Just as good food is said to promote appetite so too does one's first taste of the forbidden fruit promote carnal appetite.

One of the rites of passage for a young man in Sydney in the eighties was a visit to A Taste Of Cash. A.T.O.C. was generally regarded at the time as the city's best brothel – or should one say bordello?

A.T.O.C. was everything to which other establishments in the sex industry could only aspire.

The management was all-female. As should be the case the blokes were the punters and the women ran the show. There was therefore no standing over of workers and payment of wages was always in cash not kind. (Other less savoury establishments would pay wages in the form of illegal drugs in order to feed and maintain addictions.) Everyone knew where they stood: the house kept half of all payments, the women who did the work received the other half. The ladies were not just prostitutes: they were courtesans. Medical checks were conducted on a weekly basis and a clean bill of health had to be obtained prior to a lady recommencing work. Grooming and deportment lessons ensured the ladies scrubbed up well. Attention to detail extended to dental health and even a slightly chipped fingernail required immediate remedial action.

For their part clients were expected to shower and undertake a visual examination conducted by the lady whom they were seeing prior to physical contact being allowed. Later in the decade the A.I.D.S scare would ensure the use of condoms became mandatory but at the time what one could not see was deemed incapable of causing harm.

Opinions in the men's locker room at the Mail Exchange varied widely as to the merits of A.T.O.C.

"They all look like dental nurses," opined one mailie.

"Oh, I like dental nurses," came the reply.

"They'll suck the skin off your willy", was one of the more cerebral observations.

Gaily decided it was time to find out for himself what pleasures could be found behind the famous door in Sydney's inner suburb of Surry Hills.

Gaily rang A.T.O.C. preparatory to his first visit.

A young woman's voice answered the telephone. He enquired as to whether there were any blue-eyed blonde English girls on the staff and was told that "Kim" fitted the description. As if he did not already know he would learn that all working girls work under assumed names.

His other enquiry pertained to the payment required. A hundred and eighty dollars for an hour was an affordable amount as an occasional treat for someone on a low wage.

This was more exciting than joining the silly Trots. His drinking had been knocking him around a bit lately so he had been cutting down for the previous few weeks. He rationalised the situation by saying to himself that the hour at A.T.O.C. was paid for out of what would otherwise have been drinking money. It was a reward for abstemiousness. In reality it was swapping one vice for another but fair exchange is no robbery.

Some of the older blokes with whom he was now mixing went on the wagon for two or three months each year. It was a good way to avoid cirrhosis. Gaily was glad to be surrounding himself with wise old heads but in his own hoped to be able to put the funds thus liberated to good use.

To some extent he was revolting against the unnecessary constraints he had imposed upon himself whilst with the Trots. Those bastards had bled him white. Now he was going to spend more of his hard-earned on himself.

Having survived his probationary period with the post office he was now entitled to five sickies a year without having to produce a medical certificate. Gaily determined to have a day off work for his first visit to A.T.O.C. and then if he enjoyed himself go on the razzle to celebrate.

Phoning in sick was a formality at the Mail Exchange where the clerical staff knew a nod was as good as a wink to a blind horse. Sick leave was a legal entitlement under the award and any employer who challenged a worker's right to a day off was a mug. Gaily made the call –merely stating he was sick – and the rest of the day belonged to him.

Kim started work at ten so Gaily made a point of being at A.T.O.C. an hour early. First in, best dressed meant Gaily was wearing a Lacoste t-shirt, dress shorts and his best thongs. His dress sense at this stage of his life was more casual than smart but this would change with the passing of time.

Gaily rang the doorbell at nine sharp. He was keen as mustard. The receptionist was a stunning Kiwi girl in a miniskirt – sharp and sexy in appearance.

"Christ!" he thought, "if this is the receptionist what must the girls themselves look like?"

The receptionist took Gaily to a waiting room. The room was plushly furnished. The place oozed sophistication. It actually played an important secondary role in teaching men how to behave in the company of women.

The receptionist offered Gaily a drink.

"Is there Resch's, please?"

"Yes there is."

The receptionist brought him his beer: the old "silver bullet" – now passed but fondly remembered. (A "silver bullet" was a tin of Resch's Pilsener. It came in a silver tin hence the nickname.) A glass was provided. Attention to detail makes a huge difference.

"Kim will be with you shortly", he was told.

On the dot of ten there was a knock on the waiting-room door. In walked an incarnation of beauty straight out of a wet dream. Gaily was momentarily gobsmacked.

"Good morning. I'm Kim," said Kim – just to prove she was flesh and blood like a mere mortal.

Gaily stood and shook her hand. A kiss may have seemed too forward.

When asked to follow her to a room Gaily dutifully obliged. He not so much walked as floated. The view while ascending the stairs leading to the room was most excellent.

The rooms at A.T.O.C. all had themes. Kim opened the door to their room and ushered him in to what would be their playground for the next hour.

The room was dimly lit with a myriad of small lights shining down from the ceiling. This was the Starlight Room.

The girl wore a tightly fitting aqua blue dress which highlighted the curves of her perfectly toned body. Through the back of her dress Gaily had already glimpsed the outline of her high-cut knickers. The requisite amount of money changed hands and the girl left him for a few minutes to enable him to undress and shower. The carpet and furniture were plush, the towel white and fluffy.

Gaily quickly undressed and showered while Kim left the room to account for the first of many payments she would receive that day.

Upon returning to the room she engaged him in conversation in her clipped London accent. This was the first of many encounters he would have with posh totty.

Kim peeled off her dress to revel matching blue knickers. At this stage of her life she required no bra.

Kim invited Gaily onto the big double bed and got him to lie on his stomach – having first checked downstairs with the aid of a reading lamp.

Gaily felt her firm warm breasts rub against his back as she gave him a shoulder massage to loosen the tension in his body. It was after all a massage parlour.

Kim was several years older than Gaily. Not for her the monotony of years of low-paid menial work. In two years she would make her pile and return to London.

In the meantime Kim got Gaily to roll over onto his back. He was already hard as a rock so it was just a matter of carefully mounting him and riding him to orgasm. Gaily watched in admiration – at once spectator and participant – as the beautiful young woman bounced up and down, her firm breasts defying gravity as her lightly tanned body rose and fell on top of him.

Eager to please the girl stroked him until a second erection had been achieved and repeated the act with a similarly happy ending.

The two showered and dressed with Kim taking the now soiled towel which had been spread across the bed.

Gaily could not thank Kim enough for the wonderful service provided. He got a quick peck on the cheek for his trouble and Kim got ninety dollars.

On being let out the main exit fantasy again turned into reality. Gaily looked both ways to ensure no feminists were in sight and walked away whistling. Like General Macarthur he would return.

With the day to himself Gaily thought a celebratory

schooner of Resch's at the Criterion would be in order. He also had to be careful not to run into work types as he was meant to be sick. His luck held but on a day when he had got the daily double up with the beautiful Kim he was never going to lose.

Upon Gaily's return to work the next day he was greeted like a hero by his workmates.

The union's officials had got hold of a rank-and-file group leaflet attacking them for having sold out over the bypass issue. They were furious and two of them had visited the Mail Exchange to have a quiet word with the leaflet's author.

Most of the officials were despised by the mailies and the union representatives (shop stewards/delegates) at the Exchange always tried to resolve matters in-house rather than involve the officials.

"Must be an election coming up," said Gaily- the standing joke being the officials were only ever seen when they needed to drum up support for re-election.

In fact shop-floor elections were about to be conducted and Gaily was an odds-on favourite to win a position at the expense of one of the officials' supporters. The officials had lost a lot of support since the bypass dispute loss. Many workers were still repaying debts incurred despite its having been more than two years prior. The moneylenders who operated quite openly within the workplace had had a field day and their usurious rates of interest made it very difficult to ever repay a loan.

Gaily usually spoke at the floor meetings which were often convened over relatively minor day-to-day issues. The existing reps were in the main looking forward to Gaily's election as he brought enthusiasm and fresh ideas to the table. Only the tired old men who were thought to be in the boss's pocket would oppose him as it would be at their expense he would win votes.

Gaily would stand with the support of the rank-and-file group. This was a motley collection of Trots and A.L.P. lefties. The rank-and-file group met regularly at the Trade Union Club in Surry Hills. They were considerably to the left of the officials and slightly mad. Gaily thought the world of them.

As anticipated Gaily was duly elected as a union rep. This was a position he had coveted since joining the workforce and now he was in a position to put his politics into practice where it most mattered: in the trade union movement.

Like his C.P.A. comrade Brian Timothy Gaily had quickly won the respect of workers and management alike due to his politeness, his ability to speak and write and his enthusiasm for the trade union struggle. The officials themselves were secretly glad one of their old supporters had been outvoted by Gaily as they would try to harness the younger man's energies to their own advantage by making him sing for his supper. In the long term they thought they would be able to buy him off with a job. They had few principles themselves and could not understand those who did.

The main role of a union rep was to act as an intermediary between section managers and staff when a grievance arose. The Exchange staff had led such a sheltered existence for so long it was often a matter involving the way in which a supervisor or overseer spoke to a member of staff which led to a complaint being made to the union. In these situations a show of contrition on the part of the supervisor or overseer was usually required in order to placate the aggrieved party.

Another pet hate was overweight bags. A bag of mail

was considered unsafe to lift if it weighed more than six-teen kilogrammes. Parcel bags were allowed to weigh twenty kilogrammes.

When overweight bags were received from outside the Exchange they were often blackbanned for twenty-four hours. This involved their being piled on the floor with empty bags thrown over them to indicate the placement of a ban. Of course bags could also be tied off overweight by one's fellow Exchange workmates. Sometimes this would occur inadvertently near the end of a shift. In other cases this was done quite consciously and a ban imposed on the spot in order to achieve a square-up for a perceived injustice.

Bans could only be imposed with the approval of one of the union's officials. Similarly meetings could also only be convened in this way. The official concerned would generally give his assent as this obviated him of the need to attend in person. In this way the union reps were able to run their own race for most of the twenty years of the Exchange's existence.

One of the tricks involved in gaining the assent of the officials to take action was to know which of the officials to contact. This required a sound knowledge of the individuals concerned and the games being played amongst them at the time.

Being a union rep meant being able to attend Mail Branch meetings once a month. Here delegates and officials from the postal side of the union met to discuss the issues of the day. The Mail Exchange was always well represented as this was still where the most militant and conscientious unionists worked. It was here one got to know one's officials and mix with other reps.

The Mail Exchange was a large workplace divided into sections - each of which had its own reps. Mail Branch was a gathering of the clan. The highlight of the evening was repairing to the Star Hotel across the road. Here Trots, anarchists, Communists and A.L.P. lefties would form a united front based on a love of the cut and thrust of politics discussed over a cold drink.

The Star was to become a favourite haunt of Gaily's. Prior to the introduction of poker machines in pubs the Star was a real trade union pub. With the introduction of pokies and the decline of trade unionism it would become little more than a pokie den.

In the eighties then it had a large oval-shaped bar divided in two. The front bar was the public bar tradition-ally frequented by men only, the back bar the lounge for mixed drinking.

Although this delineation was fading Gaily could still remember the time sitting in his father's car in the car park of the Ampol service station in Baulkham Hills. Across the road was the Bull And Bush Hotel. Men would bring middies (half pints) of beer out to their wives in cars parked just outside the pub. They would then go back into the pub to drink their schooners (three-quarter pint glasses) in all-male company.

Change has occurred slowly in Australian pub culture.

Change, however, was occurring far more rapidly within the post office. Increasingly discussion centred on the closure of the Mail Exchange and its replacement by a decentralised network of mail centres throughout the Sydney metropolitan area. The fight to save the exchange was on but the events of 1979 ensured it was a battle which could not be won.

The election of a Federal Labor Government gave the labour movement renewed confidence in its ability to forge social change. However, this confidence was based on illusions in the A.L.P. to deliver change through parliamentary reform.

The postalworkers' union was historically aligned with the A.L.P.'s right-wing faction – particularly that part of the faction controlled by the Catholic Church (the Groupers). (The Industrial Groups were the industrial wing of the National Civic Council. In Victoria the N.C.C.'s political wing was the Democratic Labour Party but in NSW the N.C.C. forces stayed in the A.L.P. rather than break away.)

Just as the union's right-wing federal officials could blame their factional opponents at the state level for the introduction of the bypass system so they would blame a previous conservative federal government for the eventual closure of the Exchange. The rank-and-file would put up an almighty fight but they would be isolated and defeated.

The writing was on the wall when the employer was allowed to create interim mail centres within the mail exchange building. Instead of the exchange being divided into sections pertaining to the categories and destinations of post being processed it was divided into sections which corresponded with a suburban centre of the future.

Workers were allowed to nominate the suburb in which they would prefer to work while the mail centres were still under construction. The centre would function at its temporary address in Redfern and then when construction was completed staff and facilities would be shifted to continue business as usual.

Most people would move to the centre closest to their place of domicile. However, the centre servicing the eastern suburbs looked to be shaping as the most politically radical of the new workplaces. The promises of action and camaraderie were a major lure to Gaily. He discussed the issue with Brian Timothy.

A true intellectual, Timothy would analyse a problem from all angles – tending in the process to overanalyse. His was always a slow all-sided approach whereas Gaily would tend to rush in all guns blazing then have to beat a hasty retreat.

Another Mail Exchange worker - Steve Metho - had been attending Party meetings with the intention of joining. Timothy proposed that having a C.P.A. member in the three biggest of the new centres would give the Party the best utilisation of its limited human resources. With Timothy going to the inner city centre and Metho going to the western suburbs centre Gaily's plan to head east would actually achieve Timothy's goal. It was a case of spreading oneself thin – a concept with which Gaily was already familiar.

Metho was an interesting character. Gaily had brought a lot of people closer to the Party of whom Metho was one. He was a union rep in a different section but had met Gaily where most people would meet him: at the pub. They were both big Resch's drinkers. Metho would eventually quit the post office, marry an Aboriginal girl and go bush. Metho had always been a vehement opponent of racism – a question on which the Party was very strong. He was therefore acting in character by marrying a black woman.

Since the bypass dispute defeat the employer had suspended P.R.D.s (Payroll Deductions). This meant union dues could not be deducted automatically from wages on a fortnightly basis. It impeded the ability of the union to function as dues had to be collected manually by reps on the job. The union's cash flow and solvency were adversely affected.

One day some dues from Metho's section went missing. It was rumoured that one or other of the reps had misappropriated money. This would have been a very foolish thing to do as handwritten receipts had to be issued. Metho and another rep spent a lot of time together at one or other pub. They conducted a lot of union business over a beer. Nothing was ever proven, the money was eventually accounted for and life went on. Smear and innuendo were often used against lefties in the union movement so one could not be too careful.

"Don't draw the crabs," the old blokes at the Exchange would tell new recruits.

By this was meant "don't draw attention to yourself". It was sound advice.

Gaily's little world was further shrinking. The Mail Exchange was closing. The countries he had for years thought of as socialist had regressed to capitalism. The C.P.A. was questioning its own reason for being.

This latter was masked under the amorphous banner of "Prospects For Socialism": the title being given to an internal debate driven by a Party leadership bent on dissolving the Party and seizing its assets.

The debate was couched in terms of creating a new socialist party more attuned to the needs of the time. It would basically be a watered down version of the C.P.A. with the name to delete any reference to "Communist" and question being given to the relevance of Marxism.

Members were being demoralised by talk of the Party being unsustainable in its present form with declining membership numbers and Tribune sales.

One of the reasons membership numbers were declining was the debate itself drawing attention away from activity and towards introspection. As one member put it at the time it was "navel gazing".

If all that was required to turn around the Party's fortunes was a simple change of name then this could be achieved through a vote at Congress. An interminable dialogue of the deaf would drag on for years and end in the Party's dissolution. This is what some people wanted.

The Postal and Telecommunications branch had already folded and Gaily had been transferred to his nearest locality branch in the suburb of Parramatta.

His new branch secretary said that if ever there was a time which required the existence of a Communist Party that time had arrived. Whole branches were opposed to dissolution. The Party was split over whether or not it should continue to exist.

Brian Timothy had spoken of not throwing out "the baby, the bath water and the bath".

The push for dissolution was strongest in Sydney where the Abrahams family had their power base. The Abrahams boasted three generations of Party leaders.

In Melbourne it was a slightly different story. The dominant family in Australia's second largest city was the Daft family. The Dafts had taken the dissolutionist proposal to its logical conclusion by saying no party was necessary. Rather, they proposed a "socialist organisation" which would bring together socialists of various hues.

Brian Timothy had tried to rationalise this proposal by pointing out it was not necessary to dissolve the Party in order to form another organisation.

Like many older members Timothy had personal allegiances to the Dafts dating back decades just as others had allegiances to the Abrahams. Both families played on these allegiances to garner support for their positions.

In the final analysis it was all about money. The Party had considerable assets accumulated since 1920. Properties and other assets had been bequeathed to the Party in all good faith. In its more affluent days the Party or entities controlled by the Party had also acquired property and assets of their own volition.

The Daft family called their hand on two counts.

Firstly, they formed their own "socialist organisation" - which was in fact nothing more than a discussion group. When the Party did eventually dissolve the Dafts dissolved their discussion group into the A.L.P.

Secondly, they made a failed grab for the Party's assets. It was a premature act as the Party still existed at the time. Their foray was able to be used against them by Abrahams supporters. It further marginalised the Daft supporters thus strengthening the Abrahams' hand.

Gaily was to later get himself into strife by conducting company searches to ascertain the exact extent of the Party's assets.

However, like a lot of others he was worn out by all the negativity by which he was surrounded.

The previous year had seen the defeat of the British miners' strike. Gaily was intrigued as to the ability of the English left to respond to such a massive setback. He was also interested in visiting totty at home.

Gaily booked his flights and packed his bags.

It was Gaily's first trip overseas. His parents were very pleased for him. His poor old mother had never been overseas as her husband had seen the world as a wireless operator on Lancaster bombers.

Gaily deeply regretted having got involved with the Trots not least because his political activity had precluded him from accompanying his mother on a trip to England and France to see the Australian Rugby League team play. The annual tours were hosted by their favourite football commentator. Mrs Gaily had offered to shout her son a trip as a reward for his school results. Now Gaily was in his own little world of work and politics he had learnt to forgo the joys of seeing his team play for the dubious pleasures of attending meetings and selling papers. With the Trots he felt compelled to be active; with the C.P.A., the union and the peace movement he felt obliged. Even this month away would be a busman's holiday as he had arranged to stay with English Communists. His mother would now never experience the joys of overseas travel.

Not that the flight itself filled Gaily with much joy. It would be his first and last flight with his country's national carrier Qantas. The flight would also teach him to avoid economy class travel if at all possible. The cabin crew completely ignored him the whole way so he arrived in London starved, dehydrated and exhausted.

Being inexperienced in the ways of the world Gaily had not realised that for someone desirous of visiting northern England it would have been far more straightforward to have alighted at Manchester Airport rather than Heathrow. A long coach trip ensued which finally saw him in Liverpool. He was about to spend a month with scouse lefties.

Hailing a cab from Leece Street in Liverpool Gaily allowed the cabbie to choose the hotel in which he would spend his first night in England.

The hotel was a reasonable three star affair but was only a stopgap measure. He had been given a list of Communist Party of Great Britain (C.P.G.B.) contacts by the Party back in Sydney. In the morning he was able to ring the local Party offices and make an appointment to visit later in the day.

The C.P.G.B. in Liverpool welcomed Gaily with open arms. For four weeks he was billeted in comrades' homes, fed and watered. His hosts and hostesses were reluctant to take a penny by way of recompense.

The Party was active and vibrant but Gaily detected an underlying tension similar to what must have existed in the C.P.A. prior to the split which saw most of the pro-Soviet members leave to form the Socialist Party of Australia.

It was a similar situation to that which existed in the peace movement: Old Left versus New Left. The Old Left tended to be made up of older pro-Soviet types who placed great emphasis on studying classical Marxism and the role of the trade unions. The New Left consisted largely of younger, trendier types who were not as well-read and saw the new social movements around feminism and homosexuality as being at least as important as the unions. A third camp had a bob each way. They borrowed a little from one side's ideas, a little from the other and tried to appease both sides without success. This third group would always contain those most likely to leave if a split developed as they possessed no real ideological commitment or world view.

Gaily stood firmly in the Old Left camp. His interpretations and practice of Marxism could be traced back to the thirties when Zinoviev was President of the Third International and the social democrats were dubbed "social fascists" by the Communists.

Gaily would try not to but would still tread on a few toes in England. He was not the most gracious of guests.

Central to the C.P.G.B.'s existence was the Party's daily paper Morning Star. The Star editorial took a hard line approach. This was as opposed to the theoretical journal which drew heavily from the New Left Euro-Communist trend which had emerged in Italy. When the split eventuated the Party was able to survive as a shadow of its former self by rallying around the Morning Star. Thanks to commercial structures which had been put in place the press survived despite millions of pounds disappearing.

In Australia the liquidators would take the lot. Only the name would remain: it was deemed a liability and therefore of no monetary value.

To show his appreciation for the hospitality offered him Gaily did as much Party work as possible. More homes were letterboxed with Party leaflets during Gaily's visit than in any other month in the history of the C.P.G.B. It was a real busman's holiday.

Gaily was made self-conscious of his accent by a couple of incidents.

Once after engaging in conversation a little girl remarked, "Daddy, that man speaks just like the people in Home And Away."

On another occasion when asked his occupation "mail-sorter" was interpreted as "mouseholer".

Summer in England is notorious for making young roses bloom and old roses wilt. The most beautiful of the young roses was in full bloom at the swimming pool in Liverpool 8. Here Gaily prepared to do his laps and admire the lifesaver in her little royal blue netball skirt.

It was a funny time to be in Liverpool as the Trot Militant Tendency within the Labour Party had gained a majority on Merseyside Council. To achieve full employment people were given jobs where no work existed so, for example, the beautiful blonde rose in the netball skirt had five mates to assist her watch one swimmer doing his laps. (Gaily invariably had the pool to himself.) At the end of his stay he arranged for a dozen red roses to be delivered to the girl.

At the end of his stay also a farewell party was arranged in his honour. It was held at the Flying Picket Bar - which was owned and controlled by the left.

Gaily's drink of choice in England was always going to be cider. However, on this occasion he partook of the bitter being poured by the buxom barmaid. He had heard so much about Tetley Bitter he tried eight pints of the stuff.

At the end of the night the barmaid walked him home. Feeling a little unsteady he took the girl's hand as they walked through the roughest part of Liverpool: Liverpool 8.

"Don't hold my hand," she said. "My boyfriend's a Rasta."

Gaily left the C.P.G.B. to get on with its work. He had had a day trip to London to meet with the editor of the Star. He had established a bond with England which would last the rest of his life. Visiting England was like coming home for Gaily as he reaffirmed his heritage. He revered the women and the politics but he could never renounce his own country. He left England with mixed emotions but by the living crikey the first schooner of Resch's would taste good.

Upon his arrival home the drive to dissolve the Party had intensified and the Mail Exchange was about to shut up shop.

The battle to keep the Exchange open had been won and lost six years prior but the Party could still be salvaged if the motives of the national leadership could be exposed.

Prior to Gaily's departure he and a comrade of Indian descent – Gunga Din – had discussed the possibility of conducting company searches to ascertain the exact size and extent of the Party's assets. Upon his return they set to work.

Their efforts at the Department of Consumer Affairs and the Land Titles Office revealed a complicated company structure designed to baffle C.P.A. members and the Tax Office alike. Companies within companies had been established like so many sets of the Russian dolls available at the S.P.A.'s bookshop. There were more front groups than the Party had during its period of illegality during World War II.

Slowly but surely the picture began to emerge of an organisation with millions of dollars' worth of property and other assets. Prior to the dissolution of the Party all of these assets would be transferred into the names of the outgoing National Committee. Assets left in all good faith to the Party or purchased with funds given in all good faith would become the personal property of half a dozen individuals. In the opinions of Gaily and Gunga Din the liquidation of the Party would involve multiple acts of fraud.

Bourgeois Communists though are no different from other forms of bourgeois. They seek to protect what they view as their property at all costs. Gaily was about to find this out in no small measure. He and Gunga Din had drawn the crabs.

Mike East was a little spiv of a bloke who eked out his existence by writing articles for union journals and not paying his debts. He saved money on razor blades by not shaving and saved money on laundry detergent by not washing his shirts. Gaily suspected he only possessed one set of clothes.

East was part of the bob each way faction. His position would vary in accordance with that held by his interlocutor at the time. At meetings he would remain silent and abstain from voting on key questions. Gaily was by now on the Party's Sydney District Committee and had learnt not to trust East. Still East persisted in attempting to ingratiate himself as Gaily was one of the main spokesmen opposing dissolution.

The Criterion was not open on Sundays and Gaily had gone to the nearby Covent Garden after a District Committee meeting to avoid some of the leadership's supporters who had gone to the Star. East followed him into the Covent.

East pulled out a crumpled twenty dollar note he had just borrowed off some mug.

"Wouldn't shout if a shark bit him," Gaily thought to himself.

"What's your poison?" East asked.

"Always Resch's. You know that, Mike," Gaily replied.

"What's this I hear about you and Gunga undertaking company searches?" asked East – cutting straight to the chase.

Gaily gulped a third of his middy to make sure it was real and before East had a chance to take it back. East only drank small beers.

"What's it to you?" Gaily retorted.

"It means nothing to me but it might mean something to you to know you and Gunga are under very close surveillance," said East.

"How close is 'very close'?" asked Gaily.

East looked around furtively. Gaily thought he must have seen someone to whom he owed money. East lowered his voice.

"Put it like this: if you and Gunga keep this up you're dead meat," whispered East.

"You're just trying to put the wind up us," Gaily grinned - feeling unnerved but showing his best game face.

East named a former editor of the Tribune whom he said had arranged to have a number of the Abrahams family's political enemies murdered over the years.

"The cops always find the victim to have died accidentally without any suspicious circumstances," East concluded.

"This is outrageous, Mike," said Gaily.

"Just remember the Golden Rule and you'll be right. The man with the gold makes the rules. The Party's no different and the man with the gold intends to hang onto it" were East's parting words as he made towards the door. "Oh and by the way you owe me a drink."

"I owe you nothing," Gaily shot back, finishing his middy and ordering a schooner.

Upon leaving the pub Gaily went straight to the nearest public telephone and rang Gunga Din.

"It looks like all bets are off," Gaily told him.

He repeated word for word what East had had to say. Gunga Din sighed audibly over the telephone.

"We need to find out if these threats carry any weight. I'll ask around but discretion might be the better part of valour for the time being," Gaily went on to say. "This is pretty heavy stuff."

Gunga Din agreed: there was no point in being a martyr over an internal dispute. There were better things to die for were such sacrifice ever required.

The following Saturday afternoon there was a meeting of the Party's rank-and-file group held in the backyard of one of the inner-city comrades. The title "rank-and-file group" was used in order to deflect accusations of factionalism although everyone attending was expected to oppose dissolution. Gaily was the only one out of about thirty present who had sold Trib in the morning. Most were public servants or teachers who liked the sound of their own voices.

Gaily felt obliged to attend but was bored by the dilettantism of it all.

"They might do good work in their unions but in the Party they just talk," he thought.

Gaily occasionally allowed his eyes to wander to the nether regions of a stunning girl sitting awkwardly on the grass a few metres away. Her miniskirt was obviously not designed for wearing in such situations.

Gaily quickly glanced away. He did not wish to be accused of sexism. Several lesbians were having a good old dekko but they could look as much as they liked. It was just not fair.

Gaily looked at the faces around him. How many of these people could be counted upon when the crunch finally came?

Gaily was by now a pretty shrewd numbers man. Out of the thirty or so present there were only himself, Gunga Din, Brian Timothy, his new branch secretary Spud Ailing and a couple of people who had bothered to come down from the Blue Mountains. The only other fair dinkum Comm there was Mary Churchby – the secretary of the Sydney University Students' Representative Council and the Party Women's Collective.

Good old Mary: Gaily had had the hots for her for five years. The feeling was reciprocated. Every time they saw each other there was an almost overpowering transfer of sexual energy between the two. Sooner or later the passion they felt would have to be consummated.

When the meeting was finally over Gaily attempted to round up the troops for a drink at the local pub. Most of the others preferred coffee to beer so preferred cafes to pubs. Only Gaily, Gunga Din, Brian Timothy and Mary ended up going for a drink. The Blue Mountains people had to catch a train, the girl in the miniskirt was going out with her boyfriend and the rest preferred coffee or marijuana.

At the pub Gunga Din and Gaily told the other two about the threat Mike East had conveyed. They had refrained from discussing it at the meeting as there was obviously a spy in the ranks for the leadership to have got wind of the research they had been conducting.

Timothy was still fuming at the inaction of the rank-and-file group. He quoted Chairman Mao.

"A meeting should not be conducted unless action is to flow from it," Timothy said. Gaily had never been able to place it in his readings of Mao but who was he to dispute Timothy?

The four friends and comrades sat momentarily silent. The postalworkers had seen it all before as another part of the little world they inhabited appeared about to collapse. Whilever the Party remained they would at least have each other's camaraderie.

Mary knew how much the Party meant to Gaily. She smiled demurely at him as she sipped her cider. Mary was the older by almost ten years. Her body was fit and firm from swimming at the university's pool every day. Her long thick brown hair fell down her back and over her shoulders. A long flowing floral dress highlighted her hourglass figure.

Mary continued to study one subject a year to enable her to remain on the Students' Representative Council. It was important for the Communist presence on campus and ensured the left retained the numbers on the council as well as providing strong leadership.

Gunga Din was not much of a drinker. He liked to joke about Aussies having "pub legs" to enable them to stand all day as long as the beer flowed. He was the first to leave but would be there when the whips were cracking.

Timothy talked about a name change being an acceptable concession if the Party could be retained. Time was still on their side as the leadership wanted to absolutely run the organisation into the ground to be assured of the vote at Congress. They probably had a few more years in which to turn the situation around.

Timothy had slowed up a lot since having suffered a

stroke a few years prior. No longer did he receive "please explain"s asking why he had been seen entering or leaving licensed premises during working hours. He finished his second middy then left Gaily and Mary to their own devices.

"Will you walk me home please, Charlie?" Mary asked.

"Certainly," he replied.

It was only a few hundred metres to the little rented house she shared with her cat. (The Party had not expanded along with Sydney. Most members lived in the inner city. If anything it was contracting as older comrades in outer suburbs died and inner-city trendies took their place.)

Mary smiled and grasped Gaily's hand. Initially shocked he retracted his hand momentarily only to place it back in hers seconds later.

They kissed goodnight. Gaily was not big on public shows of affection but a quick snog seemed in keeping with the moment.

During the week Gaily received a note from Mary through the post. It said how "over the moon" she felt to be in love with him. It ended with an invitation to visit her at home on Sunday morning.

Gaily doubted the invitation being extended was to share a cup of tea. Finally it seemed likely the feelings they had repressed during more than five years of friendship were about to be unleashed.

On Sunday at ten Gaily knocked on Mary's door filled with a sense of adventure. He was wearing his regulation white dress shorts, Lacoste shirt and rubber thongs. It was what he termed "nouveau ocker".

Mary answered the door in a short, light floral dressing gown. The cup of tea appeared long odds.

Not a word had to be said. Once Mary had led him

towards her bedroom they both knew what was about to occur.

Mary flung off her dressing gown to reveal her little white cotton knickers and big firm white breasts, the nipples quivering with excitement.

She fondled Gaily's crutch but no further stimulation was required. The lower garments and shirt were quickly removed by two pairs of hands shaking with nervous excitement. Years of sexual tension were reaching their crescendo.

A Catholic upbringing and conversion to Marxism and feminism had left Mary little time for boys. Feminism in particular had provided little liberation at the personal level as heterosexuality was equated with sexism and patriarchy. No women's liberation without socialism: this was the most liberating experience either of the lovers would ever have as they worked their way through a veritable Karma Sutra of positions.

Both pairs of Mary's lips allowed Gaily to penetrate them over and over again while her breasts had him speaking perfect Spanish by midday. Her big round firm buttocks inspired him to take her from behind- a pillow under her hips further exaggerating the convexity of her bottom.

"I am woman, hear me roar" Helen Reddy had sung and Mary roared all day with multiple orgasms and laughter.

As he stimulated her with his hand they laughed at the joke told by a mutual acquaintance about the Jewish boy whose favourite finger was his middle finger: it was the one with which he hit the cash register.

Mary cooked some chops for lunch (she was the all-Australian girl from the bush) and they were ready for the afternoon session.

Next day came the telephone call.

"How do you feel?" Mary asked.

"Like I've run the City to Surf," he replied (the City to Surf being Sydney's most popular foot race – conducted over a third of the marathon distance).

"Me too," she replied.

"Me three," he said. They laughed as only lovers can laugh.

It had been quite an athletic performance on both their parts. They arranged to do it all again the following Sunday.

For two months they revelled in each other's company. The weekends belonged to them as they walked hand in hand or lay on the grass together in Sydney's magnificent public parks: the Domain, the Royal Botanic Gardens and Hyde Park.

…And the sex…

Gaily had never had and would never have such a quantity and quality of sex regardless of his liaisons with so-called professionals. It was therefore incomprehensible when Gaily did something very stupid, hurtful and destructive. He asked to call the whole thing off.

For years Gaily had maintained a dalliance with an aspiring actress who was in actual fact a barmaid. Deirdre was from a prominent Communist family and was one of the first people Gaily met upon joining the Party. It had been on his first May Day march as a Communist. At the time the girl was still at school – being four years Gaily's junior. There was no doubting her beauty but there would never be more than friendship and flirtation involved.

Deirdre's crowning glory was her thick platinum blonde hair. This fixation with hair colour would cause Gaily more grief in the course of his life than any other aspect of his personality.

He never said so at the time but here was an opportunity to have a long-lasting affair which could have ended in a happy marriage with a beautiful, deep, mature intellectual. Instead he chose to throw it all away in exchange for a dalliance with a shallow young floozy.

Gaily was too young and immature himself to realise the value of that which he discarded. He and Mary would gradually drift apart until the Party's eventual dissolution saw them go their separate ways.

More than twenty years later Gaily would be profusely apologetic when happening to run into her at a railway station. Worn out by the rigours of life her effete appearance was in stark contrast to the beautiful firebrand of his youth. Mary merely shrugged, said she had done some silly things at the time and went on her weary way. His apologies were too late.

At the time Gaily had merely shrugged his own shoulders and gone for a beer. He was not ready to make a commitment to another individual and when he did his choice would be suitably disastrous. Enter the Irish Goddess of Love.

A Taste of Cash beckoned Gaily back into the land of Strumpet Crumpet. His fling with Mary had only whetted his appetite.

It was also time for him to again cut back on his drinking so what better way to reward himself than with a visit to A.T.O.C.?

He made the requisite telephone call, was given the requisite information by the lovely lady on the other end of the line and made plans for his next visit.

The receptionist was both amused and bemused by Gaily's enquiry. Of all the ladies on the staff at the time the one who best fitted the description of the required

attributes was Colleen. Colleen it was then whom Gaily
would see upon his next visit.

Gaily's visits to A.T.O.C. had been fairly sporadic since
his first meeting with Kim five years prior. Kim had been
and gone as had the several other ladies whose acquaintance he had made.

Colleen was starting her shift at ten on Saturday morning so Gaily made a point of being first in the queue at
nine.

It was always a pleasure to visit A.T.O.C. The smell
and feel of the place could only be provided by a woman's
touch.

The fact that his visits were only occasional meant the
novelty of the event still remained as much as ever.

His pulse quickened as he approached the door in
anticipation of meeting a beautiful woman in an hour's
time. It was always a pleasure and a privilege to meet a
beautiful woman. Such would always be the case.

The receptionist was charming. Gaily recognised her
from a previous visit. She was the vivacious Kiwi girl with
great legs which served as an appetiser for waiting clients.
Her name was Raelene.

Raelene brought Gaily a Resch's heart starter. While
waiting for the girl to return to the waiting room with the
drink he had placed a fiver on the floor opposite the chair
in which he sat.

"Oh look, Raelene, someone's dropped a fiver on the
floor over there," he said upon her return.

The receptionist knelt carefully down to retrieve the
note without allowing the client to see up her skirt. Raelene was a tease but she was not cheap.

"Not that easily tricked, Charlie," she said, fly to his ploy.

Raelene left Gaily to his beer. It was Saturday and he

had the Herald with which to amuse himself until Colleen arrived.

Just before ten Raelene popped her head in the waiting room door.

"Mistress Colleen will be here to see you shortly," said the receptionist.

Gaily's level of anticipation was further heightened. Finally there came a knock on the door and in walked Mistress Colleen.

Gaily stood up and extended his right hand as Mistress Colleen entered the room. He was already renowned at the establishment for his impeccable manners.

Their hands met briefly as did their eyes. Colleen had the most beautiful grey-green eyes and a wicked sense of humour to match.

"Good morning, I am Mistress Colleen and I will be taking your class this morning," she smiled – and her Irish eyes laughed with her.

They walked up the stairs to the Japanese-themed room. This was Colleen's favourite of all the rooms as a lot of her clients were Japanese businessmen. She spoke basic Japanese and had visited Tokyo but as Gaily was to learn Irish geisha prefer champagne to tea.

Colleen had just turned thirty-five but looked no more than thirty. In fact when they went out together for the first time some months later the Irishwoman could have passed herself off as younger than Gaily despite being seven and a half years his senior.

She was short – five foot two standing on a butter box as Gaily's favourite football commentator might have said – with the long thick platinum hair and hourglass figure he so admired.

Colleen wore a tight knitted tangerine tube dress which had just managed to cover her ample behind as she led

Gaily up the stairs. Her bottom hovered provocatively in front of his face, her expensive black high-heeled shoes causing the buttocks to jut out even further than would otherwise have been the case.

The courtesan took Gaily's cash downstairs while he quickly undressed and showered. As usual the room like the lady he was seeing presented in immaculate condition.

Colleen returned with a half-bottle of champagne and two glasses. This was the first of many occasions when he would open champagne for her.

"Ah, 'tis a lovely sound," Colleen lilted.

Their glasses clinked as they toasted each other's health. Neither of them had eaten breakfast and the wine was strong and heady.

Colleen removed her dress and they lay together naked on the bed chatting. She was a consummate entertainer of men and her general knowledge and vocabulary were astounding – particularly for someone who had left school at the age of fifteen. Gaily was more than a little impressed.

For a first meeting it was a very intimate conversation they held – telling each other as they did of their very different backgrounds and upbringings.

Gaily's middle class liberal origins were in stark contrast to Colleen's Irish working class experiences. Having moved with her family from Ireland to England as a young girl she had left school at fifteen to work in retail before a stint in the public service.

Hers was a story of someone from a bog Irish background aspiring to better themselves. The poverty of her childhood drove her to succeed in the financial sense of the term. Success should not be measured by money alone but for people such as Colleen it is their sole yardstick.

One of the tricks of the prostitute's profession is to relate to their clients by drawing parallels between their respective lives. In this way a psychological bond is developed. Essentially the main aim upon meeting a new client is to sound them out, build a good rapport and hopefully have them as a regular client in the future. Although speaking mainly about herself by eliciting responses from Gaily Colleen was able to draw him out about himself and achieve her aim. However, Gaily had not achieved his.

With their hour together almost over Colleen looked at her watch and then at Gaily's level of arousal. The watch said it was almost eleven but Gaily was definitely at twelve noon. It must have had something to do with daylight saving.

"We'll have to do something about this," Colleen said, producing a tube of Lubafax lubricant.

The firm right hand with which he was to become familiar quickly brought him to a sudden climax. In the ecstasy of the moment a jet of semen shot over his chest and abdomen. On this occasion the story had a happy ending.

Colleen would often argue that clients paid for her time rather than for a specific service. Men visiting prostitutes should not necessarily therefore expect the provision of the "full service". Some men would not require it and others prefer a variation on the theme. Strictly speaking Colleen was correct as A.T.O.C. ladies were paid by the hour. However, it cut both ways as a man could request a refund if not satisfied with the services required. At times the manageress would direct a lady to provide a specific service as requested and no matter how reluctantly that service had to be given. There were of course one or two taboo acts.

At any rate Colleen had landed another fish with her not inconsiderable bait. Gaily would be back the following weekend for another hour with the redoubtable Mistress Colleen.

Mistress Colleen would be responsible for a number of notable firsts in Gaily's sexual development.

The simple act of providing hand relief had added a new dimension to his sex life as Gaily had never previously achieved orgasm by this means. Colleen had thereby granted Gaily a gift by showing him how to obtain pleasure in this manner. She told him that masturbation was a natural and healthy act which in moderation would add to the overall sexual experience. Still he would always prefer the hand of a woman to his own.

After a lifetime of abstention from masturbating the sheer novelty of the act provided welcome relief. It was only when his sexual performance with Mistress Colleen began to deteriorate he admitted to having been bringing himself to orgasm four times a day. Thereafter he was put on strict rations to ensure the maximum pleasure and satisfaction would be experienced in her company.

So much did Gaily enjoy this new acquaintance's company he became a weekly visitor to the lovely old terrace houses which formed A.T.O.C.

As the weeks rolled by Gaily began to look forward to his weekly visit as an addict would crave their substance of choice. Colleen knew how to press his buttons and Gaily responded on cue. It quickly got to the stage where if Colleen were away sick or on holidays Gaily would suffer withdrawal. Colleen's response was to make a risqué pun about "withdrawing from her". Her little plays on words were a constant source of amusement. He got to know some of the other ladies but was loyal to the woman whom he now thought of as his mistress.

Colleen continued to draw out Gaily's sexuality. When she recognised the degree of arousal caused by miniskirts or revealingly short dresses his mistress would often dress in a manner quite purposely designed to provoke. He would be encouraged by her to look up skirts and dresses during the week and report back to her what he had seen. This is not the sort of thing which should be encouraged but it had the desired effect of playing on Gaily's need for risk and titillation.

One day Colleen got him to tell her about what he had seen walking up the stairs at a railway station.

After he had given her a detailed description she said to Gaily, "I think it's time you had your bot-bot spanked young man".

His mistress got him to pull down his shorts and bend over her knee. He enjoyed rubbing against her right thigh as her open right hand came down hard on his buttocks one hundred times.

Thereafter spankings were incorporated into their weekly ritual. Gradually a Mason Pearson hairbrush was included for added effect after the bottom was warmed with the open hand. A light leather paddle the house possessed for such purposes was used by way of variation from the hairbrush. After a few months one hundred spanks with the hand were followed by four hundred strokes of the hairbrush or paddle.

Colleen always dressed to catch the eye with sharply cut skirt suits, fluorescent tube dresses or leather miniskirts. The outfits were set off by silk stockings or bare sun-kissed legs. Bright colours contrasted with straight black. Her signature piece was a choker: either black or pearl. The final touch to the ensemble was provided by beautiful earrings and killer high heels.

This was a woman with a touch of class. Her years in retail with one of the big fashion houses had not been wasted but the sexual incitement of the precocious teenage years had been superseded by the added allure of the courtesan at the smouldering peak of her powers.

Gaily had been invited to the seventieth anniversary celebrations of the Russian Revolution at the Soviet Consulate. The Consulate was located in Sydney's eastern suburbs as was Colleen's place of domicile. Gaily felt obliged to attend but not being a vodka drinker feared it might prove a trifle boring. He therefore invited Colleen along to liven things up a bit. Her presence certainly had the desired effect.

Colleen was not particularly political. Her parents were fish and chip Tories. Her own politics were in general liberal with a dash of Tory thrown in. However, as a professional entertainer she had learnt long ago to play to her audience.

Client and mistress met for lunch at a little cafe in Sydney's Kings Cross. It was a warm late spring day as they sat outdoors sipping champagne. Gaily was able to partake of a steak with an accompaniment of flies.

Colleen had the day off but had agreed to act as Gaily's escort for a small consideration. It was an unofficial arrangement as A.T.O.C. was not involved. This was to Gaily's financial advantage as the bordello's hourly rates would have set him back considerably more than was about to change hands.

The courtesan was taking full advantage of the free advertising being afforded her by dressing at her provocative best. A sheer leopard print blouse allowed the keen observer to see a black bra underneath. The blouse was matched with leopard print tights under which there appeared to be very little apart from a very firm, pert bottom. A black choker, gold hoop earrings and black heels provided the finishing touches.

Gaily had exchanged his signature shorts for David Jones blazer, sports shirt, sports trousers plus the white leather shoes made famous by Queensland estate agents. He looked sharp but there was no doubt as to which of the two was the more eye-catching.

They caught a cab to the Consulate. Colleen would always make a point of engaging cab drivers in conversation. In the words of a song popular at the time "never let a chance go by". Gaily slipped Colleen the agreed upon amount of five hundred dollars.

The function was an informal one but by invitation only. The doorman accepted their invitations and wished them a good afternoon. Had they been announced in the English fashion it would have been "Lord and Lady Muck".

The couple sauntered into the consulate's large function room. They were fashionably late. All eyes turned to look at the beautiful woman accompanying Gaily.

Most of the two hundred or so guests knew Gaily through his work in the peace and trade union movements. Most of the men present had always wanted a glamorous wife or girlfriend but had ended up with a fellow leftie. Gaily broke the mould.

The men silently admired Colleen but were too intimidated to approach her. The women on the other hand picked her profession in one.

"Tart," they thought – and they were correct.

However, when teaching someone the difference between the singular and the plural it is important to remember "tart" may be sour but "tarts" are sweet.

"Who was the girl with the tits and the tiger tights?" Gaily would later be asked by the Peace Committee co-ordinator.

It was at this function Gaily's two lives first clashed for

all the world to see. His public life was one of an impecunious left-wing postalworker. His private life saw him in the arms of courtesans.

Colleen was ostensibly his "girlfriend" but how many of the hard-nosed old lefties present would believe such a fairy tale?

Colleen worked the room like a true professional. The Soviet officials were not as backward in coming forward as their Australian comrades.

The beer, champagne and vodka flowed. Toasts to the Great October Revolution were made. Gaily made small talk to some of his peace movement colleagues with Colleen flitting in and out of the conversations.

People finally began to leave. Men who had been too timid to speak to Gaily managed to say hullo as they filed out the door. These were the same hard men who led unions in the maritime and building industries but they were intimidated by a petite Irish prostitute.

Gaily hailed a cab and they went back to the Cross. Colleen drew the line at allowing Gaily to know her residential address. Trust was still being established and she retained her right to privacy – particularly if there were a falling out between the two.

Colleen had a walk of a few hundred metres and Gaily a shorter walk to the railway station. They kissed perfunctorily and went their separate ways.

Gaily had difficulty in discerning reality from fantasy. Still it had been a pleasant afternoon spent in the company of a beautiful woman. It had been another good day to utilise his sick leave entitlements and all in the name of the class struggle. Thankfully none of the C.P.A. feminists had been there to observe the company he kept. Somewhat appropriately they would have had kittens at the sight of the leopard print outfit.

Role play had become such an important part of Gaily's sexual activity he decided to buy Colleen an authentic Castle Hill High School senior girl's uniform. To avoid unnecessary embarrassment he was able to make the purchase over the telephone using a credit card and have the items posted to him.

The uniform had changed slightly since Gaily's day but the main thing was it was the pukka article. There was a white blouse, a navy blue skirt and a little pair of white socks. He added one of his own old school ties.

Next came a visit to the lingerie section of the David Jones department store. He bought two brief pairs of silk knickers – one pair red and lacy, the other cream and frilly. Gaily visualised the knickers riding up his mistress's buttocks. This was as much a present for himself as for her.

On Saturday morning he presented the gift to Colleen. As each item emerged from its parcel it slowly dawned on the courtesan the overall impression which would be conveyed by donning such kit.

Gaily had not neglected to have the skirt's hem taken up. A friendly seamstress had transformed the skirt into a miniskirt.

The overall effect was indeed stunning. Memories of school days flooded back just as blood surged into Gaily's nether regions. Colleen picked out the red knickers on this occasion. They were a size ten and the cleft of her big round backside greedily devoured them just as Gaily's eyes greedily devoured the sight of them on the wearer.

Colleen wore the uniform down to reception when conveying Gaily's weekly donation and received rousing applause from the receptionist and her workmates in the ladies' waiting room.

Now there could be a slight alteration in roles with Colleen able to be the naughty schoolgirl and Gaily the prefect who would give ever so light a spanking to the naughty girl flashing her knickers so provocatively.

Alternatively he would don his old school uniform. It still fitted perfectly. Then she would be the prefect and spank him for looking up her skirt.

These "lessons" almost invariably ended with Gaily taking his mistress from behind. To enable him to continue to look up her skirt as he penetrated her she would pull aside the silk or cotton covering the entrance to her vagina and carefully guide his erect penis inside her before he became too frenzied with excitement.

On special occasions such as birthdays Colleen would invite one of the other ladies along to perform a "double". This would further expand the scenario enacted by adding another player to the cast.

In these situations one lady would be the teacher or headmistress, the other the naughty schoolgirl.

The naughty schoolboy would willingly make double the payment on such days as they added spice and variety to his visits. However, the presence of the second lady was a little bonus whereby Colleen had a supporting actress while firmly remaining the star of the show.

Gaily was a very loyal client. He would not have it any other way.

With all the shenanigans in Gaily's private life it was a wonder he could retain focus on the important issues in his public life.

Often he would attend meetings the day after having seen Colleen, his backside raw and red and bruised from the ferocious spanking he had received the previous day. On these occasions he would have difficulty sitting down.

His mistress would regularly warm him with one hundred spanks with her hand then follow up with four hundred strokes with a hairbrush. Thankfully punishment would always be followed with a reward.

Gaily's little world was shrinking more rapidly than a post-coitus penis.

The last hurrah was approaching in both the Party and the union.

The Party membership had been depleted to the point of no return. With the exception of a slight jump around 1975 numbers had been steadily declining since their peak at the end of World War II.

Through a conscious policy to wind down the organisation the number of financial members nationally was less than a thousand. The supporters of dissolution were now justified in deeming the C.P.A. to be unsustainable. They had created a self-fulfilling prophecy.

On average there were two obituaries per week in the Tribune for members of long standing. An organisation which cannot renew itself will inevitably die. This was to be the C.P.A.'s fate.

Demoralisation was rife. People who had sold the Tribune for years could no longer be bothered. Many branches actively discouraged new members from joining. Many resignations were received and duly accepted. It was just a matter of time.

As Gaily had foreseen the rank-and-file group had failed to provide any meaningful opposition to the Party leadership.

In his union it was a slightly different story. The union would go on albeit in a weakened state.

The peak body of the Australian trade union movement is the Australian Council of Trade Unions. In a bid to shore up their affiliates a series of amalgamations had occurred to create what were being termed "super unions".

In reality what the A.C.T.U. had implemented was what the capitalists would term a rationalisation. Fewer unions would mean fewer positions for trade union officials thus drastically reducing overheads. Fewer unions would at least in their initial stages give the "super unions" more members per union; however, this would only provide the movement with a breathing space if numbers continued to dwindle.

The amalgamations were also conducted in an irrational manner. Rather than amalgamate along industrial lines to create industrial unions workers from disparate sections of the workforce were lumped together for no obvious reason. Thus, postal and telecommunications workers were suddenly united under the same banner with sections of the building trades. Other construction industry workers came together with forestry and mining workers – and so on.

Over the years Gaily's little union rank-and-file group had gained kudos for its consistent work in opposing the worst of their union's officials. The rank-and-file group members were all highly respected in their workplaces. They had held their heads high after the bypass dispute and had taken a principled and well thought out opposing stance to amalgamation.

Elections for the union's state executive were approaching. The A.L.P. left faction did not possess the strength within the union to win back power off their own bat. Their only chance was to negotiate a deal with the rank-and-file group.

The deal involved offering paid positions to Gaily and the five other blokes who formed the hard core of the group. They would have first dibs on organisers' positions in the event of a combined left-wing ticket coming to fruition. In fact they would be the ticket's official candidates if they so desired in exchange for their support. It was the opportunity of a lifetime for the individuals concerned and a very rare opportunity for a left-wing ticket to gain a majority.

Overnight the blokes' annual incomes would more than double. However, they also knew the real power which could be exerted on behalf of the rank-and-file through the acquisition of organisers' jobs.

A union organiser does not sit in an office. If he is worth his salt he is out in the field all day organising the troops. For the worker on the shop floor he is the public face of the union. He is also the conduit between members and otherwise faceless officials.

It was actually quite a moving experience for the six mates to be offered these positions. It was a show of confidence in their abilities by the A.L.P.'s powerful left faction. The other five said an unequivocal "yes" to the offer; Gaily procrastinated.

For months Colleen had been in Gaily's lug suggesting he chuck in his job with the post office to pursue a career rather than waste his life in a lowly, poorly paid dead-end job.

His parents also continued to nag him with repeated appeals for him to enrol in university.

It was easy for him to fob off his parents by simply telling the truth: he could not afford to leave the paid workforce.

His parents countered by telling him, "We would help you, Charles".

The unstated truth was Gaily was up to his ears in debt. He detested sponging off his parents but begrudgingly accepted their hand-outs in order to maintain interest payments on credit cards and personal loans. Gaily would borrow as much as he could lay his hands on in order to see Colleen as often as possible. Love had proven to be highly addictive.

Had Gaily gone to university he would have qualified for social services. His parents offered to top up the social services to the level of his present wage so that he would effectively not be out of pocket despite not having a job. He would be able to study full-time without loss of income provided he could learn to live on the equivalent of a mailsorter's wage.

It was a generous offer on the part of his parents. It was also extremely controlling behaviour. Gaily valued his independence too much. He therefore declined the offer.

Colleen was less easy to fob off. She offered not money but that which can be bought with money. Colleen provided all the pleasures of the flesh via a beautiful body which radiated sexual energy.

The enticement for either party concerned here was simple. If Gaily could generate more income he could spend more time with Colleen – the more time the more pleasures of the flesh with the Irish Goddess of Love. It was a simple equation.

For Colleen the equation was equally straightforward. The more time Gaily spent with her the more money she earned.

Colleen had only to tell Gaily to jump and he would ask, "How high, Miss?"

The problem was resolved in Gaily's mind when Colleen announced she was leaving Australia. Gaily would chuck in his job to pursue her to the ends of the Earth: which ends would prove to be the dosshouses of Penang in Malaysia.

The difficulty would be in leaving the job without jeopardising the chances of the Left winning a majority in the union elections. He also needed to maximise the amount of money he would receive when resigning from the post office.

This second problem would be resolved by the way in which Gaily would stage-manage his own departure from work.

Gaily's mere name on a ballot paper was worth a bloc vote of five hundred such was his standing in the union. Without his candidature the left-wing ticket could not win a majority.

Gaily had a word in the ear of the A.L.P. Left's choice of candidate for the union presidency Bill Grainish. He put it to Grainish that he would run for an unpaid Executive position on the premise that when the Left won the elections Grainish would swing Gaily a golden handshake.

Grainish said the way to go about it would be to make Gaily's position on the roster redundant thereby entitling him to Voluntary Early Retirement (V.E.R.). Gaily agreed to this plan and pledged his ongoing support to Grainish and the ticket as a whole.

Gaily would never forget the meeting at Strathfield Pub in Sydney's western suburbs. The meeting was organised by a shifty Lebanese union official who had arranged to bankroll the ticket with money derived from God (or Allah) knows where. His name was Ahmed Inane and the meeting was convened to finalise the composition of the left ticket.

Inane looked directly across the table at Gaily. The meeting had been under way for half an hour or so. In the best traditions of Australian trade unionism the table was littered with empty beer glasses.

"Do you want an organiser's position?" Inane asked Gaily.

All eyes were on Gaily.

"No, Ahmed, I just want an unpaid position on the proviso that when we are elected you blokes will swing me a golden handshake."

With these few words Gaily consigned fourteen years of hard yakka to the dustbin of history. He had consciously entered the workforce with a view to becoming a trade union activist. This he had done with distinction to the point of being at the age of thirty-one on the state executive of one of Australia's largest and most powerful unions. Now when the opportunity arose to take advantage of years of activity and sacrifice he was about to walk away. He was sacrificing all for love: love which would prove unrequited.

When word began to circulate about Gaily's decision many were disappointed; a few were disgusted. A lot of his fellow workers admired Gaily and knew he would have been a wonderful trade union official. With his eloquence, energy, sincerity and politics it was a match made in heaven. Since leaving school he had coveted such a role.

For the Trots and the other ultra-leftists who inhabited the fringes of the union it merely reinforced their opinion of Gaily as an opportunist. Purer than the driven snow they refused to even participate in rank-and-file group activity. They never made mistakes because they never did anything – preferring to scream advice from the sidelines.

The left-wing ticket won a majority on the new state executive. The presidency was obtained by a margin of less than thirty votes. Other positions were won by similarly small margins. It was Gaily's only consolation that without his name at least appearing on the ballot paper the left would not have carried the day.

It would take six months to swing the golden handshake. One of his parting gestures was to get square with one of the usurers to whom he was in debt.

Gaily owed Maurice Zion and Co. five hundred dollars and was flat out repaying the interest, which worked out at one hundred and forty-four per cent per annum. Due to a technicality in the wording of the documents signed by their clients a class action had been initiated against the legal validity of those contracts.

The class action was led by the Law Society of New South Wales and the Consumer Credit Association.

Zion's clients had been asked to volunteer as witnesses against their creditor. Gaily had stepped forward.

The President of the Law Society at the time was Kevin Puller Q.C. The great man himself interviewed Gaily in the company of a dishy young solicitor from the Redfern Legal Centre Lisa Cutter.

Mr Puller asked Gaily how he had got into debt. He went so far as to ask him on what he spent his money.

"Booze, women and Marxist books," came the prompt reply.

"Ah, a middle class Marxist," was Puller's response.

"You've known a few of them in your time, Mr Puller," thought Gaily.

Gaily was not required to make a court appearance but the class action was a success so nor then was he required to make further loan repayments. Shortly after Zion and Co. was declared bankrupt.

Gaily had further infuriated the ultra-lefts by obtaining a Senior Mail Officer's position. In fourteen years of service he had gone up one rung. For this heinous crime against the working class he was deemed to have sold out by becoming a boss.

To realise the golden handshake his position would have to be abolished. Gaily was already in his mind cleaning out his desk and counting the cash.

His mother had been disappointed because the organiser's job would have given him a substantial wage increase. His father had been disappointed because he knew his son would have made a good union official. As usual though his father said nothing.

"It's your life, Charles," said his mother.

It seemed the only ones not disappointed with the decision were Gaily himself and Colleen.

Colleen had just resigned from A.T.O.C. amidst allegations of drug use. Colleen's version of what had occurred seemed a bit hazy but then drugs can do that to a person.

While Colleen still remained in Sydney she allowed Gaily to see her but only on the basis they met in five star hotel rooms. Gaily quickly gained an insight into his future dealings with her. Payment was to be five hundred dollars per meeting. The golden handshake was being spent prior to its even being received.

Meanwhile Gaily's Party branch had voted against dissolution and elected him as a delegate to what turned out to be the last Sydney District Conference. However, those opposing dissolution were by then in a tiny minority. Dissolution seemed inevitable.

The liquidators had gone ahead with their scheme to establish a new watered down version of a socialist party. Appropriately it was named the New Left Party. Someone had sat up all night to think of that name.

The new party already claimed more financial members than the old party although most of the new party members were in fact dual card carriers.

Gaily and Gunga Din sat together in the inner city town hall which had been hired for the day. A handful of other hard liners sat in their vicinity. Less than a hundred in total were present for such an historic occasion.

Mary was there looking as lovely as ever. It was a deeply emotional occasion. His own foolishness had destroyed his relationship with Mary and now the foolishness of others was about to destroy the Party which had brought them together.

Mary smiled and said hullo. There was no bitterness on her part. For this he was thankful. He wished her every happiness.

The conference finally got under way. Gaily had spent half his political life waiting for meetings to start and the other half waiting for them to end.

The Party leaders got up one by one to justify what was about to occur. They droned on and on with the same arguments they had employed for years. Gaily tuned out as his father did when reading the Herald at the kitchen table. At least his mother's nagging did not derive from criminal intent. She had always worked for her money not obtained it by acts of fraud.

The lunch break finally arrived. Gaily could not get to the nearest pub quickly enough. He chug-a-lugged seven schooners of Resch's and floated back to the hall.

Straight after lunch Gaily was allowed to outline the dissenting position. One of his mates in the post office had told him years prior one always speaks better after a few drinks and he had taken him at his word.

Gaily spoke eloquently enough. He outlined the Party's proud history, the vital roles it had played in the struggles of the working class and its centrality to the building of the unions and the mass social movements of the day. He pointed out that the liquidationists would do by their own actions what the Menzies government had failed to do with its attempt to ban the Party.

He ended with the famous quote from the Australian

poet Henry Lawson, "They needn't say the fault is ours if blood should stain the wattle".

Most of the older women in the audience were in tears by the time he finished. Only the most craven and hard-headed of the liquidationists failed to applaud him as he left a party microphone for what would be the last time.

Gaily had given it his best shot and Gunga Din shook his hand warmly as he returned to his seat.

Gunga Din gave a similarly impassioned speech but it was too little too late. The final vote was fifty-eight to two in favour of supporting dissolution at the national Congress. Gaily and Gunga Din asked for their names to be recorded in the minutes as having cast the dissenting votes. History would show who had taken the principled position.

Delegates to Congress were elected. Gaily and Gunga Din were not amongst them. They would be entitled to observer status only.

Back at work on the Monday Gaily was formally advised of the golden handshake he was to receive. It totalled eighty thousand dollars and was divided into two parts. The first part was severance pay of twenty thousand dollars which would be paid straight into his bank account. The second part was the actual handshake of sixty thousand dollars which would be paid into a roll-over account of his nomination in order to minimise taxation liability. Gaily made arrangements to open a rollover account with Barclays – they having an Australian subsidiary at the time.

Colleen had already moved to Penang where she had planned to retire. Gaily had cut out all his leave entitlements to spend as much time with her as possible. They stayed in separate dosshouses but as had been the case at the end there in Sydney the mistress required a five star room and five hundred dollars for their rendezvous.

Penang was a pleasant little place. It was the most secular of the Malaysian states. The local brew was similar to Resch's so met with Gaily's approval but Gaily had significantly reduced his intake in order to throw every spare dollar, pound or ringgit into his pursuit of Colleen. Even without drinking heavily Gaily was in self-destruct mode. Colleen was more than happy to assist him along this path.

The Party Congress was about to be held. It was a foregone conclusion what would occur. Gaily was drawn to it as one's eyes are drawn to a fatal car accident. He had come this far so he may as well be in at the death.

A handful of like-minded individuals attended the gathering held at an inner city community hall.

The key question in Gaily's mind was, "What's the Party worth?"

The whole sordid affair had been about money and the main report at Congress bore this out.

The patriarch of the Abrahams family was Abraham Abrahams. Abrahams made it quite clear all available capital was safely invested in the Vietnamese short-term money market. The funds were therefore helping build socialism while giving the C.P.A. a healthy income. Throw in the odd property here and there and the Party was worth seven million dollars.

This was almost certainly an understated figure because of hidden assets but Gaily had been warned what would happen to those who looked too deeply into these matters.

The whole thing was a farce to rubber-stamp decisions already made. Dissenting opinion had been virtually excluded by way of the delegate selection process.

Most of the delegates were so old they would soon be in their own graves but they first had to bury the very party they had helped build.

Somehow one of the Blue Mountains members had wangled a delegate's position. He was the sole dissenting voice in an otherwise unanimous decision to dissolve.

The Party assets were left in the hands of the outgoing National Executive - who duly gave themselves each a house in which to live. There was no real accountability but the rest of the funds and income ostensibly went towards a fund for deserving causes as adjudged by the executive. They had already shown which causes they deemed most worthy of support – namely their own.

Gaily's little world had been crumbling for a while but now it had finally collapsed.

By his own volition his activity in the union movement was about to end and the Party was finally officially dead. All he had left to live for was Colleen.

The golden handshake was about to be paid. For taxation purposes management had offered to allow him to stay on the payroll until 1st July thus taking him into the following financial year. He was in such a hurry to rejoin Colleen he declined their offer and accepted 30th June as his final day on the payroll.

It was a hastily made decision and one he would live to regret.

However, like the Party's demise there was a certain inevitability to both his actions and their outcomes.

He booked his flights, packed his bags and returned to Penang.

Upon his return to sunny Penang Gaily found things to be not too sunny with Colleen. She was broke.

Gaily had had his own debts to settle out of his severance pay. Colleen's situation at least meant she was willing to see him on a regular basis – at five hundred dollars a pop.

Gaily was still in Colleen's good books as prior to her leaving Sydney he had arranged and paid for a former workmate to come around with a van and take those belongings she no longer required to an auctioneer for sale.

Penang was steamy and so was the sex. With time not really an issue their sessions would last hours. The hours were filled with tease and discipline – always ending in an explosive climax. Colleen's body and legs were a golden brown, her body firm and toned. Gaily swam laps at the local pool, Colleen herself doing her breast-stroke with her head out of the water as do most long-haired beauties. It was an idyllic time but for the lack of cash. After less than three months Gaily had run through the last of his severance pay and Colleen possessed only such money as she had received from him less her living expenses. The time had come to wish Penang goodbye.

Apparently Colleen had invested most of her own savings with a property developer on Queensland's Gold Coast. A sum of fifty thousand dollars had been handed over by way of a loan on which interest of twenty per cent per annum had been promised. The developer and the money had both vanished.

There was also a little house in Brisbane on which a mortgage had been taken out. Repayments of eight hundred dollars per month were supposedly required for Colleen to retain the property.

When one is in a bit of a hole always ask someone to hand you a shovel that you may make the hole considerably deeper. Colleen handed Gaily a large shovel and he proceeded for the next twenty years off and on to dig his own grave.

Gaily agreed to go up to Brisbane and see the solicitor who was handling the case pertaining to the missing money. If a case for fraud could be made the developer could be sued and the money pursued through the courts.

Gaily also agreed to make the mortgage repayments until further notice.

Colleen said she could never return to Australia until the money was retrieved so entrusted the tasks to Gaily. The potential loss of the money was such a traumatic experience she could not stand the rigours which would be involved in the retrieval process. Rather Colleen would return to England where her family lived and seek to pick up the pieces.

Gaily said he would do his best. Ominously Colleen was already referring to Gaily's lump sum payment as "our money".

They spent their last day together at the Eastern and Oriental Hotel. Colleen had delayed conveying the bad tidings until as late as possible in the hope the Brisbane solicitor would turn the situation around. However, the correspondence received was more doom and gloom. There were also legal fees which had to be paid.

Colleen had started to smoke again. Five star hotels are all well and good but one cannot open a window. The room filled with smoke and Gaily had difficulty breathing. He had had asthma as a child but swimming had cured him of the affliction.

One of Gaily's favourite possessions was a photograph of Colleen holding a packet of Marlboro. The photograph had been taken at the Covent Garden Hotel in London prior to her coming to Australia. Gaily always said it was the best advertisement for Marlboro for which Philip Morris could ever wish.

On this particular day though Colleen was not a real

good advertisement for anything. She still looked the part with a sarong over her black bikini but was not her usual vivacious self.

"Don't always expect to have sex with a woman just because you have paid," was all Gaily received by way of explanation.

Gaily walked back to the filthy little dosshouse he had called home for most of his stay. The agreement when they went to the E. and O. was that Colleen would always retain the room for the night. They were only ever day-time lovers.

The next day Gaily saw a gorgeous platinum blonde in the street. The cleft of her bottom was clearly visible through the seat of the tights she was wearing. There were obviously no knickers involved. Thankfully Allah was a straight bloke so knickerless bottoms were tolerated in at least one state of Malaysia.

Gaily would know those buttocks anywhere. They belonged to Colleen. He ran up to their owner. She smiled that smile.

"I was hoping to run into you," said the mistress in her most endearing tones.

His heart melted as Colleen walked him into a paper shop where she proceeded to pile together glossy magazines.

"…and a packet of Marlboro Red, please. My friend is paying," Colleen said to the shop assistant.

It was news to Gaily but if it made her happy…

The bill came to sixty ringgit. He paid the money and was accorded the privilege of walking Colleen to the nearest bus-stop – he carrying the magazines for her.

"All part of the service," he smiled as she stepped onto the hot, crowded bus to go back to her dosshouse. It was one of their favourite lines.

Apart from a farewell drink that was the last they would see of each other until the following year. He had his riding instructions and she had her life to rebuild in England.

He was glad to see the last of the vermin-infested doss-house in which he had stayed. One of the few Malaysian words he had learnt was "tikus" meaning rodent. There were "tikus many many". The other words were "pang-gang halal" roughly meaning "buttocks permitted under Islamic law". He had many wonderful photographs of Colleen's bottom to act as an eternal reminder of the more pleasant moments spent in Penang. His outlook was still overwhelmingly positive and he mused about the future as Malaysian Airlines conveyed him back to Sydney. It would be good to have a schooner of Resch's at the Star.

Once back in his mother's flat in Sydney Gaily had to take firm stock of the situation.

He had sixty thousand dollars in a rollover fund. This was a huge sum of money to him: it represented three years' wages in the post office and was a reward for over fourteen years in the workforce and sharp bargaining near the end of that time.

He had been honest with his mother about the amount he had received. For her part Mrs Gaily had told him bluntly the sum was not sufficient to live on for any length of time. Her son had other ideas.

Gaily's other love apart from Colleen and Resch's was racing. Now with no Colleen in sight and no job and no Trib to sell he was free to pursue a career as a professional punter.

Gaily had fallen in love with racing at the age of fourteen. As part of his duties as an Australian father Mr Gaily had seen it as incumbent upon him to take the lad to a race meeting.

They had gone to Rosehill Racecourse one Saturday.

It was a glorious summer's day in the western suburbs of Sydney. The weather was fine and the track was good: ideal conditions for racing.

Mr Gaily had given his son a nominal bank of ten dollars with which to bet. As a minor the boy had to get his father to place bets on his behalf. As would be the case for the rest of his life he had done the form with the help of Australia's national racing newspaper the Sportsman.

Like most people attending their first race meeting Gaily experienced beginner's luck. This is what ensures one is hooked for life. He would never forget the names of the two winners he backed: Sasha and Air Voyager.

Of the two he had nominated Air Voyager as his best bet of the day. On the way home his father had asked him why he had not had a larger wager on his best bet.

Gaily's reply was very telling. From his first attempt at serious betting he had understood the merits of fixed or level stakes investment. This was a principle he was to deviate from at his peril in the future. It would prove to be a cornerstone of his success on the punt.

His first day at the races had seen Gaily turn ten dollars into twenty eight dollars: a one hundred and eighty per cent profit on turnover. Again his attitude was that of a businessman not a gambler. Mr Gaily had brought his son up to believe a long-term return of fifty per cent on capital outlay was feasible. This then would be the younger Gaily's goal when he attempted to become a professional.

Of course it is a qualitative leap from being someone who mucks around with twenty dollars on a Saturday to being a full-time professional punter. Gaily though had burnt his bridges and was prepared to risk his entire capital to maintain his relationship with Colleen.

He knew Colleen had had boyfriends and there was no

reason why he could not become the next. He also knew – were he honest with himself – their relationship would always revolve around money. Gaily was driven for the first time in his life to generate a high income. With his available capital he would not achieve this via traditional means such as shares or property. When he was about to leave the post office the union's state secretary at the time had suggested he buy a property. The suggestions had been made in all good faith. He and the secretary had been sparring partners but there was no ill feeling between them. However, in Gaily's opinion, the proposition was out of the question. Any rent he might receive based on current returns of eight per cent gross and five or six per cent net would be insufficient upon which to live. He would have to get another job: something he was loath to do after turning his nose up at what would have been his dream job as a union organiser.

Since the age of fourteen Gaily had only ever coveted two career paths: either as a trade union official or as a professional punter. He had sacrificed his ability to pursue the first path because of Colleen. Pursuing the second would enable him to win the heart of Colleen while compensating him for not having taken the opportunity proffered by the union.

With sixty thousand dollars he could give himself a betting bank of fifty thousand and put ten aside for the creation of a tipping service.

For years he had thought of a tipping service as a lucrative sideline for a professional punter. First get your fifteen minutes as a professional punter than dine out on them by selling tips to the mugs.

The difficult part was getting the fifteen minutes. Gaily knew Colleen wanted money. It was what drove her. Gaily also knew women liked successful men. Their success could be in any field – it did not matter. Success in most any field will bring with it financial gain.

Success requires confidence. Success builds confidence. Gaily was starting to come to terms with what was required to be a consistent winner. The psychological aspect was crucial. He had started to read various manuals which claimed to be able to assist the individual to tap into their creative side. For someone whose reading had been limited to classical literature and classical Marxism these books opened up a whole new world of thinking.

For too long Gaily had merely allowed himself to drift like so much flotsam and jetsam. Now instead of sacrificing his wants and needs to those of others he sought to take control of his own destiny.

As well as reading what was essentially New Age thinking derived from America he began to read Sartre. Sartre's ideas on the role of the individual within society filled a huge and glaring gap in Marxist theory. Marxism had always spoken of and for the masses. Where did the individual fit into this framework? Sartre answered this question.

Success also requires a plan. Gaily's punting plan was based on using the Sportsman as his data base to enable him to rate horses using the methods outlined by Australia's most successful punter Don Scott.

Scott had outlined his methods in the late seventies in his book Winning. Scott's successes largely relied on his class and weight ratings which looked at the grade of races a horse had contested in the past, the grade of race it was about to compete in and the weights it had carried and was about to carry.

Over the course of twenty years Scott and his Legal

Eagles syndicate took millions out of Australian betting rings. Gaily had taken Scott's ideas and improved upon them in order to give himself an additional edge. He had created his own set of criteria pertaining to the class of race being contested, its distance, the fitness of a horse, its form, its gender, the going or condition of the track's surface, the grade of race, the jockey riding the given horse and the venue at which the race was to be conducted.

All of these factors combined to provide a numerical rating which could be expressed as a percentage and converted into a rated price using a conversion factor.

To obtain the best available odds Gaily opened a telephone betting account with leading rails bookmaker Rod Marks. Trading with Mr Marks was done on what was termed a "cash positive" basis meaning Gaily had to place money in the bookmaker's bank account before he could have a bet and could only bet up to the limit of his account balance.

This suited the aspiring professional punter as one of the biggest mistakes a punter can make is to accept credit from a bookmaker. In racing parlance credit is referred to as "tick" and once someone starts betting "on tick" they can get into a lot of strife when the inevitable losing streak occurs. Gaily's parents had brought him up to be a gentleman and a gentleman always honours his debts.

One of the best aspects of betting with Mr Marks was the ability to stipulate a minimum price. Gaily's ratings enabled him to assess a price below which he would consider a horse bad value and therefore not worth the risk of backing.

The bookmaker provided the best price (termed "top fluctuation" or "top fluc." for short) on all races conducted in the metropolitan areas of Australia's five mainland state capitals: Brisbane, Sydney, Melbourne, Adelaide and Perth. The only stipulation was that one had to bet prior to prices being posted for the first race of the day.

Mr Marks would set a punter to win up to fifteen thousand dollars in Sydney and Melbourne and ten thousand in Brisbane, Adelaide and Perth with any winnings over and above these amounts being paid at Starting Price (S.P.).

Gaily knew he had to hit the ground running so consulted the Don Scott book for Scott's formula as to bet size. Scott recommended betting to take out five per cent of one's bank based on one's rated prices. For someone with a bank of fifty thousand dollars this would mean betting to take out $2,500 which would mean if a horse was rated 6-4 ($2.50) one would have a thousand dollars on it and so on. Later Gaily would revert to flat/level stakes betting but one has to start somewhere.

He also decided to bet one horse per race whereas Scott might back five if the value was available. From a logical point of view Gaily disliked the idea of effectively betting against oneself. The proof of the pudding would be in the eating.

Such was Gaily's plan for success at the races. However, the best laid plans of mice and punters can be undermined by a beautiful and unscrupulous woman.

Colleen had an alternative plan to that of Gaily: simply fleece him of his money before he had the opportunity to risk it on the races.

A few weeks after his return to Australia Gaily received a letter from Brighton in England. It consisted of a hastily scrawled note from Colleen asking him to ring her at his earliest convenience. Included was Colleen's new telephone number.

Early the morning after having received the letter he

went to a public telephone and rang the number. Colleen answered.

Her tone was distraught. There was no attempt at small talk. The woman's anger was directed at him. He did not understand. They had had such a lovely time together in Penang.

She spoke rapidly. He had further difficulty in understanding what was being said. The gist of it was she had a "life-threatening" illness and needed money urgently for medical treatment.

He panicked. All his own long-term plans were evaporating before his eyes. All his hopes and dreams for both of them were disappearing with them.

He offered to come to England to be with her but was told there was no point. He was not a doctor.

She starting raving about the property in Brisbane and cursing the developer who had stolen her life savings.

He promised to go up to Brisbane the following week to see if any progress had been made in the matter. The month's mortgage repayment had already been paid.

Colleen repeated the reference to "life-threatening illness". He asked her the nature of the illness but it was a private matter she would not discuss.

"It could be cancer," he thought.

His mother had never fully recovered from radiotherapy for her cancer. It was a dreadful disease and a horrible way to go if remission could not be achieved. Even then it usually came out of remission and eventually killed you.

"How much do you need?" he asked.

"Ten thousand dollars," came the reply from the other end of the line.

He baulked at the amount but she continued to wear him down with her hysterics. He finally capitulated.

It would take a few days for him to gain access to the money but the sum requested would be conveyed via electronic bank transfer. He would need her bank account details.

Suddenly her voice became calmer. She would get her account details and read them to him over the telephone. He had a pen and paper handy and faithfully recorded the account details. Over the following twenty years hundreds of thousands of Australian dollars would be converted into pounds and paid into that account via electronic transfer.

Gaily rang his father for advice. He explained the situation to his father using Colleen's choice of words. His parents knew of Colleen but had never met her. His mother had extended an invitation years ago for her to have a meal at the family home. It had initially been accepted but subsequently declined. A flask of Gilbey's was still in his parents' liquor cabinet. It had been purchased so Colleen could have a gin and tonic. The flask was always referred to as "Colleen's gin". It was still there when his parents died.

The father gave his son sound advice. He said Colleen should provide medical evidence before Gaily parted with the money. Like all good advice given it was not heeded. His father also said there were some friends one could not afford.

Mr Gaily knew his son was a soft touch. He also sensed Colleen was only interested in his son for any money which might come her way. On both counts Mr Gaily was of course spot on. Still it was his son's life to do with what he chose. Mr and Mrs Gaily had discussed Colleen to the extent they could with the limited information their son provided about her. They chose to believe she was or had been whilst in Australia their son's girlfriend but suspected otherwise. Gaily often thought his mother had twigged to the reality when she gave him the works of English author Patrick Hamilton in which prostitutes feature prominently.

Colleen had merely shrugged off her change of mind regarding meeting Gaily's parents by saying, "No mother likes women like me".

Gaily had the money transferred. It was a huge chunk out of his capital but he could not challenge the veracity of Colleen's words.

His punting was progressing at a very slow rate. There was a lot of trial and error involved. He would have a losing sequence, cut the size of his bets then strike a few winners but not have enough money on them to recoup his losses. He was still refining his methods but had to learn on the run.

He felt under enormous pressure. The woman he loved was twelve thousand miles away. He had to liaise with the solicitor in Brisbane and make repayments on the Gold Coast property while still in the initial stages of building his own business. He was betting in denominations fifty times larger than he had ever bet in his life. At the same time he was attempting to establish a tipping service.

Gaily had promised Colleen he would go to Brisbane to see her solicitor so being a man of his word off he went. It was the first time he had visited the state of Queensland, Brisbane being its capital. The most famous of Brisbane's hotels is Lennon's where such celebrities as Louis Armstrong and members of the Royal Family have stayed. If it was good enough for them it was good enough for Gaily so this is where he booked his night's accommodation.

The solicitor was a Mr Hay. He was a pompous flush-faced old bloke who spoke in the cant of his profession. Mr Hay gave the impression of knowing what he was talking about. The trick here is to know more about one's subject than the person to whom you are speaking.

Mr Hay had obviously had extensive correspondence with Colleen. He searched through his files to refresh his memory.

"I am a very busy man, Mr Gaily," Mr Hay said by way of explaining his lack of preparedness.

"Time is money, sir," replied Gaily.

"Couldn't have put it better myself," returned Mr Hay – not detecting Gaily's irony.

Mr Hay started by saying he was aware that Colleen had worked in what he euphemistically termed "massage parlours" whilst living in Australia and was now similarly employed back in England. He did not need to know the exact nature of her work. Whilst working in Sydney she had met a property developer named Jack Melody who had offered to pay her twenty per cent interest on any multiples of ten thousand dollars invested with him. He was to use the money for the specific purpose of building a block of flats on the Gold Coast. The crux of the matter was that there appeared to be no legally valid documentation of any transaction pertaining to the loan. Melody had skipped town after sending Colleen notes saying that payment of interest had stalled due to cash flow problems. Investigations were continuing regarding his whereabouts but at that point in time the only contact address for Melody was a post office box on the Gold Coast which had not been cleared for weeks.

Mr Hay summed up the situation with the words "Silly girl".

Essentially nothing more could be said or done to retrieve the lost money. Even if Melody could be located any legal proceedings against him would probably founder for lack of evidence. Unless other victims came to the fore it was just Colleen's word against Melody's.

Gaily paid Mr Hay Colleen's outstanding bills and

wished him good day. Gaily had made an undertaking to Colleen to go down to the Gold Coast but it was too late in the day for that so he went and had his first ever drink of XXXX beer. It was execrable stuff. How could people drink it? He went to bed longing for a schooner of Resch's and awoke the next morning with a slight headache as a result of having forced down a couple of extra pots of XXXX.

He caught the first coach of the day down to the Gold Coast and found his way to the post office. His task was to hang around the post office boxes and apprehend anyone clearing Melody's box. It was only just after seven in the morning and he had thought it fair enough if he stayed until ten as most boxes were cleared by clerks and secretaries on the way to their respective offices.

Gaily read the Courier-Mail to pass the time. Desperate men do desperate things and desperate women get desperate men to do their bidding. It was a waste of time. Gaily confirmed with the clerk in the post office that the box remained uncleared then cleared out himself.

The Gold Coast is a popular holiday resort but Gaily had no time or money for holidays. He had to go home to try to make some money. His capital had already been significantly reduced.

Back in Sydney he registered the name "Rails Run Publishing" with the Department of Consumer Affairs. He had purchased a little word processor and started to produce a racing newsletter. A Telstra 1300 line enabled punters to call for his tips from any location in Australia for the cost of a local call. He started placing small advertisements in the racing press and used the offer of a free newsletter subscription as a means of attracting clients. His service was monitored by the consumer watchdog for racing services Punter's Choice and received favourable reviews. Clients responding to his ads paid seven hundred and seventy-seven dollars per year for subscriptions to his service (the use of the number seven in one's price will increase sales he had read in a so-called "marketing" manual).

Still he only managed to break even on the exercise. Subscriptions barely covered overheads but at least the overheads were tax deductible. Gaily would not have to pay tax but then nor should someone with no income.

It was a similar story with the punt. If one could break even one should be able to tweak one's methods and produce a profit. It was just a matter of how to tweak what he was doing. There were so many variables involved. One could tinker with what was working and overlook what was not.

Two factors compounded Gaily's problems.

Firstly, he tended to overanalyse things. He was an intellectual by nature not a practical person capable of thinking and acting on his feet.

His mother used to say in her son's defence he did not have a "mechanical" mind by which was implied a lack of skill in working with his hands as opposed to work of a more intellectual bent. For Gaily though it went deeper than this as ideas were too often sufficient in themselves without seeking to give them practical application.

Secondly, there was Colleen. Gaily had an unlisted telephone number possessed by very few even of his friends and acquaintances. His parents had his number "just in case something happens, Charles" as his mother would say. Then there was Colleen. He dreaded the bloody thing ringing. At night he would take the receiver off the hook. When the occasional visitor came around he would unplug it from the wall and hide it in another room.

Still eventually the call came. It was Colleen. He had

not heard from her for a couple of months. His letters remained unanswered. He had not even been thanked for his gift of ten grand. There was no real way of knowing what was happening in England without being physically present.

Colleen was distraught. The medical bills were mounting. The "life-threatening illness" required ongoing private hospital treatment. A public hospital would have a waiting list a mile long. Could he send another ten grand as soon as possible?

He hesitated momentarily in responding.

"Do you want me giving blow jobs for fifty quid down the pier?" shrieked the voice.

It was not until being informed indirectly by Mr Hay that Gaily had come to know Colleen was back "on the game".

"Aren't you working?" he meekly responded.

"Who told you that?" came the response – at once aggressive and defensive.

"Mr Hay said something," he mumbled.

"I'm sick!" came the hysterical reply, Colleen once again on the front foot.

He capitulated. How much did she want?

"Another ten."

Colleen knew he was putty and treated him like dirt. For one who liked to portray herself in the dominant mistress role her behaviour was extremely reminiscent of a spoilt brat.

"It will be sent this week," Gaily said - relieved to end the conversation.

"Tomorrow. I can't afford these phone calls, Charlie," Colleen's voice echoed down the line.

The money would be paid tomorrow – if only to keep

the peace. As a peace activist Gaily was well aware peace always came at a price. For him it was increments of ten thousand dollars.

He put down the receiver. Overwhelmed by the situation he went to the refrigerator and took out one of the cold bottles of Resch's. Ironically he had cut down on drinking for this woman. Now even had he wanted to drink heavily he could not afford the regular benders of his post office days.

Gaily knew not where to turn but had to speak to someone about the situation. He did not feel close enough to his parents to speak with them in an open manner.

Gaily had the telephone number of one of Colleen's former workmates at A.T.O.C. He would ring her to try to tee up a lunch date. A.T.O.C. had not been graced with his presence since Colleen's departure and he had no intention of returning. Gaily would be faithful to his mistress in her hour of need.

In the meantime he went to see his local GP. The good doctor was a Pacific Islander with a surname people found difficult to pronounce so he had been affectionately nicknamed Dr Coconut. The doctor had studied at an Australian university so his qualifications were pukka. His bedside manner was pleasant although the missionaries had got to him at an early age making him unduly subjective about gambling and drinking. Practising in the western suburbs of Sydney gave him plenty about which to be subjective.

Gaily and Dr Coconut had developed a good rapport over the seven years of their association. The doctor knew of Colleen but could not approve of his patient's befriending a prostitute. Dr Coconut insisted on giving Gaily a hepatitis B injection but only after asking to see photographs of her. As a married man with daughters he secretly envied Gaily's freedom.

Gaily knew to arrive at the surgery half an hour before it opened in order to be first in the queue. There were no appointments. Once inside he gave his Medicare card to the receptionist and sat down in the waiting room. Dr Coconut was always fashionably late.

When the doctor finally appeared he called Gaily's name – ushering him into his surgery. After exchanging pleasantries Gaily explained the situation to Dr Coconut. The doctor listened intently but had seen it coming and had in any event heard it all before. Young blokes were fools where women were concerned.

The doctor's advice could be summed up in two words: "Walk away". Like all good advice it was ignored.

Gaily sought a second opinion from Colleen's former workmate Mistress Vicki. They met for lunch at the Greek restaurant Diethnes.

Gaily had liked Vicki ever since seeing her in her white towelling A.T.O.C. dressing gown. He marvelled at her youthfulness and her extraordinary beauty. Like Colleen she was blonde and full-figured. Her hair was the colour of cream - which complemented the peaches and cream of her complexion. When she would work a double with Colleen Vicki would wear a little white tennis skirt with white g-string knickers underneath. Gaily would always be fully erect by the time Vicki got him over her knee.

Outside work Vicki would always dress in a conservative fashion. Gaily mused as to the colour of her knickers when first they met at the restaurant. Disappointingly Vicki wore slacks – something Colleen would not do until premature old age.

Over lunch they discussed their absent friend. Vicki and Colleen had not parted on good terms. Vicki accused Colleen of attempting to steal her boyfriend. Despite this of anyone in Sydney it would be Vicki who best knew Colleen.

Vicki did not want to get involved in other people's problems: she had enough of her own. Indeed Vicki seemed more intent on gaining any juicy gossip Gaily could provide than being of any real assistance.

When Gaily raised the subject of drug use Vicki almost choked on her mineral water (Vicki was a teetotaller).

"You mean 'Californian snow'," was her succinct response.

Gaily was familiar with Colleen's use of this term to describe cocaine.

"Colleen always said she had never tried the stuff," replied Gaily.

"Charlie, all I will say is you are very naive and if you are throwing your money at her you may as well throw some my way," said Vicki.

"Are you making me an offer, Vicki?" Gaily responded.

"I want nothing to do with you sexually. Colleen always made it clear she owned you," came the terse answer.

"Colleen always said it was the other ladies who used – not her," probed Gaily.

"She would, wouldn't she?" smiled Vicki.

"She also seemed in a hurry to get out of Sydney," persisted Gaily.

"Colleen made accusations against some of the girls. I stayed right out of it," sidestepped Vicki.

There was obviously little point in pursuing the theme so Gaily allowed the conversation to drift onto other subjects. They finished the meal and Gaily paid the bill. He thanked Vicki for being so generous with her time as she could easily have charged escort rates but had refused his offer of money.

Vicki gave Gaily a lift to Central Railway Station which he accepted as much for the female company as anything. Life had become very lonely for him and he clung to the additional few minutes with Vicki the lift afforded.

Gaily was fond of Vicki not just for her looks and the few doubles she had worked with Colleen. Vicki had led a very colourful life in the company of equally colourful racing identities. The former girlfriend of a professional punter and (illegal) S.P. bookmaker and the former wife of the son of a top rails bookmaker she had adopted a more sedate lifestyle in middle age.

Gaily found her past romantic life created an additional bond which would not otherwise have existed. He had no reason to believe Vicki was herself any longer a drug user although by her own admission she had smoked a lot of marijuana in her younger days. This was probably a contributing factor to the anxiety attacks Vicki experienced down the track. Of course the medical profession can be relied upon to be able to prescribe a legal drug to counter the side-effects of illegal drugs. In Australia there are half a million schizophrenics or sufferers of what is now termed bipolar disorder – the vast majority as a result of long term marijuana use. Half a million schizophrenics in a population of only twenty-three million cannot be wrong.

Vicki had hinted strongly at the fact Colleen had used "snow" but then where was the evidence? He had no reason to disbelieve the woman he loved when told via her own sweet lips such was not the case. It may have just been animosity on the part of Vicki given Colleen's alleged advances towards Vicki's current boyfriend. He knew the two women had not parted on good terms. In any event his love was proving to be deaf as well as blind.

The advice of Dr Coconut and the implications of Vicki's statements would go unheeded. When someone is determined to destroy themselves no one can stand in their way.

Again and again and again Colleen would ring Gaily

with hard luck stories and he would dutifully send the requested amount for non-existent medical bills. While Gaily was self-destructing Colleen was equally intent on self-medicating. Of course if "snow" were a part of Colleen's self-prescribed medications list the drug does have a legitimate medical use as an anaesthetic. However, doctors and anaesthetists do not generally administer cocaine via the patient's nasal passages.

All good things come to an end – as did Gaily's money. When Colleen was apprised of the situation she became very angry.

"That was our money," she screamed over the telephone.

Thankfully twelve thousand miles is a fairly safe distance otherwise Gaily may have copped more than a spanking for his trouble. Having given his mistress most of the lump sum he had received only a year prior he was now accused of gambling it away.

Never argue with coppers, idiots or women – and Colleen fell into at least one of those categories. Gaily was declared persona non grata by Colleen until such time as he could come up with some more dosh.

For the first time in his life Gaily was forced to worry about his own survival. Love had become his drug of choice. Like champagne combined with cocaine love and Colleen were proving a lethal cocktail.

Gaily's attempts to placate the situation seemed only to inflame it. From one minute being at death's door Colleen suddenly found a new lease of energy with which to heap abuse and scorn on her former client. He was recalled from Coventry only to be harangued for his inability to maintain Colleen's mortgage repayments.

"You promised me I would not lose the house!" read the letter written in all upper case.

The house by the way had turned out to be a weatherboard shack in the backblocks of Brisbane for which Colleen had paid ridiculous "overs". Mr Melody had done almost as good a job on Colleen as she was doing on Gaily.

One day Gaily had gone into a branch of the bank with which Colleen held her Australian bank account. Normally he would simply pay eight hundred dollars into the account as per his instructions. On this particular occasion he for some reason made reference to the "minimum monthly mortgage payment".

"Six hundred dollars," said the teller.

"Pardon?" questioned Gaily. "There must be some mistake".

"The minimum monthly mortgage repayment is six hundred dollars," replied the teller tersely – annoyed at having her veracity brought into question.

This disclosure brought into question the veracity of someone other than the bank teller.

Gaily was shocked at the way in which his generosity had been taken advantage of in such a petty but unscrupulous manner.

"Oh! I had been told by my friend the minimum repayment was eight hundred dollars," sighed Gaily.

"I am sorry. Had I noticed the account holder's name I would not have disclosed the information. We are not meant to disclose account details to those who are not signatories to the account," the teller answered in an attempt to cover her own not inconsiderable backside.

"One can still make payments into another person's account though," observed Gaily of the irony of the situation.

"Yes," returned the humourless teller.

Gaily paid the full eight hundred dollars into Colleen's account with a wry smile. The Irish Goddess of Love's aura was glowing with a slightly less brilliant glow but a few words of blarney would rekindle the fantasy and have Gaily eating out of Her hand again – the hand which had spanked him so many times.

The fact he had been lied to greatly upset him. He had not thought Colleen capable of lying. In these types of predicaments one is logically forced to question if indeed there may have been other similar instances in the past.

The one subject which weighed most heavily on Gaily's mind was drug use – with good reason.

Gaily had established a business structure around his registered trading name Rails Run Publishing. Nominally he was a desktop publisher although his publishing skills only extended as far as two-fingered typing on a word processor and printing of very limited edition newsletters.

Word had got around the traps he was down to his uppers and he had been approached by one of his former workmates regarding a business proposition.

The proposition involved having his father murdered with Gaily inheriting his estate and bankrolling the take-over of the small suburban printing business at which the former workmate's uncle was employed. The former workmate was now dealing smack in Sydney's Kings Cross and the cash obtained via the sale of the heroin would be laundered via the printery.

Gaily was appalled. When he rejected the outrageous proposition out of hand he himself was threatened with violence. The only solution was to skip town but he was broke.

As Gaily was discovering desperate men do desperate things. He himself had joined the American pyramid selling company Herbal Death in a vain attempt to get back on his feet. The last few dollars he possessed went on this hare-brained scheme.

Gaily refused to declare himself bankrupt. He no longer had any capital but retained his pride – this despite self-destructive behaviour reflective of self-loathing.

His father's tack had now swung from encouraging his son to go to university to encouraging him to declare himself bankrupt. There was no shame as there once might have been. He would not end up in the debtors' prisons depicted by Dickens.

Gaily could not enlighten his father as to the druggy's suggestion to have him "bumped off". Neither could he tell the full story regarding Colleen. All he could do was say his initial failure was due to a lack of experience in the business world and hope his father could see his way clear to cash him back up for another shot.

Ted Gaily was a generous man and also a bit of a soft touch. Against his better judgement he made a gift of forty thousand dollars to his son. It was all the spare cash the old man had at the time.

Once in possession of the money the first thing Gaily did was buy a return ticket to England to visit Colleen. Gaily had never been to Brighton where she now lived. It was a good way to get away from the threat of violence in Sydney and try to work out what was actually occurring in her life.

Brighton is a beach resort town on England's south coast. It had its heyday in the nineteenth century. Dickens has some of his books' characters recommended Dr Brighton by their own doctors for its health-giving sea air.

By the end of the twentieth century it was going to rack and ruin. With England being located on Europe's doorstep and discount airlines cutting each other's throats for business most Englishmen could just as easily go to Europe as Brighton for holidays.

Day trips to Brighton on warm sunny days were still popular but the town had definitely had its day as being a resort for the rich. In their place had come impecunious foreign students and even more impecunious homeless English people – the latter attracted by relatively mild weather and cheap off-licence beer and cider. The streets were filthy and the whole place reeked of the shabby genteel. Small businesses depended on passing trade which was in turn dependent upon the vicissitudes of the weather.

This was Colleen's old stamping-ground. After an absence of ten years it was to that with which she was most familiar she returned. Having attained her fortieth year Colleen was revisiting her past as Gaily would at a similar age seven years later.

Loose lips sink ships and Colleen had two pairs of lurid pink lips in order to make doubly sure of sinking Gaily's ship.

Having been silly enough to tell Colleen of his father's generosity he then compounded his error by rushing back to Colleen at a moment's notice.

Women have an excellent sense of smell and Colleen could smell Gaily's money from twelve thousand miles away. To give the impression of being the hostess with the mostest she had even sought out a little guest-house near her own place of domicile. This would ensure his first visit to Brighton would be a pleasant one. As the guest-house was inexpensive it would also leave more of Gaily's money to be spent on her. If you are going to fleece someone always give the impression it is for their own benefit.

When Gaily received his lump sum from the post office his standing joke had been that Colleen was his rollover fund. Tap her on the shoulder and she would roll over. Now that money was gone but he had been given a second chance by the generosity of his father. However, it would turn out to be merely a second chance to make the same mistakes.

Gaily had learnt one thing from the past: not to fly long haul with his country's own national airline. Instead he flew British. He had visions of beautiful blonde hosties with peaches and cream complexions and the shortest of miniskirts. He was sadly disappointed.

Still what hosties there were were friendly souls and kept him well fed if not well watered. Getting a drink at all is difficult enough when one flies economy so it was with a sense of relief as well as expectation he reached HeathrowAirport.

Under instructions from Colleen Gaily caught the National Express coach to Brighton rather than lug luggage on and off trains. On the way down Gaily marvelled at the Downs which form a green belt between London and Brighton. In Sydney an attempt had been made to maintain such an area but developer capital soon ensured green turned to grey. In Sydney Brighton would have been a suburb of Sydney (in fact a suburb of Sydney is named after the English Brighton).

Alighting from the coach at Pool Valley in Brighton Gaily caught a cab to what would be his home for the following month.

The guest-house was spotless. It was run by a charming husband and wife team. Properly speaking it was a bed and breakfast. Breakfast was served at seven which was the same time the local pool opened during the week so often he missed the last of the beans if he did his laps as would have been the case at home. The room was clean, there was an en suite bathroom – he had no complaints.

Gaily had been vegetarian for five years and vegetarians are well catered for in Brighton. He had not come for the food though – unless one was referring to a nice piece of Irish rump. A vegetarian could occasionally make an exception to their dietary requirements when such succulent fare was on offer.

It had indeed been a long haul from Sydney so Gaily performed the necessary ablutions and changed his clothes.

Next came the difficult task of locating a public telephone which actually worked in a booth which did not double as a public toilet. Finding this impossible he had to settle for a public telephone which worked in a booth which did double as a public toilet. Even this took quite some finding.

He held the door of the booth open to try to partially avoid the overpowering stench. No wonder mobile telephones were becoming so popular.

He dialled Colleen's number. There was no answer. He had nothing better to do so walked back past his digs to regain his bearings and down to the seafront. It was a short walk as he was lodged in one of the little side streets which run between St James's Street and Marine Parade. The English Channel rolled in to the shore. Across the water was France. Gaily mused as to how in his teens he had had aspirations of swimming the Channel: another goal never realised.

He had Colleen's address and walked along the footpath until he came to the block of flats in which she lived. Looking upwards from street level he wondered which of the flats was hers. Colleen might just have popped out to the shops and be back home now.

The little gate at the front was ajar so he walked up the roughly hewn stone steps to the front door of the building.

It had intercom security. He pressed the buzzer next to the number of her flat. There was no response.

He turned to walk away but as he did so a couple of very camp homosexual men approached and asked him what he was doing. They seemed suspicious of his motives unless this was their idea of chatting up a pretty Aussie boy in white shorts.

He told them he was a friend of Colleen's but she seemed to not be at home. With that one of them gave Colleen's buzzer several very long presses. It was a stupid thing to do.

A stream of invective poured through the intercom telling whoever it was in no uncertain terms to go away and leave her alone. It was Colleen all right.

"Looks like she doesn't want to see you", said one of the old queers as he and his boyfriend opened the door.

Gaily was certainly not going to see her now so he walked dejectedly away. Tomorrow would be another day.

Here he was in a strange town with no idea of where to go for a drink or a meal. He bought some nuts and water from the nearest supermarket. With no refrigerator his food options were limited if he intended to eat in his room. Gaily also bought a two litre bottle of cider. He had never seen such a large bottle. It put the famous Darwin stubby in the shade: probably not a bad place for a Darwin stubby. Still jetlagged he demolished the cider and fell asleep.

The following morning he sought out the local pool to maintain the exercise routine he had established in Sydney. The pool was of the indoor variety and overheated. Still it was better than nothing. Occasionally he would go for a run along the seafront. Without seeing Colleen on a regular basis it would be a lonely existence.

He had to see her. Gaily walked back down to Marine Parade and along to where Colleen lived. This time there was no need to press any buzzers. There she was on her balcony in a black bikini. It was a glorious summer's day made all the more beautiful by the presence of his mistress sitting sipping champagne in the sun. Her platinum hair provided an eye-catching contrast with her golden tanned skin.

"Rapunzel, Rapunzel," he called out to her.

The joke fell flat. Looking down and seeing who it was Colleen got up from her chair and walked inside. No word was spoken.

Gaily waited and waited to see if Colleen would reappear or if she had gone inside preparatory to coming downstairs to see him. As the minutes elapsed it became apparent Colleen wished to avoid him.

There must be some mistake. The woman had known he was coming all this way to see her.

He knew from Mr Hay that Colleen was working in one of the so-called massage parlours but did not know which one. In his wanderings he had noticed a sex shop which boasted it was "the biggest and best in Brighton".

Supposing Colleen would work in the biggest and best massage parlour he presumed the biggest and best sex shop may be able to provide him with directions.

Gaily hated sex shops with their offensive hard core pornography but saw no alternative were he to locate the parlour. It was not the sort of question he would ask a random stranger.

On entering the shop he was glad to see a male shop assistant. It was also not a question he would ask a woman. The young bloke looked heterosexual so Gaily thought he might have a fair idea.

In fact the shop assistant nailed it – in racing parlance

picked it in one. Gaily was given the name and address of the Roman Goddess Health Studio. With nothing better to do he went and bought another two litres of cider. The cider would be a more regular feature of his stay in Brighton than his time with Colleen.

The next day saw Gaily at the Roman Goddess Health Studio just after it opened for trading. It was a small parlour – in fact at the time Colleen was its only full-time employee. Despite its name it was nothing flash either – a bit of a come-down from the bordellos of Sydney.

Gaily asked the receptionist if Colleen was on duty and ascertained she was but under a different name. The rates being charged were considerably less than those he had been used to paying in Sydney. This would translate into Colleen having to work considerably longer hours to keep herself in the manner to which she had become accustomed in Sydney. In fact Colleen was working herself into the ground but would never have anything to show for it.

Gaily asked to see her for an hour. At the receptionist's request Colleen emerged from nowhere and commenced to tell the receptionist in no uncertain terms she refused to see her former client. A barrage of invective similar to that spewed through the intercom at the flats the previous day then followed.

God knows what the receptionist made of it all. Gaily did not hang around to find out. It was not a very good advertisement for the parlour. In Sydney a lady would be sacked for such an outburst. Gaily would never go to that parlour again. There seemed no point.

Gaily wondered if there was any point in anything any more. What a fiasco! The things which had given him pleasure and his life meaning were all gone. The woman he loved had turned on him.

He wandered aimlessly through the streets. In a paper

shop he saw a copy of the Morning Star. It reminded him of the wonderful years he had spent as a political activist. Gaily bought a copy. At least he could maintain contact with his political co-thinkers in England.

There was no point certainly in further pursuing Colleen. She knew where to find him for it was Colleen herself who had booked the room at the B&B on his behalf.

Gaily wanted to get to know London better. He gave himself a day up there and visited the Morning Star offices. It was just like old times. He gave the comrades his version of what had happened to the Party in Australia. They empathised with him as similar moves were afoot in their Party. Gaily and a few of the Star faithful went for drinks at a nearby pub. It did him good to be amongst like-minded people.

Back in Brighton he ran into Colleen in the street. She acted as if nothing had happened between them the previous week. Gaily had encountered this type of behaviour amongst heavy marijuana smokers. In Sydney it was termed "flipping out".

Without giving any reason Colleen said it was impossible to see him at the massage parlour. Could he then see her privately? No, her hours were too long.

Gaily persisted and finally Colleen agreed to see him at her place but it would cost him. He asked how much she would require and without batting an eyelid the reply came back: five hundred pounds per session.

He hesitated but knew he was gone. To use a favourite expression of Colleen's "pussy power" had triumphed yet again.

Since her return to England Colleen had become a much more selfish lover. She had always been selfish. Now increasingly her selfishness had extended to her role as a provider of sexual services.

Gaily was finally allowed into the inner sanctum of Colleen's world: the little flat she rented overlooking the seafront. To get back in her good books he made a point of taking flowers and champagne for his mistress along with cider for himself. He would never be able to cop English beer.

Every picture tells a story. When Gaily opened Colleen's refrigerator all it contained was another bottle of champagne and a stale carrot.

He knew Colleen well enough by then to know she liked flowers for the home so he had brought some lovely lilies from the local florist. Colleen placed these in a vase and they went out on the balcony for drinks.

Gaily had to take full advantage of Colleen's apparent good mood. They sat in the sun with their drinks and chatted as do old friends.

When the time came for business to be mixed with pleasure they went inside and Colleen undressed her client seductively – giving the distinct impression she had performed this act once or twice before.

Colleen was wearing tights which combined black opaque knickers and sheer stockings under a black leather mini. She bent over and turned her head to observe the reaction her rear view would have on Gaily. His penis jolted to attention and she laughed at how easy it was to manipulate men.

Next she put him over her knee and brought her hand down with increasing severity on his bare backside. This was what happened to little boys who got caught looking up their mistress's skirt. Then came four hundred strokes with a Mason Pearson hairbrush – again with increasing severity.

By the time the five hundredth stroke was delivered Gaily's backside was red raw and the following day would be bruised. He was dripping pre-come.

However, before his final need could be met Colleen insisted on his performing cunnilingus on her. It was she who had taught him the location of her clitoris and how best to stimulate it with his tongue.

It was one of Colleen's rare days off so there was not the urgency attached to the usual hour sessions they had shared in Sydney. The following day would bring another twelve hour shift for her.

For the moment she could savour her lover's tongue – the pleasure coming to a shuddering climax a few minutes later. Then as his reward Gaily was allowed to take her from behind. The tights discarded he did not take long to achieve his own orgasm – bringing to a conclusion months of frustration.

It was just like old times. They went to a nearby restaurant for a late lunch and more drinks. For a few fleeting moments Gaily thought his luck must have changed. In Colleen's bathroom he had seen a cake of Lux soap. "Luck's a fortune", as they say in racing.

Colleen's days off were few and far between. As he was not permitted to visit the parlour they only saw each other on two further occasions before it was time for Gaily to return home. On both occasions they had a mutually pleasurable experience in each other's company.

The two parted on good terms. Gaily put the earlier unpleasantness down to the long hours Colleen was working. As the years went on her mood swings would increase in both number and severity. Gaily would always cut a beautiful woman plenty of slack and where Colleen was concerned he was in for the long haul. Both literally and figuratively he was a glutton for punishment.

It had been summer in England and for the first time in

almost twenty years Gaily had missed the Hiroshima Day march and rally.

Upon his arrival home he ran into an old acquaintance from the peace movement and they shared a beer together at the Star. The Resch's still tasted as good as ever.

The bloke's name was Andy. He was a member of the Socialist Party of Australia so whenever it rained in Moscow Andy put up his umbrella. He was very serious and hard-working so he had little time for the frivolities of life. He was another example of someone who made a virtue of poverty. Andy would also have had kittens had he known about Gaily's private life.

He was not a very relaxed person to have as a drinking partner so Gaily drank even more rapidly than usual.

Apparently two tough-looking blokes had disrupted a Hiroshima Day committee meeting searching for Gaily. In Andy's words, "They meant business".

From Andy's description of the intruders Gaily knew exactly who they were – the former workmate turned drug dealer and his uncle. His timing had been spot on as he had probably just missed out on being stabbed in a fit of rage. The former workmate had boasted of his prowess with a chiv.

Gaily thanked Andy for this information by buying him a beer. Gaily had had a narrow escape from at the very least a serious assault. He was quite shaken by what had occurred. His name would be slurred around the traps by the more small-minded gossips to be found in all organisations. He would be guilty by association with these no-hopers. These were the least of his worries.

Had only he aspired a little more at an early age he could have avoided mixing with such scum. One cannot foresee how one's colleagues will go bad on one with the passing of time but it is far more likely to occur in low-paid dead-end jobs.

Neither can one change the past. The question was how to avoid this situation from recurring.

Gaily always sought to avoid confrontation. He would rather a feed than a fight. He saw no alternative but to leave Sydney for good. Much as he loved the place this incident forced him to leave his home town. He would leave Sydney and make a fresh start in either Brisbane or Melbourne.

Gaily put it to Andy that this was his intention.

"Well, Charlie, it wouldn't be a bad idea to lay low for a while. There is plenty to be done in Brisbane and Melbourne."

Good old Andy was of course referring to political activity. His party had not dissolved itself. They would get a few refugees from the C.P.A. but not one C. Gaily.

In fact Gaily's unspoken plan was to pretty much break with his past while never renouncing his views, mix in new circles of mainly racing men and make his fresh start a genuinely fresh one. To do otherwise would merely be to pour old wine into new bottles.

The whole plan was hatched on the spur of the moment but to Gaily this was a good thing. For one generally indecisive he was thinking on his feet. The most difficult part would be to explain his move to his parents without any direct reference to the junkie.

In the back of his mind Gaily still doubted his own abilities and clung to his parents for financial support as required in the course of his life.

He knew he would probably inherit his parents' estate eventually and without wishing to expedite this eventuality he allowed the prospect to hamper his ability to function in the present. His parents took advantage of this situation by manipulating him with punishments in the form of threats of disinheritance and rewards in the form of gifts.

He could never be truly independent whilever this relationship persisted. One of the main means his parents used to manipulate him related to their ownership of the flat in which he lived. The sale of the flat would potentially free up valuable capital while at the same time allowing Gaily to distance himself both figuratively and literally from his parents.

Prior to his departure he would have to go into hiding so the sooner he acted on his impulse the better.

All these thoughts were going through his mind as Andy rambled on about his political activities. Were Gaily honest with himself he would admit the world Andy inhabited represented his past. For one thing one could not be simultaneously a professional punter and a political activist. One could tell the movement one required Saturdays off to attend the races but the movement would not listen. There was also the conservative morality which pervaded the left which frowned on gambling almost as much as it frowned on men patronising prostitutes.

Gaily had tuned out on what Andy had to say several beers ago but politely feigned interest while drifting off into his own thoughts. They had many wonderful shared memories though and when they shook hands to say goodbye Gaily's handshake was firm and sincere.

Gaily was still in possession of most of the gift his father had generously provided. If he could be provided with at least the better part of the proceeds from the sale of the flat he would actually be in a better position financially than when he first left the post office.

The flat was in his mother's name. It was on her he would have to more heavily lean to clinch the deal. His father was a softer touch, his mother a hard case.

With no work, no political activity and no Colleen on tap his weekends were fairly leisurely affairs. Saturdays were still devoted to the races although he was betting with greater caution and in smaller denominations than had been the case a year prior. Sunday really was a day of rest.

His parents insisted on visiting him on either a Saturday or a Sunday morning. He was very fond of his parents but had difficulty in expressing this fondness. Sunday was the preferred day for their visits but an hour of their company was about the maximum which could be tolerated without harsh words which would later be regretted being spoken.

Mrs Gaily's main concern was for the welfare of her flat. In the allotted hour each week she would perform a week's worth of housekeeping duties. By then in her sixties Gaily's mother still appeared very sprightly for a heavy smoker in particular as she vacuumed, dusted and generally fussed about cleaning.

"Your mother is a good woman, Charles," remained one of his father's stock lines.

His father loved to discuss the issues of the day with his son. Ted Gaily was a lonely old man whose main aim in life had become to spend as little money as possible. He was a dogmatic Australian Labor Party supporter for whom the A.L.P. could do no wrong. For all this he was also a decent man and his son did his best to engage the old man in conversation without losing his temper.

On the Sunday after his conversation with Andy Gaily dropped the bombshell which he expected to have a Hiroshima-like effect on his parents.

Initially shocked they quickly recovered their composure but needed time to discuss the proposition. Every decision they had ever made in the course of more than forty years of marriage had been made in this way – with careful consideration of all aspects of the problem at hand. They were an old-fashioned couple who lived as one, thought as one, acted as one and would die as one. His parents told Gaily they would get back to him when next they met the following Sunday.

Mr and Mrs Gaily were not fools. They knew their son was a gambler, a spendthrift, a larrikin, a bit of a lad. Still they loved him and wanted to do their best by him. His father had to prevail upon his wife to allow the flat to be sold but eventually they agreed to go along with their son's request. The flat would be sold and Gaily given the proceeds with which to do as he wished.

"Your mother and I have discussed your request for your flat to be sold Charles and after due consideration your mother and I agreed that it would be in your best interests for the sale to proceed. We will provide you with the proceeds of the sale and we wish you every success in the next phase of your life."

With this formal statement did Gaily's parents announce their decision to their son. Gaily had decided to try his luck in Brisbane so with his parents' reluctant support for what they privately believed to be a poorly thought out scheme preparations began for his permanent departure to the capital of the state of Queensland.

In reality Gaily was running away from himself as much as the petty crims who had threatened him with violence. The terrible thing is when one runs away from oneself one still wakes up with oneself.

Gaily rang a few of his old friends and comrades from his post office and Party days. After the business with the drug dealer he was very circumspect regarding whom he invited to his farewell party. About a dozen turned up at the Star. The Resch's and anecdotes flowed just like the good old days but in his heart Gaily knew the past was dead and buried. Usually he drank with the flies – on this occasion he drank with ghosts.

"Don't tell me what won the last, tell me what's going to win the next," one of his father's professional punting mates would say. This would be his motto.

Ironically Gaily's farewell was on 22nd April – Vladimir Lenin's birthday. Gaily would always consider himself a Leninist but the central tenet of Leninism is the revolutionary party. The Australian party had dissolved: Gaily's bitterness and anger over this criminal act would never dissipate. How then though could one apply one's ideas without a party?

Having severed ties with the trade union movement and witnessed the decline of the peace movement Gaily was thoroughly demoralised. He hoped a change would prove as good as a holiday.

The left would have to be rebuilt and from that process a new party would emerge. Gaily hoped to be able to assist in this process. For the time being though he wanted to just go to the races and be with Colleen. The races would provide him with the means by which to have Colleen as his full-time mistress. The frivolity he had missed out on in his years of political activity would be made up for in spades.

He had a final round of drinks with his mates. He was bitter about the reason those of them who had been in the Party with him were now denied this privilege. He was bitter about the catalyst for his feeling he had to leave Sydney. This bitterness had to be channelled into constructive activity which would see him win money at the track and in return the heart of Colleen.

He was not bitter about the years he had spent with these wonderful people. His farewell was the final occasion on which he would see some of them. Hands were shook and tears shed. He looked around at the familiar surrounds and recalled all the good times he had had at the Star. One day he would return to celebrate the phase of his life upon which he was embarking.

Three days later he left for Brisbane. The flat had been sold and a cheque for one hundred thousand dollars paid into his bank account. His mother was a woman of her word. Although she did not agree with what he was doing Mrs Gaily was fully supportive of her son once the decision had been made.

Gaily's mother wondered if she would ever see her son again. More tears were shed at their parting. His father looked on stoically with his usual restraint. Father and son shook hands.

Gaily spent his final week in Sydney in a room in the pub which had been his local for fifteen years. His parents had suggested this on grounds of economy. Similarly they had consulted with the Australian Hotels Association to locate good pub accommodation in inner Brisbane. It had felt strange to Gaily to have not purchased a return flight.

The flight from Sydney to Brisbane took only just over an hour. It was Anzac Day – the day devoted to the memory of war veterans. Gaily's dad had always eschewed Anzac Day. His memories of the war were best forgotten -not remembered.

Gaily was about to spend his first May Day in Brisbane. May Day was now a throwback to his past but old habits die hard.

He was meant to be doing the form but still turned up for the march and rally.

At the rally he came face to face with the remnants of the Party. A few old liquidationists had supported the Abrahams family until the bitter end. The so-called New Left Party had already failed. The liquidationists had grabbed the seven million dollars-plus in loot and run. In each of Australia's six states a little rump group still existed to give the pretence of maintaining a legacy of the glory days.

Gaily ran into the Brisbane version of the debacle. It was called Left Disconnection. Without wishing to be ageist the average age of its tiny membership was eighty not out.

The Left Disconnection comrades were all ex-C.P.A. They pretended to run their non-existent organisation from a tiny office in an inner suburb. They were lovely old people but politically they had lost the plot years ago. Their loyalty to the Party leadership had been blind in nature. The end result was to sit in an otherwise empty office watching the paint peel and the cockroaches going about their business.

One of the old comrades asked Gaily to help man the office. Not knowing at that stage what he was walking into and being a soft touch he foolishly said yes.

As has already been intimated the work involved sitting in a dirty little office waiting for the telephone to ring. On the rare occasions this occurred it was usually a wrong number.

Occasionally they would post out a little newsletter. Most of the newsletters would be returned to the sender because their mailing list was so out of date. Still they persisted in posting out to people who had long ago moved address or died. The handful of ostensibly active members saw each other on a regular basis as the circles in which they moved were of decreasing dimension. Left Disconnection had to maintain the pretence of having created something viable.

It was a pointless waste of time. One old dear maintained to Gaily that so-called "drop in centres" such as this existed throughout Italy. Until then Gaily had had no idea the Italian Communist Party had hit such hard times. They did in fact prove winged words when the once-mighty P.C.I. itself dissolved.

Gaily quickly pared back his hours of voluntary labour to concentrate on more pressing issues. Even sitting in Queen Street Mall perving at girls was more constructive activity.

Left Disconnection was a distraction Gaily did not need. His punting was on the up-and-up. He found the Brisbane racing fraternity friendlier and less cliquish than their Sydney counterparts. At Eagle Farm or Doomben racecourses on a Saturday he was mixing with successful businessmen with a knowledge of and passion for racing. This was the new circle of acquaintances he knew would be integral to his long-term success.

In his first year of trading in Brisbane he made a twenty-five per cent profit on turnover. He thought to himself "Here we go, here we go". He had had one hundred and forty bets with an average bet size of a thousand dollars. With a bit of bank interest thrown in he had made double his old wage in the post office. Ironically this was about the same amount as he would have made as a union official had he hung around.

The trick with success is to maintain it until at least one has obtained one's fifteen minutes. Otherwise as his accountant back in Sydney had observed it would prove to have been merely "a lucky year" – a statistical aberration. Would his luck hold?

The short answer to this question is "No". However, it was to be a gradual slide into oblivion but a slide into oblivion nonetheless. There would be highs and lows but eventually the lows would outweigh the highs to the point where the general downward trend would have to be admitted.

To mark his first year of genuine success Gaily returned to Sydney to celebrate his own birthday. This would be an annual pilgrimage during the years he lived interstate.

In those future years he would stay in one or other of the three to four star hotels in the Kings Cross area. However, on this particular occasion he had lashed out on the fifth star with a room at the Hilton. His favourite Star though where hotels were concerned would always remain the Star Hotel.

As soon as he had ditched his luggage in his hotel room in fact he made a beeline for the Star.

It had been eight months since he had been in the old place. It was fitting he celebrate at the Star as they were growing old together. Both had been born in 1959. Each year of his enforced absence he would note the changes which had occurred as one notices the changes in an old friend one has not seen for a year.

There would be changes of management and staff but this simple pub would always evoke vivid memories of the past. Its political character would be eroded with the passing of time but for those who knew its past and had been a part of it the Star would always retain its significance.

It would be increasingly rare for Gaily to see a familiar face but this suited him as he was very wary of running into certain people. In fact he had not even bothered to invite any of the old crew to help celebrate his birthday. If he ended up drinking with the flies it would suit him fine. The flies were better company than some people of his acquaintance.

The only person of his acquaintance he had apprised of his visit was Vicki. They remained in occasional contact via telephone and Vicki had palled up with another lady, left A Taste of Cash and gone out on her own.

The other lady's name was Sarah and over the years

the two women would work out of a range of flats in Sydney's inner city and eastern suburbs.

Vicki's plan was to fob Sarah off onto Gaily. Vicki wanted nothing to do with him and while her partner was out seeing Gaily Vicki would stay in the flat they shared answering the telephone and stealing Sarah's regular clients.

Tipsy bachelors by themselves in hotel rooms at night are vulnerable to loneliness. The working girls are experts at exploiting the vulnerable.

Vicki arranged for Sarah to ring Gaily in his hotel room. Sarah spoke with an educated Australian accent. It was almost a clipped English accent she affected. Both women had good formal educations and pleasant speaking voices. The work they performed had, however, added a certain coarseness to their vocabularies. Sarah had studied biochemistry at Sydney University – which qualified her to marry and divorce a doctor.

The divorce had been acrimonious in the extreme. Sarah was hospitalised with fractured cheekbones and her three children kidnapped. The father was still able to maintain custody as he made sure to first clean out their bank account. The wife who had been his partner for fourteen years was left with nothing.

Thus had Sarah found her way into the sex industry – with Vicki to show her the ropes. Sarah it was then who rang Gaily in his room.

Gaily was bored and frustrated. The call was a welcome distraction. Sarah described herself as "Aunt Sarah" and said she wanted to come around and visit him. It was never clearly explained to him what services might be provided. They agreed on the rate of payment and an appointment was made on the basis of Sarah visiting Gaily in his hotel room.

The session was an absolute disaster. Gaily heard a knock on his door and looked through the spyhole to see a well-dressed blonde rising forty. He opened the door.

The blonde tottered into his room. She was wearing killer heels. The lady introduced herself as Mistress Sarah.

Mistress Sarah's face betrayed the stress she had recently endured. Although still beautiful her face was older than her body and her grey-green eyes were sad. Gaily recalled her eyes were the same colour as Colleen's.

Mistress Sarah was platinum blonde. Her hair provided a striking contrast with her tight black cocktail dress. Through the dress a pair of g-string knickers could be observed covering the cleft of her pert bottom. Her figure was a petite hourglass.

The room was plushly furnished. They sat down on separate chairs and Gaily offered her a drink from the mini-bar. Mistress Sarah declined. She was a teetotaller. Tap water would be fine.

They discussed a role play scenario where the mistress would be the schoolteacher and Gaily the student. The mistress suggested he don his school uniform – to which he acquiesced.

Everything was going smoothly until Mistress Sarah produced a heavy wooden hairbrush.

Mistress Sarah asked Gaily to hold out his hands to which he reluctantly agreed.

"Now close your eyes," commanded Mistress Sarah.

Gaily did so only to open them again with a start when the hairbrush began to be repeatedly crashed all about his bare hands.

Mistress Sarah was insane. Gaily quickly retracted his hands but they were already becoming swollen and bruised around the knuckles and joints.

"You didn't tell your mistress she was exceeding your

pain threshold," countered Mistress Sarah in anticipation of Gaily's protestations.

Gaily looked at the woman with a look of incredulity.

"You are mad" is what he thought.

"Er, no" is all he said.

The frisson of anticipation which Gaily had experienced was lost in the flurry of sadistic violence.

There was no point in continuing the session. The moment had been lost. Gaily slumped dejectedly in a chair.

Mistress Sarah grabbed the envelope on the coffee table containing five hundred dollars, said a hurried goodbye and ran out the door as quickly as one can run in killer heels.

Gaily took a bottle of Resch's Dinner Ale out of his refrigerator. The Hilton did not stock Australia's best bottled beer in its mini-bars so Gaily had done a spot of self-catering. The future belongs to those who plan for it.

If he could not have a little titillation at least he could savour his favourite beer while licking his wounds. The painkiller had the desired effect and he slept the sleep of the just.

The next morning was a different story. His hands were swollen and bruised. Gaily wondered if he should have precautionary X-rays to check for hairline fractures.

Pressing the keys very gingerly Gaily rang Vicki to discuss the events of the previous day. The call was not unexpected.

On such occasions Vicki was a woman of few words.

"We thought you liked S.&M.," Vicki explained.

This was a classic case of someone attempting to provide a service they are not qualified to provide. It is a very common occurrence in the sex industry.

"Er, no" was about all Gaily could manage.

"Sarah would love to see you again," Vicki told him.

"I am sure she would," replied Gaily.

Vicki and Gaily had their birthdays within two days of each other. They had known each other for seven years so wished each other a happy birthday and agreed to maintain contact. Gaily also asked Vicki to wish Sarah all the best but left it at that. He was not one to hold a grudge but his introduction to Vicki and Sarah's idea of discipline had been an unfortunate experience.

Gaily was quietly furious. Vicki should have known better than to unleash this madwoman at him. Vicki had spanked Gaily several times in Colleen's presence and again should have been aware of his requirements.

For her part Sarah should have discussed the content of the session prior to its commencement. The intensity and duration of the session and the choice of implements to be used should all have been spoken about between mistress and client. It had been an amateurish as well as a sadistic performance.

As soon as the time difference permitted Gaily rang Colleen. Colleen was of course the epitome of concern and empathy regarding what had occurred. "Crazy tarts" was her description of Sarah and Vicki.

"I need to come straight over to see you," were her next words.

Gaily had walked straight into that one. Sitting in a hotel room by himself he was particularly vulnerable. He really craved the type of service his mistress knew how to provide. Surely a short stay in Brisbane for Colleen would not leave him too much out of pocket? It had been three years since last they had seen each other. They negotiated terms.

Colleen would come over for a fortnight and stay at Lennon's – flying business class and receiving five hundred dollars per session – sessions were to be at least twice a week for a guaranteed income to Colleen of at last two thousand dollars. Gaily would leave it to Colleen to make the necessary bookings and convey payment for the flights via electronic transfer. Upon being advised of dates he would make the hotel booking himself in person.

Back in Brisbane a birthday card from Colleen awaited him. For twenty-four years they would always remember each other's birthdays. Colleen's cards were always witty and risqué. They were generally bought from a specialist card shop in St James's Street in Brighton. Gaily's cards featured Wally Wombat and friends – a sentimental range of cards featuring scenes from the Australian bush. Gaily had bought a swag of them from a card shop in Brisbane. Valentine's Day and Christmas were also excuses for exchanging greetings.

While in Sydney Gaily had not contacted his parents. They would not want their son frittering away his money on five star hotel rooms and he did not like lying to his parents so thought it easier to send Christmas greetings from Brisbane and leave it at that. Again he felt forced to act in a secretive manner towards them.

For their part they would never fail to remember birthdays and Christmas. Despite not being religious they also used Easter as an additional excuse to send their son a card containing a cheque. Their cards reflected the love they felt for their little boy and would feature native animals or characters from the Peanuts comic strip.

Gaily reluctantly returned to his dingy nought star accommodation in Brisbane. Being a professional punter was potentially the source of a wonderful lifestyle but he had insufficient official income to enable him to rent a flat. His new accountant in Brisbane had advised him to declare his winnings as income so as a result of his successful first year interstate he would soon be able to rent a little flat in Spring Hill in preference to the squalor of the dive in Fortitude Valley.

"It's not the Hilton," mine host had told him.

"That's for sure," thought Gaily.

His initial success at the track had begun to wane and he looked at new ways of tweaking what he was doing. In his spare time he kept fit with long swims at the Valley Pool and read classical literature. He would read two books per week beginning with the complete works of Shakespeare and Dickens. This allowed him to retain a bond with his parents as initially at least they would send him books from their own library rather than see him depleting his capital by forking out money for books. They worried that their son was spending too much time reading rather than building his imaginary desktop publishing business.

If Gaily thought Colleen's arrival would enable him to put his cares aside for two weeks he could not have been more wrong. From Day One she complained about the hotel – insisting she should have been put up at the Hilton. Admittedly Lennon's had been downgraded to four star status but Gaily associated its name with quality accommodation.

Then came the demands for money. It was clear from the outset any payments received would constitute little more than appearance money. On the Saturdays they went to the races together where at least Colleen could be placated with bottles of champagne. However, the sexual contact Gaily craved was denied him.

Despite still being desirable for the first time in Gaily's eyes Colleen was showing signs of aging.

He ogled the waitresses in the racecourse dining room in their black miniskirts and Colleen made the telling admission that "that was me twenty years ago".

The most damning act on her part though came when checking out early from the hotel. Gaily was owed a five hundred dollar deposit for incidental expenses which Colleen pocketed – laughing at the mug for his naivety.

Colleen went back to England and they would not see each other for eleven years. Through all those years Gaily still lived for the moment they would be reunited. He had been treated like dirt but would come back for more. For eight of the eleven years he remained celibate. Moving on with his life was impossible for him so great was his unrequited love.

The months rolled on but Gaily's winning streak at the races appeared to have ended. Try as he might the best he could do was break even. He looked for trends which might give an edge but the trends like his money came and went.

In December he again ventured down to Sydney. Like a dog returning to its vomit he again agreed to see Sarah. She seemed saner as her divorce was now well behind her. They had a little role play as teacher and schoolboy but it would never be the same for Gaily as with Colleen. This woman was not as much fun to be with as he chose to remember Colleen as having been. She was obsessed with her own frailties – referring to herself as being possessed of an addictive personality. Alcoholics Anonymous had stopped her from drinking but the underlying problems which had caused her to drink heavily in the first place had not been addressed. She knew Gaily drank and bet on horses and nagged him constantly when in his company. Her attitude to his betting was negative and unsupportive.

The sex industry was still new to Sarah but she provided Gaily with a service of sorts and would have provided "full service" (penetrative sex) if required. He was still faithful to Colleen though and refused the offer – preferring a happy (manual) ending.

Spanking is very much an acquired art and Sarah got it pretty right but her scenarios were not as much fun. Gaily found her boring.

They went out to lunch at a cafe in the suburb of Bondi on his birthday. Gaily would rather have gone to the pub but Sarah insisting on taking him out. She felt guilty about the events of the previous year and tried to make it up to him. Sarah also wanted to keep him out of the pub. It was controlling behaviour. Gaily was glad to get back to Brisbane.

Gaily's flat in Brisbane was like an oven. He never liked air-conditioning so preferred to live in a sauna for three months. The landlord would do nothing about the wasps' nests outside so Gaily was forced to keep the windows closed all the time. It was not an environment conducive to productive activity.

He was again eating into his capital: a fatal error for someone who was supposedly in business. Gaily looked for excuses for his lack of success.

The flat in summer never dropped below thirty degrees Celsius, rising to forty degrees during the day. As his capital dwindled so did his confidence. His father wrote long letters which reflected the loneliness of his retirement years and his anger and frustration at the way he imagined his son to be living. His mother simply wrote letters filled with love imploring him to come home.

Gaily himself became increasingly frustrated with the way he was living. Put simply he had lost the plot. He twisted and turned to no avail. His frustrations were sexual, emotional and financial in nature.

He could still not bring himself to return to Sydney but his situation was becoming increasingly untenable.

When a perceived solution has proved not to work try the same thing again with a view to obtaining a different outcome. Gaily's solution to his problems in Brisbane was to run away again – this time to the capital of the state of Victoria: Melbourne.

After more than three years in Brisbane he was just about broke again so in order to make the move he was again forced to reluctantly lean on his poor old parents.

They would always be supportive of their son no matter how rash his actions. Gaily at least paid them the courtesy of a visit to discuss the matter. Having not seen him since the move to Brisbane they were delighted to see him. A baked dinner was cooked in his honour – his mother always hopeful of his starting to again eat meat.

As usual Gaily was evasive in his replies to his parents' many questions. He was still wary of certain parties knowing his whereabouts. If his parents did not know his exact address they could not inadvertently convey it to others.

At the end of dinner Gaily's father got out his cheque book and presented his son with a cheque for ten thousand dollars. Gaily thereby had the means by which to move from Brisbane to Melbourne while continuing to bet in a small way. In point of fact most of his possessions were in storage at the family home. His father hoped the money would facilitate yet another "fresh start".

The joys of renting flats at market value were still new to Gaily. He gave the landlord plenty of notice of his intention to vacate. The landlord waited until Gaily was about to board the plane to Melbourne before advising him his bond would not be refunded because of marks on the carpet.

Gaily contested the decision at the tenancy tribunal but had already left Brisbane by the time of the hearing. A typed statement he provided could not quite get him over the line.

When he got to Melbourne Gaily found the flat he had rented sight unseen to be even less suitable than the one he had just vacated. L.J. Hookem and Scalem's representative in the suburb of St Kilda had described the flat as being on the first floor of a block with a courtyard. It was in fact on the ground floor and the courtyard consisted of a couple of paving stones behind a gate which would not lock.

The place had a timber floor and the lack of carpet served to add to the echoing of his neighbours using the toilet. Petty crims congregated outside at night and the flat had the minimum amount of security required by law. Gaily was scared out of his wits. He gave two weeks' notice of his intention to vacate.

The suburb of St Kilda in Melbourne is regarded as Bohemian in character. Gaily had thought he would fit in well. He moved into a pad in Toorak Road, South Yarra and found it far more to his liking. It was quiet, secure and middle class. Trams and trains provided ready access to racecourses and the city. The flat itself was very good value and its spacious interior allowed Gaily to have his own office. He still kidded himself to be a self-employed businessman.

Melbourne is one of the world's major racing centres. In countries outside Australia racing is peripheral as a sport. The Melbourne Cup and other races conducted in the spring ensure Australian racing remains mainstream.

Gaily was working on the supposition that his move to Melbourne would change his punting fortunes. By surrounding himself with more successful and affluent punters his luck would change.

For a while the theory seemed to be working. He won the respect of bookmakers and other punters alike.

In a moment of doubt he consulted a bloke who was genuinely successful. The only job he had ever had was a year as a bookmaker's clerk – the rest of his adult life he had made his living on the punt. His consistency allowed him to support a wife and children. It could be done.

David told Gaily to identify his strengths and his weaknesses. On this basis he concentrated on jumps races and two-year-olds with some success.

David's favourite saying was, "It's the bottom line which counts".

Gaily's bottom line was looking decidedly unhealthy. His parlous financial situation caused a bout of depression for which he sought psychiatric counselling. The psychiatrist saw how passionate he was to succeed and attempted to assist him with the aid of psycho-analysis.

The political animal in Gaily craved political activity. To this end he joined Friends of the Earth – an organisation which was very big in Melbourne at the time. The organisation was full of people who would rather spend money on marijuana than soap.

Gaily also maintained contact with a small Maoist group active in the peace movement. Their activities centred on Saturdays which for him would always be the main race day so he made donations of stamps which made them happy.

More and more he craved to be back in Sydney. At the end of his first year in Melbourne he returned to the city of his birth for a week and realised how much he missed it.

At the end of his second year in Melbourne he returned to Sydney to celebrate his fortieth birthday. The psychological aspect of turning forty was enormous. He needed to be surrounded by that with which he was most familiar.

The other problem which would not go away pertained to Gaily's finances. The punt had not come good. There had been one good year which had promised so much followed by a slide which had proven irreversible.

His depression had become worse to the point of his going on sickness benefits. He would not go on the dole but the sickness benefit provided the same income as the dole.

If the no-hopers who had threatened him with violence all those years ago were still around they would presumably have found someone else to harass. He was finally reconciled with the idea of returning to Sydney. It was an ignominious conclusion to a phase of his life best forgotten.

The main thing was he was going home. In correspondence with his parents Gaily's father had mentioned Redfern as being very good value for rental property. This was a subtle hint his father expected him to live frugally for a change.

Redfern at least provided good memories for Gaily. He got a room at the Woolpack – where some of his workmates used to drink in the Mail Exchange days. The Exchange had been closed by then for fifteen years. Australia Post had replaced it with administration offices constructed on the old Exchange site.

On his first Saturday back in Sydney Gaily got a copy of the Herald to look for a flat. The formguide would have to wait. He was down to his uppers so he sought the least expensive flat available. It was a cheap and nasty bedsit deep in the heart of Redfern. He had never experienced such squalor but he took it. This dump was all he could afford. In retrospect he would have been better off staying at the pub but Gaily seemed to live his entire life in retrospect.

For those not familiar with Sydney Redfern is a traditional working class inner suburb. A large Aboriginal community lives there partaking of the drink and drugs foisted upon them by the whitefella. It had been a good suburb in which to work but Gaily had always been happy to leave it to the blackfellas as a place of residence.

The bedsit turned out to be a nightmare. It was infested with mice and cockroaches.

Gaily used the bedsit as a motivation to look for a job. He had no formal qualifications, no driver's licence and was in his forties. It was a very narrow field from which to choose.

Gaily had run into his old C.P.A. comrade John Moore while in town one day and Moore invited him to his office. Moore and his wife Natalie ran an advertising agency which was in the process of going bankrupt. The business had succeeded for a time through employing good staff but Moore's business acumen was such he gave the distinct impression he wanted to go broke as quickly as possible.

Moore was in the process of running through the proceeds obtained from the sale of the family home. He had placed his father in a nursing home rather than wait for him to die. It was later discovered Natalie had given things a kick along by tickling the peter for money with which to play poker machines.

When Natalie offered Gaily some work he readily accepted. Gaily was more than experienced in the art of losing money – both his own and other people's.

The work involved answering the telephone when the receptionist was absent, going to the pub for lunch with Natalie and not mentioning to John the amount of money his wife was putting through the pokies. For these tasks Natalie paid fifty dollars per day cash in hand.

The pub to which they repaired was the Occidental – Gaily's first work pub more than twenty years earlier. For some reason Gaily's past revolved around pubs.

The Resch's at the Occy was not as good as the Star's. On the other hand it was heavily subsidised by his mate's business.

Gaily had written a book about punting while in Melbourne and had sold a hundred or so self-published copies. Moore offered to put Gaily back on his feet by having the book professionally published and sold via the Internet as well as the post. The only problem was they were both broke.

Moore put the bite on one of his clients named Joe Cool to bankroll the venture costing it at seven thousand dollars. The way he portrayed it the offer was a business opportunity in which Cool would put up the funds as a sleeping partner with the other pair contributing labour and intellectual property.

The book was published, a web site established and mailing lists purchased. The major expense would involve the purchase of the lists and postage.

A print run of only one hundred was undertaken with an option of further runs as required depending upon demand. The lists targeted those who had already expressed interest in racing products and the (very slim) book was to retail at the very optimistic price of forty seven dollars per copy. A flash leaflet was produced and a working bee conducted to stuff envelopes. The web site was designed by work experience staff and therefore cost nothing – which from the look of it was about its actual value.

Sales of a hundred and fifty copies would result in their breaking even but Moore had crunched the numbers and their fortunes were made.

Sales totalled forty and Cool was left to join the queue of Moore's creditors.

It was time for Gaily to get a real job. Moore was in the process of declaring himself bankrupt and had discovered discrepancies in his books which could be traced to his wife's light fingers. Despite all the turmoil in his life Moore ensured his old mate's CV was presented in a "just so" manner. It was beautifully laid out by one of his staff and the wording ensured any gaps in the employment history were adequately plugged.

Gaily and Moore had discussed Gaily's job prospects over a schooner of Resch's at the Occy. Moore put it to Gaily that his best option would be to seek employment as a pool lifesaver at a public swimming pool. Gaily had a background in swimming, still swam regularly for fitness and had had a good work ethic when last in the workforce. The training required was minimal, there was a labour shortage in the industry and the work was relatively well paid. One would also have access to the facilities at one's place of employment – which in itself was worth a thousand dollars a year.

The arguments were compelling. Moore could have done worse than take his own advice.

Gaily's other adviser was Mistress Sarah. Since his return to Sydney Gaily had started to see her on an occasional basis.

Great minds think alike. Sarah's boyfriend at the time was working at one of the universities' pools which was also open to the public. The pay was good and there was plenty of work.

Due to her controlling nature Sarah took things one step further. Out came the telephone book and before he knew it Gaily was enrolled in a Royal Life Saving Society course. Two weeks later he had all the necessary qualifications to work at a public pool.

Next cab off the rank was selling himself to prospective employers. Although Moore and Sarah never met they helped Gaily draw up a short list of pools within cooee of where Gaily lived and could reach via public transport given shift work would be involved.

Moore had form letters typed up as covering letters to accompany Gaily's C.V. while Sarah marched him to bus stops and railway stations to ensure interviews were attended.

In Australia the swimming season officially commences in October. By October Gaily was working three casual jobs at various pools. He had a foot in the door.

To make himself more employable Gaily also did a gym instructor's course with the Fitness Institute of Australia. He became qualified to work in gyms but never utilised the qualification apart from applying his newly acquired knowledge to his own training regime.

Working at swimming pools proved a huge culture shock for Gaily. He had never worked in jobs where the majority of positions were casual and the majority of the workforce ununionised and illiterate. The industry was full of people who had sought to obtain careers in one or other sport only to fail and find themselves incapable of working outside the gym or pool. A few exceptions went on to become PE teachers or personal trainers. It was very depressing.

With wages coming in Gaily could at least self-medicate on bottles of Resch's Dinner Ale from the Woolpack. Occasionally he would lash out on a day off at the Star.

At the same time he became more serious about his training. One of the ironies of bloke or lad culture is the way in which booze and hard physical training are combined. It is a difficult balance to maintain – especially when one is tipsy.

Gaily still held out hope of eventually again seeing Colleen. He made do with occasional visits to Sarah but she was never able to recreate the magic of the four years he had been a regular client of Colleen's at A.T.O.C. He remained loyal to Colleen by denying himself the "full service" which Sarah was happy to provide. Instead he would only accept "hand relief" from Sarah.

Gaily had for thirteen years significantly reduced his drinking when seeing Colleen and in the years immediately following when his hopes remained high of maintaining regular contact. Once back in Sydney he started to make up for lost time by pouring down the Resch's like there was no tomorrow.

He recalled the words of the popular song "...And the tears they ran like Resch's the day John Sattler broke his jaw".

Gaily had been at the game where this incident occurred involving the former South Sydney Rugby League great. Now living in the heart of South Sydney territory he considered his behaviour appropriate to the occasion.

The next question was how to get out of South Sydney territory and into a decent flat in a suburb with clean air? The answer was to obtain full-time employment. Again Gaily had fallen victim to agents who required proof of income from tenants. Even to obtain the filthy hole in Redfern he had been forced to pay six months' rent in advance.

After six months of casual employment a full-time vacancy became available at the Bear Park Olympic Pool where he already worked as a casual.

John Moore had by this time divorced and was in the process of blowing the proceeds of a second house by continuing to pretend to be a businessman. He was thus still again able to assist Gaily with his job application.

Bear Park Pool was owned by Bear Park Council and managed by a Scottish transsexual named Norma McNobody. Bear Park Council was particularly proud to have a foreign transsexual managing their pool as this displayed their commitment to multiculturalism and sexual tolerances in a diversified workplace and community. The fact that the pool was hopelessly run by someone who had not a clue what they were doing did not seem to bother them. They just threw money into the bottomless pit that was the pool and continued to babble about multiculturalism, tolerance and diversity.

Ms McNobody conducted the job interview with Gaily. Although McNobody had a penis she identified as a woman and was addressed accordingly in formal situations.

Gaily had difficulty understanding Ms McNobody's thick Scottish accent. He always bluffed his way through the rare conversations he had with her by agreeing with everything she said whether or not he understood her. This was a good policy as Ms McNobody had a ferocious temper and would simply raise her voice when not understood. This of course made her even less comprehensible. Communication was a little difficult at times.

This situation was a little more difficult still. Gaily knew enough about the place to know Ms McNobody expected full-time lifesavers to apply for promotion to the position of supervisor. Thus was indicated a commitment to a career path with the Council.

In fact Gaily could hardly understand a word being said so thick was the accent. However, by alternating agreement with commitments to a lifelong career as a poolie he managed to sail through the interview without once drawing the ire of Ms McNobody.

"'E be good," nodded Ms McNobody at the end of the interview.

The two shook hands and Gaily remained none the wiser until a letter arrived telling him he had the job. He went to the Star and drank Resch's as if there definitely would be no tomorrow. Most of the full-time staff at Bear

Park Pool wished privately this were the case. Gaily was about to join their ranks.

The job basically entailed watching people swim up and down a pool. A few simple little water tests and rotation between the outdoor and indoor pools provided almost all the variety the schedule had to offer. It was a job for the otherwise unemployable.

Full-time employment simply provided a thirty-eight hour week and paid leave. The union presence was negligible. The supervisors were small-minded fools who constantly took out their many and varied frustrations on those directly beneath them on the career ladder. Overseeing the operation was a manageress who used internal security cameras for staff surveillance and encouraged supervisors to use two-way radios to harass lifesavers.

Ms McNobody loved confrontation. It was how she got her kicks and vented her own frustrations. Her favourite method of harassing lifesavers was to observe someone talking to a member of the public or another member of staff and contact a supervisor through an internal telephone to in turn chip the offender. Speaking and sitting were forbidden. Lifesavers had to patrol the pool on foot even when there was no one in the water! There was no accountability as the facility was viewed by Council as "Norma's pool".

The whole scene was totally alien to Gaily's experience. He was surrounded by kids who knew not their rights. As failed sportsmen they lacked self-esteem and would rather be humiliated than stand their ground. They had never heard of trade unions and would quit their job when the harassment became too much to bear. It was another nightmare for Gaily – or part of an ongoing one.

He soon learnt to assert himself or be trampled all over.

What union there was he joined. The bastards had never met the like of Charlie Gaily.

Training for his position consisted of being teamed up with a workmate and being shown what little there was to learn about policing a pool where the regulars were snooty snobs who would never follow a lifesaver's directive and where all the equipment was constantly in need of repair.

Gaily's first day of training was with another lifesaver called George. The other thing Gaily had to come to terms with was the fact that only the manageress had a surname. The American custom of not using surnames in order to give a sham sense of familiarity had crept into the workplace during Gaily's absence from it.

George was actually a casual but given the rate of turn-over of full-time staff he often worked more hours in a week than a full-timer. He was tall, strongly built, had been to a private school and had almost completed a university degree with a view to being a schoolteacher. He did lots of weight training in the pool's gym and was obsessed with his own image. George had a girlfriend but was as camp as a row of tents.

George pointed out an old man in the sauna.

"That's Michael the German paedophile," George said in a matter-of-fact way.

"Oh!" replied Gaily, "Is nothing done about it?"

"Yes, the police come down occasionally to have a word with him. They've known of him for twenty years."

A blind eye was turned to a lot of things at the pool. Every afternoon the same men would sit in the sauna watching the children learn to swim. At lunch-time they would sit in the change rooms watching other men changing. One bloke would often sit there for two hours without a word being spoken. Another fellow's favourite haunt was the urinals. The unwritten rule was that as long as there was no physical contact nothing would be said. Occasionally as George had stated a child would be touched and if a complaint was received and validated then the police might be called. Gaily would in the course of his employment witness serious assaults which would be hushed up. He found it all rather odd.

The only rules which seemed to be rigidly enforced pertained to ensuring lifesavers did not speak or sit. There was also total inflexibility regarding shift changes. One of Gaily's first requests was to be allowed to work a permanent morning shift. In the post office the shift changers would have negotiated the changes for him in return for his rostered overtime. At the pool all shift changes went through the manageress and were inevitably declined. Those attempting to better themselves by undertaking courses would be forced to miss lectures and inevitably resign from their jobs to further their studies. It was bullying at a level which would never have been tolerated in the post office.

The only positives to come from the job for Gaily were the steady income and the ability to get out of Redfern.

To reinforce the happy memories of his post office days Gaily rented a little studio flat in Rushcutters Bay – the other suburb in which he had worked for Australia Post. He drank his last bottle of D.A. from the bedsit's fridge, wished the mice and cockroaches a fond farewell and skedaddled. After another visit to the tenants' tribunal he finally had his bond refunded. Gaily was becoming an experienced campaigner for his own rights.

This newly found assertiveness came in handy at the pool where constant harassment by management had to be confronted.

Like all the other full-time lifesavers Gaily started to develop joint problems from hour after hour of walking and standing on concrete surfaces. After six months he went to see his old friend Dr Coconut who diagnosed him as having Patellofemoral Syndrome – where the femur causes the sufferer pain by coming in contact with their kneecap.

The doctor recommended Gaily be allowed to sit down for five minutes per hour but of course Ms McNobody deemed this impossible – ironically on health and safety grounds. A lifesaver could not adequately view all areas of the pool from a sitting position.

Gaily argued that surf lifesavers in Australia had the world's best practice and had towers from which to observe those in the surf. He may as well have saved his breath.

Dr Coconut predicted if not properly managed the condition could worsen. Gaily was not able to manage the condition in accordance with his doctor's recommendations and the condition did inevitably worsen.

Instead of acting in a co-operative manner the management attempted to make his life as miserable as possible. The supervisors used quite blatant verbal abuse in the absence of witnesses and found needless tasks for him near knocking off time so the traditional early mark on afternoon shifts was eliminated. His tea breaks were timed and his medical certificates' validity were challenged. It was petty, vicious stuff with the aim in mind of forcing him to resign. Gaily dug in his toes.

After another year at work Gaily's knees were in a very bad way. Dr Coconut referred him for X-rays. The X-rays showed the presence of osteoarthritis.

Under his professional duty of care Dr Coconut had no alternative but to issue a Workcover medical certificate

stating his patient's condition. The issuing of such a certificate is the precursor to the making of a formal workers'
compensation claim against an employer.

Bear Park Council was running scared. To sack someone on medical grounds is against the law: it is in breach
of federal anti-discrimination legislation.

Again the doctor had recommended a five minute
break. At first the employer acquiesced by pulling Gaily
off the job for five minutes an hour and making him perform menial tasks in the administration office or assisting
the receptionist. They went from refusing the doctor's recommendations to enforcing it dogmatically and with the
worst possible grace.

Then when Ms McNobody saw the extent to which Gaily
struggled with the electronic till in reception she recommended to Council that he should be deployed to the
vacant receptionist's position as this would be less disrup-
tive to the centre's operation.

Gaily was thus forcibly transferred into reception. The
receptionist's till was meant to balance but in his first week
Gaily's till was consistently down at the end of each shift.
Management's policy was to get the offender to make up
the difference from their own pocket. This was in breach
of the law and Gaily refused to comply. It was clear that
he was being set up to be dismissed on grounds of incom-
petence.

After a week of this nonsense Gaily again went to
see Dr Coconut. Dr Coconut issued another Workcover
certificate for stress and gave him two weeks off on the
strength of it. The employer had been refusing to accept
certificates issued by Dr Coconut for anything related to
Gaily's knee injury but were forced to accept this certifi-

cate. Again the employer had been in breach of the law by denying a worker access to their sick leave when the reason for the absence was validated by a qualified GP.

Gaily needed the fortnight off. He went to the Star every day and self-medicated on Resch's.

In his absence the employer had the good sense to back off. A meeting with Dr Coconut was organised and Gaily was able to resume work as a lifesaver with short breaks built into his schedule. The employer still refused to allow Gaily time off on sick leave for his knee injury – only accepting certificates from a doctor of their choice who had made it quite clear to Gaily he would not issue him with a certificate were he at death's door.

Finally Gaily got his day in court – or more correctly the Workers' Compensation Commission. The union had been able to do little to assist him over the eighteen months of his battle but to their credit on the day they provided a top barrister to represent him.

The barrister tore strips off the employer. His main line of attack had been with regard to their illegally withholding access to sick leave – such leave being a legal entitlement under the industrial award covering council employees. To coin a phrase the employer did not have a leg upon which to stand.

The commissioner at the Workers' Compensation Commission has the legal status of a judge. The commissioner at Gaily's hearing looked askance at Bear Park Council's representatives. Without hesitation he awarded in favour of Gaily.

In due course Gaily saw two qualified surgeons – one of Dr Coconut's choice and one of the employer's choice. He was deemed to have a permanent disability requiring arthroscopic surgery.

The employer's insurance company paid for the sur-

gery after which Gaily required five weeks off on full pay
to recover. Ms McNobody would not allow him back
to the pool until his recovery was complete so he spent
another fifteen weeks on light duties mucking around
in the council's parks and gardens section. Here he was
required to undertake an audit of the lighting and furniture in the municipality's parks and reserves. This task
was completed at a leisurely pace but he was unsupervised
and he made a point of not drawing attention to himself.
Again his post office days stood him in good stead.

To top it all off Gaily received a lump sum payment of
over eight thousand Aussie dollars.

Upon his return to the pool the manageress and supervisors left him well alone. The point had been made most
effectively.

With all the drama out of the way and a small lump sum
with which to play Gaily's thoughts turned to England. It
had been more than ten years since he had seen Colleen.
Every Valentine's Day without fail he had sent a red rose
to Colleen, her niece and her mother. Every birthday Colleen received a dozen red roses.

His florist was a Dutch girl called Betty whom he had
met more than twenty years earlier when she worked at
the Sydney Hilton's florist shop. Whenever he placed an
order Betty never failed to tell him he should try to find
a girlfriend in Australia but inertia is the most powerful
force in society.

Year after year Colleen had received a Wally Wombat
card from Gaily's now dwindling collection. In return
Gaily received somewhat more risqué cards from Colleen.

He had not seen her since the debacle which had been
her lightning raid on Brisbane. He was quick to forgive
but nonetheless slow to forget. Gaily had been burnt by
this woman so many times but had still not learnt not to

play with fire because the fire was his passion for Colleen. The gambler in him always wanted one last throw of the dice but the dice always came up "snake eyes

One of the swimmers at the pool was an English lady who suggested to Gaily he stay at a university campus while the students were on their holidays. It was accommodation of the cheap and cheerful variety.

A lot of the regulars at the pool had become very fond of Gaily having witnessed how shabbily he had been treated by the management. The lady went so far as to download information from the Internet for him.

Gaily did the rest. He was well used to transferring money into English bank accounts via electronic transfer and phoning English telephone numbers at all hours of the day and night. "Phoenix Halls here we come," he thought to himself.

The Phoenix Brewery Halls of Residence to give them their full title are located in Southover Street in Brighton. They are a part of the University of Brighton campus. Every year some of the students' accommodation is let to the general public. A couple of telephone calls confirmed the availability of a room and the cost involved. It was certainly cheap and Gaily would soon find out just how cheerful.

The pool management was glad to see the back of Gaily and the feeling was mutual. Before he left though he owed his parents a visit. They had been very supportive of him and now they were reaching the ends of their lives. Since his arrival back in Sydney he had done his best to visit them as often as possible. With a full-time job he did not choose to be evasive towards them with regard to what he was doing for a living. For their part they had never pried but they were not fools and knew their son played fast and loose. They were always genuinely glad to see him but his mother still annoyed him by offering him a meat sandwich instead of a beer.

They had lived their lives in the hope of seeing more of their son after he had left home. Up until that time they had stayed in Castle Hill to ensure his education was as stable as possible. Then they had moved close to a railway line to expedite his travelling into the city for work. When he left home his mother had purchased the flat into which he moved. There he lived virtually rent-free for fifteen years – rarely even paying the peppercorn rent requested. His parents had moved to a nearby suburb in the vain hope of regular visits. When he moved interstate they remained financially supportive of him. Now back in Sydney the least he could do was to try to visit them whenever he had a free weekend.

Gaily's parents had become frail with age. His mother had been diagnosed with cancer twenty years earlier. The diagnosis had been made early enough for the cancer to be put in remission but the radiotherapy which facilitated this took a huge toll on his mother's body. Her son always remembered her as being a full-figured woman but she had wasted terribly. The radiotherapy had caused ongoing haemorrhages which in turn led to her iron levels dropping to the point of blood transfusions being required.

His father had also suffered from cancer requiring surgery to prolong the quantity of life but it came at a cost to the quality of life. He had suffered a stroke and had become conscious of what he termed the "Shanghai Shuffle" of his gait to the point where he avoided walking in public. This lack of exercise added additional stress to his already overburdened cardiovascular system.

They had made what Gaily believed to have been a major error of judgement in moving away from a suburb in which they had lived for almost ten years to the southern beach suburb of Cronulla. Their world was shrinking and they complained repeatedly about the nastiness of one of their neighbours.

Despite their illnesses both parents remained inveterate smokers. They sat on their verandah for hours smoking and reading newspapers or listening to the radio. Their minds were still sharp but were bearing witness to the demise of their bodies. Sometimes the man downstairs would annoy them by waving or singing out to them from the street while at other times ignoring them. He was a harmless pest who should have been ignored but their rage was of the impotent variety directed as much at their own feebleness as the antics of the fellow downstairs.

They considered friends the couple across the way but Gaily saw they merely made a convenience of his parents by getting the old people to mind their child when they went out. Mr and Mrs Gaily had enough trouble looking after themselves without being expected to provide a free child minding service. In reality they had not developed a strong peer group so in their twilight years had only each other and their prodigal son.

The three Gailys sat on the balcony of the flat. His mother still managed to keep her home in immaculate order. Everything was neat, tidy and immaculately clean. Gaily's parents lived in very comfortable conditions surrounded by beautiful antique furniture hand-made by one of Mr Gaily's old schoolmates. Their bookcases were filled with titles which reflected the breadth of their knowledge and interests. An extensive library of classical literature was complemented by books on political and historical subjects together with gardening and sport.

Gaily had purposely avoided the ritual of meal times.

His parents would have had a sandwich and a cup of tea and now sat chatting with their son.

Their conversation predictably revolved around politics and sport but these remained two of Gaily's loves so he was quite literally at home. His mother remained blindly loyal to the A.L.P. but Gaily found it disturbing that near the end of his life his father was becoming disillusioned with the party he had always supported. His father had also just recently disavowed the existence of a higher power so if there did prove to be a hell after one's earthly existence his father might be in trouble.

Gaily had renewed his season ticket with his old football team St George so this provided a softer option for conversation than politics.

When he finally stood to wish his parents goodbye everyone was a little teary. The two old people knew their lives were coming to an end while their son was in the prime of life. Without mentioning Colleen Mr and Mrs Gaily knew the main reason for their son's trip to England.

They each presented him with a small cheque to help him on his way as had so often been the case in the course of their lives. Gaily accepted the cheques and the accompanying best wishes with a good grace. His father had concluded his son was incapable of managing money so rationalised the situation by viewing any gifts as advances on his inheritance. One can rationalise just about anything.

Gaily's last port of call was the Star. Any day he was not working Gaily would find his way to the Star for old times' sake and a schooner of Resch's.

Despite having changed irrevocably the place evoked such wonderful memories for him. Gaily was a God man where the word "God" is an acronym for Good Old Days. When he entered the Star he was transported back to happier times. One of his favourite lines pertained to the fact he lived in the past "because the past was better than the present".

He had surrounded himself with a coterie of fellow dinosaurs. They were mostly lovely blokes but tipsy bachelors with poor social skills who did nothing for someone already depressed except exacerbate the situation.

There was Gaily's namesake Charlie – a little Chinese barman who worked by night and drank all day. Gough the street sweeper swept the streets by night and drank all day. Victor the retired IT expert went on his own quiet Resch's benders at least twice a week. Over glasses of house red Craig the bankrupt solicitor bemoaned the people who sent him broke almost twenty years earlier. Professor Vincent the economics lecturer prepared for his evening lectures with glasses of red. A couple of others would sometimes join them – leaving a trail of b.o. in their wake.

Gaily sat listening to Craig's life story for the umpteenth time. Craig was like a cracked gramophone record with his tales of woe involving backstabbing lawyers and fast women who had fleeced him then left him for dead.

Gough was tipsy and singing the Collingwood Aussie Rules team's song. Victor was pouring Resch's down like there was no tomorrow and not saying a word. The professor's depression was getting worse and he sat wearing sunglasses despite being indoors and staring into his rough red. Chinese Charlie had not slept for three days and was laughing deliriously at his own insanity.

Only the volume of Craig's voice would vary, the tone was always the dullest monotone. As the laughter and singing continued Craig raised his voice to make himself heard. It was bedlam.

"When I had money I'd go to strip clubs in the Cross,

drink twelve beers and throw up outside," Craig laughed in the same insane manner as Chinese Charlie.

"Went to the Gold Coast with this shiela, she never told me she had a boyfriend, spent all me money." It just went on and on.

"Used to go to this restaurant in Liverpool in the nineties: mud crabs, lobsters, the works…," the voice droned on.

At this point Craig was shouting – or should one say yelling because he would never buy anyone a drink.

"The bills were coming in faster than I could pay them…" Gaily heard the same story at varying volumes every day he drank at the Star.

Thankfully it was Saturday and Gaily had an excuse to leave the party to catch the bus to Randwick Racecourse. It was a little routine Gaily had got into since landing the job at the pool. Two out of five Saturdays he would work, the other three he would go to the races. Randwick involved a bus from Eddy Avenue, the other three metropolitan racecourses a train from Central Railway Station. Racing was in his blood so he may as well learn to win although it was proving a bloody long apprenticeship.

After all these years he was still betting with Mr Marks. The form would be done hastily using the Sportsman on his way to work or at a more leisurely pace at home were he working an afternoon shift or having the day off. Then on Saturday morning the money would go on at top fluctuation. Were he able to attend the races he could see the price he obtained and watch his money go around. If at work he would race home to catch the last of the races and always it was the Sun-Herald on Sundays for the post mortem.

It was the old story. For several years he had hovered tantalisingly around the break even mark without being able to find a way of making consistent profits. On this particular day he had a grand on a four dollar winner but he had long ago forgotten the value of money. For all the suffering incurred in its absence he just wanted to crack it as a professional at what had come to be some indeterminate time in the future and the money would flow like tears and Resch's. For the time being he had enough money to fly him over to England for a few fleeting moments of pleasure with Colleen.

Memory is selective and love is blind. Gaily spent most of the flight over wishing BA served Resch's and the hosties wore shorter skirts.

Upon arrival at Heathrow he switched immediately to Colleen mode. The coach to Brighton seemed to take longer than the plane from Sydney.

Finally he got to Pool Valley in Brighton – the final stop of the coach trip from Heathrow. It was 9.30 in the morning. From his increasingly frequent telephone conversations with her over the months just passed he knew this was a good time to ring her. They would only be about a quarter of a mile apart in distance if he rang her from near Pool Valley: a quarter of a mile away from closing a gap of eleven years. The frisson of the situation was electrifying.

He collected his little port on wheels from the coach's storage compartment and thanked the driver. His mother had taught him to always thank the bus driver.

He ran to the nearest public telephone. The stench inside the booth brought back memories going back more than ten years.

It did not matter. All that mattered was the woman at the other end of the line. He visualised her washing her beautiful long platinum hair and wrapping a towel around her head as she went to answer the telephone. Colleen would be a most unlikely Muslim in her white fluffy head scarf. He quickly banished the anti-Islamic thought from his mind as he did not want a fatwa placed on him. He recalled her references to Muslim women as "slit clits" in Penang. The men there would have liked to have placed more than a fatwa on her. He was later to learn quite a few had but still remained in blissful ignorance of this woman's life despite having known her by then for almost twenty years.

The telephone was ringing. It kept ringing. Gaily was thankful it was a land line number as it would not connect to an answering service after a couple of rings as would a mobile telephone.

The telephone was finally answered. It was Colleen. She had the same sweet girlish voice as ever.

"I was just washing my hair", she said by way of explanation for the delay in answering.

"How did I guess?" he laughed joyously at hearing her voice.

They laughed together like old friends. He could not wait to see her.

"Your place or mine?" he asked – cutting straight to the chase.

Colleen knew he would be in cheap digs unbecoming a lady. They arranged to meet at her place the following day.

Gaily caught a cab up to Southover Street. For the rest of the day he floated around town familiarising and refamiliarising himself with Brighton.

His local for the following month would be the Greys. At four o'clock it opened its doors and Gaily was first in as well as best dressed. He had brought his lone Dom Bagnato suit over for the occasion. It was one of the few positive legacies of his three years in Melbourne.

At the Greys Gaily was introduced to the joys of Stowford Press cider. He supped five pints. It was not Resch's but it would suffice for the duration of his visit. His primary aim in visiting Brighton was not to drink but to renew auld acquaintance. Jetlagged and pleasantly relaxed he went back to his dingy digs and slept the sleep of the just.

The new day dawned and Gaily was reintroduced to more joy in the form of the local swimming pool. No wonder a countrywoman of his had described English pools as "chlorinated phlegm". He did his sixty laps as quickly as possible, got out and went back to his room to spruce up for Colleen. The arrangement was to meet at eleven for a quick session and then go to lunch at her favourite restaurant. He had agreed to pay five hundred pounds for the privilege.

It was a mad rush to be ready by 10.30 but there was no way in the world he would be late.

Gaily walked down to Marine Parade. He had allowed half an hour not knowing exactly how long it would take. Walking at a rapid pace he arrived early to see her sitting on her balcony.

He needed to have a second look in order to recognise her. Colleen had always been worth a second glance but this was different. They smiled and waved to each other. Gaily's face smiled but inwardly he felt only sadness. The woman with whom he had waited eleven years to be reunited was almost unrecognisable. Such was the extent to which Colleen had aged.

Gaily cast his mind back to the previous occasion they had seen each other. The ravages of time had been just starting to take their toll on this woman who relied to such an extent on her looks for her living. Colleen had joked about the sands of time going to the bottom of the hour-glass.

Now in her mid-fifties no longer did any hourglass remain. In its place were vast rolls of fat compressed into a corset which threatened to burst out of its confinement at any moment. The peaches and cream complexion had been replaced by a ruddy puffiness which despite the layers of make-up could not conceal years of debauchery.

It was the first time in his life Gaily had seen Colleen wearing trousers and flat heeled shoes rather than a skirt or dress and high heels. Her little feet had difficulty carrying the additional weight they were forced now to carry. The feet themselves – once so small and dainty – were themselves bloated. Only her beautiful hair and eyes remained as Gaily remembered them but the hair was largely hidden by an outlandish hat and the eyes with gaudy sunglasses.

He buzzed her flat and was allowed into the block in which she lived. Ascending the stairs Gaily was almost in tears at the change in Colleen's appearance. As his mother might say he was no longer any spring chicken himself but he was holding up better than her for sure and certain.

As he reached the top of the stairs he was of half a mind to turn around, run back down them and out the door to freedom. Far better to retain the memories he had of Colleen as he would always choose to remember her rather than see this caricature who was about to open the door.

He knocked. The door was opened by a blowzy, broken down, prematurely aged old tart almost incapable of walking.

Reluctantly he kissed her – not with any passion – merely a peck on the cheek. His nose came too close to her mouth and his nostrils were assailed by halitosis. He drew back his head quickly and smiled, trying to think of some compliment he could pay her to break the ice after all his years of yearning.

The only ice Colleen was interested in was in an ice bucket containing a bottle of champagne. Before even being offered a seat he was directed to the nearest off-licence with strict instructions as to the champagne she required. Colleen had switched to rosé champagne. When buying it herself she would take advantage of the three bottles for the price of two offers. As with brewing one's own beer the more one drinks the more one saves. Lugging bottles home had become Colleen's main source of exercise.

Gaily was glad of the distraction. Needing no encouragement he filed out the door to the convenience shop and got cider for himself as well as the wine for Colleen.

When he got back they sat out on the balcony together drinking. Colleen's father had recently died and Gaily had supported her with regular telephone calls and exchanges of letters at the time. Gaily's parents were in failing health so there was some empathy able to be exchanged but the old fire had finally died.

They went inside and Gaily reluctantly allowed Colleen to pull down his trousers as she had done on so many previous occasions. He was frogmarched into her bedroom where Colleen got him to lie on his back on her futon.

"What will happen now?" he wondered.

With great difficulty the woman knelt over him and started to perform fellatio. In all his years of seeing Colleen she had never brought him completely to orgasm with her mouth – only with her hand or her vagina had the climax been achieved. On this occasion then a first of sorts was achieved – but all without the use of a condom.

He recalled anecdotes from her A.T.O.C. days about clients saying they appreciated the use of condoms for the protection they afforded to which Colleen would always reply that they were for the lady's protection not the client's.

It was the clinical work of an experienced professional which took Gaily from a flaccid state to climax in three minutes. Just prior to ejaculation he expected Colleen to desist and finish him off by hand but when he could hold back no longer he was shocked to see her accept his semen in her mouth then swallow it. Standards were falling.

Colleen simply joked she knew his penis had not been anywhere dirty but he wondered about her mouth. His worst fears were confirmed when a few days later a small cold sore appeared but thankfully it cleared up in time for his next reluctant visit.

They walked to a nearby restaurant for their lunch. Gaily noticed how slow Colleen had become on her feet (the rhyming slang "plates of meat" was now most appropriate). Gone were the days of heads turning to admire the beautiful woman walking along the footpath. The best Colleen could now manage was another old duck complimenting her on her hat.

Gaily had waited eleven years to bring about this moment. Over lunch he pondered how best to end it as quickly as possible – but with a good grace. As usual he would weaken and allow inertia to enact his fate.

Colleen never missed an eye for the main chance. Having locked Gaily into an agreement to see her on a weekly basis food and drink were now being devoured in copious quantities.

"I only have one meal a day to retain my sylph-like figure," Colleen guffawed between mouthfuls.

Being paid five hundred pounds for three minutes of actual work and one's own not inconsiderable weight in French fizz and food would in cricket parlance be termed to be "on a good wicket".

Colleen continued to hold her bat throughout three courses and into the second bottle of Laurent-Perrier. Whenever they now went to lunch she would order a second bottle of champagne, put a stopper in it and take it home for consumption later. Apart from being quite rude it outlined the fact Colleen did not particularly like Gaily's company and was merely using him for money.

Unbeknown to Gaily Colleen had established a web site through which she had generated a nice income thank you for the provision of "sexual services". Accompanying blogs contained the wit and wisdom of Colleen. There was a lot of graphic detail about the services provided.

The photographs on her site were old and flattering. The site provided rates of payment based on time and fairly explicit descriptions of the services. Even for an extrovert like Colleen it did not leave much to the imagination. There was a strong Bondage and Discipline theme and some of the acts Gaily associated with homosexuality and very risky behaviour.

They left the restaurant and went their various ways. Gaily did not expect to see Colleen again until the following week but she turned up on the Sunday for midday dinner at the Greys. In fact she kept turning up like a bad penny. No money was required on these occasions although it was made quite clear to him that she was going out of her way to show Gaily a good time and provide him with company which would normally cost hundreds of pounds. The actual cost was paid in kind in the form of large meals washed down with two bottles of rosé champagne – one of which would be consumed on the premises and the other secreted in a handbag carried for the purpose. Gaily soon became familiar with the names Laurent-Perrier, Roederer and Billecart-Salmon.

The problem here was Gaily would rather have spent the time alone instead of in the company of Colleen. Colleen had become a different person. He found this Colleen to be an embarrassment with her gaudy clothes and hats and her loud and coarse conversation. One of her most annoying habits was the way in which she feigned a

London accent. Anyone less Belgravian would be hard to imagine.

Gaily was locked in a situation largely of his own making but from which he did not know how to escape.

Gone were the long sessions involving teasing and spanking. Colleen was no longer physically attractive enough to tease him and had become too lazy to mete the spankings which had formed the centrepieces of their former lovemaking sessions.

In their place Colleen performed some perfunctory act more for her own pleasure than that of her client.

On one such occasion she required Gaily to perform cunnilingus on her. Watching the mountains of fat escaping from the confines of her corset almost made him vomit. Then came the task of actually locating the clitoris in the midst of her obesity. To think there had been a time when she would refer to her neat little vagina as her Wendy House.

On another occasion Colleen told Gaily to bend over. He thought finally the old-fashioned spanking he craved was about to be provided. Instead he felt a soft, warm object penetrate his anus and begin to massage his prostate gland. It was Colleen's tongue. The act did not come as a complete surprise as it had been referred to in her blogs. She had certainly developed a very kinky aspect to her sexuality.

After he had been relieved by hand he questioned the hygiene of providing what some people term analingus, others "rose leaf".

"I didn't hear you complaining," came the reply.

It was true. Occasionally there would be pleasant moments for him but they were becoming less and less frequent.

The blokes at the Greys did not know how to handle the

situation when Colleen visited the pub. It was so far outside their experiences as to be totally foreign. Gaily gained a certain kudos in their eyes for keeping the company of such a notorious prostitute. The fellows kept to themselves on those occasions Colleen graced the pub with her presence. They were not fools though and could see Gaily was clearly unhappy. All the older men preferred to ogle the young barmaids rather than keep the company of women closer to their own ages. This might explain why most of them were still bachelors.

He was not sorry to leave England. His sorrow was for the fact that he could never again love the woman he had for eighteen years adored. Perhaps it was true the best way to maintain a friendship is to stay apart. To employ the phrase popularised by Guy de Maupassant his first "grand passion" had ended in tragic circumstances.

Gaily's return to Sydney was equally tinged with sadness. His parents' health was fading fast.

Mrs Gaily was in and out of hospital for blood transfusions with monotonous regularity. She was a frail bag of bones pitiful to see.

Mr Gaily could barely walk. Such was his difficulty in negotiating a flight of stairs leading up to their flat the couple saw no other option than to move to a building with a lift or move into a ground floor flat. They chose the second option.

Moving house is traumatic enough at the best of times. For the frail old couple it was even more fraught. They hired a removalist who had in the past provided good service. The removalists were all Maori hard men and Ted Gaily had long admired the Maori work ethic.

All the glass, crockery and porcelain had to be wrapped just as Mrs Gaily would have done it herself. All the beautiful furniture had to be handled with kid gloves so as not to be scratched.

When the time for unpacking came a couple of fragile items were broken, some furniture scratched. Gaily's parents were bitterly disappointed. The flat in the suburb of Sutherland was to be the address which would appear on their death certificates. At least in the final phase of their lives they would be surrounded by most of the objects Mr Gaily described as "old friends".

Gaily resumed his duties at the pool. When left alone by management he found it to be not too bad a job. Looking at water is very meditative and as a fit man Gaily found he could lower his heart rate at work below what it would normally be at the resting level.

His main thoughts were for his parents. He wanted to ensure he was as close to them as possible prior to their shuffling off this mortal coil. No word should be left unspoken.

To ensure this occurred he would visit his parents every Sunday on which he was not working and ring them at least once a week.

Gaily also resumed seeing Sarah every fortnight or so. Following the disappointment and frustration of England he asked Sarah if she would be prepared to provide him with full service. Sarah was quite happy to agree to his request. It had been eleven years of self-enforced celibacy for Gaily if we accept a certain American president's definition of "sex". His devotion towards Colleen was gone as a result of his recent experiences. Sarah gave him what he wanted and Gaily knew he would never fall in love with her. He could safely bonk her without any emotional commitment.

Gaily continued to remain in regular telephone contact with Colleen. They would continue to exchange cards and letters thus maintaining a charade of friendship or at times even love. He felt no bitterness towards her – he had loved her too passionately for too long to feel anything but sorrow.

The health of Mr and Mrs Gaily continued to fluctuate from bad to worse and back again but there was a certain inevitability which even the redoubtable Blind Freddie could see. His parents were tough bastards but smoking and lack of exercise had taken their toll. They clung to each other for support and to the independence afforded by continuing to live in their own home. If they could not avoid death they could at least avoid the living death of a nursing home.

Gaily took some time off to be with his parents and used their state of health as an excuse to not visit Colleen the following year.

Two years after his previous trip Gaily returned to England and to Brighton. It was a pleasant little town and warmer during their summer than Sydney during what is the Australian winter. He also wanted to be absolutely certain he no longer felt any love for Colleen. He did not. They went out to lunch, they revisited old haunts, they sat on the balcony – he in "Charlie's chair" – drinking and chatting. He paid her for the time they spent together. Gaily was reassured by the experience his judgement had been correct. His ability to love the former Irish Goddess of Love had vanished.

"…And the tears they flowed like Resch's…."

Gaily returned home to watch his father die.

Ted Gaily had been admitted to a private hospital in the nearby suburb of Caringbah. He had often joked that one of the good things about living in Sutherland Shire was the abundance of hospitals. Now he was in one and would not leave on his own two feet.

His cardiopulmonary system was in the process of shutting down. As he lay in the bed his wife kept a largely silent vigil by his side.

Every day Mrs Gaily would arise early, have breakfast, pack a lunch and make the pilgrimage to the hospital. There she would sit quietly reading the Herald. When her husband was up to it they would share little snippets of conversation.

Increasingly large and frequent doses of morphine ensured Mr Gaily spent most of his remaining hours in painless sleep. Nurses and rehabilitation staff would take Gaily's father for little walks and provide him with simple exercises but even these as the weeks went on proved beyond his ability. He was dying and the once fine mind which had been by this time ravaged by four strokes comprehended the reality of the situation.

Gaily would visit the hospital as regularly as his work permitted. The pool management made the situation as difficult and unpleasant for him as possible by questioning his right to take time off to be with his dying father. Thankfully Dr Coconut was more understanding and provided medical certificates to cover any absences.

Every day Gaily would ring the hospital in the morning to ascertain his father's condition. Every day he was met with the non-committal answer of "stable".

While still lucid his father spoke to Gaily about the anger he felt at the way he had been treated by the solicitor under whom he had been an articled clerk, the waste of his life and the regrets he felt. Gaily could only seek to calm his father by assuring him he had done what he considered the right thing at the time – which was true.

His father implored him to look after his mother when he was gone which Gaily pledged he would.

They discussed Gaily's personal finances. His father had often in the course of his life compared his son to Mr Micawber in Dickens' David Copperfield. Mr Gaily told his son that when the time came he could sell the extensive share portfolio he possessed with his blessing.

"I am not sure you should say that to someone such as I," his son replied.

Mr Gaily certainly did not lack attention from the many and varied staff at the hospital. As an ex-serviceman all his medical bills were covered by the Department of Repatriation and Veterans' Affairs ("Repat" for short). The hospital saw this as a blank cheque for every conceivable test and service they could provide.

After five weeks Gaily's father had been ascertained to have a blocked artery and a spot on his lung which proved to be a malignant tumour. Nothing could be done about either malady as the old man was by this time so frail and weak any attempts at major surgery would only hasten his death. A week later Mr Gaily went into a coma from which he would not emerge.

Gaily was satisfied nothing had been left unsaid between father and son. The only other word Ted Gaily would ever speak was to scream out his wife's name occasionally during the night. Three weeks later he was declared dead.

Both mother and son were on hand when the pronouncement was made by the nurse in attendance. The treating doctor would be in later to confirm the death.

The wasted little corpse lay quite still in the bed – ashen even prior to its cremation. A shock of dishevelled white hair partially obscured the sunken features of the face where once a full dark head of hair had graced a blue-eyed visage with a square jaw.

Gaily's mother brushed her husband's hair back for the last time. Mother and son clasped a cold frail hand and said their last goodbyes.

Mrs Gaily vowed to obtain the War Widow's Pension. It seemed to Gaily an odd thing to say in the presence of death but it reflected a desire to continue living in the absence of her lifelong helpmate.

Gaily and his mother were exhausted from the nine week ordeal. They caught a cab back to the family home and Gaily stayed with his mother for a week to ensure she could cope on her own.

A neighbour came around to assist with the preparation of meals. His mother's brother lived outside Sydney but maintained regular contact. His sister in the bush had been very fond of Mr Gaily. They would try to attend the funeral. Various friends of the family emerged from the woodwork to provide support.

Gaily was overwhelmed. He could not cope by himself and was glad of the assistance.

Funeral arrangements had to be made with Repat to cover the tab. It would be a good send-off with a wake at the local ex-servicemen's club.

Gaily was very proud to give the oration at his father's funeral. His mother had intended the funeral to be attended only by her and her son but Gaily insisted on inviting people who were close enough to the family to have sent their condolences despite no death notice having been published.

His mother tried to present a tough exterior to the world but this was largely a front. In reality the old lady was dying of a broken heart. Like the men the women of her generation were not good at expressing their emotions.

Gaily used the organising skills he had acquired in the movement to ensure the funeral was a celebration of his father's life. Central to achieving this goal was the need to have close family and friends in attendance. Most of the dozen there went to the club afterwards. It was an appropriate and tasteful celebration. The one person who let Gaily down badly was Sarah.

Gaily had been seeing Sarah on a regular basis for the five years since obtaining a full-time job. They had become quite close – despite Gaily's finding her an overbearing pain in the neck at times. As the perceptive Colleen had gleaned he got the hour he paid for plus another he did not want of nagging and well-intentioned advice. However, unlike with Colleen he at least received a service in return for his money.

In fact as a middle-aged bachelor Gaily found an hour spent with just about anyone was usually sufficient. In the words of Sartre "hell is other people".

Sarah was really only a close acquaintance not a friend. However, as her regular client she felt obliged to attend the funeral of Gaily's father. His parents had known of Sarah for years without knowing exactly the role she played in their son's life. There had only been two women in his life in eighteen years and all mothers live in the hope of their bachelor sons marrying.

Sarah also knew of Gaily's parents and of their declining health.

"I'm here for you," she had said.

"Just ring me if you need me – I'll be there for you."

Sarah had even gone so far as to ring Gaily's mother and have long heart to heart conversations with the old woman regarding her son.

The problem was a familiar one – as is usually the case

with people who make the same mistakes over and over again.

Firstly, Gaily had mistaken Sarah for a friend – just as he had with Colleen. Thankfully he had not fallen in love with Sarah but both women had only been and would only ever be his acquaintances.

Secondly, they had allowed the line between friend or acquaintance and client to become horribly blurred. Once the lady provides some of her time on an unpaid basis while still seeing the man as a client on other occasions things start becoming confusing.

At any rate at the last minute Sarah rang Gaily to tell him she would not be attending the funeral. Another client had insisted on seeing her on that particular day, she was terribly sorry but knew he would understand.

It was actually quite offensive behaviour but as usual Gaily copped it sweet. He continued to see Sarah - proving once again the power of inertia.

He also continued to work at the swimming pool. His father had left him a small amount of money sufficient to pay off credit card debts but the bulk of Mr Gaily's estate went to his wife.

Gaily was in no hurry to leave the pool. The bastards in management had been low enough to give him a hard time while he was watching his father die and he was happy to go back to work just to nark them. He was a happy-go-lucky fellow whose spirit would never be broken while they were miserable sods who got their kicks from antagonising others.

Gaily had continued to dabble on the horses: it was part of his identity. He knew he would eventually win out while the tin-pot despots of this world waste their lives building imaginary empires.

In the back of his mind Gaily also knew he would one day inherit his mother's estate. To facilitate this process he and his mother had visited the family solicitor to have the heir-apparent granted power of attorney status.

"Just in case something happens, Charles," Mrs Gaily had told her son.

The family solicitor had been shocked at the old woman's emaciated appearance. Gaily confided in Mr Myer his fear his mother's cancer had come out of remission.

"Something is certainly not quite right," Mr Myer agreed in his usual non-committal manner.

Mr Myer's concerns were echoed by one of Mrs Gaily's neighbours. However, the neighbour was far more forthright than Mr Myer.

When Gaily was visiting his mother one Sunday he was bailed up in the corridor by a complete stranger. The fellow accused Gaily of allowing his mother to starve to death. After identifying himself by his first name only he scurried back into an adjoining flat leaving Gaily more than a little rattled.

Of additional concern was the disappearance of valuable items from the family home. Gaily's aunt and uncle had noticed this on their most recent visit. Several large items of furniture had walked out the door.

A friend of one of his parents' former neighbours had inveigled her way into Mrs Gaily's life. Her nominal role was "carer". The woman was getting his mother to write cash cheques in payment for the care supposedly provided. She and the fellow down the corridor also had keys to the flat "just in case something happens, Charles".

Gaily was forced to assert his power of attorney. He relieved the "carer" of her duties, had the keys returned and shortly after had the locks changed.

A qualified nurse was hired to visit Mrs Gaily but it was

too little too late. After a series of falls the old lady was admitted to the same hospital where her husband had died seven months earlier. She did in fact have malnutrition.

The malnutrition accounted in part for Mrs Gaily's frailty and increasingly confused state of mind. However, this was only part of the story. After her husband's death the shock of the loss really hit home.

The widow spent her days moping around the home she had shared with her husband of more than fifty years. The Herald was delivered and left unread. Food was purchased and left uneaten. Hours were spent at the dining room table with head in hands. The ability to look after herself was lost along with the will to live.

Like her husband the last nine weeks of Mrs Gaily's life were spent in the hospital.

It was pitiful to watch the old lady in a fitful morphine-induced sleep reaching over to feel for where her husband would have been when they slept together in the marital couch—calling out his name to receive no response.

For the once beautiful and well-dressed woman it was an undignified way to die – a little bag of bones soiling her nappies.

Ironically the final nail in her coffin was being denied access to her coffin nails. Days after it was decreed she could not go outside for a cigarette Mrs Gaily died. After the death of her husband her smoking was the one enjoyment left in her life.

Gaily made the same arrangements for his mother's funeral as his mother and he had for that of his father. The same crowd turned out for Mrs Gaily's funeral and Gaily again gave the oration. His mother was cremated with her last carton of Rothman's. Gaily had a wicked sense of humour.

Once probate was granted Gaily suddenly became a

millionaire. He did not quit work straight away, however, as he preferred to hang around for a while just to infuriate the people who had antagonised him for seven long years. He made it quite clear to management he no longer needed the job but would leave on his own terms in his own good time. In the meantime he would turn up when he felt like it, do as little as possible while still performing his basic duties to the best of his ability and cut out all his leave entitlements. It was his way of giving management the middle finger minus the rude gesture.

While the old lady's corpse was still warm the vultures began to circle. Generous men with large inheritances attract spongers. Gaily was a very generous man and no exception to this rule.

Sarah had done exactly the same thing at the time of his mother's death as had been the case at the time of the death of his father.

"I'll be there. I'm here for you."

Then at the last minute she was unable to attend the funeral.

Once probate was granted, however, Sarah was all over Gaily like a cheap suit. At least he was able to relieve some of his grief and anger with some good hard bonking.

Colleen had maintained contact via the post and telephone throughout his mother's final weeks. Now the beautiful voice on the end of the telephone was increasingly amorous. Gaily had to check himself as to the extent to which the voice's owner had changed for the worse.

In a very vulnerable state of mind and with no source of support or guidance to whom he could turn Gaily made the first of a number of disastrous choices. He decided to visit Colleen in England accompanied by Sarah. He asked for trouble and got it in spades.

In a moment of madness Gaily offered to fly Sarah

business class to England and shout her cheap digs at Brighton University. Cheap digs are unbecoming for a lady but Sarah had her own agenda.

They negotiated a weekly allowance based on a weekly session for the duration of a two month stay.

Then Sarah announced she was desirous of trips to Rome, Paris and San Francisco – the latter being where one of her daughters resided. Gaily agreed to fund these sojourns as well despite having no desire to accompany her.

Sarah also suddenly began to incur legal fees which had to be paid for some complicated case involving the body corporate in the block of flats where she lived. Then there were huge dental bills which had to be met. From being a successful and independent businesswoman Sarah was overnight about to lose her home and her teeth.

Gaily began to have grave misgivings after the first five minutes of the twenty-four hour flight to London. The woman drove him up the wall with her inane chatter. By the time they got to Heathrow he was ready to tear out his hair – but there was not a lot to spare. He was just thankful they arrived at all after Sarah decided to provoke an altercation with Hong Kong customs officials: bad move.

Then came the coach trip to Brighton with Sarah embarrassing him with her yelling at him to run for the coach so as not to miss it – as if she could run in her tarty heels.

They did not speak much on the coach. Sarah pretended to sleep. He was glad he had cut his losses by not offering hotel accommodation.

Gaily and Sarah had a perfunctory bonk in one of the grotty little rooms and that was the first and last service provided. He at least had a drinking partner in Colleen and the blowzy old trout was her charming old self whilever the champagne flowed and the food was plentiful.

The Greys brought the three of them together. It was (another) total disaster. Colleen got plastered and Sarah sat there drinking Diet Coca-Cola reciting Alcoholics Anonymous maxims.

Gaily was mortified. He drank his Stowford in silence. All the locals including mine host and his staff saw what was happening to the lovely little Aussie they had adopted as their own but were powerless to act.

Thankfully the worst situations we encounter in our lives have a habit of eventually resolving themselves. The day after the Greys debacle Sarah announced she was off to Paris and Rome. Gaily had known for years Sarah was off so it came as no surprise.

Just to twist the knife a little bit more Colleen got some of her mates to ring Sarah on her mobile telephone in order to ascertain her whereabouts. Sarah had actually let it slip she was going to London to work. The calls revealed Sarah was still in England. Modern technology had caught Sarah out as a liar.

Gaily had wasted money on fares to Rome and Paris which were never utilised – possibly also the San Francisco connection. This in turn provided Sarah with the pretext to leave Brighton weeks before Gaily's intended date of departure.

"Oh! I would have loved you to accompany me," she cooed.

Sarah dropped her guard too often. Her real sentiments were expressed in the form of a parting jibe.

"I'm going to find younger men who can get it up," she hissed just before her departure.

The bitch really kidded herself.

Gaily still had feelings for Colleen. He was certainly a soft touch and had followed the progress of a court case in which she had been involved over the previous three years.

He had lent his moral support but had drawn the line at giving too much more support of the financial variety.

Their regular telephone conversations had continued when they were twelve thousand miles apart and Gaily understood the toll the case had taken on the woman.

As was always the case where Colleen was concerned money had been involved. Legal proceedings had been initiated by Inland Revenue (the English equivalent of the Australian Taxation Office) for alleged tax evasion. The case had dragged on and on before finally being resolved in Colleen's favour.

It was a landmark decision for all English sex workers as the court ruled that prostitutes were not liable to pay income tax given the fact they were deemed not to exist.

The stress of the case had caused Colleen's health to decline at an even more rapid rate than would otherwise have occurred.

Colleen had become unrecognisable from the beautiful jockey-sized doll Gaily had met more than twenty years prior. Her little feet and her knees had been forced to carry increasing amounts of weight to the point where the strain had become almost intolerable.

Gaily's main sexual stimulus had always been visual. Colleen no longer held any appeal for him whatsoever as the quality of her company had deteriorated along with her physical appearance.

Gaily had finally determined after twenty-two years to cut his losses by severing all ties with Colleen. Then Colleen played her trump card.

Colleen had sensed Gaily's decreasing interest in her. The woman's drug and drink addictions were so bad she felt powerless to reverse the behaviours which had led to increasing weight gain and wild mood swings.

The only remaining advantage Colleen possessed was

her experience in knowing exactly how to press Gaily's buttons.

Colleen's dream had been to change career paths by becoming a successful writer. Her first published book had, however, proven an absolute disaster. It had been an autobiography which sold only five hundred copies from an initial print run of five thousand. Colleen was a big fish in Brighton but Brighton is a small pond.

If Colleen were to continue to live in the manner to which she had become accustomed she needed to find a new means of bleeding her old client.

Gaily had already dropped his guard once since the death of his mother by agreeing to fund an ill-fated business venture involving Colleen.

Gaily had perceived a void in the English magazine market for a quality and tasteful cheesecake magazine depicting attractive women wearing miniskirts or short dresses. The shots were to be so taken as to give a glimpse of their knickers. The notion appealed to Gaily's warped mind and he knew a lot of Englishmen possessed a similar warp.

Colleen was in an ideal position to organise the project as she knew a large number of beautiful tarty women and a top photographer who specialised in cheesecake.

Gaily had paid Colleen a very generous wage to oversee the project but the wheels had fallen off when the surly old woman had provoked a personality clash between herself and the photographer. There was also Colleen's laziness with which to contend.

When one is having a good bonk one should prolong it as long as possible as one never knows when such good fortune will again occur.

Similarly Colleen knew to make the project spin out for

as long as possible in order to maximise the amount able to be gouged from Gaily.

A magnificent portfolio of photographs resulted despite tensions between secretary and photographer.

After a year there were sufficient photographs for several editions of a glossy magazine tentatively entitled "Short And Sweet". This and several other names had been registered but Colleen claimed no interested publisher could be found. That was the end of that.

Colleen had to find a new angle by which to maintain a flow of cash from Gaily's bank account into her own. One telephone call did the trick.

Colleen had made the acquaintance of the notorious London dandy Oscar Wildly. She even claimed to have had a fling with him but this is a story for another time. Colleen rang Wildly to arrange a meeting involving one of the fast women of Wildly's acquaintance, herself and Gaily.

Colleen had done this on the pretext of cheering up Gaily after the debacle involving Sarah. Of course Colleen was a cunning linguist who saw an opportunity to drive the knife into Sarah while creating a renewed source of income for herself with another member of the sisterhood to be equally remunerated.

The requisite lady was booked and a time and date set. The lady was one of London's leading Bondage and Discipline mistresses. Some kinky fun was on the agenda.

Then at the last minute the lady bailed. An executive decision had to be made. Wildly persuaded his own girlfriend Racquel to fill the breach.

Gaily was still in for a treat. Racquel was one of England's most famous pin-up girls during the nineties. She was still intoxicatingly beautiful as well as being renowned for her exhibitionist streak.

The rendezvous was to occur at Wildly's own flat. Wildly derived vicarious titillation from the occasion. He himself would be absent but he was leaving Gaily in very experienced hands where the art of tease was concerned.

Colleen and Gaily travelled to London together on the train. At Victoria Railway Station Gaily purchased champagne and flowers. First impressions count.

They caught a cab to Weird Street in Soho and rang the door-bell. Racquel answered the door.

The vision of beauty which greeted Gaily's eye took his breath away. This was not just the most beautiful woman Gaily had ever met. Racquel was the most beautiful woman he had ever seen. In the words of the Ladbrokes' advertising slogan it was "game on".

Racquel led the way upstairs to Wildly's flat. She was wearing a short blue and cream dress which provocatively just managed to cover her large, firm, round knicker-clad bottom.

Gaily smiled in anticipation of things to come. What a playmate! Large firm G-cup breasts pointed towards the empyrean. Her narrow cinched waist formed the middle of the hourglass and her pert buttocks were those one normally associated with black women. At forty years of age Racquel was still one of the world's most beautiful women. No wonder her photographs had graced the pages of newspapers, glossy magazines and the Pirelli calendar.

Gaily opened the champagne while Racquel provided glasses. Colleen just sat down and gloated to herself about the success of procuring such a stunner. Then on cue she made her usual remark about the beauty of the sound of the popping champagne cork.

Gaily was too overawed by the occasion to worry about drinking champagne. He drank in the sight of Racquel just as Colleen guzzled the fizz. His eyes absorbed greedily the long thick wavy blonde hair, the big blue eyes, the perfectly formed face, the toned body, the expensive clothes and shoes and the attention to detail required to create such a complete package.

The triangular nature of the relationship ensured it would always be unwieldy and ultimately unworkable. With one corner of the triangle being formed by Colleen good will was in short supply.

Gaily's affection for Colleen was long gone and now she had introduced him to someone far more attractive it was time for the parting of the ways.

Colleen's attitude was that this mere act of introduction created a large degree of indebtedness on Gaily's part from which she would reap the benefits. Colleen would milk the situation for all it was worth. To her Racquel was a meal-ticket.

Racquel herself lived far more in the moment. If the session went well she would commit to further rendezvous. If not there were plenty more irons in the fire.

Racquel had obtained her fifteen minutes of fame early in life then created a brand around her own image which continued to generate large sums of money.

Racquel was big on self-publicity and the Internet had afforded her an ideal medium through which to beat her own drum. Facebook in particular was a huge boon.

The session started. The role play was an obvious one. Colleen was the schoolmistress. Gaily donned his Castle Hill High uniform to regress to the role of naughty schoolboy and Racquel was the naughty schoolgirl flashing her knickers.

Racquel was such a tease. The role had been rehearsed on thousands of occasions going back well over twenty

years. On this particular day Racquel had little white knickers with daffodil yellow lace trim. She was such a tease.

Every time Gaily got a glimpse of knickers he was given
a little spanking by Colleen. Colleen was too fat and lazy
to offer more than a perfunctory spanking but this meant
Gaily had more opportunities to savour the knicker-clad
bottom as Racquel bent over various objects in the lounge
room. Racquel's knickers were sheer at the back so one
got to savour the cleft of her bottom. At one point Gaily
was allowed to engage in a little frottage. Racquel was
able to grip the schoolboy's penis as it rubbed along the
cleft. Racquel flexed the buttock muscles in order to effect
the tight grip while never at any stage being in danger of
being penetrated.

For Gaily though it was as if penetration had been
achieved. The sensation was as intense as he had ever
experienced with penetrative sex.

Just before attaining climax Colleen provided Gaily with
hand relief to avoid his coming over Racquel. This ensured
they could go to lunch earlier than would have been the
case if Racquel had had to change her knickers. Colleen
was very thoughtful where her own interests were served.

Without any preconceptions as to what was likely to
occur the outcome of their first encounter was very pleasing for all parties concerned. Gaily had no qualms about
leaving five hundred pounds on the kitchen bench for
Racquel. Colleen had already ensured her payment was
received in advance.

The three of them went to lunch at the Covent Garden
Hotel. Colleen had demolished one bottle of champagne
and was keen to wash it down with another.

Racquel on the other hand drank little but talked much
– mainly about herself. With women of such rare beauty
men tend not to listen to what they have to say and such

was the case as the very beautiful and very narcissistic English rose held forth in Gaily's company.

It was more the way it was said than the actual words. Gaily studied the movement of the rosy red lips, the expressions of the beautiful face and heard the clipped English accent without comprehending a word.

This was pukka posh totty – not some sham attempt at imitation. Gaily was in exalted company. The second grand passion of his life had commenced.

As the outing had gone so well Colleen ensured another appointment was made prior to Gaily and herself returning to Brighton. In order to really cement the link Colleen invited Racquel to meet them at her flat the following week. Playtime would be followed by lunch-time.

Gaily counted down the days until his next treat. Racquel drove down from London.

She was such a girlish girl and such a tease. Colleen and Gaily waited for her arrival on Colleen's balcony.

Finally a grey Range Rover drove up and parked opposite the block of flats. Out stepped the vision of loveliness in a floral dress. Racquel waved to her new admirer and he waved back – his face filled with joy and wonder. Colleen sighed. It would be over an hour before she could reasonably expect to be filling her own face with something far more substantial than joy or wonder.

The wind licked the hem of Racquel's lovely little dress. The dress was bedecked with spring flowers which rose and fell in the gusts of sea breeze. Passers-by stopped and smiled as the English rose crossed Marine Parade.

Gaily let Racquel in and walked the mandatory six steps behind as they ascended the stairs – behind here being the key word.

The champagne was an even more mandatory part of the ritual and two glasses were duly poured. Gaily was surprised when Racquel requested him to buy cigarettes for her but there was yet much for him to learn about the fascinating femme fatale.

Much of Racquel's background was revealed in a book with which she presented Gaily. It was the recently published autobiography of Oscar Wildly and was signed by the man himself. Gaily looked forward to expanding his knowledge of Racquel on the homeward plane trip. For the time being he was content to expand not just his knowledge as he watched Racquel smoking a Marlboro Green on the windswept balcony. Gusts of wind repeatedly lifted her dress to expose her white knickers. It was schoolboy heaven.

Gaily was roused from his reveries by Colleen declaring it was time to take a cab to Cote restaurant. Fun but not food were strictly rationed where Colleen was concerned.

At the restaurant Colleen dominated conversation in order to minimise the amount of communication Gaily was able to have with Racquel. The older woman was already becoming jealous of the encroachments Racquel was making on her territory. Accepting the inevitability of the situation she vowed to drive as hard a bargain as possible to arrange future liaisons by way of both compensation to her wounded pride and revenge for Gaily's infidelity.

At the end of the meal Gaily did not want to be separated from Racquel. They had only met a week prior and already it was time to part. Colleen did not want to be separated from the third bottle of champagne so asked a waitress to put a stopper in it for domestic consumption.

Racquel had her own life to return to – filled as it was with her many other generous admirers, the night life of Soho, holidays overseas, family, friends and endless shopping for clothes and shoes. Racquel was high maintenance and just the cost of maintaining appearances was increasing with the passing of each year.

Like Colleen Gaily reluctantly accepted the inevitable. His day in the sun would come but as with other areas of the middle aged man's life it was a long time coming. Blinded by the beauty of Racquel it was yet to dawn on him such a day would never arrive whilever Colleen continued to cast an increasingly large shadow over his life.

The next day Colleen saw Gaily off from Brighton's Pool Valley. As far as Gaily was concerned his farewell present had been his meeting with Racquel the day prior. Colleen still described herself as Gaily's "first wife" and therefore claimed first dibs on him. He had made the mistake of telling her he had included her in his will and she was intent on getting her hands on her share of his estate while he was still alive.

They had a meal together at one of Colleen's favourite haunts near where she lived and close to the coach station. Their relationship now revolved around the older woman's ability to continue to procure the company of Racquel for Gaily's delectation. As Gaily so succinctly put it Racquel was now "the glue" of whatever friendship still remained.

Colleen expressed the opinion his "infidelity" threatened to tear apart a friendship of over twenty years' standing. He had lost interest in her family, had not bothered to enquire after her mother or niece even before his meeting Racquel and seemed uninterested in anyone other than Racquel once the introduction had occurred.

Colleen portrayed herself as a loyal long-term friend who felt betrayed by his fickleness. However, she would continue to act in his best interests by acting as his go-between despite the thanklessness of the task.

Gaily countered by asserting the monogamous nature

of his mind would not allow him to love more than one woman. Forced to choose he had transferred his affections from Colleen to Racquel.

It was all a little melodramatic. Colleen felt she had to save face. Gaily was in the first throes of love with a woman he had met in the previous fortnight. Racquel could not really care less and had already spent Gaily's thousand pounds on clothes from Selfridges.

Colleen waved a teary Gaily goodbye. He managed a smile and a wave then slept off his lunch all the way to Heathrow.

On the flight home Gaily read through Wildly's book in a most voracious manner. He was eager to get to the section containing references to Racquel. In the process he got to know a lot more about her boyfriend which Gaily hoped would stand him in good stead in winning at least a share of her affections. As Colleen had made a point of telling him there was plenty of her to go around.

With forty pages to go he came across the first reference to his new love. Most of the last part of the book was devoted to Racquel. To say it was an eye-opener would be an understatement. There were things there he would rather not have known. Forewarned is meant to be forearmed but there was to be no warning Gaily of the perils which would confront him on the rollercoaster ride upon which he was embarking. To use one of Colleen's favourite expressions he was "in for a penny, in for a pound". By the time the plane stopped over in Hong Kong the book was read – its contents absorbed but its implicit warning unheeded.

Gaily always liked to be back in Sydney in September – and this particular year was no exception. September in Sydney means spring – when a young man's thoughts turn to...football. The National Rugby League finals are conducted in September culminating with the grand final on the first weekend of October.

Gaily had backed his team St George at long odds at the start of the season to win the premiership then continued to back them as they firmed in the course of the season. Saints had maintained excellent form throughout the year – having kept up their winning strike rate in Gaily's absence. They went into the finals as firm favourites, the team full of confidence.

Saints had a reputation as chokers but under a new coach this looked unlikely to recur. Gaily had them going for well over a hundred thousand dollars.

He rang Colleen and in a tactically unwise move told her what he stood to win.

"If Saints win the premiership why not fly Racquel over for your birthday?" Colleen suggested in her usual helpful manner.

"Colleen, they're certs. Make the bookings now," Gaily said with a grandiose wave of the hand missed by his interlocutor twelve thousand miles away.

Colleen started to whinge about the enormous workload Gaily imposed upon her for unpaid secretarial duties but finally agreed to his request.

It is now history St George did indeed again choke – losing both their finals matches to be bundled out in inglorious fashion. Never bet on anything that talks.

Win or no win Racquel was coming to Sydney in December. From the moment he met her it had been Gaily's intention to bring her over at some stage. What better opportunity than his fiftieth birthday?

Colleen ostensibly negotiated the terms of payment Racquel would require in order to comply with Gaily's request. Colleen not surprisingly would require exactly the same payments. Both women knew full well the besotted fool would part with just about anything in exchange for a bit of perfunctory tease providing a glimpse of Racquel's knickers.

Colleen did not mess around. Flights were to be business class, hotel accommodation of at least four star quality. There was to be a two hundred dollar a day allowance for both her and Racquel. There would be a minimum of three "lessons" or "sessions" with Gaily for each of the two weeks of their stay with each "lesson"/"session" requiring a payment of a thousand pounds sterling.

Gaily did his maths very quickly but knew it was a case of take it or leave it. He took it.

What he had agreed to amounted to an outlay of over forty thousand Aussie dollars for the company of two escorts – one of whom he did not even wish to see. He would see Racquel on at least six occasions. This was all that mattered to Gaily. He would just have to back a few more winners.

Gaily had again been able to recommence betting in denominations of one thousand dollars since the death of his mother. He loved to boast to Norma McNobody of his successes in order to just rub her nose in it a little more. He would never forgive her for the treatment he had been accorded.

Normally Gaily would never allow himself displays of hubris. It was out of character for him to behave in this manner. Now he knew he would soon be resigning he allowed himself to be a little cocky. He had to be confident to be a show of winning the hand of the fair Racquel.

The idea was for his resignation to become effective on his birthday. He would have lunch with Colleen and Racquel at the restaurant overlooking Bear Park Pool after first handing in his letter of resignation in their company.

In the two months leading up to their arrival Gaily

made a point of cutting out all his remaining leave – reserving just enough to ensure he would be off for the duration of Racquel's stay.

This latter was how he actually regarded the matter: it was Racquel who was visiting him with Colleen as her travelling companion.

The day of their arrival came around. He was at the airport to meet and greet. Racquel looked radiant and resplendent as usual despite the long journey. Colleen looked the frumpish old procuress she had become. One was the quintessential English rose in full bloom, the other wilted beyond the point of being able to be renewed.

First impressions count. First Gaily then Colleen set the tone for the duration of the visit even before they had left the airport.

Gaily could see Colleen was angry over something so proceeded to antagonise her by showing obvious reluctance to kiss her while being all too willing to kiss Racquel.

At the first opportunity Colleen drew him aside. The girl had driven her up the wall with her airs and graces. Colleen then proceeded to give a passable but very catty impression of Racquel.

Given the choice Gaily knew whose airs and graces he would prefer. As for her mannerisms Gaily was mesmerised by Racquel's quirky little facial expressions and turns of phrase. It was all part of the process of falling in love.

Racquel lived in her own little world: Planet Racquel. On Planet Racquel men fell in love with Racquel and threw money at her in the vain hope of love being reciprocated. Unfortunately Racquel was too much in love with herself but the money was put to good use to ensure Racquel remained eternally youthful and kept in the manner to which she was accustomed. Rumour had it that there were often heavy snow-storms on Planet Racquel but these rumours remained unconfirmed at the time of publication.

Colleen and Racquel were initially staying in a little four star hotel in the suburb of Potts Point. The luncheon at the Bear Park restaurant had appropriately gone rather swimmingly with lots of good food and champagne to placate Colleen. Racquel had found a gym where she could work off the little band of fat which had supposedly formed around her waist. Gaily had been able to persuade her to go swimming with him. Everyone was as happy as could be expected under the circumstances. Then tragedy struck.

Colleen was walking beside the pier at Circular Quay when she slipped on a crisp wrapper – falling heavily on one knee. After a few hours the pain from the injury became intolerable. For the duration of her stay Colleen was wheelchair-bound.

One of the consequences of Colleen's accident was the need for her to move hotels as the hotel in which both women were staying did not have wheelchair access. Gaily did four thousand dollars cold and Colleen made it quite clear she could not care less. Racquel moved into another hotel in Potts Point to keep her company then spent most of the rest of her visit shopping and going to the gym. Colleen was furious.

If a walking, talking Colleen was difficult to put up with a wheelchair-bound Colleen was positively unbearable.

Colleen accused Gaily of leaving her to her own devices all day while he chased after Racquel. The only way Colleen could be placated was with bottles of champagne which were consumed while she lay on her bed.

Gaily had quite literally gone out of his way to live out a major fantasy with Racquel. He had gone out to his old school to obtain a school uniform for her.

What he had not banked on was the grilling he received

from the lady in charge of uniform sales. Gaily let himself in for a full interrogation by telling her he had a niece coming over from England to enrol in the New Year.

The lady wanted to know when the niece would be arriving, her age, which form she would be in, if resident status had been granted and with whom she would be living.

Gaily had to duck, bob and weave his way out of the predicament as best he could while procuring his blouse, ties, skirt, socks and hat. He made sure he would not have to return for quite a while.

Once out of the uniform shop he congratulated himself on his purchases. They had been made weeks prior to Racquel's arrival and provided him with hours of titillation at the very thought of her in uniform.

The skirt was suitably modified by a local seamstress and the stage was set for him to live out the fantasy of a lifetime. He was not disappointed.

Racquel was a great exhibitionist and readily went along with her assigned role. The knicker-clad buttocks peeking out from under what had been transformed into a micro-miniskirt stirred vivid memories going back more than thirty years. In fact the re-enactment was better than the original. Racquel looked superb and really played up to her little school friend when they were both in uniform.

The injured Colleen put a real dampener on proceedings. The "lessons" became more perfunctory than would otherwise have been the case. Nothing though could dampen the sheer joy Racquel's presence gave Gaily.

The only problem was Racquel was in an unfamiliar situation and looked to Colleen for a lead. When the lead was not forthcoming the role play side of the proceedings disappointed Gaily's very high expectations.

If permitted Gaily would have spent hours worshipping at the altar of Racquel's buttocks. However, the snarling

Colleen would put an end to the kissing and fondling just when Racquel and Gaily's obvious pleasure became too much for Colleen to bear. Then it was time to return from the pleasures of fantasy to the reality of expensive restaurant lunches.

The cab journeys and meals provided awkward moments for Gaily and Racquel. With the best will in the world they had little in common apart from Racquel's exhibitionism being matched by Gaily's voyeurism. They inhabited very different worlds although Gaily's inheritance had facilitated at least a partial merging of their two worlds.

It therefore came as a pleasant surprise to Gaily when Racquel raised the subject of marriage. They were on their way to Icebergs Restaurant in the eastern suburb of Bondi – this meeting Colleen's required criteria of being wheelchair-friendly, expensive and serving rosé champagne.

Gaily was vulnerable to Racquel's vamping behaviour. In his heart he knew he was incapable of marriage and doomed to be a bachelor for the rest of his days. He wanted desperately to believe the beautiful woman's words – so he did.

They spoke of one or other party relocating to the other's country. Gaily would have loved to have had a daughter and Racquel's daughter would become his step-daughter and heiress in the event of his marrying Racquel. Gaily in thinking in terms of an heiress was presupposing his prospective wife would not render him penniless prior to his death.

Colleen laughed at the fellow's credulity while inwardly worrying about her old client's shift in allegiances.

Over lunch Gaily had eyes only for Racquel. The waves rolled in at Bondi Beach and he was sitting across the table from the most beautiful girl in the world. The English tabloids and magazines had years before eulogised Racquel as "a cracking lass" and "posh totty". What more fitting place than Bondi Beach for an Australian to savour his finest hour?

Colleen diverted Racquel's attention from Gaily to herself. The older woman was intensely jealous of her younger rival. Colleen was being hoisted by her own petard and did not like that which was of her own creation. She ordered more and more of the most expensive rosé champagne to test Gaily's generosity in the hope he would expose himself as a cheapskate while in Racquel's company.

Like the true gentleman he was Gaily never lost his nerve or his temper. For his reward Racquel gave him a wonderful farewell present.

Colleen was also present in the hotel room but Gaily recognised only the presence of Racquel. Racquel was in full Castle Hill High senior girls' uniform. Her pink high heels were definitely not regulation school shoes. Her beautiful calves were encased in long knee-length white socks. Her little blue tartan skirt constantly threatened to expose her magnificent bottom. Her pert breasts strained her white school blouse to the point where what was intended as the blouse's waist was knotted provocatively above that of its wearer. The hat was perched at a jaunty angle atop masses of long thick blonde hair.

The effect was breathtaking

Racquel bent over in front of Gaily. The skirt rode up to reveal black and white zebra print knickers. The sight of the magnificent knicker-clad bottom brought out the animal lover in Gaily.

He planted hundreds of tiny kisses all over the bottom. Gradually he began to lose control – nibbling and licking in a paroxysm of lust.

Racquel hinted that Gaily might just be overdoing it

slightly by momentarily drawing away but only for as long as it took to regain her balance and reposition herself over the edge of the room's bed.

He began rubbing against the freshly exposed buttocks and she reached behind her to unbutton and unzip his grey school shorts. Her deft hands did their work without Racquel having to turn around so adept was she at undressing men.

The bulge in Gaily's white cotton underpants manifested his innermost desire. However, there are limits to all good things and frottage was where the boundary had been drawn between Racquel and Gaily.

Boundaries are made to be pushed and Gaily pressed with all his might against the cleft between Gluteus Maximus One and Gluteus Maximus Two.

Racquel again reached back to pull down Gaily's underpants. Freed of constraint his rock-hard erection rubbed frantically along the cleft of her bottom. She clenched the cheeks so that the penis was locked inescapably in the firmest of embraces. The physical and visual stimuli combined to form a heady cocktail resulting in an inevitable climax. The bloke might just have turned fifty but the explosion which soaked the zebra print knickers was that of a much younger man.

Colleen had merely played the role of spectator while the two younger people had engaged in their act of intimacy. Her role as a participant was now completely redundant. This much had been exposed as clearly as Racquel's derriere.

While Racquel went to change her knickers Colleen sat in her wheelchair fuming at her obsolescence. The broken down old tart had to balance her anger at Gaily's rejection of her with the avarice she had for his money. Whilever Racquel agreed to retain her as procuress Colleen was assured of a steady stream of money such was Gaily's love for the younger woman. Colleen's pride and dignity were deeply hurt but her revenge on the unfaithful long-term client would be exacted by using Racquel as her meal-ticket with a view to bringing about Gaily's financial ruin.

After the high jinks in the hotel room lunch was remarkably quiet apart from the sound of Colleen demolishing yet another farmyard friend served with vegetables and gravy. Interspersed with the sounds of gluttony was the matching sound of champagne being guzzled.

Colleen's luncheon partners ate and drank little – preferring to preserve their schoolboy – and schoolgirl – esque figures.

Gaily stared into Racquel's pools of blue. He had finally met a woman to whom he would totally commit. The only problem was she lived twelve thousand miles away and was the muse of Oscar Wildly. It was all the more reason to savour the moment.

Racquel simpered just like the schoolgirl whose role she played so well. Gaily studied her every mannerism and could find no fault. Racquel had a quirky way of pouting her rosy red lips and twitching the puckered mouth from side to side. A hairdresser had put gold-coloured hair extensions through her hair and Gaily watched with fascination as they glistened in the summer sunlight. The dazzling woman was even more dazzling than ever.

Soon they would be parted for six long months – or so they would seem to Gaily.

Those six months would also see Colleen begin the process of poisoning Racquel's mind against Gaily. What little contact the two women would have in Gaily's absence Colleen would devote almost exclusively to badmouthing him to Racquel.

It was the same with the women who had been involved

in the ill-fated magazine project. As these women were mainly residents of Brighton Colleen had been more readily able to maintain contact with them than with Racquel. The knife was well and truly in Gaily's back and being twisted. Colleen was toxic and Gaily was acutely aware of the fact without being able to pinpoint how to eradicate her from his life without severing ties with Racquel. The fact was the triangular relationship was doomed from the very beginning but the lovestruck Gaily was impervious to this fact.

Ironically the main means Colleen utilised in her hate campaign against Gaily was to constantly reinforce his drinking problem in the minds of those in her tiny circle of influence. Never mind her own drug and drink-related problems. Never mind the very same problems of those whom Colleen sought to influence. The constant snide remarks in his absence and increasingly also to his face whilst in the presence of others were the only means Colleen still possessed of salving her own ego given Gaily's perceived infidelity.

At the end of her first fortnight in Sydney Racquel was already beginning to become bored. A diversion was required in order to maintain her ongoing commitment to the ill-fated business arrangement – to label it in frank terms.

Racquel's idea of oral sex was to constantly talk about it without actually initiating any action: so it seemed to Gaily. Thankfully it was the same story with her drug use: constant references to "snow" but to Gaily's knowledge no actual use of the drug during their initial Sydney sojourn.

To titillate her sensibilities Racquel had for most of her stay proposed a visit to a brothel. This did not resonate well with Gaily as any sexual activity in which he engaged he wanted to be with Racquel. Here Racquel's voyeuristic traits came to the fore.

The idea was for Gaily to perform with another woman for Racquel's entertainment. Colleen would also presumably form the other half of the audience. Voyeur and exhibitionist were being asked to reverse roles. The introverted Gaily did not like this unorthodox proposal but at the same time did not wish to offend Racquel.

Gaily's compromise solution was to see someone who did not provide the "full service" but who would participate in a role play scenario with the three of them. It was a good compromise in so far as it somewhat marginalised the role Colleen would have to play. The less Gaily had to do with Colleen the more he liked it so to this extent it was a positive move whilst also keeping Racquel happy.

For some time Gaily had read with interest classified advertisements placed in his local newspaper by a Mistress Claudette. Mistress Claudette billed herself as specialising in "O.T.K." (Over The Knee spanking).

The telephone call was made and the appointment booked. Colleen took full credit for "introducing" Gaily to the French mistress. Colleen's indispensability knew no bounds.

As usual it was a cab job and with Colleen still in a wheelchair they had developed a good rapport with a Chinese cabbie called Lee who drove a cab with wheelchair access.

Colleen made a point of having Gaily ascertain whether Mistress Claudette would require a bottle of wine (at ten o'clock in the morning). Colleen's disappointment was manifest when the reply came back in the negative.

Lee drove the three of them to Mistress Claudette's and arranged to pick them up later. Gaily was not trusted to push the wheelchair so this task fell to the reluctant Racquel. Racquel was very strong from all her gym classes but was unfamiliar with anything approximating work. Thus, did the motley trio descend upon Mistress Claudette's boudoir.

Mistress Claudette was a petite Frenchwoman who claimed to be in her late thirties. Rather uncharitably Colleen had emitted one of her many crude utterances upon hearing of her fellow mistress's supposed age.

The Frenchwoman lived in and worked from a small flat in the suburb of North Sydney. Her frizzy brown hair was long, her black shift short, her accent thick and her interest in Bondage and Discipline manifest. An array of implements were on display which in capable hands would instil pleasure and inflict pain in large and equal measure.

Colleen had an esoteric conversation with Mistress Claudette about various aspects of bondage and discipline. Mistress Claudette was somewhat perplexed as to the reason for the sudden invasion of her premises until the subject of role play arose. The emergence of the school uniforms further clarified the situation.

What ensued was a fairly short and perfunctory session which followed a predictable pattern. Gaily would be caught looking up Racquel's skirt then spanked. Mistress Claudette performed her role to the best of her ability but Racquel was becoming bored with the sameness of the sessions and all Colleen was concerned about was the eating and drinking to follow.

With payment having been made in advance Colleen saw no need to do anything other than offer Mistress Claudette a few words of encouragement from the sidelines. The Frenchwoman was experienced in the art of spanking and obviously enjoyed her work.

Gaily was glad at Colleen's lack of participation as by this time he had come to find her very touch abhorrent. For her part Colleen would never forgive Gaily for switching allegiances so sought to minimise any pleasure he may experience in Racquel's company whilst maximising her own financial gains. Mistress Claudette perceived the dynamics at play but felt powerless to intervene. It was a toxic situation into which to introduce a stranger.

The French mistress politely excused herself from joining them for lunch and Lee's cab whisked the three of them to a nearby restaurant.

Gaily would maintain occasional contact with Mistress Claudette. As part of maintaining the pretence of an enjoyable game Colleen was required to give her approval for this to occur.

To convey the impression of looking after Gaily's needs he was granted permission to see Mistress Claudette on a monthly basis. More than this would require Gaily parting with more of his money than was deemed desirable by Colleen and Racquel.

Racquel simply took the path of least resistance where Colleen was concerned: mindlessly acquiescing to her requests and demands. In bondage and discipline role play a participant who is able to act in both a dominant and a submissive role is termed a "switch". Racquel would be dominant towards Gaily and submissive towards Colleen. This in turn allowed Colleen to remain in control of the situation of her own creation. It was a lose–lose paradigm but Colleen was incapable of creating anything viable, sustainable or even mildly enjoyable. She had become the Kiss of Death. When Mistress Claudette got to know her a little better she would describe Colleen as "evil" and Gaily would agree with this summation.

How frustrating for a man to be introduced to someone so desirable only to have any potential friendship sabotaged by the one who has performed the introduction.

Unlike Colleen Gaily had at all times acted in good faith. He could hold his head high. His own lack of self-assertiveness was though a major shortcoming in thwarting Colleen's manipulativeness and Racquel's inertia. As Colleen would express it "it has always been thus so". To assert himself would be to risk losing all contact with Racquel but to rid himself once and for all of Colleen.

The trick was to make himself genuinely attractive to Racquel but for this to occur Colleen had for the time being to be allowed to remain on the scene. It seemed an impossible task but for someone in the first throes of love anything is possible. Like Hamlet Gaily thought he could "win at the odds". Colleen was his Laertes.

The ladies' day of departure back to England arrived. Colleen was in a foul mood. Racquel was on Planet Racquel and saw little of the world around her. Gaily saw Racquel was so in love with herself she was incapable of loving another.

Packing her bags was a major military operation for Racquel. Pink ports were crammed with the spoils of shopping excursions. Dockets had been retained in order for tax to be reclaimed.

The cab ride to the airport was a sullen affair filled with an awkward silence. The lopsided relationship Colleen had created for her own financial advantage obviously afforded her little joy. Colleen would seek to extinguish any joy experienced by Racquel and Gaily while raging at her own entrapment.

Gaily's entrapment was of a very different variety. On this particular day it wore a little Alannah Hill number. Gaily pondered the future as Racquel pondered a chipped fingernail. Alannah had succeeded where Gaily had thus far failed.

At the airport Colleen took French leave of the other two. Even Racquel was forced to notice the rage of her travelling companion. The younger woman would attempt to appease and placate the older without seeing the insoluble cause of the problem.

Racquel agreed to maintain contact but only via Facebook.

Gaily had been forced to open a Facebook account for this purpose and this purpose alone. He detested new technology in general and Facebook in particular. He loathed its impersonal nature, its informality and its capacity to mesmerise the minds of the masses.

For Racquel it very quickly became her main tool of trade. The miracles of cyberspace enabled her to project her image to all corners of the globe. Admirers could be picked and chosen on the basis of age, looks and social status. The so-called social media presented the narcissist with both a giant mirror and a never-ending supply of worshippers to be shunned or wooed as required.

Racquel's use of others did have negative repercussions. One of these had been when a jealous sugar daddy had hacked into her email account. This was the actual catalyst for Racquel's stated preference for Facebook as a means of communicating.

There is an old saying about beggars and choosers. Gaily fell into the former category. There were still a few in front of him in the queue of Racquel's admirers but at least he was in the queue. A quick peck on the cheek and it was goodbye for six months.

Despite the stated intentions little contact was maintained between Gaily and Racquel. To Racquel Gaily represented easy money with Colleen doing most of the work.

In the back of his mind Gaily remembered a cartoon featuring a character called Ziggy at the door of the "Introverts' Club". The caption read "please take a ticket and go away". As an introvert Gaily had related very strongly to this caricature upon first seeing it and now with Racquel in his life found it particularly apt.

For such a popular form of social media Gaily found Facebook a difficult medium to negotiate. Not even his love for Racquel could inspire him. He often joked about being the least computer literate person in the world with their own Internet site. It was six months before he learnt the basics of retrieving messages. Little notes of thanks and general salutations which may have kindled the first sparks of friendship were missed.

Gaily felt awkward in maintaining contact via the post when the girl had not provided him with a postal address other than that of her boyfriend Oscar Wildly.

Again in the back of his mind Gaily had grave doubts. His betting was assisting him in developing intuition but he was unable to utilise this new attribute where beautiful women were concerned.

Gaily knew enough about Facebook to know people who use it as their major form of communication have something to hide. People who use others ditch so-called "friends" at a moment's notice when their purpose has been served.

Gaily had no postal address for Racquel other than Wildly's place of domicile. He had been told to prefer Facebook to email.

The only attempt to ring Racquel via mobile telephone had been curtailed with a curt reference to her being about to have her nails done (!).

Gaily's problem was he did not know when he was beaten unless a Mason Pearson hairbrush was involved. He had sufficient self-esteem to pursue someone highly desirable but lacked the confidence to bring the situation to a successful conclusion.

The great Australian professional punter Eric Connolly coined the motto "money lost nothing lost, confidence lost everything lost". It was this winning confidence which eluded Gaily in matters of the heart.

However, as a Marxist Gaily knew all human behaviours are socially conditioned. Therefore self-confidence is an acquired trait. Gaily strove to acquire this characteristic so fundamental to success in all areas of life.

Winning breeds confidence. The development of professional sport at an elite level has provided the general population with an insight into the psychology of winning.

Gaily's betting was on the up and up. However, was it yet another winning streak only to be followed by the inevitable losing run? No, this was inspired betting.

Oscar Wildly described Racquel as his muse. Now Gaily too was able to draw inspiration from his love of Racquel. As Colleen had truthfully stated there was plenty of Racquel to go around.

Wildly was not jealous of other men's affections for Racquel – rather drawing vicarious titillation from such situations. Why then should not Gaily derive inspiration from the same source as the latter-day dandy?

As had been the case with his first grand passion Colleen Gaily's main motivation was to generate a high income in pursuit of a high maintenance woman.

The inspiration he derived from Racquel was clearly of a higher quality than that provided by Colleen. His betting had finally attained a genuinely professional standard.

Only two bookmakers in the Sydney ring were prepared to take him on: Luke Henry and Warren Bird. The rest were too scared to set him for the amounts he requested.

His mother's death had provided him with the capital and turning fifty had provided him with the maturity to succeed.

Oscar Wildly had also been a successful punter although he had played the stock-market rather than the horses. Gaily envisioned himself following in Wildly's footsteps in more ways than one.

Gaily adopted a favourite slogan of Wildly's: "To the glory of the warrior, the good luck of the gambler".

Apart from his love of Racquel, Gaily had two other sources from which he derived additional confidence. These were boxing and dancing.

For years Gaily had wanted to attend classes at Sydney's Fighting Works gym. However, shift work had precluded him from including these in his fitness routine. His leaving the paid workforce created the opportunity to pursue this adventurous new goal.

The gym proved to be everything he had hoped for and more. He was able to surround himself with positive and successful people. The gym's coaches had all participated in their various disciplines at an elite level.

Wednesday morning classes were conducted by Graham Peters. Peters was in his mid-thirties and over the years had held eight world titles in jujitsu and kickboxing. The Wednesday class was a boxing class and Peters was accomplished in this discipline as well. In fact he would go on to win the New South Wales heavyweight title.

Those who have succeeded at an elite level in sport understand the psychology of winning. The workings of the human mind are now so well understood as to be able to be programmed as one would programme any other computer.

By adopting Peters as his coach, personal trainer and mentor Gaily was able to gain an insight into the mind of one of the world's most successful athletes.

Because of the disciplines in which he had specialised Peters was better known overseas than in his native Australia. Over a career spanning almost twenty years Peters had travelled the world in pursuit of his titles.

His classes were interspersed with little comments which only hinted at the knowledge he had acquired at first hand. It was in one-on-one personal training sessions Gaily really got to know the bloke.

Boxing training largely revolves around high intensity interval training as boxing involves fighting rounds between which the combatants receive breaks. The personal training sessions would therefore mimic a fight by involving spurts of high intensity training between which Gaily would rest and be regaled by Peters' voluminous stock of anecdotes, pithy one-liners and homespun philosophy. Gaily fed off the success of his mentor and applied Peters' knowledge and wisdom to the profession of punting. It worked.

Gaily's other source of inspiration proved to be his dancing teacher.

Racquel had quickly come to recognise Gaily's introverted personality as a major flaw. If like attracts like then introverts attract other introverts.

To convert a middle-aged introvert into an extrovert is no mean feat. Racquel's suggestion to Gaily as to how to achieve this transformation was simple: learn to dance.

Racquel would come to regret having made this suggestion. Gaily became so enamoured of his dancing teacher he would spend tens of thousands of dollars on lessons: money Racquel asseverated would have been better spent on her.

Gaily had always understood the Murray Arthurs Dance Studios to be synonymous with the art of dance. Thus, when the beautiful Racquel made her fateful suggestion it was to the Murray Arthurs Studio in Sydney's C.B.D. Gaily turned.

The young lady charged with the onerous task of teaching Gaily was Kath Middleton.

At the time Kath was nineteen years old. Her appearance was that of an Australian version of Marilyn Monroe. Her blue eyes were the size of dinner plates and her golden blonde hair cascaded down her back and over her shoulders unless pulled back in a ponytail or put up for formal occasions. Her figure was a full hourglass and her pins those of a young dancing teacher who spent many hours per week twirling around a dance floor to the admiration of her onlookers. Her skirts and dresses were provocatively short and on warm days such as are so often experienced in Sydney her legs bare.

Upon being introduced to Miss Middleton Gaily's mind was cast back more than twenty years to the young Colleen.

After a short discussion with one of the studio's supervisors he extracted his cheque book from the "man bag" Racquel had helped him choose at David Jones.

He handed the supervisor a cheque for just over ten thousand dollars then jokingly asked Miss Middleton what it was again she taught. Gaily would always be a soft touch for a beautiful blonde.

The difference between the dance studio and any previous experience in the course of Gaily's life was that at the dance studio there were clear boundaries in place.

A sign on the studio wall spelled out "fraternisation between teachers and students is strictly forbidden". In the jungle that Gaily was used to frequenting there were no such rules.

At the dance studio Gaily would be safe from himself. As a gentleman he had no problem with respecting boundaries which reinforced basic civility and respect for women. Here he could come to enjoy the company of a very beautiful and very young woman free from the pressures created in an overtly sexual situation.

The dance studio provided the opportunity for Gaily to speak with and touch in an appropriate manner his teacher – but no more.

He found the dancing teacher to be possessed of all the positive human attributes and none of the negative ones. Her charm, wit, intelligence, beauty, vivacity and ethnicity combined to make the perfect package in his eyes. Only her age and the role she performed made her unattainable. This was good as it would ensure the longevity and the uniqueness of their relationship.

Gaily now had two muses: Racquel and Miss Middleton. One would seek to destroy him for personal gain, the other would teach him rumba, foxtrot, waltz, swing, cha-cha and tango.

Finally, Gaily was living the dream. Swimming in Sydney's beautiful outdoor pools, working out at Fighting Works gym or running in the magnificent public park the Domain were his choices as to how to begin each day.

Three days a week he would dance with Miss Middleton. Fridays were devoted to doing the form, Saturday was race day.

The Resch's at the Star had never tasted better. Still he wanted Racquel to share this wonderful lifestyle he had created.

Again in emulation of Oscar Wildly Gaily had become something of a dandy. The Australian dandy always wore tailored Dom Bagnato suits. The suits were always set off by beautiful silk ties with a racing theme.

Mistress Claudette was enamoured of dancing and accompanied him to the dancing studio. She accused him of dressing to impress Miss Middleton. Of course the shrewd Frenchwoman was correct.

Racquel and Miss Middleton inspired Gaily to lift his standards. Attention to detail at a personal level was akin to the "one per centers" sporting coaches speak of as being the difference between winning and losing.

The old world charm of the studio suited Gaily. Here the prefixes "Mister", "Mrs" and "Miss" were still in use. A young workmate at Bear Park Pool had described Gaily as a political radical but a social conservative. Just as had been Mistress Claudette's observation this too was most perspicacious on the part of the young fellow.

Gaily detested the crass Americanised society in which he lived. The vulgarity of the lumpenised masses made him angry but it was an impotent anger which he usually successfully suppressed. It could find no political expression so was therefore pointless. The American ruling class had won the day but it would prove a pyrrhic victory as humanity descended into oblivion.

Despite this gloomy backdrop Gaily continued to find great joy in his racing and dancing – or at least the company of his beautiful teacher.

Like dance racing is old-fashioned: the most old-fashioned of the mainstream sports. Its adherence to tradition flies in the face of the commercialisation of elite cricket and the football codes.

It was at the racecourse Gaily felt most comfortable. In his bespoke suits and with his large betting bank he was someone.

His other source of comfort was his new place of domicile. In order to surround himself with his parents' belongings he had moved into a large two bedroom flat overlooking the water in Sydney's eastern suburbs.

Here he had a vast library housed in timber book cases, the dining and lounge suites handcrafted more than fifty years previous, display cases filled with Waterford crystal and Wedgwood and to top it off a queen size bed hand-picked by Racquel.

During one of her softer moments Racquel had con-descended to visit the David Jones department store and assist him in selecting a bed.

As usual on this occasion Racquel had cast a large shadow in the form of Colleen and no, she never actually agreed to share the bed with him. The fact remained the bed was an ongoing reminder of Racquel.

Similarly the flat into which Gaily moved was in the same building as that in which Colleen had lived for ten years. The ghost of Christmas past haunted him along with the ghost of Christmas present. The only problem with Christmas present was her stockings were not at the foot of the bed of her choosing.

Gaily sublimated his sexual energy into dancing and punting, dousing the flames with copious quantities of Resch's. He would have liked to have doused the old flame with something slightly more flammable.

Once a month he visited Mistress Claudette. The funny little Frenchwoman would spank him in a most enthusias-tic manner then provide him with hand relief.

"It is noth-ing," Mistress Claudette would say of the happy ending.

Her liberal attitude towards providing a service to a paying client was in stark contrast to Racquel's indiffer-ence. Even Colleen had commented about Racquel's lack of enthusiasm – making specific reference to her reluc-tance to touch Gaily's person in any way. It was a pity Gaily could not find Mistress Claudette sexually attractive but his sole focus in this regard was on Racquel.

Despite his preference for Racquel Gaily still treated

Mistress Claudette with respect. One thing which set her apart from other sex workers was her lack of avarice. This accounted for her lack of material success as these women are invariably hard-nosed businesswomen.

Occasionally after dancing they had gone for a late lunch and Mistress Claudette would refuse payment for her time. On another occasion the French mistress accompanied him to the races. Gaily had to insist on her accepting payment for escort services. Racquel, Colleen and others would have insisted on payment merely for the provision of their company. Racquel in particular viewed her payments as appearance money – no further service being required to be provided.

Gaily discussed the respective merits of Racquel and Mistress Claudette with his small circle of close acquaintances. Despite presenting the merits of the two women in a manner favourably biased in its depiction of Racquel all agreed the Frenchwoman to be the better choice.

With many of his acquaintances he could not make specific reference to money changing hands but of his aunt, his uncle, his lovely young dancing teacher, the blokes at the gym, the pub and the swimming pools – none of these people were fools. These people could see Gaily setting himself up for a pratfall but he himself remained oblivious.

He continued to enjoy great success at the track and made plans to revisit England in July. Then something totally unexpected occurred.

Colleen sent him an email. Oscar Wildly was dead.

Wildly's extensive drug use was common knowledge. In fact his flouting of it provided an excellent source of self-publicity. He had written at length about the subject in his autobiography.

His tales of debauchery had made his book a best-seller.

The success had led to a stage play being produced. Ironically Wildly died of what was a suspected drug overdose on the play's opening night.

Gaily's first thoughts were for Racquel. Gaily had intended to meet Wildly but now this obviously would never occur. Racquel would be severely shaken by the loss of her intimate friend.

Slowly but surely a version of events emerged from twelve thousand miles away. Apparently Wildly had taken a "speedball": a cocktail of heroin and cocaine. Racquel had entered his flat to find him lying in a pool of his own blood.

A coronial enquiry would be conducted to which Racquel would be called as a witness. Various theories were emerging as to Wildly's state of mind at the time of his death. He may have been suffering from depression.

"Who knows?" thought Gaily.

With Colleen and the Internet as his two sources of information Gaily knew he was guaranteed a garbled mish-mash of fact and fiction.

The one person whom he wanted to hear from remained silent: Racquel. Colleen remained her mouthpiece. Gaily would often wonder how much of what Colleen attributed to Racquel was actually derived from Racquel and how much was the product of Colleen's fertile imagination. Colleen and Racquel did not maintain regular communication. They were occasional partners for the purpose of fleecing Gaily.

Colleen was not one to remain sentimental for very long. Wildly's death presented an opportunity for the main chance- which would not present itself too often. Colleen seized it with all the greed and avarice of which Gaily knew her to be capable.

After a week of mourning the ultimatum arrived. Wildly's death had heightened Racquel's profile and placed her time at a premium. Any escort work conducted by Racquel would be at a rate of one thousand pounds per session. Of course Colleen's rates for organising these treats would be charged commensurately.

Gaily knew Colleen's and Racquel's form pretty well by this time. Colleen would have at least have run it fleetingly past Racquel, at worst acting off her own bat in full knowledge no one would object to an overnight doubling of their appearance money.

The whole business was worded in what was now Colleen's standard terse and rude manner where communication with Gaily was concerned. It was conveyed via the impersonal conduit of the Internet.

He was being presented with a fait accompli: take it or leave it mug. Reluctantly he agreed to the increase in rates. Racquel could replace Gaily with a default admirer tomorrow: that much he knew. Colleen had her own agenda with a game of brinkmanship designed to destroy Gaily's relationship with Racquel while at the same time ruining him financially.

They negotiated times and places for rendezvous while Gaily was in England. Colleen made a huge point of the fact that her flat was going to be utilised as a meeting place for Gaily and Racquel. Her tone was increasingly nasty to the point of being vile. Even for a thousand pounds plus food and drink she could not contain her rage at the younger woman having usurped her place in Gaily's affections.

It would have been so much easier had Racquel agreed to see Gaily on a one-on-one basis. Colleen's procurement fee would have paid for a five star suite with money left over. For procurement fee it was: Racquel was unable to tee up her own appointments so had to have a second party perform her secretarial duties.

Colleen's presence was neither desired not appreciated but the provision of her place of domicile gave her bargaining power in continuing to make herself indispensable.

The negotiating of sessions was a game of cat and mouse. Even without Colleen's agenda Gaily had to weigh up the cost of having to see the two women together with his desire to see one of them alongside his detestation of the other. The death of Oscar Wildly meant Wildly's flat was off limits and Racquel was so secretive about her place of domicile it was pointless to suggest they meet there.

Gaily had booked his airfares and accommodation months prior to Wildly's death. Having not anticipated the increase in rates he had allowed himself a two month stay.

Gaily was increasingly desirous of knowing if there was any possibility of a meaningful long-term relationship with Racquel. Colleen had strung him along by suggesting he had moved one closer to the head of the queue with Wildly's death.

While Gaily could not have anticipated Wildly's death what he could now anticipate was the fact Racquel would be in a very fragile state. He undertook to cut her a lot of slack.

When his mother had died Gaily had felt an urgent need to acquire the wife or girlfriend he could suddenly now afford. Racquel was of his preferred ethnicity, age and social class, was possessed of great beauty and intellect and had a ready-made daughter who could eventually be his heiress.

Colleen having had more than twenty years' experience pressing Gaily's buttons thought she knew exactly what she was doing when facilitating their introduction.

"You was so depressed" had been her words at the time.

Colleen had not foreseen the extent to which Gaily would be smitten by Racquel nor her own being slighted and the reaction it would evoke.

A year after their initial meeting Racquel and Gaily were to be reunited in the little flat Colleen referred to as Chez Colleen.

If cutting Racquel some slack involved him accepting Racquel being even less responsive to his overtures then so be it. Gaily rationalised the situation by assuming someone traumatised by death would draw into themselves. Even an extrovert like Racquel could be forgiven this natural response.

In reality despite protestations to the contrary Racquel had already acquired a new boyfriend. Paddy McGinty had been sniffing around prior to Wildly's death and did not wait for the corpse to be cold before jumping into his bed.

This was unbeknown to Gaily who proceeded to fork out two thousand quid a pop plus the cost of meals and drinks for little more than luncheon companions.

Gaily was learning through harsh experience the Law of Diminishing Returns which applies in the sex industry. Beyond a certain point one received less and less for one's money until one is forking out vast amounts for virtually no return.

Having Colleen facilitate their liaisons did not help matters. The woman was incapable of organising anything of a varied or enjoyable nature but still insisted on asserting her authority thus making herself indispensable and avoiding redundancy. Racquel was Colleen's meal-ticket and Colleen was in the habit of savouring every morsel when at a banquet paid for by Gaily.

Racquel suggested the three of them go to Paris. This was quite out of the blue and displayed refreshing initiative from her. Gaily hesitated because of the additional expense which would undoubtedly be incurred. However, he need not have worried as the implementation of the suggestion was left to Colleen. Needless to say they never made it to Paris.

Colleen suggested they go to Eastbourne – a little town not far from Brighton. Colleen apparently had a favourite haunt there. Neither Gaily nor Racquel had any objection but then Colleen backpedalled by saying it would be too cold for Racquel by late afternoon.

Gaily grasped at some means of adding variety to their activities in order to maintain Racquel's interest. Somewhat cheekily he suggested a trip to the local nudist beach but Racquel suddenly adopted a facade of false modesty at the suggestion she remove her clothes.

Even a trip on the little train which runs along part of the Brighton seafront proved too difficult. Colleen again used Racquel's delicacy as an excuse.

The closest they got to Paris in fact was Brighton's French restaurant Cote. By the time Racquel found her way to Brighton from London there would often only be time for a quick drink then it was a Streamline cab to Cote. Gaily was bored and frustrated, Racquel merely bored.

The one outing out of the ordinary they shared was a day at Brighton races. Gaily hosted a table at the Ladies' Day meeting. He was certainly surrounded by a bevy of beauty with Racquel and a selection of the girls who had posed for the magazine project.

Gaily was unfamiliar with English racing form so bet only in Minties. A tip from an English barman at Sydney's Rosehill racecourse resonated with him.

"Topweights in the sprints at Brighton," the fellow had advised.

By adding a few little modifications Gaily was able to

tip his table most of the card to show a handsome profit in percentage terms for anyone who bothered to follow his selections. Such were his analytical abilities he could now walk onto any racecourse in the world and not do too much damage.

Racquel almost completely ignored him all day. Gaily continued to cut her slack because of Wildly's recent death but it was a bit rich.

At one stage one of the girls said to Racquel, "I don't know what you're being paid but you go over and talk to him".

The main attraction of the day for Racquel was the ladies' toilet. She had palled up with one of the other girls to powder their noses on a regular basis.

In order to be on time Racquel had stayed the night at Colleen's. Gaily found out there was a drug dealer plying his trade from a neighbouring flat. Colleen was a terrible influence.

Despite this she had got more of the action than had Gaily. What little role play activity had occurred served only to isolate him further from Racquel.

On several occasions Racquel had apparently allowed Colleen to spank her behind closed doors. Gaily had been left to listen to the punishment then saw the evidence in the form of Racquel's glowing red buttocks peeking out from under high-cut knickers.

Any spankings he received were increasingly designed to inflict pain rather than measured punishment.

Colleen knew how to gradually warm the backside of the recipient of a spanking. This should always be done by hand prior to one of a variety of implements being employed to take the act of discipline to the next stage. In Colleen's case though she could no longer be bothered.

What spankings Gaily received were designed to inflict maximum pain with minimum pleasure. They were acts of sadistic cruelty verging on assault as he was in no way a masochist.

Gaily copped it sweet as he did not wish to jeopardise the tenuous relationship with Racquel.

The mental aspect of their sessions was just as bad. Colleen knew full well what Gaily required but derived perverse pleasure from its denial. Racquel followed Colleen's lead thus learning to despise her classmate as someone to be contemptuously ridiculed and denigrated. Colleen was succeeding in poisoning Racquel's mind against him.

Gaily could see no way out of this toxic environment. He wanted Racquel but had to eliminate Colleen from the equation to have any chance.

He confronted Racquel and asked if she was prepared to see him on a one-to-one basis. Racquel refused his request and conveyed it to Colleen. This gave Colleen ammunition for an abusive confrontation with Gaily to try to provoke him into a pointless, unwinnable argument. He just walked away.

His fleeting association with the pyramid company Herbal Death had made him aware of "hard selling" techniques. A key component of the technique involved two salesmen confronting a potential customer. Two on one gives the two a psychological advantage over the one. They are able to bully and bluff from different angles until the victim is reduced to such a state as to part with their money just to get rid of the salesmen.

Police interrogations can run along similar lines with the use of the "good cop/bad cop" method of interview.

Gaily knew full well it was a similar story where Colleen and Racquel were concerned. Gaily wanted Racquel,

Racquel wanted money and Colleen wanted revenge. It was a simple equation.

Gaily accepted Racquel's ostensible loyalty to Colleen but made a point of using the word "toxic" to describe Colleen's relationship with them. It was now Gaily's stubbornness and ego as much as love for Racquel which would facilitate their ongoing relations until finally Gaily could take no more.

Colleen had always been good at ingratiating herself with people. Wildly's death had made Racquel particularly vulnerable to false friends and Colleen had taken full advantage of the situation. If Gaily wanted to see Racquel it would be in the company of Colleen or not at all. Reluctantly Gaily accepted his fate.

Occasional fleeting moments of pure joy made it tolerable and heartened him in his quest for the elusive heart of the fair Racquel. He felt genuine sympathy for her loss and sought to cheer her up with acts of kindness – such as continuing to pay her in multiples of a thousand pounds for her company. She had lost weight with her famous curves temporarily diminished and an occasional smile or laugh, a pout or wink and of course an occasional flash of her knickers was all the return on his money he expected or would receive.

Colleen's payments on the other hand he viewed simply as procurement fees.

Apart from grief Colleen also provided blarney to give Gaily an occasional whiff of hope where Racquel was concerned.

As well as reinforcing his having moved closer to the front of the queue with the death of Wildly her other words of encouragement pertained to his permanent place of residence.

"Racquel loves Sydney. She would like to live there four months a year were it possible," Colleen told Gaily.

Racquel rarely spoke to Gaily, choosing just to look good for him on their public forays. As a former top model Racquel did indeed always present well. Whether or not she ever uttered the words as stated by Colleen was another matter. Something may have been lost in translation.

The more likely statement was along the lines of Colleen saying to Racquel, "I'd like to go to Sydney in January. Would you come with me?"

Gaily knew Racquel did like Sydney. This much she had told him. To make her happy would give him great pleasure. With an eye to the future it would also get her away from the London party scene of which she was an integral part.

Gaily was not good at being assertive and had no desire to act in a controlling manner. However, he envisaged Racquel eventually destroying herself in the same manner as Wildly. To save her from herself in his more delusional moments he visualised Racquel relocating to Sydney to start a new life afresh.

When Colleen heard of this latest scheme she moved quickly to nip it in the bud citing price as its main source of impracticability.

"You would have to provide permanent accommodation, fly Racquel's daughter and dog over and pay private school fees. You simply could not afford to do it. Then there would be overseas holidays and a regular allowance to keep her in the manner to which she is accustomed. It's out of the question."

Gaily had made the mistakes of letting Colleen have a pretty fair idea as to the extent of his inheritance and the extent of his fondness for the new love to which she had introduced him. He had also let slip the fact he had included her in his will to which her response had been to grab as much of his estate while they both still lived.

The irony was he could have afforded to relocate Racquel had he made the offer when first they met. Now all he could do was perpetuate the toxic triangular relationship by flying both women to Sydney during the Australian summer. This was exactly what Colleen wanted and Racquel would tag along for the ride.

It was just a matter of the duration of their visit later in the year or early in the New Year and where they would stay. Gaily had again allowed himself to be manipulated by a past mistress—in more than one sense of the term.

On the basis of future favours to be conferred Gaily parted with Racquel and Colleen on better terms than would otherwise have been the case.

They had a final farewell lunch at Cote. Gaily wanted more but accepted less.

Oscar Wildly had been fond of saying, "Always leave them wanting less".

Gaily was beginning to learn what he had meant.

As had become their custom Colleen condescended to see him off from the Pool Valley coach station. By way of a farewell present he gave her the bucket he had used for his hand washing during his stay. It was filled with the bits and pieces one would otherwise chuck or donate to the universe. Shampoo and conditioner would be utilised, most other items put in the rubbish skip.

Gaily was a romantic at heart and to some extent was beginning to regret the inextricable wedge Racquel had driven between him and Colleen.

There was a certain symbolism in the token farewell present. Gaily recalled with a wry smile the great Australian play Summer of the Seventeenth Doll. The title refers to the gift bestowed upon a barmaid by a holidaying shearer each year for the seventeen years of their acquaintance.

Gaily joked there would be a "summer of the seventeenth bucket". Colleen walked him to the coach station and waved him goodbye. They blew kisses in recollection of times which could never be rekindled. Old habits die hard.

Back in the real world hard also was Colleen. She had made a point of locking in arrangements for Racquel and her travelling to Sydney the following January.

Both women wanted to celebrate Christmas at home with family then escape to the warmth of Australia as quickly as possible. With this guaranteed the three parted company.

Back in Sydney Gaily was able to revert to type. Whilever he had a quid in his pocket his was an enviable if somewhat hedonistic lifestyle.

Miss Middleton was loath to discuss his love life—real or imagined—with him. They had developed a good rapport in their year as teacher and student so matters of the heart were not completely taboo.

Miss Middleton had shared her own hopes and dreams with Gaily but found the notion of middle-aged people having amorous relations hard to cop. Even the nine year age difference between Gaily and Racquel the young teacher found frankly a little creepy. He was after all the same age as her parents – a point regularly made to ensure he kept his distance on matters not directly related to dance.

Miss Middleton nonetheless acted in the role of part-time therapist as well as dancing teacher. Colleen and Racquel placed Gaily under enormous financial and psychological pressure. Gaily made the mistake of projecting his own insecurities onto others. Therapy for middle-aged bachelors was not part of Miss Middleton's job description. Mature beyond her years the young woman merely made the point to him that she preferred to work for her money. The dancing teacher had picked it in one then proceeded to teach her student his steps in line with her role as his teacher.

Graham Peters was less subtle. At the gym Gaily could speak more openly about what was occurring. With a woman he would gild the lily for the sake of her sensibilities. The act of a man paying for the company of women will never be completely accepted - particularly by women. At the gym he could speak man to man.

The heavyweight champion was a man of the world.

"F*** them off" was Peters' succinct advice.

At the track it was the same story. Gaily was at once in love but also under immense pressure. He had difficulty retaining what Peters termed his "game face".

The bookmakers and their clerks of his acquaintance also expressed their concern. The bookies had seen men like Gaily come and go over the years. The big bank, the beautiful fast women – then nothing: they had seen it all before.

The funny thing was everyone who was familiar with Gaily's predicament felt Mistress Claudette was a better match. Although they were not aware of her exact line of work they discerned her to be less avaricious than Racquel. The men who had met her when she had accompanied Gaily to the races found her attractive. Although he always presented a case biased in favour of Racquel when speaking of the women in his life his words did not ring true with his interlocutors.

The good luck of the gambler continued to manifest

itself to the glory of the warrior Gaily. He immersed himself in activity in anticipation of again seeing Racquel in the New Year.

He attempted to open an account with one of Sydney's biggest rails bookmakers only to be told, "You're going to win and I don't want you winning off me".

He received birthday and Christmas cards from Colleen and Racquel. They received cards from him. Then it was time to renew auld acquaintance.

"The ladies" as Miss Middleton nicknamed them were only to be in Sydney for three weeks. Gaily therefore had to make the most of their time just as they would make the most of his money.

He went to the airport to meet them. Racquel had been writing a column – or having a column written in her name – in a men's magazine.

Gaily held the latest copy aloft as his guests emerged from the arrivals lounge. Racquel rarely appreciated Gaily's quirky larrikin humour.

Racquel managed a slight smile for him – enough to make his heart miss a beat. Colleen was her usual grumpy self – a circumstance not improved by Gaily's undue attention to Racquel.

They got a cab from the airport to the hotel where the ladies (heretofore we shall adopt Miss Middleton's epithet) were staying. The Diamant is in Sydney's Kings Cross area which Racquel had said reminded her of Soho. At least Colleen had said this was Racquel's opinion in her role as Racquel's conduit.

The reason they got a cab was ostensibly because Racquel did not "do" public transport. Again Gaily knew this as Colleen had told him as much.

Racquel did not speak directly to Gaily very much but

in public she always played her role to a tee. The former model always flaunted her athletic curves in short dresses or miniskirts and revealing necklines.

On what was her second visit to Sydney Racquel really made an effort to please as well as tease Gaily.

They went swimming and attended gym and aqua aerobics classes together. As well as the mandatory lunches in posh restaurants Racquel provided Gaily with a real girlfriend experience.

He was learning to live in the now: savouring every moment of this wonderful experience. He recalled the words of the song Colleen had played on one occasion in England:

"Don't stop thinking about tomorrow;
Yesterday's gone, yesterday's gone"

This was good for his ego as well. When Racquel accompanied him to Bear Park Pool his former workmates watched Gaily and Racquel swim with a mixture of admiration and envy; not that Racquel was much of a swimmer but she looked good and that was what mattered most to both Racquel herself and the men in her life. Racquel would freely admit all the gym classes she participated in (often two per day) were for reasons of pure vanity.

Gaily and the ladies visited both Bear Park and Boy Charlton Pools. While Gaily and Racquel swam Colleen looked on like some matriarchal figure.

Gaily cast his mind back almost twenty years to a younger, much smaller Colleen doing laps of breaststroke with her head out of the water in the pool at the Eastern and Oriental Hotel in Penang. What a stunner she had been in her black bikini with her long blonde hair trailing behind her. Now here was Racquel in her black one piece. His present was haunted by his past but on this visit Colleen seemed to have accepted her role as second fiddle to Racquel with a good grace. Colleen even went so far as to mention eventually breaking from the relationship thus giving Gaily hope of one day yet having Racquel to himself.

The most touching experience for Gaily occurred when the ladies came to his flat to perform housekeeping duties.

The flat was untidy but not dirty. It merely required the female touch.

Colleen's contribution was to have Gaily pour her a glass of champagne, go uninvited into his bedroom and collapse onto his bed. From this vantage point she was able to yell orders and smear makeup onto Gaily's bed linen.

An initial burst of energy consisted in telling Gaily to chuck out everything in sight. It was a tempting offer which required a great deal of restraint.

Colleen soon lost interest allowing Racquel to take charge. Gaily's flat really was magnificently furnished and his vast library gave his pad the air of being the home of a successful middle class intellectual. He hoped Racquel would be suitably impressed.

Colleen correctly observed that having Racquel there was like having one's own interior designer. Racquel cast her beautiful blue and expert eye over the lounge and dining rooms.

The furniture had been put in place by removalists more intent on getting the job done as quickly as possible than facilitating Gaily's amenity. Suggestions for altering the configuration of the furniture were made with Gaily obediently implementing them.

A sore point was the collection of boxes of memories stacked against a wall. They needed to be sorted through with what was unrequired being chucked or sold.

The clothes rack was relocated with items folded just so and placed in drawers. Racquel folded items of underwear as once Gaily's mother had done. It was a moving moment for him.

Gaily had had both a professional cleaner and Mistress Claudette in to assist on previous occasions. He had wanted the place to look not too shabby for the arrival of the ladies – Racquel in particular. Still Colleen was able to find fault by running a finger over a dusty bathroom ledge. This constant fault-finding would become increasingly prevalent as the months wore on and Colleen sought to undermine Gaily through ridicule.

Finally the job was done. In two hours Racquel had waved her magic wand to at least begin to transform Gaily's pad into a home.

Colleen had the temerity to demand an appropriate thank you to Racquel and herself for services rendered. Colleen had not so much as even been bothered to remove the bottle she had emptied. She left Gaily to take out the empty and change the linen then had herself removed by cab to continue drinking in her hotel room.

If Gaily had been wavering he was back in love with Racquel well and truly after her housekeeping performance. Racquel's parting advice had been to hire a cleaning lady but the only cleaning lady Gaily ever wanted was Racquel.

Gaily's sense of ebullience did not last long. The following day Colleen had another fall leaving her wheelchair-bound for the last few days of her stay. Brilliant blue sunny skies were replaced by a pall of grey gloomy clouds.

Colleen's mood did not improve when her travelling companion abandoned her in her hour of need.

Racquel negotiated the hiring of a wheelchair and

deemed this her contribution to Colleen's ongoing welfare. Having made this sacrifice of her time Racquel then proceeded to go shopping.

Gaily placated his old friend's anger with copious quantities of champagne. Then he too went to the department store where he was most likely to accidentally run into Racquel.

No wonder they say "There's no other store like David Jones", he thought as he just happened to pass through the Alannah Hill concession.

At the airport Colleen again took French leave of Gaily. Having had herself wheeled onto the plane by a member of the airline's staff another awkward situation ensued when Gaily and Racquel were left to make small talk.

Thankfully Racquel was able to amuse herself by looking at mobile telephone covers and junk jewellery.

Gaily was able to safely agree with her when asked if he thought pink would be an appropriate choice of colour for a phone cover.

He had learnt "yes" to be the most useful reply to her questions. If only Racquel had been equally acquiescent.

Once more their stop/start relationship was put on hold. The three participants in the unwieldy triangle would utilise the intervening six months in different ways.

Racquel would play the vamp with other men. Colleen would fume and plot against Gaily. Gaily would fantasise and seek to win enough money to keep his dreams alive.

Unbeknown to Gaily Paddy McGinty had moved into Oscar Wildly's flat from where he ran his small publishing business. McGinty had been a friend of Wildly's but was preparing to jump into his bed when he so conveniently died.

McGinty's existence had not been mentioned by either

of the ladies with Colleen having told Gaily Racquel was not interested in acquiring a new boyfriend. In fact with Racquel having passed the age of forty the youthful middle-aged woman was constantly on the lookout for men prepared to fund the lifestyle she had created for herself in her twenties.

Colleen knew she had to make the most of her association with Racquel. As Gaily was to find out nothing lasts forever.

A prisoner in her own flat for the rest of the English winter Colleen had little to occupy her mind apart from exacting revenge on Gaily while maintaining their links with Racquel. Colleen was an intelligent largely self-taught woman but had become bitter and twisted with the passing of the years.

There was only one way to hurt Gaily and that was to ruin him financially which in turn would mean his losing all ties with Racquel.

Colleen sat in her flat with her injured foot elevated and her third bottle of cheap sparkling wine beside her. Expensive champagnes were now reserved for when she was in the company of Gaily—which was now only when he was in the company of Racquel.

Colleen's decision to join the ranks of cheap wine drinkers had not been taken lightly. It was a case of economic necessity.

The more Colleen drank the more she saved. It was just like Gaily brewing his own beer years prior. Unfortunately the more Colleen drank the angrier she became as well.

Colleen was approaching her sixtieth year. Her once breathtaking looks and figure were but a memory. In her anger she wished the same fate upon Racquel.

In addition to drinking inferior wine Colleen had been forced to obtain social services in order to maintain rent payments. Had the welfare state not supported her her only option would have been to move into the family home with her brother and mother. For Colleen this would have constituted the ultimate fall from grace.

Colleen's only other source of income was Gaily. Like all greedy people motivated by negative motives Colleen's attitude to money had always been short term.

There had been a time when she could sling off at people on social services. Now Colleen had joined their number.

Colleen's business no longer existed. Her attempt at becoming a professional writer had failed. Desperately she cast around for a means of regaining the champagne lifestyle she like Racquel had enjoyed for most of her adult life.

There was only one thing Colleen could do under the circumstances so she did it. She sent Gaily an email saying after careful consultation with Racquel any future sessions with them would be at a rate of two thousand pounds per lady per day. Take it or leave it mug.

Knowing Racquel never answered her telephone Colleen then sent Racquel an email telling her what she had done.

The prostitute turned procuress finished her bottle of wine, congratulated herself on a good day's work and staggered off to bed.

Gaily had foreseen Colleen's ploy so was unsurprised by the contents of the email. The man who pays the band calls the tune. Colleen's theme song was "Money, Money, Money" and Racquel could still if need be get away with a white jumpsuit.

The almost three years since his mother's death had taken their toll on Gaily's capital but he chose to continue to pursue Racquel despite the increasingly onerous terms and conditions.

After a wonderful first year on the punt he had upped the stakes and started to bet to prices rather than betting level/flat stakes. Betting to the bookmakers' prices involves weighting one's bets according to available odds. The theory is that the market reflects reality therefore the shorter the price the greater the runner's chances.

This is true within a certain range of prices but when applied to odds on shots is a disaster as odds on favourites have a notoriously poor strike rate.

Gaily knew all this from his studies of Don Scott's works going back thirty years but had remade mistakes and relearnt the basics at great expense.

Although not unexpected the email from Colleen had the effect of intensifying the pressure he felt to generate an income of multiple hundreds of thousands of dollars/pounds per year.

Racquel had hinted at the income her prospective husband would have to generate when referring to a fellow who "only earned one hundred thousand pounds a year – it's not as if it's five hundred thousand or anything".

Warning bells should already have been sounding when at the races one day Gaily had won eight hundred dollars.

"One shoe," came Racquel's dismissive observation.

Gaily felt the need for a break from racing. Having months prior booked flights and accommodation he packed his bags and flew business class to England. Nothing is too good for the workers.

As an aspiring professional Gaily was still developing the mentality required to be a successful businessman. He was still staying at the same tired old digs in Brighton at which he had stayed when he was broke.

Hundreds of thousands of dollars and pounds were being dissipated on women who expected to travel first class all the way at his expense.

It was good for him to start spending a bit on himself for a change. The truth was he had been ill-prepared for inheritance and Colleen in particular had taken full advantage of the situation.

He at least knew what to expect from that quarter. He could do without the barely concealed contempt, the psychological games and the increasingly blatant grab for money. In reality he would prefer to do without Colleen altogether with her vulgar behaviour, outlandish hats and clothes, poor personal hygiene and obese body.

Just as he had been unready for inheritance so it had taken two years to acclimatise to Racquel's presence in his life. Her beauty was intimidating, her demeanour arrogant and her life chaotic.

He had had his chance with her however slim. In her own mind she had already moved on to other conquests. If the stupid Australian was silly enough to throw ridiculous amounts of money at her only to be further hurt Racquel would accept them in her usual "couldn't care less" manner.

Graham Peters had told him he was punching above his weight and now he was on the ropes. Were he not careful he would soon be down for the count. Emotionally and financially he was drained. Far better to throw in the towel.

As he knew himself the trouble was Gaily never knew he was defeated – or at least would not admit as much. For someone with such poor self-esteem he was driven now not by ego but by the desire for self-destruction. Racquel was the ultimate femme fatale.

It was with this negative and pessimistic outlook Gaily looked to renew auld acquaintance. Of course one look at Racquel dispelled all possibility of his calling a halt to proceedings. He was in for a penny, in for a pound all right.

Their time together was all too predictable. There

would be histrionics as to whether Racquel could or could not make it down to Brighton. Then Colleen would give the Gettysburg address outlining what a favour Gaily was being granted. Reluctantly the two ladies would acquiesce to give Gaily the privilege of their company.

Gaily would be compelled to buy champagne. Racquel was a light smoker so a packet of Marlboro would be thrown in on top of the four thousand pounds in fees.

Colleen would feign her fake Belgravian accent in a perfunctory schoolmistress role. Racquel would put on her little school uniform. Gaily would be (literally) bursting with excitement: then nothing.

On a couple of occasions Racquel would spank Gaily with a hairbrush simply because she was in a bad mood. This is the least opportune time to administer corporal punishment.

Gaily would allow Racquel to spank him because it was Racquel. However, it was an unsatisfying experience made additionally annoying by the fact Colleen knew how to administer a satisfying spanking but would not direct Racquel.

Gaily's frustration was increasingly heightened. He thought back to the days at A.T.O.C. when Colleen would slowly warm him with her hand then introduce the hairbrush or paddle, gradually increasing the intensity of the punishment in direct proportion to the engorgement of the penis rubbing against her right leg.

Then when the level of pain and pleasure Gaily was experiencing had reached a crescendo he would be allowed to seek relief inside his mistress.

For the young man this had been a wonderful service provided on an almost weekly basis. It was within his budget and served to draw him out sexually and emotionally. This went on for four glorious years.

Compare this with the amateur hour service Colleen now provided. There was no comparison.

Racquel may not have known better but Colleen certainly did – choosing to withdraw her labour due to Gaily's infidelity to her.

Colleen countered with the warped logic of his possibly enjoying what one did not want. Gaily's frustration grew in inverse proportion to his erection. The occasional hard whacks dealt by Racquel had the opposite effect those administered to an already warmed backside would have had despite its being Racquel administering the punishment.

This was exactly what Colleen wanted. Gaily was paying them both large sums of money for pain without pleasure. With Colleen acting in an advisory capacity Racquel was learning how not to administer corporal punishment. Being none the wiser Racquel merely presumed Gaily to be impotent when what was required was stimulation of a slightly varied nature provided in a Colleen-free environment.

Thus, Colleen's mere presence was having a detrimental effect on Gaily's health. Not only was his sexual performance impaired but he had begun having bouts of vomiting and diarrhoea – but only at those times of the year when he was in regular contact with Colleen. When Colleen was in his life vomiting and diarrhoea would ensue. When Colleen was a safe twelve thousand miles away he would make a complete and rapid recovery.

His cholesterol and liver function tests told a similar tale. When in contact with Colleen the readings would shoot up to dangerously high levels. When they were apart the readings would normalise.

The fatty restaurant meals Colleen enjoyed only served to exacerbate Gaily's problem. On several occasions having partaken of a meal he would go into the restaurant's toilet and bring it straight back up again.

Colleen was killing him – which was her intention. For ammunition in this psychological warfare she had the services of one of the world's most desirable women. A scantily clad Racquel was dangled in front of him and there were times when he could not manage an erection no matter how willing the flesh. On those occasions his virility returned it was time for lunch.

No wonder Mistress Claudette had described Colleen as "evil".

When demanding a higher rate of pay for these dubious "services" Colleen had written to him making light of the matter. Some models wanted ten thousand pounds to get out of bed, Racquel only required two thousand to get into bed.

After two years of increasing frustration and payments Gaily saw this as just another one of Colleen's blandishments. His friends and acquaintances were telling him to walk away, his body was telling him to run away.

If only Colleen were the one to walk away things would be different. He knew Racquel had no great liking for Colleen. On one occasion Racquel had placated Gaily by saying one day Colleen would be dead. The inference was then the wedge driven between them would be removed and they would be free to finally enjoy each other's company and friendship.

Colleen's presence made such a friendship impossible. For the time being Gaily accepted this fact. However, he would not be the one to end the arrangement if this meant severing ties with Racquel.

There was nothing there but like the proverbial drowning man Gaily clung to an imaginary straw.

On the final four days of his stay he treated himself to a

five star hotel. It was about time he started spending some of his dwindling capital on himself.

Brighton's only five star hotel is the Grand. There was a time when it had lived up to its name and star rating. Like a microcosm of Brighton itself those days were long gone. In reality it was quite a nice four star hotel.

Gaily reluctantly invited the ladies into his room. Racquel was welcome, Colleen was not.

Drinks were ordered and consumed. Colleen looked for fault in Gaily's every action. The room had not been serviced and was slightly untidy. Gaily put the ubiquitous black bucket to one side and poured the champagne but it was not sufficient to placate Colleen. With every sip of the wine she became louder and more obnoxious towards him.

Racquel had taken a strong painkiller for period pain. One glass of champagne left her woozy.

To entertain themselves they took photographs of each other but the whole scenario was so staged and perfunctory as to be farcical.

Eventually Racquel fell asleep on Gaily's bed. Initially it was amusing and allowed him to take photographs of the sleeping beauty.

It soon became apparent Racquel was out for the count and any attempt at activity involving the three of them would be out of the question.

An awkward silence ensued between Colleen and Gaily. Gaily could no longer be bothered engaging Colleen in conversation so the two sat in a silence punctuated by an occasional snarling remark from Colleen attempting to incite an argument.

Racquel slept on and Gaily had no choice but to order more drinks to pass the time. Colleen became increasingly obnoxious and by the time Racquel awoke he was on the verge of having hotel security remove her from his room.

Racquel was both refreshed and apologetic. At least the girl had some manners.

They went for tea at Cote and Racquel had to rush off to catch a flight to Spain. Her departure truncated a largely forgettable and profligately expensive day.

Gaily received the usual peck on the cheek before watching his inamorata melt into the sunset.

"You can't buy love," the by then half-sozzled Colleen had laughed at him.

He paid the bill and begrudgingly slipped Colleen an additional tenner for a cab. She bagged the remaining wine for domestic consumption and left him to it.

The eternal optimist had expected at least his meagre quota of fleeting pleasure from Racquel but had been largely denied even this. He was also running horribly late for farewell drinks at the Greys.

Gaily had made the acquaintance of about a dozen regulars at the quirky little pub on what was known as "Muesli Mountain" in Brighton. They were mainly older lefties who had taken to and accepted Gaily as one of their own. Each year the Greys looked forward to its Australian pilgrim's return.

It was after eight when Gaily finally got to the pub. The following day was a working day for most of the regulars and they had come and gone.

Gaily had wanted Racquel to accompany him but Colleen had intervened and put the kibosh on the suggestion. It was a pity Racquel was incapable of speaking for herself.

The barman informed Gaily he had missed around ten people wanting to have a parting drink with him. Mark rattled off the names. They were all good and decent people whom Gaily would not now see prior to his departure.

Gaily had several nightcaps with the barman and trudged his weary way down Southover Street to his digs.

What should have been a fun day filled with joy and happiness had been ruined.

Someone was trying to send Gaily a message but he was not listening. The next morning he handed in his key at the university digs and caught a cab to Colleen's. He need not have bothered.

He went to give her the few bits and pieces left over from his visit but she ordered him to take them up the road and dispose of them in the council skip. The woman's ingratitude and rudeness knew no bounds.

It was a constant case of placating her with booze and money. They went for drinks and the snarling subsided long enough for him to be able to escape on the coach back to Heathrow.

Having flown business class he was able to be fed and watered courtesy of Sir Richard Branson. This was after running the gauntlet of goons and lesbian gropers conducting the war on terrorism at Heathrow. Being of Anglo appearance had its advantages as did wearing Dom Bagnato.

The free drinks went down well and the airline staff turned a blind eye to the Australian with the wobbly boot. Twenty-four hours on an aeroplane is a bloody long time.

Racquel was still uppermost in his mind. He wanted to know once and for all if there was some way of achieving an ongoing relationship instead of this on again, off again business.

In the back of his mind he knew the answer but it was an answer he did not like so it remained pushed to the very back of his card index file mind.

To resolve the question Gaily decided to invite the ladies to Sydney for a lengthier stay than they had previously experienced. This would enable Racquel to really savour summer in Sydney. He in turn would have to find a way of spending more time in England. How this could be done either from a logistical or a financial point of view he had no idea. Love would find a way.

"The universe will provide", as the New Agers say.

He discussed the matter with his herbalist and naturopath Kelly Waterston. Having been given Racquel's surname his lesbian friend looked Racquel up via the Internet.

"Nice tits" was Kelly's professional assessment.

It was hopeless. He just had to go for broke and see what ensued. "Broke" would always be the key word where women like Colleen and Racquel were concerned.

"Broke" was also what Gaily did not wish to become. His punting fortunes had been on the decline for the previous year or so and he was experiencing difficulties turning the situation around. Even after adjusting his staking method his strike rate was still well down on previous years. Einstein's definition of insanity again came to mind.

Gaily wrote to Colleen suggesting she and Racquel visit Sydney in January and February. A mealy-mouthed reply came back giving the appearance of extreme reluctance to accept.

Racquel was very busy and would have to be consulted. A daily allowance would be required as had previously been the case. "Sessions" (which Gaily translated to mean "luncheons") would be on a weekly basis. She would get back to him.

Gaily knew there would be no change out of one hundred thousand Aussie dollars – probably more.

The requisite initial amount for airfares and accommodation was transferred into Colleen's account as Gaily had so often transferred money to her in the past.

He had tried to keep a lid on expenses by suggesting they stay for a total of seven weeks. Allowing for the fact

Colleen – and more particularly Racquel – would want to spend Christmas and New Year in England this still meant they would be in Sydney until the final week of the Australian summer. Colleen called him a cheapskate.

Once the airfares and accommodation were assured Colleen was in a position to really up the ante in the Abuse Stakes.

As was her custom Colleen asked Gaily for a letter stating that the funds which had been transferred were a gift to cover living expenses and rent.

This was an obvious lie and Gaily was no longer prepared to lie in order to cover Colleen's enormous backside.

Somewhat cheekily he wrote back with a letter "to whom it may concern" stating the funds transferred had been for the provision of sexual services. As is often the case Gaily's larrikin humour was not appreciated.

Colleen completely overreacted. Her response was a long abusive email referring to him as an "asshole" (sic) and someone who was obviously in need of treatment for their mental illness.

Colleen then threatened to refuse to convey Racquel's travel documents to her thus ensuring her inability to travel.

One of them was mentally ill and it was not Gaily. The alarm bells were suddenly ringing loudly and clearly in Gaily's ears.

Gaily's illness was not mental but physical. It was, however, psychosomatic in origin. His vomiting and diarrhoea became more frequent and was accompanied by terrible insomnia which no amount of Resch's could overcome.

Colleen decided to give the ratchet another twist. Racquel had incurred large legal expenses as a result of Oscar Wildly's death and required an advance on the daily allowance Gaily had agreed to pay her whilst she was in

Sydney. In addition there were unpaid debts of Wildly's which required payment.

These were such blatant lies even Colleen should have blushed were her face not already a ruddy, blowzy crimson from broken capillaries.

Gaily knew Racquel had lawyer friends who would be more than happy to work pro bono in expectation of things to come. Things to come which never eventuated were Racquel's stock in trade.

Gaily also knew from discussions with his father that debts die along with the deceased.

This was one of the rare occasions when Gaily asserted himself.

"Things are different in England," Colleen retorted when he rang her.

Gaily told her Australian law was based directly upon the Westminster system. What applied in Australia would be equally valid in England.

Colleen knew whilever she had Racquel as her trump card she would have Gaily's measure.

Although caught out as a liar she simply reiterated her threat to block Racquel's ability to undertake the flight. Gaily capitulated and sent a lump sum amounting to half the allowance of two hundred dollars per day for seven weeks.

Colleen then insisted on receiving the same amount for herself as she was after all his "first wife".

Colleen's resentment was actually inflamed by Gaily's openness as to his true feelings for the self-proclaimed first wife. In his correspondence "Yours sincerely" had come to replace "Love". No fool when it came to semantics Colleen understood perfectly the intended shift in emphasis being conveyed. Words matter and Gaily always chose his carefully and precisely even if the subtle truth behind his words conveyed offence to some people.

Gaily was left not knowing whether or not Racquel was to be allowed to again visit Australia. He tried to placate matters by ringing Colleen. The call was made on his own birthday which he thought may make Colleen soften her attitude towards him. He was wrong.

After a torrent of abuse the telephone was slammed down in his ear. Ironically he had just received risqué and humorous birthday cards from Colleen and Racquel. It was at once so tokenistic and hypocritical he wondered why Colleen even bothered.

He went to the Star for his birthday party. Ghosts of his past came to haunt him and drink beer at his expense. Then they would disappear for another twelve months. His freeness with money he had not earned only served to attract spongers and fair-weather friends.

The ghosts attempted to justify their presence by attempting to be sociable. He half-listened to anecdotes of events from twenty and thirty years previous. He switched off completely when being regaled with stories about their escapades with the bargirls of Thailand.

Gaily thought back to the times when like himself they had been fit, strong, young political and trade union activists. Now in late middle age his former comrades were old men prematurely aged by decades of poor "lifestyle choices" as contemporary vernacular would now term it.

Gaily thought of Colleen and the manipulative role she was playing with regard to Racquel. He cast his mind back to the beauty she had once possessed. He flattered himself with a sense of superiority in having attempted to win Racquel while his old mates made do with low maintenance Asians, "Asia Minor" he laughed wryly to himself with regard to the bargirls' ages.

How much more appropriate to pursue a beautiful

woman in her forties like Racquel. He had taken good care of himself and with what remained of his inheritance deserved the finer things in life – such as Racquel.

The beer flowed and the conversation dried up. His old mates together with Colleen represented his past. Racquel represented his future. Having reached this happy conclusion his meditations could be transformed into actions on the morrow.

As the sun set in the west so Gaily caught a cab east. He had shaken hands with each of the ghosts and they in turn wished him "all the best".

"We should do this more often," one of them had offered – knowing full well they would not see each other for another twelve months.

The morning after the night before is accompanied by sobriety. In Gaily's case sobriety was accompanied by the stark realisation Racquel may not in fact be returning to Sydney.

He had sent her a Facebook message gently hinting a certain party may have been seeking to impede her travelling plans. Unsurprisingly there was no reply.

In the absence of any communication from England Gaily had no alternative but to simply get on with his own life. It was a fairly enviable existence largely consisting of swimming, running, dancing, drinking, the gym and the races. Why Racquel would not wish to share such a wonderful lifestyle was beyond Gaily's comprehension. The only explanation he could come up with was the toxic role being played by Colleen.

Just before Christmas he again discussed the matter with Kelly Waterston as he loaded up on supplements prior to the Christmas/New Year break.

Kelly treated the matter a little more seriously than had

initially been the case. Kelly suggested Gaily see her girl-friend Kristina Falcon in her professional capacity as a sex therapist.

Kelly and Gaily got on well. They had been neighbours back in their studio flat days. Kelly had seen the adverse effects the ladies had had on his health and hoped Kristina would be able to help Gaily resolve the situation.

Unfortunately Kelly and Kristina were about to go on holidays so Gaily would not be able to see Kristina until at least a week into the ladies' visit. He rang Kristina, made the appointment and hoped for the best in the time intervening.

Christmas can be a somewhat lonely time for people who live by themselves and Gaily was no exception.

He felt particularly vulnerable given the deafening silence emanating from England. That it was part of Colleen's psychological warfare against him he had no doubt.

On the morning of Christmas Day he went for a run in the Dom then did the form for the Boxing Day races. It was still well before midday when he cracked his first stubby of Resch's.

Gaily found Good Friday and Boxing Day the only two days of the year when he was at a loose end. His routine was thrown out of kilter and he was cooped up in the flat for most of the day. Under these circumstances the Black Dog often paid him a visit.

Instead of a sense of joy at the prospect of Racquel's impending visit he was filled with a sense of foreboding. Had Colleen booked the flights and accommodation? Would Racquel even turn up?

Gaily checked with the hotels at which he presumed they might stay. There had been a booking made at one of the hotels at which they had stayed two years prior.

This was somewhat reassuring but Gaily remained unconvinced. Seeing would be believing.

With no flight details he was unclear as to whether or not he could or should attempt to meet them at the airport. Of one thing he was certain: he had no desire to ever again see Colleen.

He felt under enormous psychological pressure. His vomiting, diarrhoea and insomnia were worse than ever. He would wake in the middle of the night screaming the word "no".

Finally, the day on which the hotel receptionist had said the ladies were due to arrive did itself arrive. It was only a few days into the New Year and one of those beautiful warm January mornings so prevalent in Sydney prior to the onset of higher humidity the following month.

Incoming flights to Sydney from London commence to arrive at around six in the morning. Gaily allowed two hours for the ladies to negotiate customs and be driven to their hotel.

At eight he rushed into the hotel foyer in expectation of seeing Racquel. Neither she nor Colleen had been sighted.

The hotel was located in an avenue just off Sydney's Kings Cross "strip".

Dejected, Gaily continued on his usual route to the nearby paper shop, supermarket and dry-cleaner. He presumed Colleen had carried out her threat to block Racquel's ability to travel. Colleen may have even pocketed the money intended for airfares.

Gaily did not care about the amount involved. It would be the last time Colleen would get a cent or a penny out of him. With regard to Racquel he had done his best and he could only but hope their paths might cross down the track.

He walked home from the shops and was gradually filled with a sense of relief. Colleen had finally been excised from his life. After five good years and twenty bad ones he could cut his losses and get out of the sordid mess.

Gaily ditched the groceries and hung up his freshly laundered shirts. He had a light snack and walked back up to the Cross to catch the train into town. Once there it would be a well-worn path to the Star for five schooners of the best Resch's in Sydney.

Just as a precaution he again checked at the hotel reception to ensure Colleen and Racquel had still not arrived. The receptionist vividly remembered both Gaily and the ladies from two years prior. Even in the Kings Cross area a hotel had rarely become witness to the drama that these three had managed to create.

"They're here and they're broke," came the pithy announcement from the receptionist. "They've gone out," she concluded in anticipation of Gaily's response.

Gaily continued on his pilgrimage to the Star but was brought to a sudden halt when out of the corner of his eye he spotted two vaguely familiar women.

One was an obese older woman draped in heavy gaudily-coloured clothes more suited to an English winter and topped off with an outlandish hat. The other was much slimmer and younger and more suitably attired- like a model in a summer fashion parade at Selfridges. It was of course Colleen and Racquel.

Racquel caught Gaily's eye far more than Colleen. He could not help himself. He ran across Darlo' Road to greet her.

The body language was terrible and the spoken word worse. Racquel drew back at Gaily's approach and Colleen intervened as if to shield her from possible attack.

Racquel was in no danger but the same cannot be said for Gaily. It was Colleen who went straight onto the offensive.

"Where were you this morning? You should have been at the airport."

"After your last email I didn't even know if you were coming," Gaily retorted.

"Miss Racquel is very upset with you," Colleen continued – speaking as was so often the case on Racquel's behalf.

Racquel took her cue.

"Yes, Charlie. You should have been at the airport. We've come all this way to not have anyone to meet us when we arrive."

There was no point in his arguing further. Colleen had played him off a break with the threat to deny Racquel her travel documents then ceasing all communications for almost a month.

Racquel had found her tongue. Colleen was happy for her to use it in the knowledge Gaily would listen to and obey Racquel whereas Colleen now had no control over Gaily unless Racquel was involved.

"Anyway, more importantly Charlie we've arrived without any money. When could we be paid the remainder of our allowances, please?"

Colleen stood by quietly knowing she was about to benefit on a dollar for dollar basis from Racquel's words.

"I have some money at home. I will need to go to the bank in town," came the meek reply.

"When can you get it to us, Charlie? We honestly do not have a penny on us. We are totally reliant on you, Charlie," Racquel said in the voice of a very experienced button pusher.

Gaily hesitated momentarily to calculate the time he

would need to go to the Star, drink what had become by then five urgently required beers, go to the bank and get back to the Cross. Colleen scowled menacingly. Racquel smiled and fluttered her eyelashes. The latter had the desired effect.

"I can be back here by four," he said.

"Good day, Charlie. We will meet you in the hotel foyer at four o'clock this afternoon to receive the balance of our allowances," came the somewhat patronising reply.

The nightmare had begun in earnest. Over the following seven weeks he would feel the life force drain from his body as the money drained from his bank account. There would be a few fleeting moments of pleasure but these would be completely overshadowed by grief.

Filled with a sense of foreboding Gaily dutifully went to the head office of his bank to withdraw the requisite funds. First cab off the rank though was the Star for the drink which refreshes.

To make matters worse Gaily had sprained his ankle at the gym.

"Bloody jump squats," he thought to himself when the injury failed to heal overnight.

He hobbled around town as best he could seeking in his mind to make a positive from a negative. With the gym and the dance studio out of bounds at least he could still swim. This would translate into more time with a swimsuit-clad Racquel.

Gaily knew Racquel did not like the amount of money he was spending on dancing as this money could have been better spent on her. He had made the mistake of telling Colleen the price of Murray Arthurs lessons and she in turn could not get into Racquel's ear quickly enough to create additional mischief.

When Gaily returned to the hotel the ladies were waiting for him. He was sufficiently well organised to be able to simply hand them each an envelope. It was a discreet business transaction – or so Gaily had intended.

Colleen tore open her envelope and frantically began counting the money. Each envelope contained four thousand, nine hundred dollars in hundred dollar notes representing a hundred dollars per day for seven weeks.

Racquel took her cue from Colleen and followed suit. Gaily sat there stunned watching two sex workers counting wads of what had formerly been his cash. They were in full view of reception staff and anyone else who may happen to wander past.

Colleen constantly sought new ways to embarrass and humiliate her old client. The inference which could also be drawn was Gaily would short-change them.

Gaily knew who was short-changing whom so was surprised when this very accusation was made.

"It's three hundred dollars short," Colleen barked at him. "Miss Racquel could you please confirm?"

Racquel turned to Gaily. Colleen always played the nasty role while Racquel was sweetness personified. These roles corresponded with how he wanted to perceive the two women so his desired perception actually reaffirmed their assumed roles in his undoing.

"Yes," cooed Raquel, "I'm afraid the little boy has not been able to count our pocket money correctly."

Gaily could not comprehend the source of his error. He looked at his accusers with a perplexed expression on his face.

"The travelling time," Colleen snapped at him. "Two days here, one day back. Miss Racquel has brought this to my attention."

Colleen had dispensed with the need for complete sentences. A few fragmentary words would suffice. In the era of email, text messages and Twitter this perfunctory, dismissive form of address had become the norm.

"Your rudeness is only exceeded by your rudeness" Gaily recalled from How To Win Friends and Influence People.

However, he said nothing apart from apologising for his error. He would have to owe them the money.

"Did you want to go for a drink?" he eventually managed in an attempt to change the subject.

"No but you could get me a bottle of pink bubbles," Colleen replied. "I see they have cheap Laurent-Perrier in the Crest."

The Crest was a nearby pub with a bottle shop.

"Like her hide to trawl the bottle shops looking for plonk," Gaily thought to himself but said nothing.

He went to the Crest for the wine. When he returned the ladies had gone to their rooms. The reception staff by then knew the score. They gave him Colleen's room number. Gaily took her the wine – expecting no thanks and receiving none. It was a war of attrition.

He desperately wanted to see Racquel but Colleen told him she was jetlagged and to ring in the morning.

"Class dismissed," Colleen told him in an attempt to inject humour into a situation which possessed none.

Her words harked back to happier times. Filled with feelings of loneliness and despair Gaily walked back to his pad for his late afternoon stubbies.

"I'll ring you in the morning," he had said.

"As you wish," came the reply.

Racquel and Colleen had at least one thing in common: they lived for the moment – "in the now" as the New Agers say. With money in their handbags they had no reason to see Gaily again until their profligacy led them to require more.

In the morning he rang the hotel and asked to be put through to Racquel. When Racquel did not answer her phone the call reverted back to the switchboard. Reluctantly he asked to be put through to Colleen.

Colleen had been temporarily appeased by the previous day's payment. Racquel had apparently gone in search of a hairdresser.

Gaily asked when they might meet for their first session. Colleen suggested the following day at eleven.

This would mean another visit to the bank. However, this time it would be worth it. Gaily felt an intense hunger for a glimpse of Racquel's knicker-clad bottom. Absence had definitely made his heart grow fonder and his memory selective.

He had taken the liberty of inviting Mistress Claudette to join them. Ideally Gaily would have preferred a one-on-one session with Racquel. However, Racquel's insecurities led to her insisting on Colleen's presence at all times when they met.

Gaily had hoped the Frenchwoman's presence would inspire Racquel to participate in their sessions more enthusiastically than would ever be the case with Colleen leading the way.

Mistress Claudette was a most enthusiastic spanker whose firm right hand also ensured a happy ending for her clients. She would provide Racquel with a positive example of what Colleen was no longer prepared or able to provide.

When Gaily informed Colleen of the invitation he had extended she said she would have to seek Racquel's approval.

Gaily gave the matter no further thought until the following morning. Upon arrival at the hotel the reception was again unable to locate Racquel for him. He was eventually directed to Colleen's room. Colleen did not beat around the bush. He was to ring Mistress Claudette and tell her her services were not required. Racquel had been deeply offended at having the value of her time equated with that of Mistress Claudette.

Gaily went to use the hotel telephone beside Colleen's bed.

"Haven't you got your mobile?" the harridan snarled.

He was being denied access to a telephone in a hotel room for which he had paid. It was one of those rare occasions when he was in fact carrying his mobile – ironically in case Racquel happened to call.

Gaily rang Mistress Claudette on her mobile. She had been on the way there but would turn around and go home. The French mistress was too polite to express anger but Gaily knew that unlike the other two women she really did need the money as she had been having difficulty just paying her rent. Gaily was very apologetic and promised to make it up to her. He could not be too specific as to the reason for the change of plan given Colleen's proximity. However, again the little Frenchwoman was not a fool.

At least he was about to see Racquel. The beautiful vamp had finally managed to find her way back from the hairdressing salon where her tresses had been washed for her by a young minion.

Racquel always presented well. Gaily's look was one of adoration when she entered Colleen's room. Racquel was so used to this his admiration went unnoticed by Racquel but was very much noticed by Colleen.

After a quick peck on the cheek it was back down to business. Gaily continued to gaze in awe at Racquel in her little white cotton sundress as he handed each of the two women an envelope containing two thousand pounds in cash.

Butter would not have melted in her mouth as Racquel counted her payment for services unrendered. The simple but expensive dress, the long shiny hair, the beautiful lightly made-up face, the lightly tanned pins, the pink heels. What was not to like? Gaily was about to discover the answer to this question.

"Charlie, there are only two thousand pounds here," Racquel began.

"Yes, that was the agreed amount for sessions," Gaily replied.

Gaily saw anger rapidly manifesting itself and despite ignorance as to the reason for this braced himself for the impending explosion.

Racquel launched into an hysterical diatribe. The basis for her attack on Gaily was an alleged agreement for all the agreed upon payments to be made in one lump sum. Racquel was screaming and sobbing at this insulting treatment of only paying her for that day. She would not be treated in this manner, had copped it from other men but would never again tolerate such disrespect. In tears Racquel ran from the room threatening to turn straight back around and return to London.

In truth it was a Royal Command performance worthy of a far greater actress then Racquel. Nevertheless it left Gaily shaken and probably more genuinely upset than the princess who had just exited stage left.

It was of course a complete set up instigated by Colleen. He turned to her. She looked at him with a smug mocking smile on her bloated painted face.

"I meant to tell you that was part of the terms and conditions," she said with as straight a face as could be managed.

He mumbled something about cash flow but knew he had again been outmanoeuvred. He told Colleen the rest of their lump sum would be paid within a week and to fetch Racquel.

Colleen's victory over Gaily was like all her victories over Gaily pyrrhic in character. The moment had been lost. They went to a posh restaurant for lunch.

For Gaily there was a certain sameness about the restaurants they frequented. The same could be said of their luncheons.

Colleen would engage the waiters with conversations conducted in her best faux Belgravian accent. Racquel would order the cocktail with the most risqué name. Homosexual men and old ladies would compliment Colleen on her hat. Heterosexual men would sneak what they thought were subtle glances at Racquel. Racquel and Gaily would listen to and watch Colleen devour vast amounts of food and drink. Gaily would attempt to engage Racquel in conversation and pay the bill.

Gaily had been quite shaken by the violence of Racquel's tantrum. The theme of violence was maintained when he allowed the ladies into his home. What he thought would be a playful spanking was in fact a violent assault.

When one allows another person to spank them a large degree of trust is involved. From her years of experience with Gaily Colleen was aware of the boundary beyond which the inflicting of pain would provide no pleasure. Her indiscriminate use of a cane and her encouraging of Racquel to act likewise constituted a breach of trust. The relationship between Colleen and Gaily had gone beyond being toxic and had become abusive.

Kristina Falcon had returned from holiday so Gaily made an appointment to see her. He felt locked into his arrangement with Colleen and Racquel for the duration of their stay but knew for the sake of his health he had to sever all ties with Colleen as soon as was practicable.

Severing ties with Colleen would be a great source of relief for Gaily. Severing ties with Racquel would be far more difficult. The latter was something he wanted to avoid if at all possible.

Miss Falcon equated Racquel with Colleen. She viewed all workers in the sex industry as being by definition "prostitutes" regardless of the nature of the services they provided.

Gaily would indeed have to tough it out for the duration of the ladies' stay. It would though have pleasant moments which would provide lasting memories. Gaily would cling to these moments just as he clung to the possibility of an ongoing friendship with Racquel post-Colleen.

Kristina Falcon was a brilliant psychoanalyst. The therapist was able to recommend reading material and exercises to facilitate Gaily's ability to make decisions. His lack of assertiveness was viewed as his major deficiency.

Miss Falcon also provided a fresh pair of eyes with which to view his racing methodology. The therapist listened carefully as Gaily explained how he arrived at his final selections and staked his money. She in turn provided suggestions as to how to further tweak his methods.

This was what Gaily had always craved: someone off whom to bounce ideas. Ironically it was as a result of his problems with Colleen and Racquel he had finally found such a person.

Each week for the duration of the ladies' stay Gaily would see Kristina Falcon. Each week they would review the progress made with an emphasis on any changes in attitude towards Colleen and/or Racquel. Miss Falcon would also assign new homework after reviewing the previous week's efforts.

Together they went over Gaily's relationship with his parents, friends and acquaintances. He was forced to acknowledge how his own decisions had been influenced by other people and the consequences of these decisions on himself and others.

Therapist and client also reviewed his progress on the punt. By going back to basics Miss Falcon oversaw a fresh start in this area of Gaily's life. She saw his passion for racing and saw how much it meant to him. Gaily knew to begin small when testing something new but the early results were very promising. After so many years he also knew what to look for as clear trends began to emerge.

The role the therapist was playing with regard to his racing was the role Gaily had hoped Racquel would fulfil. He had hoped not only would she fall in love with him but with the sport he loved. On both counts he had been disappointed.

Racquel had accompanied Gaily to race meetings on several occasions but always with Colleen in tow. To her credit Colleen had a reasonable grasp of racing. They had attended meetings together more than twenty years prior in Penang.

Gaily had calmed down a great deal since first meeting Racquel. He was no longer intimidated by her beauty but had lost early momentum in his quest for her love because of her breathtaking looks.

He had no objection to booking a table in the members' dining room on a Saturday but knew the ladies' company came at the requisite price. Gaily increasingly wondered what he had to do to amuse Racquel. Clearly racing bored her.

Even were there to be a parting of the ways at the end of the seven weeks he wanted to part on the best possible terms. Life is long and if a temporary separation could achieve a long term rapprochement on more favourable terms so be it. Gaily had known Racquel for two and a half years and still wondered what made her tick.

He had racked his brains trying to come up with ways to amuse her. Time and money had slipped through his fingers. The one activity he thought might do the trick was a trip to the zoo.

Colleen was loath to agree to this suggestion as she had provided Gaily with an itinerary consisting of luncheon appointments. After a perfunctory visit to Chez Charlie a cab would take the three of them to one or other of Colleen's favourite restaurants.

Gaily and Racquel were obviously bored with this arrangement but Colleen would only approve of the zoo visit if it were deemed an additional paid outing thereby providing additional payments to herself and Racquel. Gaily reluctantly acquiesced.

The zoo proved such a winner with Racquel a second visit was arranged. Despite the additional expense Gaily would treasure the memories of those two days for the rest of his life.

Racquel was in her element. Gaily witnessed her girlish, childlike streak to an extent he had not before seen. Her joy in turn provided him with great joy.

On the first of their two excursions Racquel wore a very light, frilly white cotton dress. Under the dress she wore a pair of white cotton knickers decorated with red love hearts. In fact the whole purpose of the dress appeared to be to highlight the knickers at every available opportunity.

When Racquel sat down the knickers were exposed at the front. When Racquel stood or walked the knickers were exposed at the back by the slightest gust of wind.

Gaily and the ladies travelled to the zoo via ferry. On the famous harbour they were able to sit on the deck of the ferry in the summer sunshine. The natural sea breeze in combination with the ferry's slipstream produced powerful gusts of wind.

Racquel leant over the ferry's rail. Suddenly Gaily was not being transported to Taronga Park Zoo but back in time to his youth. His transports were those of pleasure and enraptured fascination as he was mesmerised by the rise and fall of Racquel's dress. As with the sun in the sky the rising of Racquel's dress signalled the beginning of a wonderful day.

Colleen took what was occurring in good humour. The attraction of Racquel's exhibition was literally obvious for all to see. It was the younger woman's moment in the sun.

Regardless of what was going through her mind once the trio entered the zoo Colleen had to conserve her breath for the day's walking. Without knowing where they were headed Racquel led them from one enclosure to the next. It was a metaphor for her life.

Sometimes racing ahead, sometimes slowing to pay attention to a creature which took her interest the breeze ensured Colleen and Gaily had Racquel's knicker-clad bottom to guide them. Gaily made bloody sure he never lost sight of it as the wind licked the hem of Racquel's dress.

This was Racquel's first opportunity to see Australian native wildlife in a simulated natural environment. The joy the girl derived from the experience though could never be simulated.

They stopped for lunch. Racquel had packed some food prepared by her own fair hand for Gaily and herself. Again it was a genuine act of kindness and thoughtfulness which could not be feigned.

They shared a tortilla with a sweet pastry by way of

dessert. Racquel spoon-fed Gaily the pudding. They had been some of the more enjoyable moments with which she had provided Gaily in the various restaurants they had visited to perform this maternal act in public. Despite being a feigned piece of role play it was part of the girl-friend experience Gaily craved.

Colleen put a dampener on proceedings by hand-ing Gaily a receipt for shop-bought sandwiches. He was having too good a time to do more than fob her off with a promise of reimbursement for the trifling amount while secreting the screwed up piece of paper in his pocket.

They soldiered on with Racquel again leading the way but by mid-afternoon the out of nick Colleen could walk no further. Reluctantly Racquel and Gaily agreed to call it a day on the proviso of a future visit.

The zoo trip had been Gaily's idea and showed what could be achieved if given a little freedom in planning ways and means of entertaining Racquel. More and more he was coming to view Colleen as an encumbrance and hindrance.

Their second visit to the zoo came only two days later thus maintaining the momentum of their initial trip. On this occasion Racquel wore a bright pink cheerlead-er's uniform with hot pink hot pants under the skirt and matching running shoes. The girl certainly knew how to catch the eye.

For one whose reputation preceded her there was an innocent joy in Racquel's appreciation of the zoo's inmates. Taronga Park is a large zoo so as soon as one creature began to cloy on her Racquel would be off skip-ping or running to the next enclosure.

To justify her existence Colleen attempted to co-ordi-nate their movements but anything involving Racquel had to be spontaneous in order to succeed. Racquel's attention span was short but her joie de vivre was large as life itself. This was the magnetic personality with which Gaily had fallen in love.

All good things come to an end. The birds, animals, reptiles and insects had all been graced by the fleeting presence of the great English beauty. A giraffe had been fed by her hand, a koala admired, a performing seal applauded.

Only one creature remained unseen: Gaily's totemic brother the wombat. Finally the resident wombat was located. The wombat is a nocturnal animal so the poor fellow was asleep. Despite Racquel's best efforts he would not awaken. Oblivious to the beauty he would behold the wombat's slumbers continued.

"...But it doesn't do anything, Charlie!" Racquel shrieked in exasperation.

"...Out of the mouths of babes..." thought Gaily to himself.

For those two days Gaily was able to erase from his mind the bad memories of his experiences with these two women. As with the highs Racquel might have experienced from snow so Gaily came crashing back down to earth from his zoo-induced euphoria. The insomnia and digestive problems returned. His body was telling his mind all was not well.

Gaily had often joked with Colleen she was both his mentor and torment. However, as the years had worn on the former role had almost entirely given way to the latter. The time had come for the parting of the ways.

In conjunction with Kristina Falcon Gaily had drafted a carefully worded letter to Colleen severing forthwith all ties with his mistress of twenty-five years' standing.

Although Gaily realised the necessity of the break it

was still a gut-wrenching act to write the letter. With the therapist's assistance he ensured the letter contained a balance of love, passion but also finality.

Gaily had always lived life with passion and had never before had to completely sever all ties with another individual. He therefore ensured the valedictory letter made explicit reference to the many good times they had shared and the memories he would always treasure while outlining the gradual breakdown of their relationship.

Colleen was one of only two women Gaily had every loved. The other was Racquel. Given the triangular nature of his arrangement with the two women it was also necessary to address a letter to his new love.

Given also the fact it had been Colleen who had brought them together it had not been possible to adhere to some very good advice quoted by Anthony Trollope in one or more of his novels.

Gaily recalled the words of the old song:

"Make sure you're off with the old love
Before you get on with the new."

Again in hindsight it was good advice which had gone unheeded. In Gaily's defence theirs had been primarily if not exclusively a business relationship. Still Gaily felt the need to word his letter to Racquel in such a way as to keep the possibility of a rapprochement alive were this at all possible.

It was one of life's "what if"s. If Colleen had accepted Gaily's switching of allegiances there could have been a different outcome. Of course if Colleen had never introduced him to Racquel he would probably have never met her.

Then again if your aunt had testicles she would be your uncle. Along the same lines Gaily was fond of joking how some people only ever backed four horses: Gunna, Coulda, Shoulda and Woulda. On this occasion he was guilty of the same error of judgement.

Stubbornly refusing to accept the reality of the situation he wrote a letter also to Racquel. Realising at least the necessity in Racquel's mind of involving a third party he suggested that future trysts involve a lady of Racquel's choosing but not Colleen.

In both letters Gaily referred to the increasingly toxic nature of his relations with Colleen. This toxicity in his stated opinion was responsible for the poisoning of Racquel's mind against him.

The therapist gave her approval to the wording of both letters but would have preferred he sever all ties with Racquel as well as Colleen. This Gaily point-blank refused to do.

Miss Falcon suggested he present the letters to the ladies just as they were departing. This would prove awkward and would virtually rule out a long and emotional parting conversation with Racquel.

On the day this was ruled out in any case by Gaily's distraught state of mind. Colleen saw the state he was in and told him not to bother about accompanying them to the airport.

He helped them into a cab and went to hand Colleen her letter which she promptly refused. Racquel also declined the envelope addressed to her.

Racquel blew a perfunctory farewell kiss and the cab drove off. Gaily felt a huge sense of relief as a result of both their departure and their not having accepted their letters.

He was left with a basket Racquel had handed him containing items of food she had not managed to consume. Racquel had been going to make him another tortilla but with her impending departure this had not eventuated.

The basket was a memento of her recent presence. Salt, eggs, garlic and muesli were strange reminders of this beautiful woman who had entered his life almost three years earlier. He smiled as his delving fingers came across a bottle of "Gun Oil" lubricant amongst the items of food.

Gaily's life had been turned upside down but also changed forever. He recalled her appearance an hour prior which had enabled him to dry his eyes and calm down to some extent.

Racquel had been wearing a little pink number. Her goddess-like body radiated more than usual due to fake tan. Any intended parting conversation was negated by the fuss she was making about a broken fingernail. If anything Racquel had been more distraught than Gaily.

Only Colleen had remained calm amidst the chaos of her own creation. With her hair up, her brief kit and golden glow Racquel had reminded him of Jane Fonda as Barbarella. Colleen had reminded him of Madam Defarge.

Now they were gone. Gaily walked home from the little hotel where his guests had been staying for the previous seven weeks.

Prior to his departure he shook hands with the hotel manager. In what would have to be the ultimate twenty-first century token gesture the manager offered him Facebook friendship. Gaily thanked him and wended his weary way home.

Gaily would in fact take the manager up on his offer only to be sickened by some of the offensive material which came his way. This only served to reinforce his attitude towards Facebook.

There were more important things about which to worry. Gaily rang his aunt and uncle to report he was assessing the damage caused by Cyclone Colleen and Cyclone Racquel.

They pressed as to the extent of the damage and he conceded the extent of his losses.

His aunt urged him to move out of his beautiful rented flat and put all the belongings he had inherited into storage. Gaily knew panic was not the appropriate response.

He looked around the flat. Room by room he observed the material possessions which had transformed this rental property into a home.

Gaily still retained all the things his parents had bequeathed him. The shares and property they had left him he had largely squandered in his pursuit of Racquel. They had meant little to him as they possessed no sentimental value and he was a sentimental bloke.

Superimposed over the family heirlooms was now the visible memory of Racquel. A photograph of her flaunting her bare legs sat on his dressing table in a frame which had once contained a photograph of Colleen. Souvenir pairs of knickers in various hues were draped over a chair. A packet of crisps from which Racquel had eaten sat on top of a display cabinet.

Gaily could not bring himself to dispose of anything-even uneaten crisps- which would serve as a reminder of this most tumultuous phase of his life. To the crisps, photograph and knickers he added the basket of goodies Racquel had earlier given him.

Her school uniform lay discreetly on his bedroom floor – neatly folded and placed inside a David Jones shopping bag. Gaily wondered if he would ever again see her in uniform – or for that matter ever see her again at all.

He opened his refrigerator and emptied the basket of

its perishables. Inside was some "Charlie's" brand fruit juice he had used to make Racquel a drink. Gaily recalled how much he had appreciated this humorous touch when she had handed him the juice to mix with her vodka.

Inside the refrigerator was of course also some Resch's beer. The sight of the stubbies jolted him out of his reveries.

Gaily recalled the words of Henry Lawson about beer making a man feel as he should without beer. There was no point in attempting any serious task for the remainder of the day. He closed the refrigerator door, checked the time and went into town for a drink. His life was returning to normal.

Karl Marx defined life as "struggle" and Gaily knew exactly what his namesake the good doctor meant. Inheritance had transformed Gaily's life into a struggle to retain sanity and solvency.

The Star would always be where he would repair to regain the former in preparation for maintaining the latter. It was a place for meditation – in the absence of his ratbag drinking mates.

Thankfully on this particular occasion the pub was sans ratbags. The lepers were out the back feeding the poker machines and he had the bar to himself to drink and think.

The bar staff were aware of the ladies' visit and the effects it had had on their favourite customer. They served him with their usual courtesy but knew to give him space. Discretion is a very important attitude to possess when working in an industry heavily dependent upon black money to keep the pokies ticking over.

The barmaid drew him a schooner of Resch's and Gaily drew breath and gulped it down, ordering another and tipping her generously. He had known the barmaid for more than ten years and like all the pub's mainly Asian staff she marvelled at his ability to knock back beer after beer.

"First of the day," he smiled and took his favourite window seat.

The races were on the television monitors around the room but they were of the Mickey Mouse variety and Gaily took little interest. Maidens at bush meetings were about as good an investment proposition as the pokies.

He turned over a coaster and started performing some simple arithmetical calculations on the back of the coaster. This was totally unnecessary but confirmed what his bank balance already told him. All up he had blown a million dollars in his bid to win the heart of the fair Racquel. More than half of his inheritance was gone.

Gaily had his fifth schooner as was his wont. He thought of Racquel on her way home to London and looked out onto the faces of the needy and the greedy as they rushed along Goulburn and Sussex Streets.

Like Lawson he "sorrow[ed] for those owners of the faces in the street" ("Faces in the Street": a poem by Henry Lawson). The owners of these faces did not drift past though as had their predecessors in Lawson's poem. They were in too much of a hurry to get home from jobs they hated, see spouses they disliked, have sex with strangers or eat food they knew to be bad for them.

Regardless of ethnicity their lives were those of coolies living lives of quiet desperation. Gaily vowed never to return to their ranks. He was still possessed of sufficient capital to be the master of his own destiny.

Gaily went home to a pad filled with memories of what might have been. He looked out over the water and listened without interest to people on talkback radio talking drivel about football and cricket. They lived their lives vicariously through the highs and lows of the teams they followed.

Gaily's passions were racing and Racquel. His head swirled with the clip-clop of horses' hooves and high heels. It had been an emotionally exhausting seven weeks culminating in the ladies' departure that morning. He had his final beer for the night and went to bed to sleep the sleep of the just. His dreams were filled with thundering hooves and pink Louboutins.

With the ladies not having accepted their respective letters it was back to Kristina Falcon for more advice on how to proceed.

The therapist agreed with Gaily that Colleen's letter should be sent to her residential address via registered post.

Racquel's letter posed more of a problem as Gaily's only address for Racquel was Oscar Wildly's former abode in Soho. He had been instructed by Racquel not to use this address and would respect her wishes. He was yet to discover why this request had been made.

To finalise the matter once and for all Gaily sent the contents of Racquel's letter to her via email. Whether the girl ever received or opened the email he did not know. In case such was the case Gaily further watered down the wording of the original letter.

Thus, he had placated the therapist and excised Colleen from his life while leaving the door open for Racquel to re-enter his life at some indeterminate time in the future.

Of more immediate importance to Gaily was the recouping of the million dollars he had invested in pursuit of Racquel. Miss Falcon was still confident in his ability to retrieve the money at the track. They worked together on a weekly basis tweaking Gaily's selection and staking methods.

He had always wanted someone off whom to bounce

ideas regarding racing. An unlikely set of circumstances had resulted in his wish being granted in the form of a sex therapist. Gaily thanked Racquel for having been responsible for bringing Kristina Falcon into his life.

The sending of the letter to Colleen had one immediate effect. Literally overnight the vomiting and diarrhoea Gaily had experienced over the previous three years ceased. His blood tests normalised without any adjustment to his diet.

Colleen had almost destroyed Gaily. He had pulled back in the nick of time. His illness had been almost entirely psychosomatic in nature.

Gaily had additional reason to thank the timeliness of Kristina Falcon's entering his life. Here again there was a beautiful example of synchronicity. Without his long-term association with his naturopath Kelly Waterston he would not have known where to turn in his hour of need. Doors were beginning to open.

The first response Gaily received to his conveying of the letters to the ladies was to be "defriended" (sic) by Racquel on Facebook. The poor fellow was so unfamiliar with the medium he did not at first comprehend the reason for his no longer having access to Racquel's Facebook page.

Upon having the explanation provided to him by a third party he was deeply saddened and not a little angry. Gaily attributed Racquel's action to the slander campaign Colleen had conducted against him.

Given the opportunity he would redeem himself in Racquel's eyes but he was doubly gladdened he had sent the Irish bitch to Coventry.

Gaily continued to work on tweaking his racing business. With the assistance of Kristina Falcon clear trends were beginning to emerge but he required at least six months of results for the trends to become meaningful.

There had been one final moment of self-destructive madness in the month following the ladies' departure.

"Why are you destroying yourself?" the therapist had asked.

Gaily replied that it had been an aberration but it had been a two hundred thousand dollar aberration involving odds on favourites.

He retained faith in himself but the warning signs were still present. Genius is a two-edged sword. It was the fine line between insanity and genius about which his mother had warned him as a child. Recognising her son's emerging talents the wise old lady was also aware of his ability to attain greatness or crash and burn later in life.

Kristina Falcon and Kelly Waterston recognised Gaily's positive side and sought to draw it out as Colleen had tapped into his sexual consciousness all those years prior. The difference here was the therapist and naturopath were steadying influences whilst the prostitute had proven almost fatal.

Before the ladies' arrival Gaily had seen fit to make travel and accommodation arrangements for holidays in England during the following July and August. Given the parting of the ways which had so recently occurred he felt very much betwixt and between.

His fears were confirmed when he received a card and letter – purporting to be from Racquel but in fact obviously from Colleen. There had been a very lame attempt by Colleen to disguise the handwriting but he knew the form too well.

The card entreated him to accept the fact he was being ignored while the letter enumerated the ways in which he had shown himself to not be a gentleman. It concluded with an expression of gratitude ostensibly from Racquel towards Colleen saying Colleen would have to find Racquel a more suitable match. The whole fabrication was signed "Racquel" in a hand clearly not hers.

Miss Falcon had directed Gaily to put all the mementoes of Colleen and Racquel in a box. The contents of the box were to be disposed of when Gaily felt ready. Into the box went cards, letters, photographs and items of clothing.

He would not part with anything which reminded him of Racquel but was slightly more flexible where Colleen was concerned. When Colleen moved back overseas Gaily had gone to an auction and purchased books and records which Colleen had arranged to be sold. Twenty years later these same records were again disposed of at auction with Gaily being the seller rather than the buyer. The books he donated to the universe.

Gradually his life was turning around. Miss Falcon warned him to avoid situations whilst in England where he would be likely to run into Colleen. He told her if this occurred he would simply ignore the woman. In his own mind he had made a clean break from his former mistress.

Gaily was keen to begin work on his first novel. Miss Falcon encouraged him in this endeavour.

In England he would be free of the many and varied distractions of Sydney. In Brighton there would be no outdoor swimming pool and no Fighting Works gym. The Greys pub did not open until four during the week. For the first time there would also effectively be no Colleen.

Gaily wondered if there would be any Racquel. He sent her an email but there was no reply. Gaily still pined for her and every day checked his email in vain for the elusive reply.

Eventually the day of departure arrived. Although he did not own an airline Gaily agreed with Sir Richard Branson about the benefits of holidays. Used wisely the time is possessed of therapeutic qualities. A farewell drink at the Star, more at the airport lounge and he was flying. There might be restrictions on carrying booze on one's person but in one's person is a different matter.

Like a microcosm of most people's lives the flight passed quickly and uneventfully. The coach to Brighton was all too familiar. The only difference was he would not be rushing to a telephone to ring Colleen upon arrival.

The university digs were also all too familiar – only shabbier than the year before. It would be the last year he would stay in Southover Street. He needed to start spending money on himself rather than other people. It was what Kristina Falcon termed "self-love".

Brighton itself was also as usual a little more shabby and a little less genteel than the previous year. Brighton was a small town and inevitably he knew he would run into Colleen. It did not take long.

On the second day of his visit Gaily avoided a confrontation in the Marks and Sparks food hall by putting his tub of salad back on the shelf and running out the door. Thereafter Marks and Sparks was declared a no-go zone.

His days were spent writing with a long drinks break in the Mariner in the city centre. At four o'clock stumps were drawn for the day and a hasty retreat beaten to the Greys.

It was a simple existence. The blokes at the pub were identical in type to the blokes back at the Star. Their company was well and good in small doses. However, the whole scenario lacked that which he most craved in England: the company of an English rose.

After a fortnight or so it finally dawned on Gaily Racquel was not about to contact him. He therefore had to come up with a Plan B.

When they had been Facebook friends Racquel had mentioned to him a Bondage and Discipline mistress of her acquaintance who traded as Madam Rose. At least this was Gaily's recollection of her name.

Gaily resorted to that highly reliable source of information the Internet search engine in order to locate the mistress in question.

Somewhat perplexingly he discovered two Bondage and Discipline mistresses with similar appellations both of whom were based in London: Madam Rose and Madam Rosa.

He therefore procured their telephone numbers and rang one of them.

Madam Rosa spoke with a thick southern European accent. Overcoming the slight language problem he managed to make an appointment with the mistress.

Madam Rosa worked out of a flat near London Victoria railway station and charged one hundred pounds per hour. This seemed remarkably inexpensive for the services of one of Racquel's friends. He therefore made an appointment for one hour the following day. Face to face was always the best way to do business and when one is dealing with a sex worker the face to face business may be conducted in the horizontal rather than the vertical. Gaily presumed all of Racquel's friends would be what she would term "hot" – birds of a feather etc. One never knew one's luck in the big city and it had been a long drought.

Gaily experienced a slight frisson at the possibility of meeting one of Racquel's friends. He went up to London filled with expectation. As instructed he rang Madam Rosa upon his arrival from outside the block of flats in which she resided. The telephone did not answer. He went to a nearby pub for a half making sure to leave his mobile on. A text message came a quarter of an hour later advising him of the number of the flat. Its tone was apologetic and told him she was ready to see him.

He entered what was a security building and caught the lift up to the appropriate floor. Behind the door he heard voices including that of a man. This gave Gaily the creeps as he stood by his conviction men should only be punters where the sex industry was concerned.

Nervously he rang the doorbell. The voices fell silent. A dumpy brunette in a cheap, grubby teddy answered the door.

This was Mistress Madam Rosa? Reluctantly he entered the flat where the girl led him to a small bedroom filled with Bondage and Discipline paraphernalia. Alarm bells began to sound in Gaily's head.

The girl went to kiss him on his lips but he averted his face in order to avoid any contact with her mouth. She repeated the action but received a similar rebuff. God knows where those lips might have been. It did not bear too much thinking about. Paramount in Gaily's mind was getting out of the place as quickly as possible.

He handed the girl a hundred pounds in cash. This was not intended as payment for any services likely to be rendered. It was ransom to facilitate his escape.

Madam Rosa left the room with the money and closed the door behind her. At any moment Gaily expected it to re-open and a man with a gun or knife come in and demand his wallet, watch and mobile telephone.

The door did re-open but it was Madam Rosa.

"You no undress love?" she said in her thick accent.

"No, I'm not feeling the best," he replied truthfully.

Gaily had come to see her for one primary reason and that was to see if she knew Racquel. A couple of quick questions ascertained the fact Madam Rosa had never heard of Racquel.

The girl picked up a giant dildo and a heavy riding whip. The whip was so heavy no modern jockey would contemplate using such a thing.

"You pull down trousers. I whip you, stick toy up your bum then we have sex," instructed Madam Rosa.

It was a tempting offer which Gaily considered for almost a full nanosecond before declining.

"Really, I don't feel very well. I think I might leave," he said.

The girl started to become angry but Gaily knew the magic words.

"I don't want my money back," he added.

This had the desired calming effect and he quickly made good his escape. By process of elimination Madam Rose would be next cab off the rank.

However, sufficient unto the day is the evil thereof. Gaily went back to the nearby pub for a pint prior to wending his way back to Brighton.

The following day he rang Madam Rose. A woman with a clipped London accent answered the telephone. Gaily identified himself but his reputation had already preceded him.

"Did you want Racquel's telephone number?" Madam Rose asked him.

At least he was getting somewhere. "Somewhere" proved to be a little flat in Mayfair's Shepherd Market.

Given the basis upon which he and Racquel had parted ways Gaily declined the offer of a telephone number. Instead he made an appointment for a midday session with Madam Rose to be followed by a meal at the Renaissance Hotel. Although The Renaissance was a half hour ride in a taxi it was his choice because it was well known to both parties. This was where Gaily had taken Colleen and Racquel on many occasions – a fact about which Racquel had not been backward in regaling Madam Rose.

On the morning of their initial rendezvous Gaily rang

ahead prior to boarding his train. Madam was all too happy to wear a miniskirt. In fact she went so far as to ask him if he had any preference as to how she should dress. His response had been all too predictable.

What could not be predicted with any certainty was where this would all lead. In the back of his mind Gaily hoped to renew contact with Racquel with the assistance of Madam Rose. Failing this he would be able to enjoy the company of the mistress herself. It was a win–win paradigm.

First impressions count as Gaily had learnt through harsh experience. As Kristina Falcon had remarked he presented well. His attention to detail was punctilious: the suit, the tie, the shoes, the grooming and the flowers for Madam. The hallmark of good taste is understatement. It was the complete package.

Gaily rang Madam Rose again from Hyde Park Corner. He received precise instructions as to locating her flat. A quarter of an hour later he was ringing her door-bell.

A stunning middle-aged brunette answered the door dressed in a provocatively short skirt, a tight blouse and heels.

"Come in, Master Charles," smiled Madam Rose with her Belgravian purr.

He entered the house and they hugged in the manner of people already well acquainted. Madam led Gaily upstairs revealing in the process a pert bottom partially clad in white knickers.

They discussed his requirements regarding their first session together. Gaily knew what a Bondage and Discipline Madam would consider light discipline might still test the limits of his pain threshold. He also discerned Madam Rose to be a consummate professional who understood the need for clear boundaries to be set in place. These boundaries would always be respected. A gratuity of eight hundred pounds was agreed upon.

They then acted out the familiar classroom scene with Gaily being spanked for looking up the beautiful mistress's skirt.

Madam Rose began by warming Gaily's bottom with her bare hand. Then having removed his shorts a flurry of blows commenced employing a Mason Pearson hairbrush then a leather paddle.

Each successive whack was infinitesimally harder than the previous. Madam was able to gauge the effectiveness of the punishment from the gradual engorgement she could feel occurring against her leg.

The final few slaps brought the session to a crescendo by taking Gaily past his pain threshold. Sensing this to be the case Madam Rose desisted from her labours leaving her new client with a red and raw backside.

For tolerating his punishment so well Gaily was rewarded with a kiss. Madam Rose was another example of someone who understood the need for conveying good first impressions.

After changing into slightly more appropriate attire the mistress and her new client repaired to the restaurant for lunch. Despite being slightly older than Racquel Gaily noted how Madam Rose was still capable of turning heads when in mufti.

There was almost as much leg on show in public as there had been in private and very shapely pins they were too. The lower half of the legs gave some hint as to their owner's profession encased as they were in tight black glossy boots ending at the knee. A little white dress left little to the imagination. A hint of knicker here and a leopard print jacket there and the effect was complete.

Madam Rose knew how to play to her audience. If

Gaily wanted to hear about Racquel he had come to the fount of all knowledge.

Madam Rose and Racquel went back more than ten years. They had shared a flat together – and that was not all they had shared together. At one stage they had been more than just good friends.

However, recently Madam Rose had distanced herself from Racquel due to Racquel's alleged use of smack.

Only a quirk of fate had seen Madam Rose and Gaily not brought together three years prior. The late Oscar Wildly had arranged for Madam Rose to meet with Colleen and Gaily on that fateful day.

At the last minute Wildly changed his mind and arranged for Racquel to fill the breach.

What might have been: Woulda, Shoulda, Coulda and Gunna were again contesting the "What Might Have Been Stakes".

Madam Rose told Gaily things he did not particularly want to hear.

Madam Rose alleged Racquel had been at Oscar Wildly's flat at the time of Wildly's death. This was in contradiction with what Raquel had told Gaily. She said that she had found him in a pool of his own blood the day after he had died. It also contradicted a statement made to the coroner.

Madam Rose claimed to have witnesses who could validate her assertions. Were these assertions true Gaily had fallen in love with a perjurer.

The mistress further asseverated part of the reason for Racquel's distancing herself from Gaily throughout her last visit to Sydney related to her having covertly brought over Paddy McGinty.

Gaily interrupted Madam Rose to ask where the money came from to facilitate payment for airfares and accommodation for this additional visitor.

"You," came the simple reply.

Again, were these assertions correct Gaily had effectively subsidised overseas holidays for a freeloader. This would explain Racquel's urgency for payments in advance then her reticence to see her benefactor or afford him access to her hotel.

Lunch with Madam Rose had provided Gaily not just with food and company of the highest quality but also much food for thought. He had no reason to disbelieve the Bondage and Discipline madam.

Again, were what she had told him true he had been played for a mug to a greater extent than he had thought possible. He had also been dealing with people devoid of morals.

There would be one more twist in the saga prior to his return to Australia but for the time being he had heard more than enough.

Gaily was only able to see Madam Rose on one further occasion before departing England.

Again they enjoyed each other's company. It was over lunch at the Renaissance Madam Rose dropped what for Gaily was a bombshell. The blonde bombshell Racquel had married Paddy McGinty.

Racquel had rung her old friend to convey the joyous tidings after the fact. It had been a small ceremony attended by only a handful of people. Madam Rose thanked Racquel for the invitation.

The wedding and the marriage received little or no media coverage. It was a far cry from Raquel's usual attention-seeking behaviour.

Gaily also wondered why Racquel's new husband had not sought greater publicity for the acquisition of such a trophy wife. There was after all only one reason for marrying a woman such as Racquel.

Unlike Racquel Madam Rose made it quite clear to Gaily she had a boyfriend. There could therefore be no misplaced expectations regarding the nature of their relationship. It was a business relationship based upon the provision of specific services in exchange for money.

If Gaily wanted more he would have to look elsewhere. Gaily did want more. He wanted what other men had but had eluded him all his life.

"I do have a friend Susie though," Madam Rose had proffered. "She's on holiday at the moment but I could send you photos of her. If you like her we could fly her to Australia to visit you."

This offer sounded rather familiar to another he had made to Colleen three years prior. Had Madam Rose been Racquel on the fateful day he had met the now married woman things may have turned out very differently.

For one thing Madam Rose would have tolerated Colleen for all of five minutes on a good day. With the toxic influence out of the way Racquel may still have found her way into Gaily's life. However, this would have been on very different terms and conditions from those negotiated by Colleen.

A triangle involving Madam Rose, Racquel and Gaily would probably have worked well for all parties concerned. They would probably have genuinely enjoyed each other's company.

The fact of the matter was this had not occurred. What had occurred had severely traumatised Gaily. He had suffered emotionally as well as financially.

Although Madam Rose was obviously a far more honest and sincere person than either Colleen or Racquel Gaily was now very wary of anyone working in the sex industry. It was an unregulated jungle.

In any event he now lacked the funds to lavish on Madam Rose he had lavished on Colleen and Racquel.

Gaily sensed the Bondage and Discipline mistress felt she had missed an opportunity – which was the case. Mistress Claudette had harboured similar regrets. Kristina Falcon was correct. In the final analysis it all boiled down to money.

Thankfully Madam Rose was not a bitter person. Gaily parted with Madam on good terms. There was the basis for ongoing friendship. They would maintain contact. For the time being though they would resume their separate lives twelve thousand miles apart.

It could be worse. Gaily returned to the relative safety of a life which revolved around training, drinking, dancing and racing. It was at once a lifestyle both sublime and sublimating.

From a philosophical standpoint Gaily knew there to be no such animal as absolute freedom. However, this life he had finally managed to forge for himself left him far more the master of his own destiny than could ever be possible for the average punter.

Every day Gaily gave thanks to his parents for the capital he still possessed. After severing ties with Colleen he felt wealthier than when he had possessed three times his current capital.

For the first time in his life he was tapping into his subconscious mind. To this end he continued his work with Kristina Falcon.

Graham Peters had impressed upon him the importance of trial and error in achieving one's goals. Only in this way would ultimate success be attained as incorrect methods were eliminated and one edged closer and closer towards perfection in one's area of expertise.

Gaily synthesised the knowledge of the university-trained therapist and the self-taught champion fighter. The result was an increasing ability to pick winners and back them for an optimal return on capital outlay.

He began to rebuild his capital base as a direct result of his own efforts. His political world view told him it was essential to develop survival skills in a changing world. Many would not survive , the majority would struggle. The self-made man would not only survive but thrive.

Gaily's confidence grew. The self-confidence he had lost in his youth began to return. Integral to this process was the role being played by his dancing teacher Kath Middleton.

Miss Middleton had yet to be subjected to the slings and arrows of outrageous fortune. The young woman exuded a joy and a confidence which was irresistible in its infectiousness.

Gaily gave her a copy of Breakfast At Tiffany's.

He inscribed it with a quote from Miss Holly Golightly: "Anyone who ever gave you confidence, you owe them a lot."

Gaily was slowly but surely surrounding himself with a circle of successful and positive people. He knew there was a direct correlation between confidence and success. The greater the degree of well-founded confidence the greater the likelihood of success. He dubbed his circle of supporters Team Gaily.

Success in one area of life carried over into others. He was adjudged the most proficient student at his first dancing tournament.

His main role had been to make Miss Middleton look good. This was not difficult.

Warren Bird offered him a job but Gaily was having too

much fun and fobbed him off until after another overseas trip and dancing tournament.

Gaily was enjoying unexpected success in Bird's football tipping competition. This created a potential problem as in England it would be difficult to obtain access to the information which in Sydney would be at his finger tips.

Graham Peters had taught him, "Losers find excuses, winners find solutions".

Kristina Falcon had taught him to think in a slightly more New Age manner. Gaily asked the universe for help and the universe duly provided.

One of Luke Henry's clerks agreed to convey cuttings from the football programme to him via email. The magazine did not have an online edition and Gaily was loath to learn how to use a tablet or Iphone. Thus Gaily avoided having to acquire the despised gadget.

His back-up plan was provided by an old mate purchasing the magazine on his behalf and reading the required articles to him over the telephone. Despite its unconventionality the plan proved an effective means of obtaining the required information.

Just before Gaily's departure for England an unfortunate incident occurred.

Craig Magoo had been a member of the unofficial "Bachelors' Club" at the Star pub for the previous few years. He was one of the most boring and depressing people Gaily had ever met. Gaily tolerated his presence more out of politeness than anything else. Gaily's father would have termed Magoo "a real cheer up merchant".

Their fellow middle-aged bachelor Victor adopted a more tolerant approach than Gaily.

"He's not a bad man," Victor had said in Magoo's defence.

Gaily though had learnt from harsh experience to be very wary of toxic people. His fear of failure made him acutely aware of Magoo's ability to poison his mind with negativity. Just as people such as Kath Middleton lifted his spirits so the Magoos of this world could drag him down.

Magoo had not been seen for several weeks. When he failed to respond to Victor's text messages Victor knew to trawl through the Telegraph's death notices until he found Magoo's name.

Magoo had been dead a month. The Bachelors' Club membership had been reduced by twenty-five per cent. Its only other surviving member, Gough, dimly recalled Magoo saying something about having cancer. The cause of death would remain a mystery as Magoo was a passing acquaintance whose funeral had already been conducted. He had been several months younger than Gaily.

Magoo had never got over a business failure compounded by a spending spree on prostitutes. He had spent the last eleven years of his life bemoaning his bankruptcy and an inability to ever turn the situation around.

While Gaily could empathise with the fellow's plight he had found his behaviour depressing in the extreme. Day after day Magoo would recite the same hard luck story over and over again. He would drone on for hours about his misfortunes.

Magoo had been a slow drinker because as he would often tell his audience he was broke. For a time this had worked as a cue for Victor to buy Magoo another glass of rough red until Victor finally twigged he would never have the favour returned.

Gaily was sick of drinking in pubs. His increasing aspirations sought new outlets for expression outside the constraints of the walls of pubs frequented by the likes of Magoo. Gaily knew his drinking held him back from more constructive pursuits but it was a habit into which he had fallen at an early age.

With this in mind he hopped on an aeroplane to travel twelve thousand miles from the home of schooners to the land of pints. It was not before partaking of a few of the former at his beloved Star pub.

The trip was Gaily's Farewell to Brighton Tour. In line with his new policy of spending more money on himself and less on others he had booked a room in a four star hotel on Brighton's seafront.

After about five minutes in Brighton he wondered what the bloody hell he was doing there.

The hotel itself was everything he had requested: clean, quiet and secure. However, one step outside took Gaily into the Third World.

The Greens had obtained a majority on Brighton Council and had won the local seat in Parliament. The result was the transformation of footpaths into obstacle courses where pedestrians were forced to dodge cyclists, dogs, dog droppings and other refuse.

From his Australian experience Gaily knew the Greens to be Trots in disguise. They were incapable of providing leadership out of the crisis of capitalism. On the contrary their anti-working class stances antagonised council workers into taking industrial action for better pay. This in combination with the Greens' environmental tokenism led to Brighton becoming a filthier hole than was previously the case.

Gaily sought refuge in his hotel room to concentrate on his writing. It was after all a working holiday. He did though make a point of renewing auld acquaintance. The Greys pub had barely survived a lean winter and their new management could not confidently plan for the future.

The new landlord did his best to confirm Einstein's

definition of insanity by replicating the previous management's failed attempts to resuscitate a dying business.

Gaily made time for drinks and lunches with the people who had so kindly allowed him into their lives over the previous eight years. However, privately he already considered them the ghosts of his past.

The real clincher occurred when he caught sight of Colleen in the street. Twenty years prior he would have given her a second glance because of her stunning beauty. Twenty years on he required a second glance to simply recognise her.

His former mistress was morbidly obese. Her small frame and little feet were almost incapable of carrying the load requested of them. It was a terribly sad although somewhat predictable sight for Gaily.

He pondered the self-loathing one must possess to engage in such flagrant self-destruction. Gaily broke into a run to escape the possibility of her noticing him as she slowly lumbered along. The hatred Colleen had displayed towards Gaily was now being directed inwards at herself. It had indeed been a lucky escape for him.

London beckoned. It was good to be reunited with Madam Rose but there was a certain sameness in the relations Gaily had enjoyed over the years with sex workers.

His experiences had been overwhelmingly negative and extremely traumatising. The women seemed largely motivated by greed and hate. The more money he had thrown at them the worse they had treated him and the more rapacious they had become.

This had certainly been the case with Mistress Sarah, Colleen and Racquel. Mistress Claudette and Madam Rose were not greedy by nature but were still obviously miffed by the amounts Gaily had lavished on Racquel. Gaily in turn was upset with himself for having spent so much on Colleen when he no longer desired her company. In pursuing that which he had fervently desired he had been forced to accept the company of someone equally undesirable. The resulting disaster should not have been entirely unpredictable.

Mistress Claudette was back in France with her family. Gaily maintained contact with her but only at a very superficial level. The Frenchwoman had briefly visited England but had quickly assessed the situation and advised him to obtain an English girlfriend.

Madam Rose was very attractive as well as being sexually compatible. However, as previously stated the English mistress had been honest enough to tell Gaily straight out on the first day they met she had a boyfriend. This was a precaution in case he had any ideas about transferring his affections from Racquel to her.

Part of the attraction of Madam Rose for Gaily was her connection with Racquel. This is what had brought them together in the first place. Madam Rose was his conduit with Racquel. Were he ever to be reunited with Racquel under more favourable circumstances it would be as a result of Madam Rose's intercession. In the meantime Gaily enjoyed the company of the English mistress and the services provided. In fact his pleasure was magnified by the vicarious aspect involved in being with one of Racquel's former lovers.

Gaily jokingly asked Madam Rose if she had any single girlfriends. The unexpected reply was in the positive.

A blind date was arranged by the mistress whereby Gaily could meet the totty hairdresser who had recently separated from her husband. Madam Rose even offered to act as Jill's chaperone – an offer which Gaily gratefully accepted.

This was to be the first actual date Gaily had been on

for almost thirty years. He was more than happy to shout the two ladies lunch as this would be the only money with which he would have to part. It was very kind of Madam Rose to tee the whole thing up in this manner but even if he were to hit it off with her friend there may still be a service for her to provide.

Gaily was also glad of any excuse to escape Brighton. He had overstayed his welcome and would be pleased to leave the filthy hole behind for good.

He was finding the company of the older men at the pub increasingly irksome. It was the same as in Sydney – only worse because there were more of them.

There were the lonely who were obviously so desperate for company their desperation was repellent and only acted to compound their problem. None of them were interested in racing and viewed Gaily as something of an oddity whereas he himself thought of his passion for racing as part of what it means to be a man.

There were the single and those who should have been. They seemed more interested in pet dogs than women. During the final weeks of his stay he sought out other pubs or drank with the flies in his room. It was as much as he could do to be civil. Still those of them who were aware of what had occurred with Racquel and Colleen had been tremendously sympathetic and supportive in Gaily's hour of need. The time was overdue for him to move on to the next phase of his life and this had to be undertaken with dignity and respect for others. His most enduring memory of Brighton would be of an almost unrecognisable Colleen so obese she could barely move. He could not allow this to tarnish the reputation he had earned amongst the many good and decent people whom he had had the privilege of knowing over the years.

He felt the same about the Star in Sydney although the Star possessed a far greater sentimental attachment.

Brighton was his past but Sydney would always be a part of his life even were he to become an expatriate.

Unless in the company of racing men Gaily was bored by the company of other blokes. A beautiful woman would always provide a dash of excitement. He looked forward to his double date in the knowledge he shared Madam Rose's tastes in women. Another door was opening: would it be the door into the boudoir of an English rose?

Then another unexpected occurrence intervened. Madam Rose rang Gaily to tell him Paddy McGinty was dead. Racquel would have to front yet another coronial enquiry. The cause of death was suspected to be an accidental drug overdose compounded by the effects of alcohol.

This had happened on the eve of Gaily's first date with Jill. He had already been given strict riding instructions by Madam Rose not to mention Racquel while in Jill's presence. Under the circumstances these would be very difficult instructions with which to comply.

Madam Rose obviously rated Jill and Gaily a good match. One of her few faults was to get a little bit ahead of herself. Thus, she had rushed in to fill the void formerly occupied by Racquel and Colleen. In similar fashion she already had Jill and Gaily an item.

Jill was a career hairdresser in her early forties. The Madam had described her as being "more of an English rose than Racquel". This was high praise indeed. Madam Rose was a pretty good judge of these things.

The sun shone on the City of London as Gaily waited on the steps of the Renaissance Hotel for his two luncheon partners.

Two stunningly beautiful and elegantly dressed women approached. Gaily removed his sunglasses to better appreciate the spectacle. They were both of a certain age – not in their "first youth" as the great English writers may have said. However, far from detracting from their respective appearances maturity had only served to draw out the beauty which lies dormant in one's youth.

Gaily was momentarily dazzled – the brilliant sunshine created the illusion of haloes as it reflected from the ladies' respective crowning glories. Proving there really is something for everyone in this life one was brunette, the other blonde. On attaining focus Gaily recognised Madam Rose in the company of a blonde English rose. The latter was presumably Jill. To employ a term often used by Graham Peters Jill was "smokin'".

The lady accompanying the mistress was in fact Jill and Jill was everything Madam Rose had described multiplied by a factor of X. Gaily was reminded of his father teaching him "X" was the unknown factor. Profound beauty is impossible to quantify because of the subjectivity involved but Jill certainly possessed it in spades.

Introductions interrupted further reveries. Gaily was introduced to one rose by another. Jill's eyes were a deeper shade of azure than the summer sky, her complexion more peaches and cream than the desserts named after Dame Nellie. Her long hair was the blonde which had caused Gaily such grief but would always retain its allure. Even by her own standards the hairdresser had obviously gone to great pains to ensure its lustre, length and colour were pleasing to the discerning eye. Jill's tight cream dress was a little long for Gaily's liking but he had to check himself in remembering Jill was not a "worker". The dress encased the firmest of hour-glasses while the open shoes flaunted what Dickens would have termed "the neatest of ankles" – literally supporting a great pair of pins. It was a very promising start but as in racing it is not how one starts which counts but how one finishes. The professional punter felt the familiar rush of adrenalin as the race commenced – in yet another pursuit for the love which had proven so elusive.

They entered the restaurant. It was magnificent. Gaily paused momentarily to silently give thanks to Colleen for introducing him to such a wonderful realm for the courtship of the fillies of London. The old mare certainly knew a thing or two when it came to the nosebag.

He quickly regained focus. This was not difficult given his current centre of attention. Gaily knew this was not a time to dilly-dally as he had to make the most of the opportunity with which he was being presented. His departure from England was imminent so first impressions would count then fate would do the rest.

It was of no small advantage to have Madam Rose in one's corner. Her girlfriend was obviously predisposed in Gaily's favour. The fact Jill had agreed to turn up at all boded well. The Jills of this world have a virtually unlimited gene pool available to them.

Jill had recently divorced so Gaily was catching her on the rebound. Her marriage had gradually withered to the point where by mutual agreement she and her husband had separated. Their children had attained their respective majorities so their parents no longer felt the need to maintain the pretence of marriage.

Madam Rose had impressed upon Gaily the fact that there had been no acrimony involved in her friend's divorce. The mistress had done this in order to allay any fears Gaily may have had about Jill being "damaged goods".

On the contrary as Gaily had replied at the time he would be the more likely of the two to carry emotional baggage despite having never married.

The lunch proved a glorious celebration of two people being brought together for the first time by a mutual friend. Champagne was the obviously appropriate drink to accompany the fine food and company. Gaily was able to utilise the vast experience he had accumulated in the purchasing of the fizzy stuff. Jill was greatly impressed. Madam Rose merely gave a knowing smile.

The luncheon was notable for its lack of agendas. The three of them were there by choice. No money was changing hands. No games were being played apart from Madam Rose's footsie under the table with Gaily. For him it was all a refreshing change from his previous experiences with other women.

With no ulterior motives they were able to enjoy each others' company. There was the hairdresser experienced in the maintaining of light conversation, the brilliant dominatrix with her wide range of knowledge and experiences and Gaily with his larrikin banter. It proved a perfect mix.

It later dawned on him how little he had to try in order to leave a favourable impression. Gaily had learnt in other areas of his life how trying too hard actually has the reverse effect to that intended. It is only when the mind is disengaged the power of genius can be unleashed. This is an immutable law of life.

Certainly he had paid close attention to his appearance but this itself had become second nature.

The same could be said of his luncheon partners. Both ladies had forged their careers based on maintaining appearances: one of them placing emphasis on her own appearance, the other using her professional skills to optimise the looks of others while also maintaining her own.

Gaily had been paid a huge compliment. The key question in his mind pertained to whether or not Jill would like to see him again. Then the further question would arise as to the basis upon which they would again meet.

Gaily was not interested in one night stands or holiday flings. He wanted to commit and hoped Jill was of like mind.

There was also the problem of the tyranny of distance. Long distance relationships do not work. Sooner or later one or other party has to relocate unless it is possible to spend part of the year together in one country and the rest of the year in the other.

Gaily recalled the words of the bookie Luke Henry when they had discussed Gaily's personal life. The wise old boy had told him he had a good friend in Madam Rose after she had told him he had had a lucky escape from Racquel.

Just as Colleen had known Racquel would be to Gaily's liking so Madam Rose knew he would find Jill attractive.

Racquel and Jill had much in common. They were both blue-eyed posh totty of similar age with long blonde hair and hour-glass figures. Again Madam Rose was at pains to emphasise Jill's lack of emotional baggage. The hairdresser had also taken a genuine interest in their conversations as opposed to Racquel's indifference.

More questions had been raised than answered by their first encounter but life has a habit of answering questions once they have been asked. One merely has to await the reply.

It had been a promising start to a new friendship and the furthering of an established one. However, the same could be said for his first meeting with Racquel. The difference was the good will displayed by Madam Rose and the fact she would not become insanely jealous were Gaily to fall in love with Jill.

Gaily returned to Brighton with great expectations. The next day his sexual fantasies were abruptly interrupted while he walked down East Street.

The manageress of one of the little boutiques accosted him with some bad news. He had remembered her as being a friend of Colleen's.

The woman told him Colleen was in hospital on life support. Her entire cardiovascular system was in the process of collapse.

Gaily was upset but not surprised. The human body is capable of tolerating only a finite amount of abuse. Years of poor diet, heavy drinking and lack of exercise had finally caught up with his former mistress.

Gaily had severed all ties with Colleen eighteen months prior. Would he be being untrue to himself by going to visit his former friend on her deathbed? On the spur of the moment he decided he would be more untrue to himself were he not to visit her.

He rang the hospital and on the basis of the very limited information he was able to ascertain got a cab straight there. It was almost too late.

Despite the parting of the ways Gaily still felt a bond towards the woman who had been a part of his life for a quarter of a century. Colleen would never again play any role in his life. This much was obvious as Gaily entered the hospital ward from which Colleen would not emerge alive.

What met his gaze was by then a familiar sight. Gaily had witnessed both his parents die in similar circumstances. After all he had been through very little was capable of shocking him. Given Colleen's physical condition it was a predictable end.

Gaily's former mistress lay gasping for breath. Her bloated body heaved convulsively. Colleen's body had been penetrated in many and various ways over the decades but never quite in this fashion.

Breathing apparatus, nebulisers and drips formed a bewildering maze of tubes to the untrained eye. The Judaeo-Christian basis of the English health system dictated the terminally ill had to have their lives prolonged until finally they were allowed to drift away on a wave of morphine.

Freed from the constraints of the corsets she had been forced to employ in recent years simply to fit into clothes Colleen's final hours were being spent as a heaving mass of blubber. Every laboured breath caused her massive rolls of fat to wobble uncontrollably under the flimsy sack of the oversized hospital gown.

Gaily's parents had died in similar circumstances. Their corpses had been tiny emaciated bags of bones ravaged by decades of heavy smoking. Colleen was the victim of her own avarice and gluttony.

He approached the bed as he had approached her bed on hundreds of previous occasions. Now there could be no love or lust – merely loathing mixed with pity.

Their eyes met. Colleen recognised her old client but was incapable of speech. Her grey-green eyes which once gleamed so seductively expressed shock then acceptance of his presence.

Gaily grasped the dying woman's hand and squeezed it. The hospital staff present realised the poignancy of the moment and averted their eyes. No friends or family were present.

"I forgive you," he whispered.

Colleen's eyes expressed cognition of his words. A slight smile momentarily crossed her face which Gaily reciprocated.

Half an hour later he was ushered out of the ward. Colleen had shuffled off this mortal coil.

Gaily felt no further responsibility incumbent upon him. He left the hospital with a clear conscience. The next of kin could sort out the mess. His only feeling was one of bewilderment as to how Colleen's life had unravelled to this extent. He caught a cab to the Greys and had a pint in memory of his former friend.

When Gaily returned to his hotel there was a message from Madam Rose asking him to ring her at his earliest convenience. Intrigued, he rang her straight away.

Madam did not beat around the bush. Jill wanted to see him again prior to his departure. There was also some juicy gossip regarding Racquel and Paddy McGinty which she would convey when they met.

Gaily again booked a table for three at the Renaissance's Gilbert Scott Restaurant. He had a fair idea what to expect when next they met.

Madam Rose was living up to the old bookmaker's description of her as a true friend. Such friendship sometimes needs to be rewarded. Gaily had no problem with this concept.

The deal put to him involved his flying Jill and Madam Rose and the mistress's boyfriend to Sydney. They would only require economy class seats so it would be about the same cost to him as when he had flown Racquel over. In fact it would be only half as expensive as Racquel had always been accompanied by Colleen.

Madam Rose began to speak more rapidly. They would only require two hotel rooms as Madam would share a room with her boyfriend. One of the hotels at which Colleen and Racquel had stayed would probably be nice.

None of this came as a surprise to Gaily. He had anticipated something of this nature. The manner in which the proposition was put to him was far less rapacious than had been the case where Colleen was concerned.

Gaily hesitated. He mumbled the name of what was in his opinion the best of the hotels at which Colleen and Racquel had stayed.

Jill smiled at Gaily. He further weakened and said he would agree to the proposal put to him by Madam Rose subject to him winning first prize in Warren Bird's football tipping competition. He also suggested as it would be their first trip to Australia a fortnight's stay would be sufficient.

Madam Rose knew Gaily had incurred a significant depletion of his capital so did not press the matter further. The mistress genuinely wanted to see her friends happy and secretly hoped Jill would eventually relocate to Sydney. The same thought had momentarily crossed Gaily's mind but he knew to put it to one side.

It had been a little bit cheeky of Madam to swing a free holiday for her boyfriend but they would be two couples for two weeks. This was the thinking behind the move and it was intended to create a win-win paradigm whereby Gaily would have Jill to himself for a large part of the time.

When Jill went to the Ladies Madam Rose told Gaily about the death of Paddy McGinty. It was a similar story to that of Oscar Wildly but for the fact drink as well as drugs had been involved.

There would be a toxicology report, a coronial enquiry and in all probability a finding of death by accidental overdose. Racquel would then inherit her late husband's entire estate.

Colleen had in one of her franker moments referred to the path of death and destruction Racquel left in her wake. Madam Rose had told Gaily he had had a lucky escape. Now Oscar Wildly, Paddy McGinty and Colleen were all gone.

Upon Jill's return the three friends had one for the road and went for a slightly tipsy walk. The Madam along with the rest of the world had to avert her gaze from Gaily and Jill having a quick snog. Gaily generally viewed public shows of affection very grimly and thought the kiss was shared in a subtle manner. To employ his own turn of phrase it was about as subtle as a hand grenade in a bowl of porridge. Such is the stuff of mature age schoolboy crushes.

With the parting of the ways came a new sense of hope for Gaily. One cannot choose one's relatives but one can choose one's friends. Actually he had chosen his family pretty well. It was his so-called friends who had let him down.

A new circle of positive people were being attracted to him in place of the toxic negative forces of his past. Some of the toxic individuals had already managed to poison themselves to death.

The London belles saw Gaily off at the railway barrier. He netted a farewell kiss from each of them. Consulting his watch he saw he was seconds out from his fifteen minutes of fame.

Gaily flew back to Sydney, but not before buying Jill a Mason Pearson hairbrush as a farewell present. He maintained contact with Jill through Madam Rose. Several weeks after his return he won the hundred and five thousand dollar first prize in the tipping competition. It was his finest hour thus far as a professional punter.

Gaily was straight on the telephone to Madam Rose.

He suggested she and her friends come over for a fortnight during the Australian summer.

This was the same duration as Racquel and Colleen had stayed for in Sydney on their first visit together. It was only just long enough to give people visiting Sydney for the first time a glimpse of the harbour city. Then if they liked what they saw they could return for a longer visit.

The necessary arrangements and requisite payments were made. They returned to their everyday lives until January arrived along with Gaily's English visitors.

He was always the gracious host and met his visitors at the airport. They were jetlagged but otherwise well. Even at their worst the two English roses stood out in the crowd as they made their way through the packed arrivals lounge.

Madam Rose's boyfriend was a likeable sporty chap of similar vintage to Gaily. They developed an instant rapport with each other. Everything was set for a wonderful two weeks of fun in the Australian sun.

They were the best two weeks of their lives. They went running, walking and swimming together. They wined and dined as two couples. Gaily took Madam Rose's boyfriend to the gym and the pub. The girls bonded by going shopping together. Gaily was able to show Jill off to men of dubious sexuality at the Boy Charlton Pool.

Sensing sexual tension Jill condescended to provide relief with hand and hairbrush. He had insisted to Madam Rose his seeing the mistress as a client would be inappropriate under the prevailing circumstances. His fidelity to his new squeeze was duly rewarded.

Madam Rose was pleasantly surprised at Jill's ability to read the situation and respond in an appropriate manner. However, Gaily's needs were fairly basic and required only a willingness on Jill's part in order to be met.

The two weeks vanished. The time had come for Gaily's guests to depart.

"We must do this again," they said in unison – and meant it.

Jill appeared a little teary and had to be assuaged by Gaily's promise to see her again in June. The money was rolling in and he was confident of his ability to come to the same ongoing arrangements with her. They would discuss it when next they met.

Jill had already met with a hairdresser friend of Gaily's and discussed her relocation to Sydney. They looked to the future with optimism.

Gaily had long craved success in one of the world's toughest professions. Having attained this success he wanted an English rose with whom to share it. In Jill it seemed he had found such a woman.

His three guests had returned back to the old country. Gaily returned to his own little world.

He was already planning the date of his own return to London based on the quietest part of the Australian racing calendar: mid-June through to the beginning of August was the ideal time of the year.

This time he would do it in style. Madam Rose had introduced him to a five star hotel in the West End. In years to come this would be his playground when he and Jill took their annual holidays from Sydney.

Gaily was already visualising the wonderful life he would share with Jill when the telephone rang. His mobile was sitting on his dining room table and he had been in his study daydreaming over a copy of the Sportsman. He ran to answer the call thinking it might be Jill.

The caller indeed possessed the posh totty voice which he so adored but it was not Jill. It was Racquel. They had not spoken for eighteen months.

Gaily held no grudges. He was genuinely pleased to hear from the woman he had so passionately loved. Racquel had married and lost her husband since her last communication with Gaily. He was only aware of this through Madam Rose.

Gaily did not know if Racquel would even be aware of his knowledge of these events. He sought a lead from her call but received only a torrent of distraught babble.

Gaily calmed Racquel down as best he could. From what he could make out the widow was fed up with her life in England and wanted to relocate to Sydney. She was genuinely sorry about the way she had treated Gaily and wanted to make amends. It had all been Colleen's fault. He had been correct all along in saying Colleen had poisoned her mind against him.

Racquel said she wanted to move to Sydney to make a fresh start. The only problem was there might be difficulty in obtaining permanent resident status. There had also been a recent spate of unforeseen expenses which had left her short of cash.

Gaily knew to tread warily where Racquel was concerned. He asked her to jot down the details of what she was proposing. A permanent move to another country would mean a major upheaval in her life – and having Racquel back in his life would mean a potentially bigger upheaval for Gaily than for Racquel.

A week after his request a letter arrived addressed in Racquel's unmistakable loopy hand. The tone of the letter was calmer than had been her voice on the telephone. However, the gist of the request was the same. Racquel required financial assistance to relocate to Sydney then would need some ongoing means of generating an ongoing income to maintain her lifestyle.

They exchanged correspondence. Finally Gaily had

established the regular communication he had so craved when first they had met.

Gaily looked at the pile of letters all written in Racquel's quirky hand which sat on his desk. He took the box containing mementoes of their shared past from its hiding place. Looking over the cards, letters and photographs his memory became increasingly selective.

Gaily went to the Star for a few schooners of Resch's to clear his mind. This was when he was at his most meditative. There was only one course of action to be taken.

It was early evening in Sydney when Gaily left the pub. It would be late morning in London. He was now again in possession of Racquel's telephone number. He rang Racquel and told her to expect a letter from him in the next week sent via registered post.

Gaily drank his usual quota of stubbies and went to bed. He wanted to sleep on what was going through his mind.

After breakfast the next morning Gaily wrote to Racquel with a formal proposal of marriage. This would be dependent upon the future Mrs Gaily moving to Sydney on a permanent basis. He also offered to pay all costs associated with Racquel's relocation and the payment of a weekly allowance for her living expenses once they were married. The amount of the allowance he quoted was based upon Gaily's most wildly optimistic business projection.

A week later Gaily's telephone rang. It was Racquel. She accepted his proposal, could not wait to get out of London, could not wait to be back in Sydney and could not wait to see him again. They would have to stay in touch on a daily basis now until finally they were reunited.

Gaily hoped Jill would understand.

Some people never learn.